About the Authors

Susan Carlisle's love affair with books began when she made a bad grade in maths. Not allowed to watch TV until the grade had improved, she filled her time with books. Turning her love of reading into a love for writing romance, she pens hot medicals. She loves castles, travelling, afternoon tea, and hearing from her readers. Join her newsletter at susancarlisle.com

Born and raised on the Wirral Peninsula in England, **Charlotte Hawkes** is mum to two intrepid boys who love her to play building block games with them, and object loudly to the amount of time she spends on the computer. When she isn't writing – or building with blocks – she is company director for a small Anglo/French construction firm. Charlotte loves to hear from readers, and you can contact her at her website: charlotte-hawkes.com

With a background of working in medical laboratories and a love of the romance genre, it's no surprise that **Sue MacKay** writes medical romance stories. She wrote her first story at age eight and hasn't stopped since. She lives in New Zealand's Marlborough Sounds where she indulges her passions for cycling, walking, and kayaking. When she isn't writing she also loves cooking and entertaining guests with sumptuous meals that include locally caught fish.

The Surgeon Collection

The Surgeon's Passion

SUSAN CARLISLE

CHARLOTTE HAWKES

SUE MacKAY

MILLS & BOON

First Published in Great Britain 2023
by Mills & Boon, an imprint of HarperCollins*Publishers* Ltd,
1 London Bridge Street, London, SE1 9GF

www.harpercollins.co.uk

HarperCollins*Publishers*
Macken House, 39/40 Mayor Street Upper,
Dublin 1, D01 C9W8, Ireland

ISBN: 978-0-263-31966-8

MIX
Paper | Supporting
responsible forestry
FSC™ C007454

THE BROODING SURGEON'S BABY BOMBSHELL

SUSAN CARLISLE

To Jeanie.
The best sister-in-law I could have ever wished for.

PROLOGUE

THEIR NIGHT OF passion had started so innocently.

Dr. Gabriel Marks had taken the only open seat at the dining table. The petite young woman with the light brown hair and quick wit he remembered from the committee meeting six months earlier sat to one side of him. She smiled and said hello, as did the rest of the committee members.

Their chairperson had organized the dinner for those members flying in that evening. The next day they would all be attending the meeting at the High Hotel at Chicago's O'Hare Airport.

As a transplant surgeon, Gabe was honored to serve on the liver committee of the National Organ Allocation Network. The group met twice yearly to discuss issues involving liver donation and policy. The professionals who made up the committee, as well as family members of patients, came from all over the country and represented different areas of liver transplantation. What they did was important and saved lives.

If he remembered correctly, the woman dining beside him was Zoe somebody, a former registered nurse who now worked for the Liver Alliance, a group that educated people with liver disease and assisted patients needing a liver transplant. The Liver Alliance did good work. He'd had some dealings with the group in the past regarding patients with special considerations, but he'd never met Zoe before joining the committee.

The discussion around the table was lively during their meal and he appreciated Zoe's quick wit and infectious laugh.

The next morning, they had acknowledged each with a warm hello but had sat on opposite sides of the table during the six-hour meeting. When Zoe had spoken up, her remarks had been intelligent, enlightened and spot-on. He'd been impressed.

After the meeting had adjourned he'd headed to the airport to catch his plane home. But his quick check of the flight board revealed his plane had been grounded because of thunderstorms. Gabe was watching the word *Canceled* cascade down the panel when a groan of dismay had him turning around. It was Zoe.

She looked at him, her face screwed up. "Sorry. I hadn't meant to be so loud. This wasn't in my plans."

"It never is," Gabe responded.

"You're right about that." She looked up and down the concourse. "I guess I'm going to spend the night in the airport."

"I bet if we hurry we can get a room in the hotel before everyone figures out what's going on." Gabe turned back the way they had come.

"A room?" Her voice squeaked.

He gave her a pointed look. "I meant a room apiece. Are you always so literal?"

She grinned, walking past him at a fast clip. "I knew what you meant. I just wanted a head start if there was only one left."

He chuckled and hurried to catch up with her. A short time later they had rooms for the night. As they walked toward the elevator Gabe said, "I'm sorry, but I've racked my brain and still can't come up with your last name."

"Avery. Zoe Avery." She chuckled. "That came out sounding a little James Bondish, didn't it?"

He laughed. "Maybe a little bit. Would you like to meet for supper? Unless you have other plans." He rarely had a night free of paperwork and he wasn't going to spend this one by himself. Not when he liked this woman and was fairly confident she'd accept his invitation.

They entered the elevator. "What other plans would I have but to channel surf?" she answered with a grin.

Her mischievous talk appealed to him. As a transplant surgeon at a San Francisco hospital, he didn't have many people in his life who dared to speak to him so freely. He found it refreshing.

The elevator doors opened. As she prepared to exit, he held the doors open. "Meet you at seven in the hotel restaurant?"

"There's not a wife who's going to be mad at me, is there?" Her playful grin belied the serious concern in her eyes. Had a date ever lied to her about being married?

"No wife. How about your husband?"

"No. Not one of those either." There was a sad note in her reply, yet she cheerfully confirmed, "See you at seven, then." She waved as he stepped out.

Gabe took a moment to appreciate the gentle feminine sway of her hips, anticipating the evening to come.

He was waiting at the restaurant entrance when Zoe strolled up. There was a bright smile on her face. "Sorry, I didn't have anything else to wear." She brushed a hand across the front of the simple navy dress she'd been wearing earlier in the day.

"You look great to me." And she did. Something about her pulled at him. He wanted to know her better.

She grinned. "Thanks. You know the right thing to say to a stranded woman."

He chuckled. "If we have to be stuck somewhere, I'm glad it's a place with hot running water."

"I'm surprised you didn't say food."

"Now that you mention it, that's important too. Our table won't be ready for a few minutes. Would you like to wait in the bar?"

"Sure." Zoe walked ahead of him. She was a tiny thing with a powerful personality.

He ordered their drinks and carried them to a small table. They sat and talked about that day's meeting until the waiter came to get them.

Zoe stood, brushing against him as she moved to avoid someone sitting next to them. Gabe's blood heated. He had no doubt her movements had been unintentional, but his body reacted just the same. It had been some time since a woman had gotten to him on so many levels so quickly.

The waiter showed them to a corner table and handed them menus. They discussed what they would order and were ready when the waiter returned.

After he'd left Gabe remarked, "If I remember correctly, you're a patient advocate with the Liver Alliance and live in the Washington, DC, area."

"That's a good memory. I'm impressed. You were paying attention."

Feeling ashamed, he said, "Apparently not when you said your name."

"It's okay. It happens."

"So have you always been with the Liver Alliance?"

"I went to work in an ICU when I was fresh out of school. I worked a lot with liver patients and really liked it. I decided to go back to school and become a liver transplant coordinator. About a year ago I needed something with regular hours. The Education Chair position came open and it was a perfect fit. Good, stable hours, a tiny office, and I'm still working with the people I love."

Gabe nodded. "And you like living in DC?" He didn't normally quiz his dinner dates, but his curiosity about Zoe was uncharacteristically strong.

"I do. There's always plenty to do. Museums to visit, music festivals and just the excitement of being in the center of our government."

Her enthusiasm for the area was contagious.

She leaned back and looked at him. "And you're from San Francisco. Pretty city."

Obviously, she'd been paying more attention than he had during introductions. "Yep."

"That's a pretty tough commute for these meetings." She ran her finger down the side of her water glass, leaving a trail of condensation.

What would it feel like to have her do that over his chest? He shifted in his chair. They were having dinner. That was all. They didn't really know each other. "I try not to schedule surgery for the day I get back. It makes it easier to deal with the time change." Gabe took a sip of his drink then said, "You seemed pretty upset about not flying out tonight."

"Yeah. My mother has the beginnings of Alzheimer's and I don't like to leave her alone overnight. I'm worried she might not handle being by herself."

"You worked it out?"

"I did. I got a friend to go over and stay with her." Worry flickered in her eyes as she glanced away.

"She's why you needed the job with regular hours. I understand caring for someone with your mother's illness can be difficult." He was an only child whose mother turned to him often for help and emotional support, but she still possessed her mental faculties. If she didn't and he had to provide her with constant care even while he traveled...?

Zoe looked at him again, brow furrowed. "It is. I hate watching her wasting away. And good care is costly."

"My mother is all I've got. My father died before I was born. I can only imagine how I would feel if she got sick."

Her eyes took on a dark look before she said, "Growing up without a father can be tough. Do you have a stepfather?" Zoe seemed to have changed the subject on purpose.

"Nope. Mom never remarried." He'd often wondered why. She'd always said it was because his father had been the love of her life, but he'd thought there might be more to it. As a kid, he had overheard her tell a friend she felt like she might be doing Gabe a disservice by not marrying. That she worried her decision not to do so had left Gabe with no male role model or father figure.

"She must be a great mom," Zoe commented, bringing him back to the present. "You seemed to have turned out all right."

His mother had been and still was a good mother, but truth be known, his grandmother had been the primary adult during his formative years. His mother had worked full-time to provide for him. "Thanks for saying so. But lately she's been applying pressure to become a grandmother. It gets old."

Zoe's head turned to the side, her look quizzical. "You have no interest in making her one?"

"No. I'm not good family material. My job, my career, doesn't leave me any room for a family. I'm far too busy. More than one girlfriend has accused me of being a workaholic. A wife and children deserve a full-time husband and father. I decided long ago that that drama wasn't for me."

A peculiar expression came over her face, but before he could ask what was wrong, the waiter brought their meals. Zoe started talking about places she had visited and would like to go to and he dismissed her unexplainable expression in favor of her entertaining conversation. When they were done with their meal, Gabe said, "It's still early. Would you like to go to the jazz bar downstairs?"

She hesitated a moment. It really mattered to Gabe that she said yes. She finally quipped, "Why not? It sounds like fun."

Relief washed over him and he smiled. Why was it so important that she go? He placed his hand at her back and guided her out of the restaurant toward the circular stairs. His hand fit perfectly in the hollow of her back. At the club, he asked for a table close to the band.

They had been there a few minutes when Zoe touched his arm. She leaned in close and said into his ear, "I needed this. Thanks for asking me."

He smiled, glad she was having a good time. His body tightened with awareness. It was overreacting, big-time. Or was *he* overly conscious of his body's natural response to an attractive woman he genuinely liked? They were both single and old enough to know their own minds, so why shouldn't they enjoy each other's attention?

Several couples moved to the open area of the floor. On impulse Gabe asked, "Would you like to dance?"

"I'm not very good." She sounded more disappointed than rejecting.

He stood and offered his hand. "You don't have to be. Just follow my lead."

Zoe smiled. One he would remember. "Hey, I can do that."

Gabe held her hand as they stepped out onto the floor. Pulling her into his arms, his hand went to her waist. It was so small his arm almost wrapped all the way around her. The top of her head came to just below his chin. The sweet scent of her filled his head and his body stirred. He resisted the strong urge to pull her tight, but firmly squelched the idea. His arousal would be evident. This was the nicest evening he'd had in a long time and he had no intention of ruining it by scaring her off.

The sultry sound of the saxophone swirled around them.

She looked up, commanding his attention. "I'm impressed. You've a surgeon's touch even on the dance floor, gentle and skilled."

"Thank you, ma'am." He brought her a little closer in spite of his resolve. There were other things he was good at he'd like to show her. He needed to squelch those types of thoughts too. Gabe missed a step.

Her hand squeezed his shoulder when she stumbled.

He looked at her, mumbling, "Sorry."

"I'm sure it's your partner," she said.

Searching the depths of her eyes, he muttered, "I assure you it isn't."

"I've not had much opportunity to dance since my prom, years ago."

Her eyes were so green. "You're doing great."

She stared back. They continued to move slowly around the space. It wasn't until there was a mumble going around the room that he forced his attention away from her seductive gaze. The music had stopped. They were the only ones still on the dance floor.

Zoe looked around. Her cheeks were spots of red. "Oops. I guess we got carried away." She focused on him. "It's been a long day and time I head upstairs. It's later in my time zone than it is in yours."

"Okay." Gabe hated to let her go. He held her hand as they returned to the table. She picked up her bag and he left a few bills on the table for their drinks. "I'll see you to your room."

Zoe grasped her bag with both hands. He would have liked to have one of them in his. Somehow it seemed to belong there. What would she do if he kissed her? Would she push him away? Did he dare take a chance? He'd regret it if he didn't.

They entered the elevator and rode up to her floor without a word. The need to touch her, hold her gnawed at him. Tension, thick as a wool blanket in the winter, lay between them. She glanced at him once, her soft, questioning eyes uncertain. He was painfully aware of what he wanted but did she feel the same? The decision must be hers.

At her door, she pulled her keycard from her purse and turned to face him. "Thank you. I really enjoyed this evening. Especially the dancing."

Was she flirting with him? Testing the water?

She gave him a long look as if reaching a decision. With a blink, her hands came to rest on his shoulders as she stood on her toes and kissed him.

That was all the encouragement Gabe needed. He reached out, pulling her against him, his mouth crushing hers, his tongue finding a warm welcome. Her arms wrapped his neck and she hung on during the most passionate kiss he'd ever received. He wanted her. Right now. Based on her actions, she wouldn't deny him.

He steadied her on her feet and growled, "Key."

Zoe put it in his hand, her lips finding his again. He had no problem with that. Backing her against the door and with a minimum amount of fumbling, he managed to get the door opened and them inside.

It closed with a click behind them. Zoe's legs wrapped around his waist. His hands cupped her butt as he stumbled toward the bed, his blood boiling and his body alive with desire for her.

He eased her down onto the mattress, moving over her. Had he ever been this hot for a woman? Supporting himself on his hands, he searched her face. She stared back.

He saw the second doubt creep in. Gabe gently kissed her. "I want you. Badly."

Silent for a moment, she whispered, "Make me feel good tonight, Gabe. Forget everything."

"I can do that." His mouth took hers while his hands worked to remove her clothes.

She followed suit with equal frenzy. Her moans of desire combined with the kneading of her fingers on his bare back made him more aroused than he'd ever believed possible. Their mating was blistering, fast and very, very satisfying.

Hours later Gabe rolled over. His hand brushed warm, soft skin. *Zoe.* His body stirred once more. He wanted her again.

"Mmm…" she murmured before her kisses teased his chest.

His hand skimmed the rise of her hip. "Damn, I don't have another condom."

Her hand brushed his length as she murmured, "I'm on the pill."

Unable to go without her any longer, he saw to her pleasure then found his. Having no barrier between them felt so right.

When he woke again, Zoe was dressed and stuffing her belongings into her luggage. "Where're you going?"

"I have to catch my plane." Her back remained to him.

"You've already rescheduled?" He was still in a haze.

"They texted me." She did glance at him then. "I have to go. I need to get home to Mom."

Gabe could see the glass wall rising between them. Unbreakable. All the warmth they had shared last night was now frigid air. Zoe was embarrassed by her behavior. It shouldn't bother him. He wasn't looking for forever, but he didn't like the idea of being something she regretted.

"Zoe—"

"I have to go." She was out the door before he could untangle the sheets from his body.

CHAPTER ONE

ZOE CLUTCHED THE restroom door handle in the conference area of the High Hotel. It had been almost six months since she'd seen Gabe and she was hiding from him. She suspected he was impatiently waiting for her in the hall. Not facing him wasn't a choice she had. Her entire world had changed in that amount of time. Her mother was worse. And Zoe was pregnant.

Guilt hung on her like a heavy necklace of stones she wore all the time. She should have told Gabe. It wouldn't have been that hard to contact him. She'd used him to escape her life for a night and now there was a baby to consider. He'd deserved better on a number of levels. When she'd kissed him at her hotel-room door she hadn't planned on becoming the "drama" he had been adamant about not having in his life.

He knew now. He'd seen her protruding belly when she'd stood. She'd heard his gasp from halfway across the meeting room. There had been no mistaking his shocked expression when she'd glanced back. Would he care if it was his? Did he want to know? Regardless, he deserved to be told he was going to be a father. Even though he'd stated a family wasn't for him.

She paused before pulling the door open. Hopefully Gabe had already returned to the committee room. At first she had thought the stomach rolling had been a virus.

After a few weeks she'd had to admit it might be something else. But couldn't believe it. She'd been taking the pill. She'd dragged her feet about buying a pregnancy test because she'd just been unable to wrap her mind around the idea she might be expecting. She'd thought of contacting Gabe the moment she'd seen the test was positive, but had immediately found an excuse not to. Each time she'd convinced herself she had to tell him, she'd come up with a reason not to call him. Too tired, working too late, her mother needed her right that minute, and the list went on. The truth was Gabe had said he wasn't interested in being a father and she felt guilty for her part in involving him.

How would he react when he found out? She'd vowed after each of their committee's monthly conference calls to call and tell him. As time had gone by, she'd decided he deserved to hear the news face-to-face. Their semiannual in-person meeting was soon and she'd planned to tell him then. What she hadn't counted on was not seeing him the night before. She'd fully expected to have a chance to tell him in private before their committee meeting. Sadly that hadn't happened.

Her fingers flexed on the handle. What if Gabe had found someone special since they had been together? The idea disturbed her more than it should have. Any relationship he might have could be hurt when the woman learned of the baby. Just another reason Zoe shouldn't have put off telling him. She hadn't intended to hurt him. Ever.

Was he mad? Glad? Would he believe it was his? She'd been such a coward.

Her body had hummed with tension all morning as she'd anticipated telling Gabe. More than once she'd had to remind herself to breathe. Had even had to force herself to eat a bite or two of the croissant she'd gotten off the breakfast buffet. Despite being five months along, morning food still didn't always agree with her. Her temperamental tummy was made worse by nerves strung so taut they would hit a high note if plucked.

She had glanced at Gabe several times. His gaze had met hers on a number of those. When it had, ripples of pleasurable awareness had zinged through her. She wasn't sure if it was the flapping of wings in her belly or the baby kicking, but her body had a definite reaction to the sight of him. She was still attracted to him. There had been an uneasiness in his eyes, but a glint of pleasure as well. Had he been glad to see her before she'd stood up, revealing her condition?

Their night together had been memorable. Extremely delightful and erotic. She'd let go like she'd never allowed herself to do before. Her life had been becoming more complicated and she'd just wanted to live a little. Gabe was there, tall, dark and handsome with a Southern drawl, her fantasy come to life…almost.

Her dream man would want to marry and have a family.

Yet despite that one character flaw, she'd wanted Gabe to give her the attention she'd craved. Had been greedy about it. Being with him had made her feel alive, desirable and carefree. She'd taken shameless advantage of their night of passion. The fear it might not come her way again had had her agreeing to things she was normally cautious about.

Not only was Gabe easy on the eyes but intelligent, thoughtful, funny and a great conversationalist. He really listened. She liked him, too much. Now fate had them in its grasp. Like it or not, against all odds, they were having a child together.

Finding the right man had been difficult for her. She refused to settle or compromise. She wanted a man devoted to her, who would feel the same way about their family. More than once her mother had said Zoe was dreaming of someone who didn't exist. Zoe resisted that idea, knowing her mother was jaded from being an abandoned wife and mother. Still, Zoe believed there could be a happily ever after out there for her. She just had to find the right man.

The one time Zoe had thought she had, she'd ended up devastated. While confident their relationship had been progressing toward marriage, she'd caught Shawn having dinner with another woman. When she'd confronted him, he'd announced they didn't want the same things out of life. That no man could live up to her expectations. That Zoe had an unrealistic view of life and relationships. To believe a man could be devoted to just one woman was antiquated.

Other men had implied the same thing. She still vowed not to lower her standards, even when she realized her pledge might mean she'd never have the family she'd dreamed of. Gabe's assertion about not being interested in a wife or family only meant he wasn't any different than the other men she'd been interested in. They'd all been like her father and left when life had turned inconvenient.

She'd fully accepted Gabe was not Mr. Right when she'd let go of her inhibitions that night, confident in her birth control.

Zoe lightly banged her forehead against the bathroom door, her hand aching from the prolonged tight grip on the handle. She just wanted that one man who would love her forever. If that was being too picky, so be it. As her mother's condition gradually deteriorated, it was becoming more difficult to date, even if she had a chance. At least now, with a baby on the way, she had one of the two things she'd always wanted.

With a sudden surge of resolution, Zoe gripped the handle even tighter, her knuckles going white. She had to face Gabe. It was time. She ran her free hand over the rise at her middle, unable to keep the smile from forming despite her anxiety. When she had finally accepted she was pregnant, she'd been filled with joy. The only disappointment was that she didn't have a husband to share her happiness with.

She rolled her shoulders back, forcing them to relax, took a fortifying breath and stepped out into the hallway. As she suspected, Gabe was there. Waiting.

Gabe gasped when Zoe stood. He felt like he'd just been sucker punched in the gut. His throat constricted as his heart recovered and went into high gear, pounding like a drum against his ribs.

Zoe was *pregnant!*

It was obvious beneath her pink dress.

For the past two hours she'd been sitting across from him, so involved in their committee's discussion she hadn't left the table. At least he'd assumed that was why she hadn't stood until the midmorning break.

Gabe clamped his mouth shut and swallowed, trying to slow his thundering heart. Tearing his gaze from Zoe's rounded middle, he glanced wildly about the conference room. *Was it his?*

Numerous times over the last months he'd thought of her. Of their night together. More than once he'd picked up his phone with the intention of calling her, only to put it down, afraid his intrusion into her life wouldn't be welcomed, especially after the way she had left the morning after.

He'd hoped to get to the hotel earlier so he could talk to her but his flight hadn't cooperated. His surgery schedule hadn't either. Instead of coming in the night before, he'd had to take a morning plane.

After he'd gasped, Zoe had glanced back at him before she'd hurried toward the conference-room exit. *Was she running from him again?*

Standing, he'd pushed his chair away with so much

force he'd had to catch it before he could make his way around the table. He'd been stopped by one of the other committee members but had ended that conversation in short order.

He'd stalked down the hall toward the restrooms, his best guess for where she'd gone.

It could be someone else's.

His heart did another tap dance. Zoe could have found someone just after they'd been together. He shook his head. His gut told him that wasn't the case. Maybe it was the way he'd caught her uncertain look before she'd headed from the room.

The unending fascination he still felt for her hadn't been part of his plan for a one-night stand, but it was there anyway. Now it appeared that night had had bigger repercussions than the memories that haunted him.

Gabe stationed himself across from the women's restroom. Zoe had to come out sometime.

When the door finally opened, Zoe stepped into the hall and Gabe met her in the middle of it. Despite the large area around them, the space seemed to zoom inward until it was just he and Zoe.

"Is it mine?" His words were low and harsh.

She nodded, before she looked away then back to him. "You don't have to worry. I can take care of it. I won't make any demands on you."

Gabe's head jerked back in disbelief. "What? Of course I'll help. This is my child too."

"It was an accident. I can take care of us." Her hand brushed her middle. "You don't need to feel obligated in any way. I just wanted you to know about the baby." Her voice grew stronger and she tried to step around him.

He blocked her path. "Yes, I can tell how eager you were to tell me. Must have been damned near impossible for you to keep it a secret all these months." He almost winced at the sarcasm in his voice. "You should have told me. Not blindsided me."

Zoe put a protective hand on her middle. Her eyes turned sad. "I wanted to. Tried. Sorry."

At the sound of footsteps, they both glanced up the hall in the direction of the committee room. It was one of the other members coming their direction.

"Please, let's not make a scene," Zoe begged.

Gabe took her elbow. He was gentle yet firm. "Come. We need to talk." He led her to a small alcove some distance down the hall from the restrooms.

Bile rose in his throat as Zoe stepped as far away from him as the space would allow. Just months ago, she'd been so alive in his arms. He took a deep breath in an effort to regain control, perspective.

"This isn't the time or the place for this." The desperation in her eyes and tone was unmistakable.

He glared at her. "Would you have ever told me if you hadn't had to? Did you really think I wouldn't notice? Did you manage to forget I've seen all of you, knew your body down to the smallest detail?"

Heat filled her cheeks. It was plain she remembered as well as he did, perhaps more clearly.

Gabe watched her closely. "Why didn't you tell me?"

Her hand went over her middle again. "This wasn't supposed to happen. I take full responsibility. I just thought you deserved to be told to your face."

"It seems to me that you could have at least picked up the phone and called."

"I know I should have, but I just kept making excuses. Then I knew I was going to see you here, but you didn't come to the dinner last night…"

The tension in his shoulders eased. She must be under a lot of pressure. Could he believe her? "I got stuck in surgery. Look, you're right. Now isn't the time for us to talk. We're expected back in the meeting. When does your plane leave?"

"Just after the meeting." Zoe glanced at the opening as if anxious to leave.

His voice softened. "You can't change it?"

"No. I have to get home to see about my mother. Just being gone overnight has become a problem. I've got to go." She shifted toward the opening.

"Okay. We'll have to figure something out later. But we *will* talk." He nodded his head toward the opening. "Why don't you go back ahead of me? I'll be along in a minute. I'd rather there be as little talk as possible."

With a curt nod of apparent agreement, she slipped past him and hurried away.

He was going to be a father. Gabe's chest had a funny ache in it. Was it joy? Being a father had never been in his plans. He'd always been so careful. Zoe had changed that.

He'd grown up without a father. That had been the deciding factor in his decision to forgo the family route. Yet now that his plans for his life had just been rewritten permanently, he was determined no child of his would grow up not knowing his father. Zoe could protest that he wasn't obligated all she liked. If she'd thought that feeble opposition would make him walk off as if nothing had ever happened, she'd badly underestimated him.

More annoying still was his body's reaction to her nearness. She'd been standing so close. Her soft floral scent still lingered in his nostrils. That fragrance would forever be hers. Memories washed over him. Zoe soft and willing in his arms. The sweet, lilting moan she'd made as they'd joined. It was a night he'd replayed over and over in his mind. Yet this wasn't the outcome he'd planned. But one he would accept. Deal with.

In the last few minutes his world had altered irreversibly. In a few months he would be a father. Next month he would be in a new job. A very visible one. He needed to look professional, be in control of his life. Gabe took a deep breath, gathered his emotions. Life had just grabbed him by the tail.

Zoe made her way back to the conference room on weak knees. Gabe had been right. They didn't need to return at the same time, especially after one of the committee members had caught them arguing. Had the woman overheard what they'd been talking about? Yet Gabe's sensible suggestion that they enter separately troubled her. Was he ashamed of her?

Maybe it was best. They shouldn't draw attention to themselves, so that they'd have to explain what was going on between them. All she'd planned to do was tell Gabe and now he knew. She didn't expect anything more from him and had made that plain. They would part ways today and that would be it. He'd have his life, his career, on the West Coast and she and the baby theirs on the East.

Except Gabe had said he wanted to talk. Would he be making demands? She had been surprised by the ferocity in his tone when he'd stated he would be in his child's life. Where had that come from? Especially after he'd told her he wasn't interested in a family. It must have been the shock of learning he was going to be a father. That was all it was.

She had just settled her shaking body in the chair when the moderator called the meeting back to order. Gabe slipped into his chair a minute later with an apologetic nod in the chairperson's direction. Zoe refused to meet his look, the one she felt on her. The rest of the day would be long. Picking up her pen, she doodled on a page of her agenda to keep herself from glancing at him. The few times she dared to look, his thoughtful light blue gaze was fixed on her. She still found him attractive.

At their lunch break, Gabe started her way but was stopped by someone asking him a question. That gave her the chance to grab her meal and hurry back to her place, avoiding interacting with him again.

By midafternoon the meeting was ending. Zoe hadn't heard much of it. She had been busy berating herself for failing to think through the consequences of not telling Gabe sooner.

"Dr. Marks," the chairperson said, and the room erupted in clapping.

Zoe's head jerked up. What had just been said? She gave a half-hearted pat of her hands as she watched Gabe. He smiled, nodding, as he looked around the room.

His gaze met hers briefly before he said, "Thank you. I look forward to becoming the head of transplants at National Hospital."

The earlier fluttering in her stomach took off like a covey of quail. Gabe would be moving to the East Coast. To the same area as her!

She stared at him in disbelief.

He shrugged.

The rest of the people in the room stood and gathered their belongings. Zoe didn't move. She'd believed Gabe would be three thousand miles away when he'd talked about being involved with their child. Now he would just be down the road. He might want to see the baby not only during the summer, while taking a few weeks of annual vacation, but regularly. He could even want part-time custody. This situation was spinning out of her control.

By the time she pulled her thoughts together, the room was practically empty. Gabe was still being congratulated by a couple of people when she was ready to go. In a stupor of shock, she snatched up her purse and grabbed the suitcase handle, hurrying out, unable to think clearly.

Gabe had upended her envisioned future as a happy single parent.

"Zoe."

She looked over her shoulder to see him striding toward her, and walked faster.

"Wait up," he called.

"I need to catch my plane." She had too much to process. Needed time to think.

Gabe pulled level with her. "But we need to talk."

"If you wanted to talk so badly, why didn't you tell me you had accepted a job that had you moving for all intents and purposes into my backyard?"

His mouth gaped in shock as he grabbed her arm, forcing her to stop.

"Maybe because I was too busy trying to recover from the bomb you dropped on me."

He did have her there. She inhaled and said on the exhalation, "I think we both need some time to consider what we need to do." His touch made her tremble, triggering memories of his hands all over her that night. How was she supposed to think?

"I already know what I want," he snapped. "I intend to be as much a part of my child's life as possible."

"Does it matter what I want?" Zoe jerked free, took hold of her luggage handle again and started out of the hotel attached to the airport by a tunnel that led under the street.

Gabe matched her stride. "You didn't think I'd want to know my child, did you?"

"I thought you deserved to know he or she existed, but I never imagined you'd want to be involved as closely as you're talking about." She kept increasing her pace, lugging her bag behind her. "You made it perfectly clear you weren't family material before we went to bed together."

"Oho, so that's it. You didn't think I'd care about being

a father. It so happens that now that I am one I intend to be one. You have a problem with that?"

"I don't know. I might if you keep applying this much pressure all the time," she hissed.

"If I keep… You've had months to adjust to having a child. I only just learned I'm going to be a father." His frustration was loud and clear.

Guilt assaulted her. "I'm sorry about that. It wasn't fair, but you can't expect me to make a life-changing decision for my child while I'm on the way to the airport."

They continued through the tunnel into the terminal. Gabe remained beside her, larger than life. Why couldn't he give her some space? She was already tied in emotional knots. She needed to get away, get home and regroup.

Zoe had other things to consider besides Gabe's newly found parental outrage. Her friend had just sent a text to say that her mom was anxious, constantly searching the apartment and asking for Zoe.

Her thoughts were too scattered. She needed to consider carefully everything she said or agreed to. What happened would affect her and her child forever. "Gabe, I'm not talking about this right now. You're moving across the country and you need time to get settled into your new job before you agree to shoulder the responsibilities of fatherhood. Responsibilities you need to carefully weigh first. Meanwhile, I need time to handle other issues in my life."

"Is there someone else involved here?" His question was a demand. "Are you involved with someone?"

"No, nothing like that." She glanced at Gabe in time to see him visibly relax. What did it matter to him if she had a boyfriend—or a lover, for that matter?

He touched her elbow to steady her when she rocked back as they headed up the escalators to the security area. Heat zipped through her. "You need to hold the handrail."

"I'm perfectly capable of taking care of myself. Pregnancy doesn't make me feeble-minded." She'd covered her reaction to him with feistiness she didn't completely feel as she pulled her arm from his hand.

"Neither does it mean you shouldn't be careful or unwilling to accept help."

Zoe's look met his. Gabe's didn't waver. He appeared sincerely concerned. She had to admit it was nice to have someone care about her welfare. So much of her life revolved around helping others, her patients and her mother. Being worried over was a pleasant change. They stepped off the escalator and continued down the concourse. "I promise I'll be careful."

She looked ahead. A young woman with a baby strapped to her chest was pushing a rented luggage cart piled high with bags. Standing on the front, holding on, was a boy of about four. Seconds before they passed Zoe, the cart wobbled and the boy fell backward onto the unforgiving floor with a sickening thud. The mother screamed as blood flowed.

Even as the accident registered in Zoe's mind, Gabe was down on one knee beside the child. The boy's screeching echoed off the high glass ceiling as the mother pushed Gabe's shoulder in her effort to reach the boy.

He half turned, catching hold of her as he said in a level, calm manner, "Ma'am, I'm a doctor. Don't move him. You could make it worse. What's his name?"

"Bobby. Bobby's his name," the woman said between crying huffs.

"Bobby, hush. I'm Dr. Gabe. I'm going to help you." Gabe continued to speak softly and reassuringly to the boy.

Zoe noticed a diaper bag sitting on top of the woman's luggage pile. Grabbing it, she opened it and searched until she found a diaper. Laying it as flat as possible on the floor, she carefully slipped it beneath the boy's head, then held his head steady to stop him from squirming.

Gabe nodded to her then said, "Bobby, I need to see if you're hurt anywhere else. Your mom's right here. She can hold your hand, but you must be still."

The boy's crying quieted, although tears continued to roll down his face.

A crowd circled them yet Gabe's full attention remained focused on the child.

The mother moved to the opposite side of the boy, going down on her knees beside Zoe. Taking his small hand, she said, "I'm here, honey." The baby on her chest started to cry and she patted her on the bottom. "Don't cry, Bobby. You're making me and Susie cry too."

The boy gave her a sad smile. His chest shuddered as he struggled to stop sobbing. The mother's eyes were wild with fear as she stared expectantly at Gabe.

"Bobby, do you have a dog?" he asked, reaching for and pulling his suitcase to him.

"Uh-huh." The boy grew quiet and watched Gabe.

Nimbly, Gabe unzipped a side pocket and removed a stethoscope. "What's his name?"

"Marty."

"Marty—that's a good name for a dog. Did you give it to him?"

Zoe shifted closer to the mother. Placing her fingers on the pulse of the boy's wrist, Zoe checked his heart rate.

"One-ten," she told Gabe. Thankfully it wasn't very high.

Zoe looked up to see a security guard hurrying in their direction. When he arrived she said, "I'm a nurse and he's a doctor." She nodded in the direction of Gabe. "Call 911. This boy needs to be seen at a hospital."

Thankfully the man didn't waste time arguing and spoke into his radio.

Meanwhile Bobby was saying, "No, my mom did. I wanted to name him Purple."

Gabe grinned. "Purple. That's an interesting name. Is he a purple dog?" While he spoke to the boy in a low tone, Gabe listened to his heart, checking his pulse and looking into his eyes.

"There's no such thing as a purple dog," the boy stated. "It's my favorite color."

Gabe chuckled and patted Bobby on the shoulder. "I'm sure you'll be playing with Marty soon." He spoke to the mother. "I think he'll be fine, but he may have a concussion and need to stay in the hospital overnight for observation."

Blinking, she swiped away the wetness on one cheek.

"I'll see that you're taken care of. Don't worry," Gabe assured her.

Seconds later the emergency medical techs arrived. They relieved Zoe and she stood. Her hands were a mess and one of the techs handed her a wet towel to clean them.

Gabe had been tender with Bobby, even able to distract him, which was a talent in itself. He showed promise at being a good father. Caring concern was every bit as evident in his interaction with the boy and mother as it had been during the night they had shared. Maybe it wouldn't be so hard to accept him as part of her and the baby's life. If he was truly serious about it. Her fear was that when reality set in he might change his mind. Right now, he was just being noble.

Gabe was busy giving the EMTs a report about what had happened when Zoe found her bag and headed to the nearest restroom to wash her hands. When she came out, Gabe stood nearby.

She checked her watch and shook her head. "I have to go. It's almost time for my plane. I have to get home."

He didn't look pleased with her putting him off once
again. "I'll be in touch."

"Okay." She pulled a card from her purse and handed
it to him. "My phone number is on it. 'Bye, Gabe."

CHAPTER TWO

Two DAYS LATER Gabe was on his way out of surgery when his phone rang. "Hey, Mom."

"Hey yourself. I've not heard from you in weeks." His mother sounded eager to talk.

"I've been busy."

"Too busy to check in with your mother?" Her tone held a teasing note but there was also some scolding as well.

"I've been trying to wrap up things here. Planning a move at the same time has kept me tied up." Along with finding out he would soon be a father...

"I'm so proud of you and pleased you'll be moving closer. I don't see enough of you."

With his schedule, he couldn't promise it would be much different, but he did need to tell her about the baby. At least that would make her happy. "Mom, I'm glad you called. I've got some news."

"I hope it's good?"

"It is. I'm going to be a father." Even though he'd had a couple of days to adjust to the idea, the words still sounded strange.

"You are! I didn't even know you were seeing anyone!"

Gabe chuckled. His mother was as excited to hear the news as he had expected she would be. "I'm not really." He didn't want to get into it.

"Okay... Well, when is she due?"

"Sometime after the first of the year."

His mother shot back, "You don't know the exact date? Is it a boy or a girl?"

He really didn't know much. He and Zoe were going to have to really talk. Today. "I'll have to ask Zoe."

"I'm guessing she's the mother?" Curiosity filled her voice.

"Yes, her name is Zoe Avery."

"Where did you meet her?"

"At a professional meeting." He wasn't surprised his mother was full of questions.

"Gabe, I'm guessing this wasn't planned?" It sounded more like a question than a statement.

"It wasn't, but we're working all that out." His pager went off. He was needed in ICU. "Mom, I've got to go. I'll call you soon. I promise."

"Okay. I love you, son."

His mother might not have been around much, but he *had* known he was loved. His child would at least know Gabe cared, even if he couldn't be there for him all the time. He'd learned early from his mother that sacrifices were necessary to survive and succeed in a profession. That focus was important to get what you wanted. For him, that was to build a renowned liver-transplant program.

He checked on his patient in ICU the nurse had paged him about and increased the dosage of pain medicine, before giving instructions to his physician's assistant to notify him if there were additional issues. Then he headed to his office for some privacy. It was time he and Zoe had that overdue conversation. He just hoped she wouldn't try to evade it. They needed to discuss things whether she liked it or not.

She answered on the second ring.

"Zoe. It's Gabe. Please don't hang up."

"I wasn't going to." The soft voice that he'd know anywhere as Zoe's sounded distracted.

"Uh… How're you doing?" He felt like a teen calling a girl for the first time. It mattered too much.

"I'm fine."

His chest tightened. She didn't sound like it. "Are you feeling okay?"

"I'm fine and so is the baby."

He was relieved to hear that. It amazed him how quickly she and his unborn child had become so important to him. "Uh, what's the baby's due date?" He'd been so shocked to learn she was pregnant he'd not thought to ask earlier.

"January twenty-second."

"My father was born in January." He shook his head. That was an odd statement. He'd not thought of that in a long time. "Do you know what it is yet?"

"No. I'll find out soon."

"You'll let me know as soon as you do?" Why should he want to hear so badly? How much time would he spend being a father anyway? More than Zoe apparently thought he should. Fatherhood wasn't what he'd planned for his life but now he had to adjust and adapt. He was determined to be the best father he could be.

"I will if you want me to."

He would like to tell his mother the sex. She would be so excited. Would start buying clothes. "Zoe, how did this happen?"

She tittered. "Why, Doctor, I thought you, of all people, understood the birds and the bees."

The Zoe with a sense of humor had returned. This was ground he was comfortable on. He huffed. "I don't mean the physical process. I thought you had things handled."

"I thought so too. I guess the pill failed." She sighed. "Or maybe the condom was bad. I don't know. I just know

I'm pregnant. I'm sorry, Gabe. I realize this isn't what you wanted."

It wasn't, but he could tell by her tone that she hadn't planned it either. "Maybe not, but I'll deal with it. Meet my responsibilities."

"This baby needn't ruin your life. I have things handled. I can raise it. I want to. There's no reason for you to change your lifestyle because of us. I know this wasn't in your life plan."

"You're not going to handle this alone. I'm here to help. I should help."

In the background, a woman called Zoe's name. Was that her mother?

"I'll be right there, Mom," Zoe said in an exasperated tone.

"Is everything okay?"

"Yes. And no." Zoe sounded bone weary. "Mom's Alzheimer's has really progressed. She's more confused these days. More demanding."

The faint sounds of Zoe's name being shouted again reached Gabe's ear.

"Sorry but I've got to go," Zoe said. "'Bye."

The click of them being disconnected was the last he heard.

The next day between surgeries he couldn't stop himself from texting her.

Is there a good time for me to call?

A few minutes later he received her reply.

Tonight. No later than ten-thirty my time. I have an early meeting in the morning.

Gabe typed back.

Will call at ten.

He needed to discuss his trip to her part of the world the next weekend. He would be looking for a house and wanted her to set aside some time to see him and discuss the baby's future.

His phone buzzed. He was needed in the emergency department. There had been a car accident. It turned out that his patient was a teenage girl who required surgery right away.

Hours later, Gabe left the operating room and checked his phone. He groaned. It was already after ten-thirty. Remorse filled him. He'd promised Zoe he would call her earlier. This was just another example of why he shouldn't have a family. He was so focused on his job. A wife and children deserved better than leftovers and afterthoughts. He would soon be a father. Where was he going to find the time? He had to show Zoe how serious he was about being a parent.

His child. Somehow that sounded weird and right at the same time.

Regardless of the time, he needed to talk to Zoe, even if just to make plans for the weekend.

She answered on the first ring. "Hello." The word was said quietly as if he had woken her.

He remembered her voice sounding like that the night they had spent together. "It's Gabe."

"I know."

Was that because of caller ID or because she recognized his voice? He hoped the latter. Now that he was actually speaking to her, he was a little unsure. "I'm sorry I'm late calling. I didn't think you'd be asleep yet. There was an emergency and time got away from me. How're you doing?" he finally asked.

"Fair, all things considered."

"Has something happened to the baby?" Gabe's middle clinched at the thought. He was surprised at how quickly his mind had gone that direction.

"No. The baby is fine. The doctor said today it measures just right. Heartbeat is strong."

An odd feeling washed over him. He was relieved to hear it. "Was everything all right with your mom after last night?"

"Yeah, she was just confused. She gets more anxious and demanding these days. She's asleep now."

"That must be stressful." He couldn't imagine what he'd do with his job demands if his mother required his attention like Zoe's did.

"I don't wish this disease on anyone."

Gabe had heard Alzheimer's was difficult to deal with, but this was the first time he'd known someone facing it daily. "Do you have any help?"

"Not really. My sister lives about four hours away and travels for work, so she can't come often." There was a pause, and then she asked, "Do you happen to know how the boy from Chicago is doing? His mother was beside herself."

"She was, but she was much better after she knew Bobby was going to be all right and they had a place to stay for the night. I spoke to her the other day and Bobby is doing just great."

"You called her?"

Gabe grinned. "Don't sound so surprised. I did. I like to keep track of my patients. She said if it weren't for the stitches in his head she wouldn't even know anything had happened."

"Good. I'm glad to hear it. You were good with him. Both as a doctor and a person."

"Thanks. I like to see that my patients get complete care. You weren't half-bad yourself. Using the diaper to stop the blood flow was quick thinking."

"It's my turn to say thanks."

The self-assured Zoe had returned. Smiling to himself, he got down to business. "I wanted to let you know I'll be in town this weekend, looking for a place to live. I'd like to see you. Discuss things without being interrupted."

"Look, Gabe, I appreciate what you're trying to do, really I do. But you don't need to feel obligated. I'm fine. I can take care of the baby."

His blood ran hot. Why did she keep pushing him away when he was offering to help? Did she expect he'd be satisfied with a phone call here and there and a few school pictures? It was time to make himself clear. "Zoe, I have every intention of being an active parent in my child's life. You're not going to push me out of it. I'll gladly handle my share of the expenses. I not only want to be involved, I *will* be involved. Let's try to keep this between us and not drag others into the situation."

Silence lay heavy between them.

She must have gotten his less-than-subtle hint about hiring a lawyer. He didn't want to go there but he would if he had to. Growing up without a father hadn't been fun. At baseball games there hadn't been a man in the stands cheering him on or coaching on the sidelines. When he'd liked his first girl and she had wanted nothing to do with him, there had been no man to listen and offer advice based on experience. His mother had tried but it just hadn't been the same. Those memories only made him all the more determined to be a present father to his child. It was his child, his responsibility.

After his and Zoe's night together, he'd like to believe

they had parted friends, albeit uncomfortable ones, but civil nonetheless. He wanted to build on that. He had no interest in angering Zoe, so he volunteered in a conciliatory tone, "I'll be looking at houses most of the day on Saturday, so how about having dinner with me that evening?"

"I can't. I don't have anyone to watch Mother."

"Then I'll pick up something and bring it to your place. I'd really like for us to talk about this." He wasn't letting Zoe run from him forever. He saw another call was coming in. He'd have to get it. "The floor is paging me. I'll be in touch on Saturday."

By Wednesday, Zoe had red-rimmed eyes, a runny nose and was sneezing.

"Of all the times to get a head cold," she murmured as she headed down the hall of one of the local hospitals to see a patient. She already had her hands full with life and her job, and to feel awful was almost more than she could take. Since Gabe's call, she was still trying to sort out her thoughts and feelings.

The reality of him moving to the area, of seeing him on a regular basis was slowly seeping in. Against her better judgment she looked forward to seeing him again. That was a road she needed to close but how could she when their lives were becoming more intertwined, both personally and professionally? Her life was changing so fast she was racing to catch up. What more could happen?

She sanitized her hands using the liquid in the container by the patient's door and pulled out a mask from the box on the shelf nearby. Mr. Luther was her most difficult patient but one her heart went out to. Why, she didn't know. He didn't make it easy. It could be Mr. Luther was the father figure she was missing in her life or that he just didn't have anyone else. He reminded her of a bad-tempered grandfather who hid his huge soft spot well.

For some reason she was the one person he would listen to. Maybe he sensed she liked him despite his rough outer shell. Regardless, she was determined to do whatever she could to help him.

Knocking on the hospital door, she waited until she heard the gruff "Yeah."

She took a deep breath to fortify herself for what was coming. Pushing the door open, Zoe entered the dark room where the TV was blaring. The sixty-four-year-old man who sat in a chair beside the bed didn't even look her way as she entered.

He'd been in and out of the hospital for months with advancing inflammation of the liver caused by hepatitis C. Because of it he had a yellow tint to his skin and eyes and ongoing nausea and fatigue. It didn't look like he would have any improvement without a transplant. She hoped that Gabe might help her there. When the time was right she'd ask him. With any luck, Mr. Luther would be transferred to Gabe's care at National Hospital and listed for a transplant.

"Hello, Mr. Luther. How're you doing this morning?"

"You know as well as I do how I'm doing."

She might but she wouldn't let him get away with ignoring her. "Do you mind if we turn the TV down?"

"I do but I guess you'll do it anyway."

Zoe grinned as she found the remote and lowered the volume. She'd learned long ago that his bark was worse than his bite. "I need to give you a listen and have you sign a couple of forms so I have permission to look at your chart."

"The others here have already listened to me today."

"You know how this works by now. I have to do my own listening and looking at lab results if I'm going to help you get better. I'm your advocate. I don't work for the hospital. I work for you. I'm here to help you."

"Aw, go ahead. You will anyway."

Zoe stepped to him. Pulling her stethoscope out of her pocket and placing the ends in her ears, she proceeded to listen to his heart. It sounded steady and strong, which pleased her. She then listened to his lungs and checked his pulse rate. Removing her small penlight from her lab coat pocket, she said, "I need to look in your eyes."

"I was afraid of that." Mr. Luther lifted his face to her.

She pointed the light in his eyes. What she found there she wasn't as happy with. The whites still weren't clear.

"Well? Will I be getting out of here soon?"

"That's not for me to say. Your doctor here makes those decisions. But I will be in touch. If I don't see you here next week, I'll be calling you at home to check on you." She didn't have to keep such close tabs on him, but as far as she knew, there was no one else to do it. Zoe placed her hand on his shoulder. "Please do what they say, Mr. Luther."

He grunted. "Always do."

She looked back at him as she went out the door. He was going to need a liver transplant much sooner than the doctors had originally estimated.

As she traveled to different hospitals to check on other patients and completed paperwork in her office over the next few days, she continued to search for reasons not to see Gabe while he was in town. The longer she could put him off, the better. Dealing with him was the last thing she needed at this point in her emotionally and physically overloaded life.

Preparing for her baby's birth, dealing with her mother's rapidly deteriorating condition and now the urgent need to get Mr. Luther on the fast track for a liver transplant... If only Gabe would stop pressuring her to make decisions about her baby's future, decisions that could wait until closer to the due date. If Gabe sincerely wanted to help her, maybe she could convince him to give her those precious three months before her baby was born to deal with her other problems by priority. Would he understand her genuine need for time and distance? Or would he be self-centered, accusing her of trying to push him out of the baby's life?

On Saturday afternoon, her mother had gone to her room for a nap and Zoe was trying to get some much-needed rest on the sofa. The cold was taking its toll on her. She'd just closed her eyes when the phone rang. Anticipation zinged through her. Would it be Gabe?

"Hey," he said when she answered, not giving his name. It wasn't necessary. Zoe would have known his voice anywhere. "Have you changed your mind about going out to dinner?"

"No." Even to her own ears she didn't sound welcoming, yet blood whipped through her veins at the mere fact she was speaking to Gabe.

"You sound awful. What's wrong?"

"I woke with a cold the other morning."

"Are you taking care of it? Getting enough rest?" His concern somehow made her feel better. She liked knowing Gabe cared about her, even if it was just because of the baby.

"Yes. I'm just tired."

"Then I'll pick up dinner. Bring it to you. What's your address?"

She gave it to him.

"I'll see you in about an hour and a half. 'Bye."

Knowing she was about to see Gabe again caused her stomach to flutter. Despite feeling bad, she still rushed around, putting her apartment in order in anticipation of his visit. Her life was already a tightrope and Gabe was tying complicated knots in it as well. With one more tiny twist she might snap.

Zoe finally settled on the sofa to wait for him. She hadn't missed his poorly veiled threat about getting a lawyer involved if she didn't talk to him. The nervous waves in her stomach crashed harder, despite him brushing off his threat with a dinner offer. He'd made it plain he didn't want a wife and children the night they had been together. His declaration of lifelong bachelorhood over five months ago contradicted his current insistence on being involved with their child. How long would his sense of obligation last? Until "his" child started making demands on his time? Would he still be sharing parental duties when they started to interfere with his career? Maybe he didn't mind being a father as much as he hated the thought of being a husband. If that was the case, she was left with the conclusion he would never marry her.

That hurt. It shouldn't, but it did.

She had no doubt Gabe wouldn't consider marriage as a practical solution to their situation. In the unlikely event he did, she would say no. Being wanted because she was the mother of his child wasn't good enough. When she married it would be for love. Her hand went to her middle. Right now, her focus would be on the baby. She wasn't going to let Gabe continue making immediate demands that would needlessly confuse her life further.

The door buzzer woke Zoe. Panic filled her. She'd had every intention of having time to apply some makeup and fix her hair before Gabe arrived. She stopped in front of a mirror on the way to the door and pushed at her hair, creating some order, before she checked the peephole, getting a distorted view of Gabe. Even then he looked amazing. Why couldn't he be everything she *didn't* want in a man?

Zoe unlocked and opened the door. Gabe had two large white bags in his hands and one small brown one. She'd never seen him casually dressed. The white-collared shirt he wore rolled up his forearms set off his dark hair and California tan. Jeans hugged his slim hips and loafers covered his feet. He could be a model for a men's cologne ad. He took her breath away.

For seconds, they just looked at each other. He broke the silence. "May I come in?"

"Yes." Zoe pushed the door wider.

Gabe entered, looked around, then headed toward the kitchen table, where he set the bags down. "You sit down and rest. I'll get things on the table. Just tell me where they are."

Zoe closed the door and followed more slowly. Her apartment went from small to tiny with Gabe in it. She needed to get a grip on her attraction to him or she would lose control of the situation.

Her mother joined them, looking from Gabe and back to her, perplexed.

Zoe put a reassuring hand on her mother's arm. "Mom, I want you to meet a friend of mine, Gabe Marks."

"Friend" might be stretching their actual relationship, but she didn't want to explain more.

Gabe came around the table with a smile on his face. "Mrs. Avery, it's a pleasure to meet you."

Her mother smiled. "Hello."

"I brought you some dinner. I hope you're hungry." He pulled a chair out from under the table and held it for her.

"Thank you. I am." Her smile broadened as she sat.

Zoe sank into a chair.

Gabe returned to the bags, continuing to remove cartons. "Zoe, I hate it, but I forgot drinks."

How like him to take control and look comfortable doing it. "I have iced tea made."

"Sounds great." He looked at her mother and smiled. "That work for you too, Mrs. Avery?"

Her mother grinned, an endearing expression Zoe hadn't seen in some time, and nodded to Gabe. The devil was charming her mother out of her fog.

Zoe stood.

"I said I'd get things." He waved her down and headed into the kitchen. "Just tell me where they are. Plates? Silverware?"

"I don't feel that bad." Zoe joined him. Gabe took her by the arm and gently led her back to her chair.

Her body trembled at his touch. She sat, forcing him to release her. If he had noticed her hypersensitive reaction to him, he didn't show it, much to her relief. She had to somehow smother her physical desire for him. She couldn't spend the rest of her life fighting it and hiding it from him.

"You may not feel very bad at the moment, but you don't need to exert yourself any more than absolutely necessary. You don't want to get worse." His tone said he'd accept no argument.

Zoe huffed then gave him directions to which cabinet and drawer he needed. He soon had the table set and was heading into the kitchen again.

"Glasses?"

"Cabinet next to the refrigerator."

After the chinking of ice dropping into glasses, Gabe brought two drinks to the table and returned to get the other. He took the seat at the head of the table. For some reason that held significance. As if he was taking on more importance in her life than she wanted.

"Who are you?" her mother asked. In a different situation Zoe might have thought it was funny. Her mother might be as overwhelmed by Gabe as Zoe was, but in this instance she was afraid her mother just didn't remember.

Gabe answered before Zoe had a chance to. "I'm Gabe."

"Oh, yeah, that's right."

He didn't miss a beat and started opening containers. "Would you like a piece of fried chicken, Mrs. Avery?"

"Yes, that would be nice."

Gabe picked up her plate and placed a piece on it. "How about potatoes, green beans and a roll?"

"Please."

Gabe finished serving her plate and put it in front of her. "Mrs. Avery, did Zoe tell you that I'm moving to the area?"

She looked at Zoe. "No, she didn't. You'll like it here. Henry and I moved here when we were newlyweds."

"So you've lived around here for a long time," Gabe said as he scooped food onto another plate.

Zoe watched her mother become dreamy-eyed as memories surfaced. "We had the best time together."

That was until Zoe's father had left and never returned. In her mother's illness she only remembered the good times, but Zoe clearly recalled the hurt and devastation her father had left behind. She never wanted to live through that again.

"I'm sure you did." Gabe smiled at her then opened the brown bag. He looked at Zoe. "I forgot. I made a special stop for you." He pulled out a plastic container of liquid. "Chicken soup. Let me get you a bowl and spoon." Before she could say anything, he was on his way back to the kitchen. When he returned, he poured the soup in the bowl and placed it and the spoon in front of her.

He'd made a stop just for her? When had someone last made her feel so special? The soup smelled heavenly. She met Gabe's expectant expression. "Thanks. This hits the spot."

"Who're you?" her mother asked.

Zoe couldn't help but chuckle this time. She was asking herself the same thing. Was there another man like him? If there was, she'd never met him.

"I'm Gabe."

"That's right. Did you know that Zoe's having a baby?" She looked at Zoe.

Gabe looked at her as well. "Yes, ma'am, I see that."

"She'll be a good mother. She's a nurse, you know." Her mother's attention returned to her food.

"I do know." He continued to watch Zoe. "I also think she'll be a good mother."

"Are you Zoe's boyfriend?"

"Mom!"

Gabe's eyes questioned her as if asking permission to answer. Was he wondering how much her mother knew? It was time to come clean. "Mom, Gabe is the baby's father."

Her mother studied him closely. "You will get married." That wasn't a question but a statement.

Embarrassment flooded Zoe. She couldn't even look at Gabe. "Mom! You can't go around telling men to marry me."

Her mother ignored her and went back to eating. "This is good," she said, not missing a beat. As if she hadn't created a cloud of tension in the room.

It took a few minutes for Zoe to find the courage to even glance at Gabe. He seemed to have taken the exchange in his stride.

After their meal Zoe settled her mother in her room to watch TV and returned to find Gabe had cleaned up the table. "I'm sorry about that. I don't expect you to marry me. I've never thought you should."

"Don't worry about it," he said in an even tone. "I put some coffee on. I hope you don't mind. It's been a long day." He hung the washcloth up.

"I'm not surprised. You pretty much came in and made yourself at home." She hadn't meant to sound irritated, even though she was…a little.

A shocked look came over his face. "I'm sorry. That

wasn't my intent. I hadn't eaten since early this morning, having looked at houses all day. Plus, I knew you didn't feel well and I guess I just got carried away."

Was she being too sensitive? He had her so out of sorts she'd not even thought about him, his needs. This situation couldn't be any easier on him than it was on her. If she met him halfway then maybe it would be better. She could at least try. "Why don't you go have a seat in the living room and I'll bring you a cup of coffee. How do you like it?"

"Black is fine."

With coffee in hand, she found Gabe sitting on the sofa, legs stretched out with his head back and his eyes closed. Was he asleep? Why did it seem so natural to have him in her home?

He quickly straightened when she set the mug on the table closest to him. He ran his hands through his wavy hair. "Thanks. I'd rather do two transplants back-to-back than look at houses all day."

She settled in the chair facing him.

Gabe took a sip of his coffee.

"Did you find a place?" Was it nearby? Could she handle him being so close?

"I did. It's out in Vernon Landing."

Zoe breathed a sigh of relief. It wasn't as local as she'd feared. The traffic alone would make him think twice before he just showed up. She wouldn't allow that anyway. He was right—they needed to talk. They needed to at least agree on visitation guidelines before the baby was born.

"I'm glad you found something." She couldn't help but ask, "When will you be moving in?"

"Two weeks."

Her heart did a thump-bump. "That soon."

"Yeah. I'm to start my new position on the first of the month."

Zoe had hoped for more time to adjust to the idea of him living nearby.

"I know this is going to be an adjustment," he remarked as though he could read her mind. "Neither one of us planned how things have turned out."

That was an understatement if Zoe had ever heard one. Her hand went to her belly.

"Zoe."

She looked at him.

"I have no intention of taking the baby away from you. All I want is to be in his life. See him or her occasionally. Do my share financially."

That declaration did make her feel better. He sounded sincere, not threatening. Having him help financially would be nice, especially since her mother was going to require ever more costly care as time went on. However, she wouldn't let Gabe think for a moment he could do as he pleased where the baby was concerned. "You know, you can't just show up here unannounced."

He put his mug down, placing his arms on his knees with hands clasped between them, and leaned toward her. "I would never do that."

"We're going to have to set rules and guidelines. I'll be raising him or her." How matter-of-fact she sounded pleased her. *She* was in control of this discussion.

"Agreed. But big decisions like schools, medical care, moving out of town should be discussed with me." Gabe's dark expression warned of his unwillingness to negotiate.

"Moving?" That he had given the future that much thought startled her. She was going to have to make a change of living space soon.

His expression didn't waver. "I won't allow you to take him or her to the other side of the country to where it makes it hard to be a part of their life."

She appreciated his rights as a father, but she wasn't

going to build her world around his wants. She started to say as much but he cut her off. "When I get settled, why don't I get a lawyer to draw up an agreement? That way we'll both know where we stand. You can make a list and I will too. Then we can compare and come to a satisfactory compromise."

Zoe considered his suggestion with care. She had intended to tell him his role in their child's life wasn't to dictate how she would raise her child, but doing so would result in arguing about it. "All right. I can do that."

Gabe stood. "Then I'd better go. I have a bit of a drive to the hotel."

Zoe rose too and followed him to the door. "Uh, Gabe, before you go, could I ask you about something?"

He looked at her. "Sure."

"I hate to ask you this before you even started your new job, but I have a patient, Mr. Luther. He's medically fragile and his liver is failing. He could really use your expertise. He can be a difficult patient but he's getting sicker and sicker..." She'd had other patients sicker than Mr. Luther, so why was she so concerned about him? He would end up being like the other men in her life and just pass through—but she still wanted the best for him.

"Email me his file and I'll have a look."

"Thank you." Why did she believe Gabe would make it all right? It would be so easy to lean on him in her professional life as well as her personal one. But could she count on him always being there?

His gaze met hers, held. Heat built in her. That same effect he'd had on her during their night together was there, curling around her, tugging her closer to him. Gabe's hand gently brushed a thread of hair away from her cheek. "You're welcome. I should go. Take care of yourself. Please tell your mother I said 'bye. See you soon."

That sounded like a promise. Zoe couldn't help but wish

for more even as she told herself that was the last thing she needed. She closed the door behind him. Something about Gabe made her want to ask him to stay longer. Yet she knew those feelings, if she acted on them, would only make matters worse.

CHAPTER THREE

GABE STEPPED INTO an empty conference room at the hospital and tapped Zoe's number on his phone for the second time that day. A couple of days had passed before he'd allowed himself to call her, convincing himself he should check on her, the baby. He could have texted, but for some inexplicable reason he was eager to hear Zoe's voice.

She'd sent the files as he had requested. He was still reviewing them, but he'd already decided to examine Mr. Luther as soon as possible. Why hadn't Zoe at least called or texted him about the patient she was so concerned about?

After a number of rings there was still no answer. What was going on with her? Had something happened to the baby? To Zoe? Her mother?

He was thousands of miles away with no way of knowing. Why didn't Zoe answer? He would try her one more time. If she didn't pick up he'd call the police and have them stop by her place. Gabe touched the green icon and listened to three rings.

On the fourth a breathless voice said, "Hello?"

Relief flooded him, the tension ebbing away from his shoulders. "Zoe, I've been calling you all day."

"Gabe, I don't need this today."

"What's wrong?"

There was an exasperated sound on the other end, and

then Zoe said, "Mother decided to cook bacon. She left the pan on the burner. The kitchen caught fire. I'm at the hospital right now."

His gut felt like someone had it in their fist and was twisting it. "Is she all right? Are you?"

"They're treating her for smoke inhalation. She'll be in the hospital at least overnight. The fire alarm went off and one of the neighbors called the fire department. They got there quickly or it could have been much worse." She paused. "I'm fine and the baby is too."

He said gently, "It may be time to find your mother a place where she'll have full-time care."

"I know, but that's costly. I can't afford an apartment and pay for a place for her to stay. Her insurance doesn't kick in until she is fifty-nine and a half. That's another seven months. I'll just have to figure something out until then. The doctor has just come in. I have to go. 'Bye."

"'Bye." He spoke into silence.

Unable to stand not knowing what was going on any longer, Gabe took the first opportunity he had and called again around midmorning the next day. He tapped his pen against his desk in his apprehension about how she would react to his suggestion that she come and live with him. Zoe answered on the first ring.

"How're things today?" he asked.

"Better." She sounded tired.

He wished he was there to hold her. Whoa—that wasn't a thought he should be having, or the type of relationship they had. "That's good to hear. I'm concerned about you. Are you taking care of yourself?"

"I told you—the baby's fine," she informed him, as if he hadn't just asked about her welfare.

Did she think he was only concerned about the baby and not her? "I want to know about you as well. Have you been able to make some plans?" Would she consider his idea? For some reason it really mattered to him that she accept his plan.

"A few. The doctor said Mom could stay in the hospital a week. That'll give me time to look for an assisted-living home for her. I don't want her to make any unnecessary moves. She's already confused enough."

Strength and determination had returned to Zoe's voice. "Can you go back to your apartment?"

"No. It's so damaged it's uninhabitable. I'll have to find a new place."

This was his opening to offer his solution. "I have something I want you to consider and I want you to hear it out before you say anything. Right now, your most urgent problem is twofold: finding somewhere your mother will be safe and that has adequate full-time care, *and* somewhere for you to live. Let me help."

"Gabe, I'm not taking money." She sounded iron-rod strong. "I can handle things on my own."

"Please hear me out." Why wouldn't she let him help her? Zoe's independence would get her into trouble one day. "I'm sure you can, but if you'll listen, I think you might find my plan practical and helpful."

She huffed then said, "Okay. What do you think I should do?"

"I think you need to move in with me."

"What!"

He jerked the phone away from his ear.

She came close to yelling, "That's not going to happen. No way."

Gabe interrupted, using his giving-order-in-the-OR voice. "Just listen. You need to find a place for your mother. Money is an issue. If you stay at my house, where I have plenty of room, you'd be able to pay for a place for her while you wait for her insurance to start."

"Thank you, but I don't think so." Her words sounded as though they were coming through clenched teeth.

"Why not?" He'd offered a practical solution. Couldn't she see that?

"Because you don't need to be involved in my problems, my private life." She sounded as if he should have known that.

"If it'll make you feel any better, I'm interested in seeing that my child comes into the world with a mother who hasn't been sleeping on a couch in someone's living room. Who isn't stressed out over finances. It'll just be for a few months. We'd only be housemates. You can pay rent if you like."

"I appreciate your offer, but I don't think it would work." Her voice had calmed, but her resolve was loud and clear.

What was that supposed to mean? It was a practical solution. "Just think about it."

"I have to go. Mother's calling me. Her nurse has just come in."

Silence filled his ear. He wasn't surprised that she'd shot the idea down and ended the call. If nothing else, he'd learned Zoe was stubborn.

Zoe resisted the impulse to kick something. How dared Gabe think that she would move in with him? She didn't even know him. Just because she was having his child, it didn't mean he had any say over her life.

Up until a week ago they hadn't really talked, and even then all they'd done was agree to make lists of what they wanted. And have a lawyer make it legal. She mustn't forget that part of his idea. She should have rejected his idea outright and told him what he could and could not do when it came to his rights. Instead she'd meekly agreed to avoid an argument.

Now he was trying to move her around like a pawn on a chessboard. She wasn't having it. Taking care of her mother, her baby and herself was her job, her decisions to make. She didn't need or want him butting into her life anytime he pleased. Besides, if she started letting him make major decisions about her life, what would she do when he got tired of playing daddy or didn't have time for her when the next crisis cropped up? One thing she had learned was that she must be careful who she depended on.

Two days later Zoe wasn't feeling nearly as confident. Since she couldn't return to her apartment, her renter's insurance was paying for a hotel room until she found a place to live or for fourteen days, whichever came first. Her priority over the weekend had been to locate a place for her mother to live. That had turned out to be more difficult than anticipated.

She'd visited every assisted-care facility in the immediate area. Responsibility weighed heavily on her about having to put her mother in a home. She had found one that would be suitable, but it was way beyond her budget. Guilt squeezed her heart.

Between searching for facilities for her mother and her full-time job, there hadn't yet been time to look for a place for herself. Her apartment manager told her that there wasn't an empty apartment available in the complex. Since her lease was almost up, Zoe would have to look elsewhere. Fourteen days in which to see to her mother's needs and find a new home for herself, not to mention getting packed to move. There simply wasn't enough time. She was almost at her wits' end.

Her workload was heavy, but she'd managed to squeeze in checking on Mr. Luther. He'd been discharged from the hospital, where he'd been treated for stomach pain and fatigue. These were just symptoms of a larger issue that wouldn't get better without a transplant. It was time he be admitted to National Hospital for a transplant workup. Thankfully he wasn't so sick he couldn't go home until that time, but that wouldn't be the case for much longer. When she could think straight again she must talk to Gabe about him.

That night at the hotel while Zoe sat eating takeout food, her phone rang. It was Gabe. She hated to admit it, but his unwelcomed suggestion was starting to look like the only answer. "Hello."

"It's Gabe." He sounded unsure. Was he afraid of her reaction after his last call?

"Hi." She was so tired and disheartened she was glad to have someone to talk to, and Gabe was a good listener.

"How're things going?"

She loved the deep timbre of his voice. There was something reassuring about it. "They could be better." Zoe sounded as down as she felt. She refused to show weakness. Appearing needy wouldn't help her either. Gabe was already making plans regarding the baby she'd not counted on.

"Your mother?"

"She's actually recovering well." For that Zoe was grateful.

"What, then?"

"I've been out looking at homes for her." Her hand cradled her baby bump. The weight of her responsibilities was growing.

"And?"

"They were awful. I can't stand the idea of putting Mother in one. I hate myself for having to do it." Why was she spilling all of this to him? What was it about Gabe that made her want to lean on him? Their relationship was nothing like that, yet she was becoming more deeply involved with him each time they talked.

"What's happening with your mother isn't your fault. You know for her health and safety she needs to be in professional care where she'll be safe and well cared for. What occurred a few days ago proves it. You're not abandoning her. You're doing it because you love her."

His voice was gentle and reassuring, washing over her tight nerves like a warm balm. "Thanks for saying that. I just wish it wasn't necessary."

"You didn't find any place you liked?"

"I found the better of the evils." If only she had the money to put her mother there. Even if she emptied her savings she'd still be short. It was just as well there was no room available. She'd have to settle on one of the other places that weren't as nice as Shorecliffs House.

"So, will you move her in when she's able to leave the hospital?"

"Yes. I'm making arrangements tomorrow."

"I'm glad you found a place for her. Any luck on a new apartment for you?"

"I haven't had time to worry about that. I'll be good in the hotel for at least a few more days. I have to see what I can salvage out of the apartment. I know the living-room furniture will have to go. It smells too much like smoke. I can keep the tables and such, but everything has to be wiped down and packed up." It wasn't a job she was looking forward to, even if she would just be overseeing things.

"You'll have some help with that?" Concern filled his voice.

She pushed pillows behind her and leaned back against the headboard. "The insurance company has a crew coming in. I just have to find some place to put what's salvageable, like another apartment."

"I'm sorry this happened."

She could imagine him pulling her into a hug. "Me too,

but at least it made me face the inevitable. Mom needs more help than I can give her."

"Tough way to figure that out." Sincere sympathy surrounded his words.

"You're not kidding." Why was it so easy to talk to Gabe? She should be putting distance between them, not making him a confidant.

There was quiet on the line before he said, "Have you thought about my offer?"

She'd suspected that question would come up before the call ended. "Gabe, I'm not living with you."

"The invitation remains open if you change your mind. I'll be moving your way on Friday. I hate it but I've gotta go. Surgery is paging me. 'Bye."

Suddenly Zoe felt utterly alone. He seemed to always be rushing off somewhere. If only Gabe could have talked to her longer. She needed his logical reasoning because she hated the idea of her mother going into a care home. There was no one else to lean on. Her sister was out of the country. Zoe hadn't even been able to get in touch with her to tell her about the fire. Zoe had friends, but they had become rather distant since she'd had to spend so much time with her mother. Now that she needed someone, Gabe was filling that spot. It was odd. They knew so little about each other, yet they seemed to click.

She ran her hands over her belly. They certainly had clicked that one night. He'd been easy to be around then and he was now. Too easy.

Zoe stuffed her leftover meal into the paper bag and threw it in the garbage. Going back to bed, she slid between the bedsheets. Curling into a ball as she hugged a pillow to her, she let the tears she'd held in check flow. What would it be like to have strong, sure arms around her? Comforting arms? Someone to share her pain with?

That was what she'd always dreamed of. Gabe's face popped into her mind. She couldn't depend on him. He didn't want a wife and family. Just like her ex-fiancé and her father. She couldn't let her heart be hurt again like he had so easily done. She had to wait for the right man to give her heart to. The one who wanted the same things out of life that she did.

She did have her baby. Zoe smiled. Another person to take care of but she was looking forward to it. Would her child have Gabe's big blue eyes and dark hair? Or look more like her? In a few short months she would know. Hold him or her in her arms. Out of all this darkness there would be a shining star. With a slight smile on her lips, Zoe fell into an exhausted sleep.

The next afternoon she received a call from Shorecliffs House, the assisted-living home she couldn't afford. The administrator said they had a room opening after all. Before the woman had hardly finished, Zoe had said she would take it. When the conversation was over Zoe put her head against the wall and tapped it a few times. She knew what she had to do. The only way she could afford it was by moving in with Gabe until her mother's insurance would cover the cost.

Backing down and agreeing to Gabe's plan put her in a vulnerable position. There must be ground rules. Above all else they would not be sharing a bed. Ever. That rule couldn't be broken regardless of how tempting it might be.

With a lump in her throat she worked to swallow, Zoe pushed Gabe's phone number. He didn't answer, so she left a message. "Please call me."

A few hours later, while working at her old apartment, her phone rang. With shaking hands and banging heart, she said, "Hello?"

"Hey, what's going on?" He sounded distracted.

"That proposition you made about me renting a room from you—did you really mean it?"

"Yeah, I really mean it. Wouldn't have offered if I didn't." He seemed totally focused on their conversation now.

"It looks like I'm going to need to take you up on a room. But there have to be some rules."

"Such as?"

"I pay rent. I have my own room. I'm strictly a room-mate. I'll only stay until my mother's insurance starts. We lead our own lives without reporting in to each other."

"Okay." He drew the word out. "Do you mind if I ask what changed your mind?"

"The home I wanted to put Mom in had an opening. I had to jump at the chance when they called. Having a roommate is the only way I can afford it. I don't have time to look for one, so…"

"I see." By his tone he did.

"The arrangement will only be temporary. I'll be out in six months, tops. I'll have found my own place by then." Hers and the baby's.

"I don't have a problem with that. My house is plenty big enough for us both. My bedroom is on one side of the house while the other two bedrooms are on the other. We might meet in the kitchen occasionally.

"With my new position, I'll be super-busy, so I probably won't be around much. I'll be moving in on Friday. Why don't you let me make the arrangements for the movers to pick up your furniture?"

"I don't really have much. Everything I own smells like smoke. The insurance had to give me money for clothes. I'm at the apartment, boxing up family pictures and such now. I'll put whatever I decide I don't need in storage. I think my bedroom suite and Mom's should be all right but the mattresses may have to go. Anyway, I don't need to bore you with all that. I'll figure it all out and get back to you."

"Zoe, I already have my movers coming. You have enough going on. Let them take care of moving your stuff as well."

"You've got your hands full with your own move. I'll take care of mine." She had to start setting boundaries now. This she would do for herself. At least she could feel in control of one area of her life.

He huffed. "If that's the way you want it. Let me know when you're ready to move in and I'll make sure you can get into the house."

Someone in the background called his name. To them he said, "Yeah, I'll be right there. I need to do it myself." He spoke to her again. "I've got a case that needs my attention, so I've got to go. Take care of yourself."

Gabe didn't like the thought of Zoe handling her own moving arrangements or of her lifting boxes, but with her attitude, he wouldn't be doing himself any favors by pushing her further. He decided to keep his distance, trying not to think about what she was doing and why. He made a point of not calling her, even though he was anxious to know how she was doing.

Had her mother's move gone well? This personal interest in Zoe perplexed him. It wasn't like him. He put it down to the fact that she was the mother of his child. And he genuinely liked her. If he didn't hear from her soon he'd be forced to call her. On Thursday evening, he flew to Richmond and resisted the urge to try to see Zoe. If he hadn't heard from her by Friday evening he would call.

Early the next day he was standing on the porch of his new home, waiting for the movers to show up. He didn't have many belongings, had never cared much about what his home looked like as long as it was comfortable. With his more-gone-than-home lifestyle, he had never felt the need to decorate his places.

Apartments had always been where he'd lived as an adult, but with a child coming, a house had seemed like the right thing to buy. A boy needed a backyard. Or a girl. The idea of having a place for his son or daughter to play like he'd had appealed. He may not have had a father but he'd had a good childhood. He looked around him at the tree-lined street with the sidewalk running along it and the other houses with their green lawns and shook his head. A subdivision wasn't where he'd ever dreamed he'd be living.

Next thing he knew he'd be driving a minivan. The very idea made him huff. Yet he'd made a step in that direction today. He had sold his sports car and picked up his new four-door sedan. His argument to himself was that he was being practical, because it would be easier to get a car seat in and out of.

A moving van pulled into his drive. The large truck held his meager belongings—bedroom suite, kitchen table, sofa, boxed kitchen items and household goods. There would be a large amount of space in the house sitting empty. Maybe what he needed to do was hire an interior decorator to come in and suggest what he needed to buy. A few hours later the movers had left, and he was searching through a box for the coffee maker when his phone rang. His heart beat faster. It was Zoe. "Hey."

"I just wanted to let you know that I'm not going to move in until Sunday."

He was both disappointed and surprised. "Oh, okay. Why not earlier?"

"I've had to deal with Mother. And the guys can't help me until Sunday afternoon. I've spent most of the morning organizing what needs to go into storage and packing up the rest."

"Guys?" What guys was she talking about? She wouldn't

let him help her; instead, she'd chosen to ask some other men. There was a pang in his chest he didn't want to examine closely.

"Some friends from work," came her offhanded answer.

"It sounds like you have everything in hand." Could she hear the testiness he felt?

"Why I'm calling is to see if it's all right for me to come over and see what my room looks like. I need to decide what to bring and what to store."

His ego took another hit. She was only interested in seeing the house, not him. It occurred to him he was taking this all too personally because he was operating on the assumption they were more than merely accidental parents. Which they weren't, so why was he feeling this way? He had to get control of his imagination, be ruthlessly realistic about the foundation of their relationship. Starting now. "Sure. That'll be fine."

"How much longer do you think your movers will be? I don't want to get in their way."

She was all business. He could be that as well. "They left hours ago, so you're welcome anytime."

"Great. Please text me your address. I'll see you later." She hung up.

Gabe lost track of the number of times he'd checked his watch since Zoe had called. It amazed him how excited he was at the thought of seeing her again. The doorbell finally rang as he finished unpacking the last box in his bedroom.

He wiped his hands on his jeans and hurried to the front of the house. Through the pane glass of the door he could see Zoe. His heart beat faster. She was as amazing as he remembered. Her head was moving one way then another as if she was taking everything in. Pulling the door open wide, he stepped back and said in a welcoming manner, "Come in."

Zoe gave him a slight smile. "Hi. I like your house. It's...big."

He wasn't sure how to take that statement. Was she being complimentary or expressing relief they wouldn't be living in close proximity? Or both?

With a tentative step, Zoe entered Gabe's new home. Stepping into his living space symbolized how drastically her life was changing. It wasn't an unpleasant feeling, just one of uncertainty. As if she'd been forced to open a door without knowing what lay behind it.

It was a new redbrick home in an exclusive neighborhood that she'd only driven through a couple of times. She was a little surprised he'd chosen the area and such a large house. This was a subdivision of family homes, not where single men tended to live. Gabe didn't impress her as a spacious-home kind of person. So why had he decided on this one?

It did have one appealing advantage, though. It was large enough they would most likely have little or no contact while she resided here. That was what she wanted. To get through the next few months then move on. Or at least that was what she was going to keep telling herself.

She ran her fingertips over the smooth wooden door with its beautiful glass panels and large oval in the middle. A hardwood floor gleamed in the shaft of afternoon sun flowing in through the open doorway. Beyond the foyer was a sunken living area with a fireplace filling one wall. She took a timid step forward. Along the back were tall windows, revealing a circular brick patio and manicured yard. Her breath caught. It was perfect. If she'd been picking out a house this would have been the one she chose.

The corner of her mouth lifted a little. The living area's massive space held only a leather sofa, matching chair and large TV. How like a man to have only the essentials. What would it be like to snuggle up on that sofa next to Gabe in front of the fire? Something she wouldn't be doing. "You have a beautiful home."

She watched his lips curve up. Was he pleased with her compliment? Did it matter to him what she thought?

"Come on in and I'll show you around."

He led her through the living area, giving her time to admire the backyard anew through the windows as she followed him into the kitchen by way of a bay-window alcove that served as an eating area. A small table and two well-worn chairs were stationed there. The kitchen was spacious, furnished with all the latest appliances. She could only imagine what a pleasure it would be to cook for a family here. Hardly the galley-sized kitchen she'd been using.

It was a shame that no woman would share this house with him. If it was her... No, those thoughts were better left alone. That was one place she didn't need to go. He'd already made it clear what he wanted out of life and that didn't include her.

From there he pointed down a small hallway. "That's my suite and the way out to the carport. This is the way to your side of the house."

It might be, but she was afraid it wouldn't be far enough. Just being near him had her dreaming of what could be.

They crossed the living area and went through an arched doorway into a hallway that ran from the front of the house to the back.

"You have a choice between two bedrooms. You can have them both if you want them." Gabe turned to the right, bumping her as he did so. He grabbed her before she rocked backward. "Whoa there. We wouldn't want you to fall."

Gabe's hands were brand hot on her waist. He watched

her intently for a moment. His eyes focused on her lips before he released a breath he'd apparently been holding and let her go.

Zoe tingled all over with the desire to have him touch her again. Living in such a virile man's home wouldn't be easy.

He led her into a sunny room at the front of the house. It was larger than she'd had in her apartment. The street was out the front window and a neighbor's house could be seen in the distance through the other. "There's a full bath right there." Gabe pointed to a doorway. "The other room's down this way."

He didn't give her time to look before he walked out into the hallway. He acted as if he was making a point to keep as much distance as he could from her. Zoe caught up with him by the time he reached the doorway of the other room. This one was as large as the first but the view was nicer. From the window facing the back she could see the yard and trees.

"There's another bath in here." Gabe stood in the entrance and flipped on a light switch. "This bath isn't quite as large as the other one but it's a nice size."

He sounded almost apologetic. Did it really matter to him what she thought of it?

As she pondered those unsettling questions, he added, "You're welcome to store anything you like in the room you don't use."

"I appreciate that, but I've already put stuff in storage. I'll just be bringing my bedroom suite, a chair and TV. That should be enough. The less I bring, the less I have to worry about moving the second time." It was important she be practical about the arrangements because she *was not* living here long.

She caught sight of Gabe's odd expression a second

before he glanced away. "Whichever one you don't take I'll make the baby's room."

Her look met his again. "The baby will be living with me."

"I know that, but he or she will be regularly visiting me. I'll need a bedroom for my child."

His assertion solidified her resolve that when she was settled they were going to sit down and decide on Gabe's visitation schedule. His insistence on being involved wasn't going to overrule what she thought best for her baby. This was *her* baby. She would be making the final decisions about raising her child, regardless of what Gabe wanted. However, she knew this wasn't the time to broach that issue. She was juggling far too many things as it was. "We'll talk about your visitation rights later."

"Just because you keep putting it off, it doesn't mean the issue will go away. Or me, for that matter." He arched an eyebrow in challenge.

Before her temper got the better of her, Zoe headed for the front door. "I've got to get going. It's been a long day."

"Have you eaten? I could call for Chinese takeout or pizza."

She didn't slow down. "I have to go. I'll just do drive-through and go to bed early."

"Do you need any help moving? I can meet you Sunday morning."

Why did he keep being so nice to her? "Uh… No, I have it all taken care of. You've got your own stuff here to worry about." She walked out the front door but stopped on the porch. "By the way, did you have a chance to look at Mr. Luther's file?"

"I did. I plan to talk to his primary doctor just as soon as I can."

She stepped to him and touched his arm briefly.

That was a mistake. Even that had her blood humming. "Thanks, Gabe. I really appreciate it."

He glanced down before his earnest look met hers. "No problem, but still no promises."

"I understand." She smiled and removed her hand. "I'm grateful for any help you can offer him. See you on Sunday." She closed the door behind her and headed for her car.

As she slid into the driver's seat, Gabe stepped out onto the porch, his face unreadable. As she drove away, Zoe looked in her rearview mirror. Gabe was still standing there, hands in his pockets.

Why was she already missing him? He truly was a decent guy. She couldn't think of another person who would have been as understanding or helpful as he had been under the circumstances. Still, she must not forget he was only being so generous because of the baby. What would it be like to have someone like Gabe to come home to at the end of a weary day?

At least for a short while she and the baby had a nice place to live and, better yet, her mother was in a safe place that provided quality care. That was what really mattered.

Not the feelings Gabe brought out in her.

CHAPTER FOUR

LATE SUNDAY AFTERNOON, Zoe led the way in her compact car to Gabe's house. A couple of guys from work, John and Rick, were helping her move. They had managed to stay right behind her despite their trucks being heavy with her furniture and boxes of possessions.

She was grateful that Shorecliffs House encouraged residents to bring their own furniture when they moved in. Having familiar belongings around had definitely made her mother less anxious. To Zoe's surprise, her mother seemed content with her new residence.

In a few months Zoe would be living in her own place as well. If she could find the right small house she would buy. A child needed space, other families around them. A neighborhood similar to Gabe's.

She had managed to salvage the end tables in her living room. With those and one comfortable chair she'd bought with some of the insurance money, she planned to set up a small living area in her bedroom. That way she wouldn't disturb Gabe when he was home. If she didn't take steps to keep her distance, she could easily become too involved in his life. That wasn't what he wanted and she would respect that.

As Zoe pulled into the drive, Gabe stepped out onto the front porch. Had he been watching for her? She pulled as far up the driveway as she could so the two trucks would be as close as possible to the front door. Moments later she climbed out of the car and started toward him.

He wore a T-shirt and worn jeans with tennis shoes. His casual dress somehow made him even more attractive. It would be nice to have him greeting her when she came home every day. What was wrong with her? That fantasy she shouldn't entertain.

She joined John and Rick, who were already in the process of untying ropes securing her furniture. Gabe came down the two steps toward them.

"Gabe, this is John and Rick." She pointed to one then the other. "They work with me."

He shook hands with the men. "I'll get this end," he said to John as he pulled her headboard off the truck. Gabe maneuvered the bulky item, and then he led the way into the house with John carrying the other end.

Zoe pulled a box off and carried it inside. Gabe was on his way out of her room when she entered.

"You don't need to be carrying that. Give it here." His hands covered hers as he tried to take the box.

Awareness zipped through her. It was always there between them. Even the simplest touch from Gabe had her thinking of that night they had spent together. "I'm fine. It's not that heavy." She gave it a tug, removing his hands. "These guys can't spend all evening here. I need to help."

"Then why don't you just tell us where to put things and let us handle the moving?" Gabe followed her back to the room.

John glanced at them then slipped out the door.

She set the box down. "You need to understand right now that you do not tell me what I should or shouldn't do."

"And you need to think less about proving your independence and more about what's good for the baby. Now let us handle it."

Anger washed through Zoe as he left before she could

respond. A minute later Rick and John entered with the footboard. Gabe was right behind them with the rails. Gabe and John put the bed together while Rick returned to the truck. She pointed to the wall she wanted the bed against. Rick returned with a couple of boxes stacked on top of each other. All the men left once again. Zoe started removing bedsheets, pillows and a blanket from a box. She'd stay put and start unpacking if it would keep Gabe from making a scene.

All three men made a couple more trips to the truck.

After one trip she and Rick were left alone. He asked, nodding toward the doorway, "Who is this guy you're renting from?"

Before she could respond, Gabe entered the room with an end table and said in a tight tone, "I'm the father of her baby."

John came in right behind him. He and Rick looked at her with wonder then back at Gabe.

Holding up a hand, John said, "No offense, man. We just wanted to make sure Zoe was safe."

"None taken." Gabe's voice still held a hard note. "I'm sure she appreciates having friends who care about her." Gabe set the table down and stepped beside her.

"Come on, Rick." John tapped him on the shoulder. "We only have a couple more boxes."

"Why didn't you tell them who I am? Are you ashamed?" Gabe asked.

Zoe couldn't have been more shocked. Why would he believe that? He was an excellent doctor, well respected in his field, smart, had good taste in homes and, most of all, was a wonderful lover. Where had he gotten the idea she might be embarrassed by him? She couldn't imagine any woman not being proud of being associated with him. "I can assure you that's not the case. I just don't broadcast my private life. John and Rick are my friends but not that close."

"They sure sounded protective of you. I thought there might be more going on." His tone implied he might be jealous.

No man she knew even came close to measuring up to Gabe. She turned her head and gave him a questioning look. He had to care on some level to have those feelings, didn't he? Warmth flowed through her at the possibility. The self-assured man for once needed her reassurance. She stepped toward him. "Gabe, there's nothing to—"

"Well, that's it," Rick announced as he and John came in with a box apiece.

Zoe stepped away from Gabe but she felt his attention on her as he said, "Thanks, guys."

John and Rick headed for the front door, and she and Gabe followed.

There Gabe shook their hands, saying, "Thanks for your help. I appreciate it. I know Zoe does too."

There he was again, speaking for her. It made them sound like a couple. They weren't. "I do. I don't know what I'd have done without you guys." She hugged John then Rick. "I owe you big-time."

"Maybe you can make it up to us by bringing us some of your peanut-butter cookies. They're the best in the whole DC area."

Zoe was both flattered and embarrassed by such high praise of her cookies. She promised them a batch as soon as she settled in. They said their goodbyes.

"Thanks again," Zoe called and waved. She turned to see Gabe standing in the front doorway, leaning against the frame. Her nerves buzzed. Not only was she alone with him, she was now living in his house. She walked toward him. "Well, I guess I'll go finish straightening my room."

"Wouldn't you like to sit down for a few minutes? Have

something to eat. Not that I have anything here. I was going to order a pizza."

"I should get some unpacking done. I have to be at work early in the morning. I've been gone for a week." For some reason she needed to get to her room, take a moment for herself without Gabe nearby.

Gabe followed her more slowly into the house. Had he made the right decision by inviting Zoe to live at his house? Could he have offered a different solution to her living arrangements? He'd never counted on this attraction roaring through him. He had to keep his emotions in check. Focus on the baby and not the mother. It would be tough, but he would manage it.

Zoe was hiding from him. He was as certain of that fact as he was his name. She wasn't the type to run from problems. She had more than shown her ability to handle difficult circumstances. Yet he didn't doubt his judgment. He'd give her space. He still had boxes of his own to empty.

While he worked in the kitchen, he listened for sounds from the other side of the house. There were none. It was as if Zoe wasn't even there. Unable to stand it any longer, he walked softly to her room. As he was about to knock on the open door, he saw her. She lay sound asleep curled up in a ball on the half-made bed. After the last few days she'd had, or the week, she must be exhausted. He spied a blanket on the cushioned chair near the rear window. Picking it up, he placed it over her.

Zoe moaned and pulled the edge of the blanket up under her chin.

She looked so peaceful. Beautiful, with her eyelashes resting against her creamy skin. This was the woman who was the mother of his child. Would she look like Zoe? *She.* Did he want a daughter? Could he be a good father to a daughter? Girls needed special care. He wasn't even sure he could give what was needed to a son.

Zoe would make an excellent mom. He had no doubt of that. The care and concern she'd given the boy at the airport when he was hurt and the love she'd shown her mother all indicated he was right. As open and expressive as she had been with her friends when she'd thanked them for helping her was just another sign of her capacity to love. He could take lessons from her.

He'd been jealous of John and Rick when they had arrived. Had been resentful of the carefree way she'd treated them, especially when she seemed so guarded around him. He would like him and Zoe to at least be close friends. They had been friends at least during that one fateful night. Surely they could build on that beginning? Their baby at least deserved that kind of parental unity.

Unfortunately, standing here and staring down at Zoe wouldn't win him any friendship points if she woke. Unable to stop himself, he ran the back of a finger along her cheek. Zoe sighed. She truly was lovely. Before he got into trouble, he slowly lowered his hand and backed out of the room.

A couple of hours later he was waiting for his pizza to arrive when a loud "Dang it," followed by a crash, came from the direction of Zoe's room. Gabe ran across the house and down the hall as fast as the twists and turns would allow. When he reached the doorway, his heart almost stopped. Zoe teetered as she stood on the cushioned chair with a hammer in her hand. Around her on the carpet was a broken frame and pieces of glass. She rocked back. Gabe rushed forward, catching her against his chest.

The feel of her in his arms brought back erotic memories: hot kisses, tender caresses and willing woman opening in welcome... Desire like he'd never felt before washed over him. He must master his libido or he'd scare her.

As he lowered her to the floor, his protective instinct

propelled his hands to her waist to steady her. The curve there was no longer tiny, but knowing the reason for the change excited him all over again. Without thought, his hands moved to her middle. The gentle bulge fascinated him. *His child.* He'd never planned to have one, but now he was and everything about the miracle filled him with awe.

Zoe leaned back against him for a second then straightened.

The part of him better left dormant reacted once more to her nearness. His lips brushed her temple.

She stiffened and stepped away. "I'd better clean this mess up."

"I have a pizza coming. You're welcome to some." He moved to the door. "Don't stand on anything again. Call me if you need to do something above your head."

Zoe went down on her knees and started picking up broken pieces. She still hadn't looked at him. "Okay."

Her tone implied she wasn't promising anything.

"Zoe." He waited until she looked up and into his eyes. "I mean it."

Her expression went hard. "I heard you. But I thought I made it clear to you earlier you have no right to tell me what to do while I'm here."

He wasn't going to allow her to push away the importance of what had almost happened just now. "Then I suggest you think through what you're about to do before you act on it. You or the baby or both could have been seriously hurt if I hadn't been here to catch you."

"Ow!" She stared at her hand.

He took an involuntary step toward her. "What happened?"

"I cut my hand." A stream of blood ran over her palm.

"Give me that." Gabe took the pieces of glass from her and dumped them into a trash can nearby. Cupping her elbow, he helped her stand. Reaching over his shoulder, he grabbed a handful of his shirt and pulled.

"What're you doing?" Zoe asked, the pitch of her voice rising in alarm.

"Taking off my shirt to use as a bandage," Gabe explained impatiently, his words muffled by the material covering his head.

"Isn't that a little dramatic?"

Pulling the shirt off, he retorted, "Not if you don't want blood on the new carpet or one of your towels." He glanced around. "Even if we could find one." He wrapped the shirt around her hand and applied pressure. "I have a first-aid kit in the kitchen. Go into the bathroom and clean up. I'll be right back."

Gabe returned to find Zoe had obeyed his instruction, which surprised him. He had fully expected her to argue or defy him. Putting the kit on the counter, he opened it. After a quick search he found a bandage and removed the covering. "Let me have a look. I want to make sure you don't have any glass in the wound."

"I cleaned it well. There's nothing there. Hand me the bandage and I'll put it on."

Gabe ignored her, seizing her hand and turning it palm up. The bleeding had stopped but there was a fine line of red across the pad, gaping slightly at the center. He looked closely for any slivers. "Does it hurt anywhere?"

"No." Her breath brushed his bare shoulder, setting his pulse humming.

They were so close. Her sweet scent filled his head. He reached for the bandage and applied one end of it. "Hold this end."

She placed her finger where he indicated, and he pulled off the paper cover of the other adhesive strip, smoothing the bandage into place. Her hand felt so fragile, soft. He ran his fingertip along the line in the center of her palm. Zoe shivered.

Her gaze met his. Time hung suspended. Their faces were so close. His attention fell on her full lips. He'd wanted to taste them earlier but had stopped himself. Here was his chance again. All he had to do was lean forward the least bit to experience them. Did he dare? Would she let him?

Want like a live sizzling wire buzzed through him. His gaze met Zoe's again. She was watching him, eyes wide with questions. Did she need his kisses as much as he wanted to give them? His mouth moved toward hers as if it had a mind of its own.

The tip of Zoe's tongue darted out to dampen her bottom lip before her eyes fluttered closed. His blood heated and his body jerked to attention. Her actions were the confirmation he'd been waiting for. There was no stopping him now. A second later his mouth found hers.

The touch of Zoe's lips was all he remembered and more. So much more. Her mouth, plump and inviting, pulled him in. This wasn't the flurry and fiery urgency of that one torrid night. Instead it was slow, easy, experimental, answering questions and creating so many more.

Zoe sighed softly and leaned into him, her hands running up his chest. His arms circled her waist, bringing her against him. Gabe deepened the kiss. Zoe opened for him, eagerly greeted him. Her fingers played with the hair at the nape of his neck as his hands roamed her back, before pulling her tighter. She tasted so good.

The doorbell rang.

Zoe jerked away. Her eyes were wild like a startled animal looking to escape. "We shouldn't have done that."

Gabe leaned to kiss her again. He hadn't had enough. "We've done far more."

Her hands fanned across his chest, pushing, stopping

him. "Gabe, we don't want the same things. You don't want a spouse or the full-time responsibility of a family. I do. We aren't living together. I'm your roommate. I only moved in here because I couldn't think of what else to do. If you cannot respect my boundaries, I'll have to find another place to go."

Anger flared in him. It was obvious she felt the attraction he did. The spontaneous spark of their kiss was undeniable proof. Yet she was steeling herself, refusing to act on it. His eyes met Zoe's, held. "Don't go. I'll keep my hands to myself. I'll stay in my half of the house."

The bell rang again.

"I'd better get that before the delivery guy leaves." At the door he stopped and turned back to her. "Just know this. You'll have to do the asking next time."

Zoe stood in the bathroom, shaking. Her heated blood zipped through her trembling body. She looked into the mirror. A woman who had been thoroughly kissed stared back at her. Bright eyes, rose-tinted cheeks and swollen lips all told the story. Zoe ran her fingers over her still tingling mouth.

Every fiber of her body wanted to rush to Gabe and tell him she wanted him to touch her again. Kiss her. Love her. Yet her coldly rational mind said no. There would be nothing but pain if she once more allowed her body to overrule her heart. She couldn't let her desire for him control what she really wanted.

Gabe hadn't even suggested marriage as a convenient means of helping her with the responsibilities and mounting expenses of being pregnant by him. Oh, he was being noble, very nice, and even willing to "pay his share" of the expenses of her pregnancy, but nothing more. From what she'd learned about Gabe, he would have done the same for any other woman he'd accidentally impregnated.

Even if he had asked, she wouldn't have accepted. What if he left her when he felt his obligation was over? She wouldn't survive. Nothing but a commitment born of love was enough for her.

Her breath had caught when he'd pulled off his shirt. She'd seen him shirtless before but the light had been dim. This time she could make out every nuance of his wide, muscular shoulders. She'd not missed the flex of his arm muscles as he'd applied the bandage or the light dusting of hair in the center of his chest narrowing into a line leading beneath the waist of his jeans. Large enough to carry heavy loads, both physically and metaphorically, it would be so easy to let him share her burdens without that all-important commitment of love.

Gabe smelled of male heat and his own special musk. His scent surrounded her. She was tempted to inhale deeply, memorize it, only to realize she already had. His tender touch had undone her as his finger had traveled over her palm. She wanted more of his kisses. Longed for his lips to cover hers again. All her vows to herself had evaporated like water on a hot day the second his mouth had found hers. There had been no thinking, only feeling. Only Gabe for that one eternal moment.

Thankfully the pizza guy had arrived, snapping her back to reality.

"Food's in the kitchen if you want any," Gabe called.

She was hungry and had to face him sometime. Also, she'd made her reasons for rejecting him crystal clear. There was no purpose in avoiding him with the ground rules of their relationship established. The aroma of cheese and tomato sauce drew her to the kitchen.

Gabe had pulled on another shirt and now sat at the table with the pizza box open and a slice in his hand. A canned drink sat in front of him.

"I haven't had time to go to the grocery. Help yourself

to a soda. If you'd rather have water, the glasses are to the right of the sink."

Apparently, Gabe had recovered from their moment in the bathroom. He was treating her like the roommate she'd asked him to. So why wasn't she more pleased about it? "Thanks."

Gabe didn't even look her direction while she filled her glass with water and took her chair. He pushed the box toward her. She selected a slice. "We haven't talked about any house rules."

He gave her an incredulous look. "There are no house rules. You're free to do as you please. Treat it as yours. There don't have to be rules for everything."

His aggravation rang clear in his tone. Had she pushed him too far? Her common sense kicked in. All she'd done was hold to her vow, hold her ground about what their relationship would be while she lived here. His ego was no doubt bruised, but what was he really after? The best she could tell was sex while he waited for his child to be born.

"Thanks. It would be nice to use the kitchen. I like to cook healthily, especially for the baby."

"Then cook to your heart's content." He took another bite of his pizza. After swallowing, he asked, "Do you mind if I ask you a question?"

What was he after now? Was he going to put her on the spot about what had happened a few minutes ago? Her feelings about him? "No. Ask away."

"Why did you pick the room you did?"

That particular question was totally unexpected. Why would he care? "Because of the view. I like the trees and the yard."

He nodded thoughtfully.

Gabe had her curiosity up now. "Why do you want to know?"

"I just wondered if you saw the front room as a nursery and chose the other for that reason." He watched her.

"Truthfully, I didn't, but it would make a lovely one with all the natural light."

"Then that's what I'll make it. I need to do something with this place. I was thinking of hiring an interior decorator to help. Unless you would like to do the room. After all, you'll be here for a little while after the baby is born."

"I'll think about it." Could she stand to see her dream nursery become reality and then leave it? Yet the thought of bringing the baby home to a pretty little world excited her.

Gabe didn't offer any more conversation. And she couldn't find a comfortable way to initiate one. She didn't like this stilted silence between them. He must be angrier about her rejection than she'd first thought.

"Do you want another slice?" he finally asked.

She shook her head.

Closing the box, he stood. "Well, I'm going to call it a night. I need to be at the hospital early on my first day." He walked to the refrigerator, opened it and put the box inside. "I'll see what I can do about Mr. Luther as soon as I can. It may not be tomorrow. Night." With that he went down the hall toward his room.

Zoe sat looking out at the dark patio, feeling deflated. Something was missing. Something she hadn't known was special until it had gone. Zoe glanced in the direction Gabe had gone. She wanted it back.

"Hey, I forgot to give you this."

Zoe jumped at Gabe's voice. She hadn't heard him returning. He was barefooted and bare-chested with only a pair of sports shorts riding his slim hips.

He slid a key across the table toward her. "You'll need that."

"Uh…thanks."

"I'll see about getting you a garage door opener as soon as possible so you can park in the carport."

"Okay."

"Night, Zoe."

"Good night." She watched him leave, wishing she was going with him.

After putting her glass in the dishwasher, she straightened the kitchen and put the chairs back into place before going to her room. Stepping into her bathroom brought back memories of Gabe's kiss. Would it be like that every time she went in? She feared it would.

Moving in with Gabe had been a calculated risk. One she'd believed she could handle, but it was proving more difficult than she had anticipated. Yet her mother now had the quality care she needed, deserved, so the risk Zoe was taking with her heart was worth it. At least living with Gabe was temporary. Knowing there was a time limit on the intense temptation did help.

Tonight was an example of why she needed to strengthen her resolve to keep their relationship on a business basis. There would be no more moments of weakness on her part if she could prevent it.

After a hot bath she crawled under the covers. She'd never felt more alone in her life. Gabe was only steps away, but she wouldn't go to him. What would it be like to sleep with her head on his shoulder? Heaven. Yet she couldn't allow herself even the pleasure of that fantasy because it would weaken her self-control.

CHAPTER FIVE

GABE HAD FORGOTTEN what it was like to start a new job. The stress, anxiety and the feeling of always being one step behind. He didn't like that. Knowing what was happening in his sphere of influence was important to him. Indirectly Zoe had accused him of being controlling. In her case and with his patients, he believed it was more about caring. Either way, he was determined he would be placed on the surgery schedule sooner rather than later. The more surgery he did, the faster his career would grow.

Even in the OR there was an adjustment period. It would take time to put a staff together that would interact smoothly with each other. For now it would be trial and error. Yet this was the position he'd been working toward his entire professional life. What he hadn't planned for was becoming a father while trying to create the finest liver-transplant program in the world.

Worse was his growing desire for his "roommate."

It had been three days since he'd seen Zoe and he didn't anticipate slowing down long enough to see her anytime soon. If she'd been worried they'd have too much time together, these past few days had proved her concern groundless. As far as he could tell, she was asleep when he came home and getting her morning shower when he left. He'd known his job would be demanding and had accepted it. That was just one of a number of reasons why he wouldn't make a long-term commitment to a woman.

Since he'd not seen Zoe after giving her a house key, he'd left his garage door opener on the kitchen counter because he had not had time to get another. He wrote her a note.

This is for you. Sorry I didn't think to give it to you the other night. Been busy. Call me if you need something.

When he pulled into the drive late that night, Zoe's car wasn't parked in her usual spot, just to the right past the front door. A light burned in the kitchen. She must have taken him up on his offer to park in the carport now she had a door opener.

He studied the glow in the window. At least Zoe had thought about him. He'd been living with his mother the last time he'd come home to a light left on for him. There was something about it that said, *I care about you.*

As he entered the front door, a wonderful smell filled the air. Making his way to the kitchen, he discovered a plate of cookies with a note beside them. He dropped his keys and picked up the piece of paper.

Made some for the guys. Thought you might like a few.

Gabe took a bite of a peanut-butter cookie. "Mmm." His grandmother used to bake them. His mother never had much time for that sort of thing. Most of her efforts revolved around her job. Her actions had taught him that success was only gained through hard work and personal sacrifice. Picking up the plate, he flipped off the light and headed for his bedroom with a smile. He would eat the rest before he went to bed.

The next morning he left another note.

Thanks for the cookies. They hit the spot.

Note-passing wasn't as satisfying as seeing Zoe, but at least they weren't ignoring each other.

How good her cookies were was on his mind as he started his rounds just after noon. The first patient he planned to see was Mr. Luther. Gabe had contacted Mr. Luther's physician, Dr. Patel, and they had agreed that he should be transferred to Gabe's care. Mr. Luther's health had deteriorated to the point where a transplant was the only option. The hepatitis C had taken its toll. Following Dr. Patel's instructions, Mr. Luther was admitted to National Hospital for an evaluation before being placed on the liver transplant list.

Gabe rapped his knuckles on the door.

A gruff voice called, "Come in."

Gabe pushed the door open. "Mr. Luther, I'm…" He stopped short. Zoe stood at the bedside of a grizzly man who obviously hadn't shaved in a number of days.

"Gab—uh… Dr. Marks, hello." Zoe's smile was cautious.

His heart gave a little extra beat. "I hadn't expected to see you."

"I wasn't sure if I'd see you either." She looked at him shyly.

"Thanks for the cookies. They were great."

She glanced toward their patient, who was looking from one of them to the other with curiosity, and said to Gabe, "It's part of my job to keep tabs on Mr. Luther."

The older man pointed first at Gabe then at her and

back again. "I'm guessing you two know each other, him eating your cookies and all."

Gabe nodded, stepping forward and extending his hand. "I'm Dr. Marks. Dr. Patel has thoroughly reviewed your case with me."

"So you're why I'm in one of these dang uncomfortable beds again." He didn't sound happy but shook Gabe's hand.

Zoe placed her hand on the man's other arm. "Mr. Luther, Dr. Marks is going to help you. If you want to blame someone, it should be me. I asked him to see you."

Gabe couldn't believe how big a heart Zoe had. She was emotionally invested in her patient far more than was required by her job. Was Mr. Luther an exception to her rule or did she, as Gabe suspected, care deeply about all her patients, and Mr. Luther in particular? What would it be like to be under her umbrella of loving concern? *Focus on your patient*, Gabe sternly ordered himself. "She did ask me, and the first thing I need to do is examine you. Then we'll run some tests."

"More of them, you mean," the man grunted.

Gabe shrugged and removed his stethoscope from around his neck. "Now, would you lean forward for me?"

The man did as he asked and Gabe listened to his heart. He then had him breathe deeply as he checked out his lungs. "I'm going to turn this overhead light on. I need to look at your eyes."

The switch was on Zoe's side of the bed and she flipped it on.

"I've not spoken to his nurse yet, so I don't know his vitals, Zoe. Would you mind getting his BP for me? Check his pulse points?" Gabe placed his stethoscope around his neck and removed a penlight from his pocket.

She laid the folder in her hand on a chair and went to work.

Gabe looked at the man. "I understand you were diagnosed with hepatitis a number of years ago."

"Yeah." Mr. Luther nodded.

"When did you first seek help for it?" Gabe looked into his eyes.

"Maybe six months ago."

"He was referred to the Liver Alliance by Dr. Patel three months ago," Zoe said, as she placed the cuff on the patient's arm. She pumped the cuff then listened through her stethoscope for his pulse. Done, she looked at him. "One-thirty over ninety."

Gabe nodded. "Not perfect but not as bad as I expected. Mr. Luther, have you been a heavy drinker in the past?"

The man glared at him. "I've drunk."

Gabe gave him a pointed look in return. "You do understand that there can be no drinking again if you have a transplant."

"I'm not even sure I want a transplant," the man grumbled.

Zoe looked up from where she was checking Mr. Luther's pulses on his feet. "Mr. Luther, you need to think hard about that. Without it you'll die."

"Gonna die one day anyway."

Gabe slipped his penlight back into his pocket. "That's true, but without a new liver you have at best a couple of years and you'll get increasingly sicker. There won't be much quality to your life. We're going to do the workup on you to consider listing you for a transplant, but you need to know that your attitude will affect the decision-making. New livers are hard to come by. If you're not going to do your part to keep a new liver healthy, you'll not be listed."

"Yeah." The man picked up the TV remote. "I'll think about it." He nodded toward Zoe. "I'd better not hear that you've been giving Avery here a hard time or you'll answer to me."

"Noted." Gabe made eye contact with Zoe and nodded toward the door. She gave the man a concerned look and followed him out.

Zoe closed the door behind her and looked at him with such hope. "So what do you think?"

Gabe shook his head slightly. "I'm really concerned about his compliance. He's a gruff bear, I know, but to be listed, the committee must know he'll do what he's supposed to do."

"I'll talk to him. Make it clear."

"*He* has to want this," Gabe stated emphatically. "You have done all you can do for him by bringing him to my attention."

Zoe glared at him. "I know that."

"Even if he does agree to cooperate, I can't guarantee he'll be a candidate. I'm just one person on a committee of eight."

She touched his arm. "I appreciate you trying."

Gabe nodded. He hated that he couldn't give her more encouragement. "I have to go. I have other patients to visit."

That evening, Gabe found a note from Zoe waiting on the counter.

There's supper in the refrigerator if you're interested. Thanks for all you're doing for Mr. Luther.

He felt himself smiling, unable to contain his satisfaction. Why was this particular patient so important to her? Even though he'd not given Zoe much reassurance on Mr. Luther's prognosis, she was expressing her gratitude by cooking for him.

He'd not eaten since lunch, so he was tickled to have a home-cooked meal. His day had been so exhausting he'd not even bothered to get drive-through. Zoe's cooking, even though it would be rewarmed, was heaven sent. He could get used to this treatment.

Gabe had just sat down at the table when the patter of feet drew his attention. Looking over his shoulder, he saw Zoe. He smiled, glad to see her. Her appearance, on top of her meal, was totally unexpected.

She wore a short fleece robe tied above the rise of her belly. His gut clenched with pride. That bump was his child. Had he ever seen a more beautiful sight? Zoe's hair was mussed as if she had been running her fingers through it in angst. Was she nervous about approaching him? Why should she be? She'd recovered her self-control the moment the doorbell had interrupted their bathroom interlude.

"Hey," Gabe said. "Thanks for the meal."

"You're welcome."

"Sorry if I woke you." He picked up his fork, ready to take a bite.

Zoe said softly, "I've been waiting up for you."

She had? Hope, warm as a fire, welled in his chest. "Really?"

"I wanted to talk to you about my rent."

Disappointment smothered his anticipation. She wanted to talk about that now? Shaking his head in refusal, he turned back to the food. "I've had a long day. Make that a week. I'm in no mood to talk business now."

Zoe moved around the table, facing him. "I have to pay for my mother's housing, so I need to know what my budget will be."

That made perfect sense, but it didn't give him the energy to hash out her rent right this minute. "Then make it a dollar for this month. When I get time, I'll figure something out."

She leaned toward him slightly, giving him an amazing

view of cleavage. Her breasts were larger than he remembered. Pregnancy had changed her there as well.

She announced with more volume than necessary, "I'm not just paying you a dollar!"

With effort, he turned his attention to cutting his pork chop. "Then you decide what you can afford to pay when you work out your budget. Right now, I'm hungry and don't want to talk about it. Instead, why don't you sit down and keep me company? Tell me how your mother's doing."

He glanced up in time to catch her perplexed look as she slowly sank into the other chair.

She didn't immediately start talking, so between bites he asked, "So? How is she?"

"Still confused but otherwise okay. The staff assures me she's adjusting quite well."

A moment of silence followed, and then Zoe remarked, "You know, you really should take better care of yourself. You're eating like you haven't had anything all day."

He shrugged. "That's pretty close to the truth."

"Gabe!"

"Yeah?" He met her look as he poked his fork at some green beans.

"You've got to do better than that. You can't keep that up."

This was the tables being turned. He was the one who normally scolded her. Now her anxiety was for him. He liked it. "Thanks for your concern. I do appreciate it. But I have my hands full at work. I've had to hit the ground running every day since I started. Hopefully it'll get better soon." He cut into the pork chop again. Lifting the piece on the end of his fork, he said, "This sure is good."

"I'm glad you like it. You know if you don't start taking care of yourself you won't be healthy enough to care for your patients."

He finished off the last of the roasted potatoes, wishing there were more. She was a good cook. Or maybe the food was made better by the fact that someone had cared enough to think of him. It would be so easy to get used to, even if she'd done it out of gratitude. "Zoe, I know you look after the welfare of others all the time, but I can take care of myself. I'm all right."

"What makes you think you can give me a place to live for virtually nothing because you're concerned enough to help me, but I can't respond in kind?"

She had him there. It made him feel good having someone waiting for him at home who would talk to him over a freshly cooked meal, instead of always eating carryout or fast food in front of the TV. Yet Zoe had made it very clear that she was only renting space from him, that they were not "living together." It was time to move the conversation off him. "Give me until this weekend to think about the rent and I'll have a figure. Will that do?"

"I can wait that long. There's one more thing I wanted to talk to you about."

Gabe almost groaned out loud. He was in no mood for this. If he had to have a discussion with her, he'd rather discuss whether or not she preferred being kissed on the neck or behind the ear. "And that is?"

"I noticed you haven't bought any food. I'm planning to stop by the grocery on my way home tomorrow. Would you like me to pick up some things for you?"

"Uh… I usually eat at the hospital or get takeout." She frowned at that, so he amended, "But you've made an excellent point about taking better care of myself. I do need to have something here. If you don't mind, could you get a few boxes of mac and cheese, some frozen dinners and protein bars? That should hold me until I can get to the store myself. Take the cost out of your rent when we settle on the amount."

She turned up her lip and looked down her nose at him.

"That's your list? As a doctor, you should be ashamed of yourself."

He shrugged. "You asked."

"I did. Well, I'd better get to bed." She rose. "Night, Gabe."

He watched her walk away. The more distance she put between them, the cooler the room became. If only he was going with her. "Good night," he whispered when she was out of sight.

Gabe finished his dinner, put the dirty plate into the sink, flipped off the light and went to his lonely room. With any luck, he was so tired he would go to sleep quickly and not think about the desirable woman just steps away. Was this what his life would be like? Always wishing for more?

Two evenings later Gabe came home before it was dark for the first time in a week. He'd had a replacement garage door opener for the one he gave Zoe delivered to the hospital, so he was now able to park beside Zoe's car in the carport. There was something strangely intimate about their cars sharing the same close space. He shook off that thought. Zoe didn't want that. Had made it very clear. Still, that didn't mean he hadn't lain awake late into the night, thinking about her.

Entering the house, he inhaled the delicious aroma of lasagna. He must be doing something right in Zoe's eyes. As he took another deep sniff, his stomach growled. Following the scent, he fully anticipated finding Zoe standing in the kitchen. Disappointment washed over him. She wasn't there. He headed toward her side of the house but along the way his attention was diverted out the window to the patio. There she was, sitting in a cheap fold-up lounger. Her head was back, her face lifted to the late-afternoon sun. Was she asleep?

Her head turned. Had she sensed he was there? Their gazes met through the glass, held. Zoe reminded him of an old master's painting where the yellow light surrounded her feminine form as if she was a heavenly being. That was the thought of a lovesick man. Which he was not!

Zoe blinked and half lifted the hand lying over their baby and waved. Gabe smiled and headed in her direction. She was a temptation he should stay away from but was drawn to as if he were in her gravity field. Stepping out of the French doors of the living room, he strolled across the patio.

"I'm surprised to see you home so early." Zoe looked back over her shoulder at him.

"I decided it was time to come home at a decent hour." He continued moving until he was facing her then nodded his head toward the house. "Something smells delicious. Do you have enough for two?" Did he sound as pitiful as he felt?

She smiled. "Yes. I made enough so that I'd have some to leave in the refrigerator for you."

Even after their somewhat strained conversation a couple of nights ago, she was still trying to take care of him. Doing it despite her insistence that they were nothing more than roommates. He suppressed a spark of hope she'd changed her mind and managed to answer in a neutral tone, "Thanks. That's really nice of you."

"It's the least I can do since you're helping me out."

That explanation left a sour taste in his mouth. He would've liked it better if her kindness was motivated by a more intimate reason. Why did he keep wishing for more? She'd made it so plain on numerous occasions there would be nothing between them but the baby. He needed to accept it and get on with his personal life. Maybe it was time to ask about the available female staff at the hospital.

Zoe was saying, "I'd better get up and take it out before it burns. If you hadn't come home it really might have. The sun feels so good." Zoe swung her feet off the lounger to the bricks. "The day is so beautiful I couldn't pass up the chance to be outside. I saw this lounger in the grocery and had to have it."

Gabe stepped closer. "I'm sorry there's no patio furniture. I've never had a need for it before."

"This is such a nice space I'd furnish it before anything else." A shocked look came over her face. "I'm sorry. That's none of my business."

"Why can't it be? As far as I'm concerned, you can have a say in how I furnish the house where our child will be spending a lot of time. I don't know anything about that stuff. How about going with me to pick something out? You'd have a better idea of what I need than I do." He wasn't sure what had made him extend the invitation, but any reason that might coax her into spending time with him was worth a try.

She looked at him as if weighing the pros and cons. "I guess I could, if you really want me to."

"Tomorrow work for you?" The question had just popped out. He'd had no intention of doing it that soon.

"I have to visit Mother first thing in the morning, but I could go after that."

"Great! We'll go visit your mom then head for the furniture store. I've not seen where she's living, and I'd like to."

"Why?" She watched him suspiciously.

"Why what?"

Her look didn't waver. "Why would you want to go with me to visit my mother?"

He couldn't really answer that, so he settled on, "Because I like your mother and she'll be the grandmother of my child. Also, you've practically gone into debt because of the quality of this place, so I'm curious."

Zoe shrugged then pushed off the lounger. When she teetered backward, he caught her elbow and helped her stand. Her chuckle was a nervous one. "Thanks. I'm getting more off balance by the day. If you want to go, you can. I need to get the lasagna out." She walked toward the door.

Gabe followed her. *And more beautiful.* In the kitchen, he watched while Zoe removed and cut the pasta. He could hardly wait to taste it. To resist digging in before it made it to a plate, he busied himself with the dishes.

"I'm impressed. A man who knows how to set the table correctly." Zoe picked up a plate and returned to the stove.

"My grandmother taught me. She'd be happy you noticed." He took glasses from the shelf and filled them with ice.

"Not your mother?"

"Mom wasn't around much. She was busy making a living. I spent a good deal of time with my grandmother in my early years." Why was he telling her all of this? He didn't make a habit of sharing his personal life.

"You must've missed your mom."

He had. She'd told him throughout his childhood that it must be that way since his father was gone. Gabe's child was never going to know that feeling if he could help it. But would that really be possible with his current job, the future demands of his career? "I did, but it was what it was."

Zoe looked at him for a moment as if she understood everything he wasn't saying. Moving to the table, she set down the plate of food. "Go ahead and start. It's better hot." Picking up the other plate, she returned to the stove.

Gabe finished pouring the tea and took his place. Zoe had included a small salad and a piece of toasted bread as well. The aroma was divine but still he waited for her.

Zoe joined him with her plate in her hand. "I told you to go ahead and start."

"And my grandmother taught me that the cook deserves to be waited for. Sorry, her teaching trumps what you want."

Zoe smiled. "Smart woman."

"She was. I miss her every day." Zoe reminded him of his grandmother, who had been the most giving and caring person he'd ever known until he'd met Zoe.

"Tell me about her." Zoe placed her napkin in her lap and picked up her fork.

"I guess she was like every other grandmother. Tough when she needed to be but loving all the time." Gabe took a bite of the hot lasagna and his taste buds screamed with joy. Zoe could get a permanent job cooking for him. He would miss her when she left. That looming event he didn't want to think about. "This is wonderful. I didn't think anything could be any better than the meal last night."

Her eyes twinkled and her cheeks turned rosy. She enjoyed a compliment. Had the other men in her life not done that enough? He'd like her to always look at him the way she was now. In spite of her curt refusal to allow a personal relationship between them, her happiness mattered very much to him. But why?

"I'm glad you like it," Zoe said with a hint of shyness. As if she hadn't been sure he would.

"Anyone would."

"Not anyone."

There it was. Just what he'd suspected. "Has someone said you weren't a good cook?"

Zoe made a sound low in her throat. "Oh, yeah, in no uncertain terms."

Annoyance hot as fire flashed through him on her behalf. "Like who?"

"My ex-fiancé. Nothing I prepared for him seemed to

suit. He always complained. Too salty, too hot. I guess that's one of the reasons he's my ex. Along with a few other, larger character flaws."

She'd been engaged? Had cared about a man enough to want to marry him? It shocked Gabe how much that bothered him. If she'd married that guy, they wouldn't be sitting here now. Wouldn't have had that night or be expecting a baby. He would have missed knowing Zoe. He swallowed hard and put his fork down. "What happened?"

"I caught him out to dinner with another woman. Turned out he was a jerk. He made it embarrassingly clear in front of the entire restaurant that I wasn't who he wanted. That I was too old-fashioned. Wasting my time waiting for a knight in silver armor to ride up and pledge to love me until death did us part. That expecting the man who said he loved me to be faithful and plan to be with me forever was naive nonsense. He said I needed to grow up. What a fool I was! I know what I want, and I have no intention of settling or compromising."

Gabe had the sudden urge to hit something. If her ex had been there he would have punched him in the face. Although he was pretty sure he wouldn't like the answer to the question before he asked it, he couldn't stop himself. "What do you want?"

"To find someone who will love me for who I am. Who'll put me first in his life and grow old with me." She looked at him. "To have that happily ever after."

Her answer was worse than he'd expected. She wanted everything Gabe was confident he couldn't provide.

CHAPTER SIX

ZOE WOKE THE next morning to the sun shining through her bedroom window and the birds chirping. She stretched. Now that she was well into her second trimester, she was feeling more energetic. A flutter in her middle made her pause. She couldn't stop a smile of happiness curving her lips. The baby was kicking. Butterfly taps, but they were there nonetheless.

At dinner after she'd told Gabe she was holding out for a man who would love her unconditionally and commit the rest of his life to their marriage and family, the conversation had become stilted, punctuated by awkward silence. His reaction had not been a surprise. It had merely reinforced his original revelation that he had no interest in getting married and having a family. With his logic, his career wouldn't allow it. When she'd risen to clean the kitchen, he'd insisted he would do it. Sensing Gabe was still uncomfortable with her answer, she'd left him to it and gone to bed. She'd slept well and deeply.

Thinking about the way their evening had ended, she feared their visit to her mother's and the shopping trip might be tense as well. Debating whether or not to spend the day with Gabe, she was surprised by the smell of frying bacon wafting into her room.

Gabe was cooking?

She pulled her robe on and tugged the belt tight, making certain she was completely covered. More than once when she'd been talking to Gabe about rent, she'd caught his gaze slipping to the V of her robe. His hot glances had brought to mind passionate memories that would have weakened her resolve if she'd allowed herself to revisit them.

The scent led her to the kitchen, where Gabe stood at the stove with his bare back to her, the view of wide shoulders with thick muscles tapering to a trim waist and slim hips clad in well-worn jeans hung low. She swallowed. He had such a nice behind, was a magnificent specimen of a male. Her fingers twitched with the temptation to touch him. Would he mind if she did? The question set off mental alarm bells. She must stop tormenting herself with fantasies of forbidden pleasures.

She stuffed her hands into the pockets of her robe and cleared her throat. "Good morning."

Gabe half turned. "Morning. I don't have your culinary talents but I can cook eggs and bacon. Interested?"

Zoe battled to master her physical reaction to him as she shrugged in what she hoped was a nonchalant manner. "Sure."

"Have a seat. I'm just getting ready to do the eggs. How do you like yours?"

Apparently, whatever had been bothering him last night was forgotten. She took what had become her place at the table. "Scrambled."

He smiled. "Scrambled it is."

She liked this cheerful, relaxed version of Gabe. This was the man she'd gotten to know in Chicago. The charmer. She suspected his charisma was at full force.

Gabe placed a plate with fluffy eggs, two slices of crisp bacon and buttered toast in front of her. It looked as delicious as it smelled. She gave him a genuine smile of gratitude. "Thanks."

He soon joined her with a plate twice as full as hers in his hand. Over the next few minutes they ate in a companionable silence. Zoe was glad their camaraderie had returned. Slowly chewing bacon and studying him as he ate, she decided she'd like it to always be that way between them. She watched as his gaze met hers. He raised a brow.

"Thank you. This is wonderful."

Gabe looked pleased. "You're welcome."

His phone that was always nearby buzzed. He picked it up. "Dr. Marks."

As he talked she continued to eat, paying little attention to the conversation. "I'll be in this afternoon to review the charts." Gabe ended the call.

"Problem?"

"I implemented a new protocol. It's not popular, so I'm getting some pushback. Do you have a certain time that you have to be at your mother's?"

"It's Saturday, so I can go whenever I wish."

"Then do you think you can be ready to leave in half an hour? I have to go in to the hospital later." He picked up his toast.

She pushed at her eggs. "Then why don't you just go pick out furniture while I go see Mom? Cut down on your stress."

"No, I've got time. I just need to check the charts after shift change this afternoon."

She was amazed at his dedication to detail. "You really oversee all the details."

"It's important that my program be cutting-edge."

She pursed her lips and nodded. "Or you're just a bit of a control freak."

He grinned. "And maybe a little bit of that as well."

* * *

An hour and a half later they were walking into Shore-cliffs House.

"This looks nice," Gabe said as he held the front door open for her.

"It is, but I still hate that Mom can't take care of herself anymore and, worse, that I can't do it either."

Gabe's arm came around her and pulled her into a quick hug before dropping away.

"You're doing the best you can for your mother. She knows you love her."

Zoe wished his hug had lasted longer as she held back tears. "I hope so."

They walked down the long hall and took the first right, stopping in front of a door on the left. Zoe knocked. Pushing it open with some trepidation about what she would find, she was pleasantly surprised. Her mother sat in a cushioned chair near the window. A book lay on her lap. Zoe's heart lifted. Her mother had always loved reading, but Zoe hadn't seen her pick up a book in months. Even if she wasn't reading, at least she'd thought to try. "Hi, Mom."

Her mother looked up. A smile came across her face. "Hey, sweetheart."

Relief washed over Zoe. Today her mother recognized her. The doctors had told Zoe there would be times when her mom would know her and then her memory would fade again.

"How're you?" Her mother was having a good day.

Zoe smiled and kissed her on the cheek. "I'm doing fine." She sank into a nearby straight chair.

Her mother looked to where Gabe stood. "You brought someone with you."

"Hello, Mrs. Avery. It's nice to see you again," Gabe said as he stepped forward.

Her mother gave him a blank look but soon the brightness of recognition filled her eyes. "I know you. You brought chicken."

"That's right." Gabe sat on the edge of the bed. "How do you like your new place? It's nice, and your daughter has done a lovely job of furnishing it."

"I want to go home," she said earnestly.

Zoe's chest tightened. She hated hearing those words. Gabe reached over and took her hand, giving it a gentle, reassuring squeeze. She appreciated the support. It was good of him to notice her distress. "I know, Mom, but right now this is the best place for you."

"Can I go home?"

"Mrs. Avery, do you dance?" Gabe asked.

That was an odd question. Zoe was thankful for his timely redirection of her mother's thoughts, but was perplexed by the new topic of conversation he'd chosen.

"Dance?" her mother asked in a tone Zoe hadn't heard in a long time.

"I noticed on the activity board on our way down the hall that there's a dance on Saturday night. I was wondering if you were going." Gabe leaned forward as if greatly interested in her answer.

Her mother actually blushed. Zoe couldn't help but smile.

"I don't know."

"I bet there are a number of men who would like to dance with you," Zoe said to further encourage her. "I also saw that they have game day, music and people coming in to sing."

Her mother gave her a bleak look. Zoe had lost her again. She forged forward. "We're on our way to buy some furniture."

"Furniture?" her mom said.

"Yes. For my patio," Gabe answered.

"He wants me to help him pick it out." Zoe watched closely, hoping her mom would come out of the place she'd disappeared to.

Her mother looked down at her book.

Together they struggled to converse with her mother for the next fifteen minutes. Her memory came and went all the while. When Zoe became frustrated, Gabe stepped in. She admired his patience. More than once her mom had asked what his name was and each time he'd clearly and calmly told her. Finally, her mother showed signs of frustration.

With a heavy heart, Zoe said, "Mom, it's time for us to go." She kissed her mother's soft cheek, straightened, hoping her mom would say goodbye. All she got was a vaguely puzzled smile. Gabe followed her out of the room, softly closing the door behind him.

As they walked down the hall on their way out, he took her hand. "I know how increasingly difficult visiting her is for you."

Zoe blinked back tears. "It is. I hate that she's losing her memory in general, but I know soon it will be to the point that she'll stop recognizing me altogether." She laid her hand over her middle. "She'll never really know her grandchild. The baby won't know her."

"Then you'll just have to make a special point to tell him or her about your mother." Gabe stepped ahead of her and held open the front door.

"You make it sound so easy." Zoe stepped past him.

"Never said that. My mom never talked about my father much. I wished she had. I don't feel like I know him."

She had a father who had decided he didn't want her. Zoe wasn't sure which was worse—never having a father to begin with, or having one who didn't want you. "My father left us when I was ten. He went to work one day and didn't return."

"I'm sorry. That must have been awful."

Her chest tightened. "It was bad but at least I had him for a little while. The worst is knowing it was that easy to walk away from us."

"Sounds like both of us might have father issues. Not a great thing to have in common, but something." There was sadness in his voice.

"I guess you're right." She looked at him. "Thanks for coming with me." Somehow Gabe's supportive presence had made it easier. She was starting to depend on him. That mistake she had to constantly guard against. He hadn't made any promises to her. He could be gone just as easily as her father, but Gabe was there for her right now.

"You're welcome," he was saying. "I'm glad to see your mom has a quality place to live. You're doing the right thing."

"Then why do I feel so rotten about it?"

Gabe stopped her. Waited until she looked at him before he said, "Because you can't do anything to make the situation better."

She nodded. "I guess."

They arrived at the car.

"So where should we go for this furniture? You're the person who knows the area." Gabe unlocked the doors.

After a minute Zoe answered, "I guess Abrams Furniture is the best place to start. It's the biggest furniture store in the area. Turn left out of the parking lot."

Thirty minutes later, Gabe parked in front of the entrance to the large building with windows showcasing furniture for many different rooms of a house. Gabe held the glass door open for Zoe to enter.

They were quickly greeted by a middle-aged woman. "Hello. What may I show you today?"

Gabe smiled. "We'd like to look at patio furniture."

The lady was quick to return his smile. "Come this way. I'm sure we have something you'll like."

They followed her along a path leading through groupings of sofas and chairs, then dining-room suites, toward the back of the store. The smell of new furniture and polished wood was nearly overpowering. Along the way they passed the nursery section. Before Zoe was the most perfect white crib. Beside it stood a matching chest of drawers, changing table and even a rocker.

She stopped, unable to resist running her fingers along the top of one side of the crib. The image of pastel ruffled drapes on the windows as the sun beamed in filled her mind. A white rocker sat nearby. When she had her own place this would be what she'd like to have for the baby. She was so mesmerized by the pictures in her head, she had to hurry to catch up with Gabe. He waited by a door leading to the outside.

"Did you find something you like?" he asked as she walked by him.

Zoe shook her head. He was already more involved in her life than she had intended to allow. She wasn't going to open her heart to another man who didn't share her dream of commitment and marriage. Heart still healing from her failed relationship with her ex, she certainly wouldn't repeat it when she already knew how Gabe felt.

The woman was waiting for them in the middle of the large covered area. There were all kinds of chairs and tables suitable for outdoor use. Some had metal frames while others were made of wicker. Many appeared nice enough for inside use. There were numerous cushions, in every color choice, both in floral prints and plain fabric. The space was almost overwhelming.

"What do you think would be best on the patio?" Gabe asked her.

"Oh, I don't know. There's so much here. Let me look

around some." She shouldn't be making these types of decisions with him. She wouldn't be staying at his home long. Furniture implied longevity, and that she wouldn't have.

Gabe walked around from one grouping to another. She joined him, making her own path through the jumble.

She wasn't sure what was best for him, but she did know what she liked. "I prefer the wicker look."

"Then that's what we should look at," he said as if pleased.

His attention turned to the saleswoman, who was swift to direct them toward a space with nothing but that style of outdoor furniture. A particular suite caught Zoe's attention. It included a table with a large orange umbrella and four black chairs. Next to them were a matching two-person settee, a lounger, and two chairs with orange cushions and a low table situated between them. The entire set was perfect for Gabe's patio. Classical, yet functional. Zoe headed straight for it.

"Why don't you have a seat and see how it feels?" the saleslady suggested. "See how comfortable it is."

Zoe took a seat in one of the chairs at the table. Gabe sank into an armchair with high sides. It accommodated his large body as if tailor made for him.

"So what do you think?" Gabe looked at her.

"I like this chair. It's sturdy enough, which you'll need if it's going to be outside all the time. But do you really need all of this?" Zoe waved her hand in a circle.

He shrugged. "I have plenty of room for it, so why not? Come try the lounger. You'd use it more than me."

She lowered her voice so the saleswoman couldn't easily hear. "I'm not going to use it that long."

"Please just try the lounger and tell me what you think." There was a pleading note in his voice.

The saleslady must have picked up on it as well because she said, "I'm going to let you two discuss this. If you need me I'll be right over there." She pointed toward the door through which they had exited.

With some annoyance Zoe sat on the lounger, pushed back until she was comfy and put up her legs. It would be the perfect place to read a book, feed their baby. *Their* baby. When had she started thinking of the baby as theirs instead of hers? She glanced at Gabe, shaken on a disturbing level. How did he think of the baby?

She had to stand. Those thoughts weren't ones she needed to have. Heartache, disappointment and disagreement were all they would bring between her and Gabe. Zoe shifted on the cushion, moving to get off it.

Gabe quickly rose and offered her a hand. "So what do you think?"

"It's very nice," she murmured.

He raised a brow in question. "Should I get it?"

Though reluctant to do so, Zoe nodded. "I think so."

"Now, that wasn't so hard, was it?"

She was grateful he didn't give her time to respond before he walked off toward the saleslady.

If Gabe furnished the rest of the house as nicely as the patio, their child would have an amazing place to visit. She wouldn't have to worry about the baby having what he or she needed. Gabe would see to it. In fact, he was quite willing to let her see to it, but she mustn't give in to that temptation. It would be too easy to think and act as if Gabe's house was hers as well and, worse, as if he was.

Gabe was kind, caring and generous. He'd be a good father based on that. Even if he didn't think so. A child deserved both a mother and father in their life. As long as she and Gabe could agree on how the baby should be raised, he or she should have a good life. Not the perfect one like Zoe dreamed of, but a good one nonetheless. What they had to do was remain civil. When their emotions became involved that was when heartache and anger would take over and create strife. She couldn't let that happen.

Zoe followed Gabe and the saleswoman into the building. As they walked past the nursery furniture, she made a point not to look at it, sighing. It would be nice to bring the baby home from the hospital to a finished nursery, but that wasn't the plan. When the time was right she'd set one up. Until then, she'd settle for a cradle in her bedroom.

She joined Gabe at the counter where he'd just finished paying for the furniture.

"All done." Gabe turned to her with a pleased smile. "Thanks for your help."

The saleslady said as they headed out the door, "It has been a pleasure to help such a nice couple."

Zoe's heart caught. A warm feeling raced through her. She looked at Gabe. Was there any chance that one day that could be true? He was an honorable and steadfast person. Just the type of man she'd been looking for...

She started to correct the woman, but Gabe placed a hand at her back and said without missing a beat, "Thanks for your help." To Zoe he said, "How about an early lunch before we head home?"

Gabe settled onto a metal chair on the patio of a local restaurant after seeing Zoe properly seated. The sky was bright and there was a slight breeze, making it comfortable outside. They had both ordered a sandwich, chips and a drink. He'd carried it to the table on a tray, thoroughly delighted with their morning together.

Visiting her mother had been difficult for Zoe and he was glad he could be there for her. Shopping, even for something as mundane as furniture, wasn't high on his list of fun things to do but he'd enjoyed the trip with Zoe.

The only catch in the morning had been when she'd resisted sitting on the lounger. She was using the fact she wasn't going to live at his house long as an excuse to avoid taking any interest in it. He wanted her to feel comfortable while she was there. To his amazement he was in no hurry for her to do so. He would miss her.

Zoe captured his attention when she said, "This is one of those places I've always wanted to go but have never taken the time."

Her light brown hair glowed in the sunlight. There was a touch of color in her cheeks, giving her a healthy look. "Being pregnant seems to agree with you."

Her look quickly locked with his as her hand moved to her middle. He'd come to expect her to do that anytime the baby was mentioned. "It has been easier than I expected, despite the first few months of morning sickness."

Something close to guilt assaulted him. "I'm sorry."

"It's not your fault."

It had better be. His eyes narrowed. "Who else's would it be?"

"I…uh…only meant there's nothing you could have done about it."

"I was just teasing you." Reaching across the table, he brushed away a stray strand of hair from her cheek with the tip of his index finger. "I know what you meant. I still haven't gotten used to the idea that I'm going to be a father."

"You might need to. It won't be that much longer," she said softly.

"Have you picked out names?" Gabe watched her closely. Would he like them? Would she care? Or ask for his suggestions? She didn't have to.

"I've thought of a few." She picked up a chip.

He watched her closely. "Such as?"

"If it's a boy I'd like to name him either William or Michael."

"Those are both good strong names. My father's name was Gabriel Harold." He didn't miss the slight upturn of her lip at the last name.

Zoe said with a dip of her shoulder and an unsure look, "I like Gabriel."

He grinned. "Not a Harold fan?"

She shook her head. "Not really."

Gabe took a bite of his sandwich. He'd like his child to have a name from his side of the family. But it wasn't a demand he believed he could make. "What about girls' names?"

"I was thinking Laura, Mandy, Maggie. My mother's name is Sandra. I wasn't going to make any real decision until I knew the sex."

"And you'll find that out when?"

She glanced at him. "This week. I have a doctor's appointment on Wednesday. I could have known a few weeks ago but I had to push the ultrasound back because of Mother."

Gabe gave an understanding nod. "What time?"

"What time?" Zoe gave him a quizzical tilt of her head.

"What time are you going for the ultrasound? I'll need to make sure I don't have a surgery scheduled." At her flabbergasted look he added, "I told you I wanted to be there."

"Is that really necessary?"

Why would she care if he went? "Is there any reason I shouldn't be there?"

Zoe didn't look at him. "No, not really, but I can just call you when I'm finished."

"I'd like to be in on the surprise as well." Why did it matter to him that he be there for the actual event?

"Okay." She didn't sound convinced but at least he wasn't going to have to persuade her further.

"You know, I've never lived on this side of the country," Gabe said, picking up his sandwich.

Zoe's face brightened. "You'll love it here. There's so much to see and do. Of course, there's everything in Washington but there are historical homes, battlefields, museums and all the seasonal events."

"Do you go to see those things?"

"I used to stay pretty busy attending concerts and festivals until Mother got worse. I've not got to do much of that in a long time." Sadness filled Zoe's eyes.

"Then maybe we should do some of those things before the baby gets here."

An expectant, hopeful look came over her face. He had her full attention. "Would you have time?"

Would he? He had no idea. "I could try."

"I'm sorry. That wasn't a fair question. I know you're busy."

He'd disappointed her. Just as he had other women he'd been interested in. Except it really bothered him that it was happening again with Zoe. There just wasn't much time in his life for extracurricular activities. He wasn't being fair to Zoe to suggest there was. He wanted to make her happy. Maybe he could work something out in a few weeks. He checked his watch. "I'd better get you home. I'm due at the hospital."

"I'm ready." She stood and pushed the chair in.

She didn't say much on the trip home. He pulled up to the front door. "The deliverymen said they could be here today at three. Will you be around?"

"Yes."

"Great. Do you mind seeing that they get the furniture in place?"

"I can take care of it." Zoe climbed out of the car. "Thanks for lunch and going with me to see Mom."

"No problem. See you later."

The doorbell ringing brought Zoe out of sleep. It took her a few seconds to clear her head enough to get off the bed and head up the hall.

She hadn't been surprised when Gabe hadn't even gotten out of the car before he'd left for the hospital. For a moment at lunch she'd hoped that what he said might be different from what he felt. That he would take time for himself. Do something other than work. Then maybe they could do some touristy things together, but as quickly as the hope flickered it had been snuffed out.

Part of knowing Gabe was accepting those types of things weren't high on his priority list. She, on the other hand, believed they were important for a balanced and happy life. With that in mind, she wanted to make the most of the beautiful day, so she took a walk around the neighborhood before settling in for an afternoon nap. She'd forgotten all about the furniture being delivered until the bell rang. She opened the front door to find two uniformed men waiting.

"We're here to deliver your furniture. Would you show us where it goes?"

"Through here." Zoe opened the door wider and led the way through the living room to the patio.

The men followed quietly, nodding as they surveyed the area, then left her. Soon they returned with the armchairs.

"Where would you like these?"

Zoe pointed to the area that received the most sun. They returned to the truck. While they were gone Zoe moved the chairs into position. In just a few minutes all the furniture was sitting on the patio. Even the umbrella was in place and up. She turned around and smiled. The floral and striped cushions with the matching colors added interest. The patio looked perfect. Gabe should enjoy using it. If he took the time to appreciate it. Until she moved she planned to make the most of the lounger as often as possible, starting that afternoon.

One of the deliverymen asked, "Where would you like the rest of it to go?"

"What? I didn't know there was any more." She followed him into the house.

He pulled a paper out of his back pocket and studied it. "We have a whole room of nursery furniture that's supposed to come to this address."

Zoe's heart jumped. Gabe had bought nursery furniture? She'd not seen him even look at any. Maybe he'd done it online.

"Oh, okay."

"So where do we put it?" The man sounded as if he was losing patience.

"In here." Zoe showed him the empty front room.

He left again and returned with his partner. They had a chest of drawers in their arms. Zoe's breath caught. It was the chest in the group she'd liked so much.

"Where do you want it?" one man grunted.

Zoe looked around the room for a second, totally disoriented by what was happening. "Uh, over on that wall." She pointed to the space between the window and the door. Still in a daze at what Gabe had done, she watched as the men brought in the rocker and changing table.

Gabe had been paying attention when she'd admired the crib and had even noticed how much she liked the set. Had any man ever been that in tune with her? He may have little time to spare, but when he was with her he was totally present.

On the next trip, the men brought in the pieces of the baby bed. One returned to the truck and came back with a tool bag. In less than thirty minutes the bed was together and the mattress in place.

"Where would you like this?" one of the men asked.

"Catty-corner, between the windows." She pointed to the area.

They did as she requested. Soon Zoe was showing them out. She returned to the nursery, taking a seat in the rocker. Feeling overwhelmed, she looked around the room. It would make a perfect nursery. She imagined the walls decorated and envisioned the drapery for the windows...

A tear ran down her cheek. The room would be so beautiful. But it would never be hers.

Zoe didn't have a chance to talk to Gabe about what he'd done because he wasn't home when she went to bed. She couldn't question his commitment to his job. Gabe seemed more than willing to put in the hours required. He'd earned her respect for that alone, but then, there was much to admire about Gabe. Too much for her comfort.

Midmorning the next day she was sitting on the patio, reading a book, when the sound of footsteps on the bricks drew her notice.

A moment later Gabe joined her with a glass in his hand. After placing the drink on the low table, he dropped into one of the chairs facing her. "Mornin'. Mind if I join you?"

It was his home. Gabe didn't have to ask her. "Sure."

She stared at him. Every feminine cell in her body stood at attention and tingled. He acted rested and relaxed. His hair was still damp and tousled as if he'd dried it with a towel and done nothing more to it after his shower. A T-shirt fit close to his chest and his jeans were well-worn with holes in the knees. He was gorgeous.

As if unaware of her admiration, he placed his feet on the table, crossed his ankles and leaned back in the chair.

"It looks great out here. I like the way you arranged everything."

Zoe was pleased by his praise. Too much so. "I'm glad you do. I didn't know how you would want it."

"I had no doubt I could trust you." He grinned.

"Why didn't you tell me that you were buying nursery furniture?"

He pursed his lips and shrugged. "Maybe because I thought you might argue with me about it. I needed something for the baby anyway. You don't like it?"

"I like it very much."

A smug look covered his face. "I thought you might. I saw you looking at it."

He had noticed her interest. She confessed, "I was thinking about getting it for the nursery at my place."

"Why don't you fix up the room the way you like it? You can take it all with you when you go. I'll get more furniture."

"I couldn't do that."

"Sure you can. The baby'll be coming home to this house. He or she needs their own space. Wouldn't it be nice for it to have some continuity from here to your house?"

That really wasn't necessary but Zoe liked the idea of having a special place for the baby from the beginning. "I had planned to just use a cradle for the few weeks I'm still here. I'll think about finishing the nursery."

Gabe picked up his glass, took a long draw on the iced tea and set it down again. "Good. I promised I'd come up with a figure for your rent. But before I give you that I'd like you to consider a proposition."

Her heart leaped. Proposition? What kind of proposition?

"I've been thinking, and don't want to offend you, but you've been cooking meals, even doing some shopping, and I appreciate you have your own job to deal with, but I've not had time to find a housekeeper. If you'd be willing, and thought you had time, to just keep things straightened around here for a little while, then I would forgo the rent altogether. I don't want to imply that I think you should be my housekeeper or anything..."

Zoe hadn't expected this. The extra money she would save would make a nice down payment on the house she wanted. She enjoyed cooking and was doing that for herself anyway. The housekeeping wouldn't be that much. Gabe wasn't home long enough to get anything dirty. Plus, he was neat. She was already taking care of her side of the house. "I think that would work."

"Excellent." He stood. "Then I'm going to catch up on some reading and watch the ball game."

"Okay. I'll make lunch in a little while."

"Sounds great." He strolled to the house.

They were acting like a married couple on Sunday afternoon now. It should have made her feel uneasy but instead there was a satisfaction there, contentment. She looked into the living area at Gabe. He was sitting in his chair with his legs stretched out and his attention on the TV. Wouldn't it be nice if it was always this way between them? It was a wonderful dream. But just a dream. Gabe had never mentioned his feelings regarding her. He was a decent man but that didn't mean he cared for her the way Zoe wanted him to.

CHAPTER SEVEN

GABE STUDIED ZOE. She'd been reading for the last couple of hours while he had supposedly watched TV. Even though he wasn't outside with her, he was very aware of her movements. From his chair he could see her better than she could him. Was she aware of how many times her hand went to the rounded area of her stomach? Just from that small action he had no doubt she loved and wanted their baby.

Her gaze met his through the glass. She gave him a small smile before she returned to her reading. Only by a force of will did he stop himself from getting up and going out to kiss her. Or more. But he'd promised not to touch her again unless she initiated it. He would keep his promise even if it killed him.

Sometime later Zoe came in and quietly went to the kitchen. Now he was listening to her moving around as she prepared a late lunch. Something about having her in his home, being around her, sharing meals and even picking out furniture seemed right. She brought a softness to his life that he hadn't known he had been missing. Did he want to let it go? Was he capable of hanging on to it?

Would Zoe consider staying if he asked? They got along well. But she wanted a husband. Could he offer her that? Be the husband she needed? What if he didn't measure up to her expectations? Could he even be the father to his child that he should be? How would he ever know? He'd had no firsthand experience, not seen a father in action close-up. Could he find enough balance in his life to make it work? Which would be worse: not taking the chance or failing?

Zoe brought him a plate with a sandwich and salad on it.

"Thank you."

She smiled. "You're welcome." She continued outside to the table.

He watched her. She hadn't invited him to join her. Would she mind if he did? One of the things he liked most about having Zoe in the house was sharing meals and conversation.

Taking his plate, he went to join her. Zoe didn't look up as he approached. He'd like to know her thoughts. "Do you mind?"

Her head jerked around. "Uh, sure. It's your patio."

Annoyance ran hot through him. "I wish you'd quit thinking like that. This is your home for as long as you stay. I want you to treat it that way."

"I'll try."

"Don't try. Accept it." He took a chair beside her.

She pushed a leaf of lettuce around on her plate. "It just seems strange to live with someone you know so little about."

"What do you want to know?" He bit into his sandwich. Was it so good because of the sliced ham and cheese or because Zoe had made it?

"I don't know," she said slowly, as if giving it thought. "What's your favorite color?"

"Green." *Like your eyes*, but he didn't say that. "What's yours?"

"Red. But I'm supposed to be asking you questions."

He grinned. "Ever think I might like to learn a few things about you?"

"Okay, then. Do you like a dog or a cat?"

"Dog. Big dog. And you?" He looked up from the fork he was filling with salad and raised a brow in question.

"I always wanted a Labrador retriever but didn't have a good place for one to live." A dreamy look came over her face.

"Nice dogs. Good with children, I've heard."

She focused on him again. "Favorite vacation spot?"

"I like the beach but the mountains are nice too. What I like is to be active and learn something wherever I go."

"Learn something?" She pulled her sandwich apart and took the cheese off it.

"Yeah, I like taking trips centered around a subject where there are lectures and visits to places where events happened. History, social service, medical missions."

Zoe nibbled at the cheese and then said, "I haven't done that. Maybe I've been missing out on something." She paused in a pensive manner before asking, "Where have you been on a medical mission?"

"I've made a couple of trips to South America, another to Arizona."

"Oh!" Zoe jumped.

Gabe leaned forward, concern making him study her. "What's wrong? You hurt somewhere?"

Her smile turned to a sweet, reflective one. "The baby kicked."

He looked to where her hand rested. Despite being a doctor, the action filled him with awe.

She hissed and looked at him. "There it was again."

"May I feel?" he asked softly. The need to know the small life growing in her would take him to his knees, begging, if that was what it took to get her to agree.

She nodded. He placed his hand where hers had been.

There was nothing. Zoe flinched again but he didn't feel anything. Placing her hand over the top of his, she moved it slightly and pressed. A second later there was a thump against his palm. His gaze snapped to meet hers. At that moment she took his heart.

He leaned forward with the intention of kissing her. But he'd promised. "Zoe…"

She wanted and deserved assurances he wasn't prepared to give. He needed space. Gabe stood and picked up his plate. "Thanks for sharing that with me."

Zoe looked at him with big wide eyes before he stalked away.

Fifteen minutes later he was on his way to the hospital.

Wednesday morning Zoe sat in the obstetrician's office, waiting for the nurse to call her name. She'd not seen Gabe since Sunday afternoon. He'd been gone Monday by the time she'd gone to the kitchen. She'd heard him come in once but it had been late and she'd already been in bed.

His new job might be demanding but the thought had crossed her mind that maybe he was dodging her. She wasn't sure why he would be but something about the way he'd abruptly left on Sunday made her question his actions.

She'd texted him the time of the appointment and the address. Maybe he'd changed his mind about being there. She wasn't sure how she felt about that. His insistence had taken her by surprise. Although she knew she shouldn't, she wanted to share the moment of discovery with him.

A nurse standing at the door leading back to the examination rooms called Zoe's name. She searched the entrance to the outside of the building as disappointment filled her. Apparently Gabe wasn't coming. After all he'd said about being involved and the one time she'd agreed, he wasn't taking advantage of it. She'd let herself believe… What, she wasn't sure. That there might be a chance for them?

That Gabe could really care about the baby beyond being honorable? Or that he could want to be there for her? All of it was just wishful thinking. Nothing based on reality.

She followed the nurse back to the examination room. Inside she sat on the table with shoulders slumped and waited. Her situation with Gabe reminded her of her relationship with Shawn and her father. She hadn't been able to depend on them. They were unreliable, would hurt her. She saw it one way when in reality it was all another. With Gabe she needed to keep what was truth separated from wishful thinking.

Zoe had been waiting a few minutes when there was a quick rap on the door. Fully expecting the doctor, she was shocked to see Gabe step in. She couldn't deny the joy surging into her chest. He had come.

"I'm sorry I'm late. I got tied up at the last minute," he said, puffing as if he'd been running. He came to stand beside her. "Have I missed anything?"

His breathless enthusiasm made her smile. He was acting like a kid looking for a piece of candy. "No. The doctor hasn't been in yet."

"Good." He sank into the only chair in the room.

Moments later the door opened and this time it was her doctor. He gave Gabe a questioning once-over.

Gabe stood and offered his hand. "Gabe Marks. I'm the baby's father."

Zoe didn't miss the proud tone of his voice. Another gentle wave of happiness washed over her.

"Nice to meet you," the doctor said, then turned to her. "This visit is the one where we do the anatomy ultrasound. The question is, do you want to know the sex?"

Before Zoe could speak Gabe said, "I'm more interested in knowing if Zoe and baby are all right."

Tears sprang to Zoe's eyes. She'd not expected that statement.

"That I can let you know as well, but I don't anticipate a problem with either one of them." The doctor smiled at her.

"That's good to hear," Gabe said, then looked at her. "We do want to know the sex, don't we?"

Zoe nodded.

"Okay," her doctor said. "The tech will be in in a few minutes to do the ultrasound. Then I'll be back to do the examination." That said, he left, closing the door behind him.

"Are you okay?" Gabe asked now that they were alone.

"Yeah. Why?"

"You just had a funny look on your face a few minutes ago." Either she'd revealed too much or he'd been watching her too closely.

"I'm just excited."

Gabe took her hand. "I know this wasn't what either of us planned, but I have to admit that bringing a new life into the world is pretty amazing." He kissed her forehead.

The tenderness of the moment dissolved when there was another knock at the door, but the lingering contentment would last a long time.

Gabe held the door open for the tech, who was pushing a large machine on wheels. "Hi, I'm Sarah. I'll be doing your ultrasound." She positioned the machine beside the exam table. "Are you Dad?" she asked Gabe.

"Yes."

"Then what I'd like you to do is sit in the chair until I get everything all set up. Then you can come and stand beside Mom." She started getting the cables organized.

A perplexed look came over Gabe's face. Zoe couldn't help but grin. Her guess was that Gabe did most of the ordering in his world and to have this woman in control of the situation had to go against the grain. Despite that, he did what the tech requested but watched her with narrowed eyes.

"Let's get you further up on the table." The woman helped Zoe scoot back. "Now, please pull up your shirt."

Zoe did, revealing the roundness of her belly, made more pronounced by lying down. She looked over at Gabe. His attention was fixed on her middle. There was something telling and intense about his focus. Seconds later his gaze rose to meet hers and his eyes softened. What was he thinking?

Soon the tech squirted a glob of gel on Zoe's belly and had the transducer moving over her skin. The swishing sound of the baby's heart beating filled the room. "Okay, Dad, you can come and stand beside Mom."

Gabe didn't have to be asked twice. When he was beside her, he placed his hand over hers where it rested on the exam table, curling his fingers into her palm. It was as if he had to be touching her. For a man who had asserted he didn't have time or room in his life for a family, he seemed very interested in her and this baby. Maybe he didn't know what he really wanted.

The tech continued to watch the screen as she moved the transducer over Zoe. "All right, I understand you want to know what gender this baby is. Let's see if we can find out."

Zoe glanced at Gabe. He was watching the screen intently.

Before Zoe could look back the tech said, "I believe with that anatomy it's a boy."

Pure joy filled Gabe's face. He squeezed her hand and breathed softly, "A boy."

Zoe looked at the screen. There was their baby boy. Would he look like Gabe? She hoped so. Tall, dark-haired with magnetic blue eyes. What child could go wrong with that combination?

A ringing sound had Gabe letting go of her hand and digging into his pocket. He looked at the cell phone and stepped away from her. Just that quickly the special moment evaporated.

"Dr. Marks." He listened then said, "I'll be right there." He ended the connection and considered her, his face grave. "I have to go. I have to be there to supervise."

His mind was already somewhere else.

"I know." Zoe did understand. She was glad that at least he'd made it there for their special moment.

He moved around the machine and slipped out the door. Zoe watched it close between them. It was just one more reminder nothing had changed and she shouldn't get her hopes up.

Gabe would have never thought he'd be this absorbed in a baby. Was it because the child was his or because Zoe was carrying it? Or both? There had always been an attraction between him and Zoe, but in the last few weeks it had grown into something more. A feeling he didn't want to put a name to or analyze, but that was taking control nonetheless.

He'd hated to leave her so abruptly, especially after his almost too late arrival. They had shared one of the most surreal moments of his life. He had been watching his son on the screen. More than that, he'd shared it with Zoe. For heaven's sake, he was a physician and he'd gone through the OB rotation in medical school, but this time it was his child.

Although it was late in the evening before he headed out of the hospital, he still had a stop to make. Less than an hour later he pulled into the garage beside Zoe's car. With a smile on his face, he picked up the brown bag in the passenger seat and climbed out of the car. Would Zoe think his purchase was silly or give him an understanding smile? It didn't matter which, because he'd been unable to help himself.

There was a light burning in the kitchen but no Zoe. With the bag in his hand, he went to her hallway. "Zoe." There was no answer. He took a few more steps toward her room. "Zoe?"

Seconds later the sound of music playing met his ears. She must not be able to hear him. He went to her bedroom door. "Zoe." Still nothing. Now he was getting worried. Had she passed out? Fallen in the shower?

He stepped to the bathroom door and jerked to a stop. His throat tightened and his heart pounded. Zoe stood in front of the large mirror over the sink. She had her night-gown pulled up to below her breasts and was looking down while her hands slowly roamed over her expanded middle. A serene smile of wonderment lit her lovely face.

Gabe shifted.

Her head whipped toward him, her eyes wide. She reached for her gown.

"Please, don't." His words were soft and beseeching. "You're so beautiful. Breathtaking."

Zoe's hands stilled but she watched him with unmistakable wariness.

Gabe placed the bag on the counter and slowly stepped behind her. Their gazes locked in the mirror. There was a question in her eyes. His arms circled her. She trembled when his palms touched her warm, smooth skin. Would she push him away?

His heart thundered in his ears when her hands covered his, her fingers interlacing with his. She moved them down and around until they cupped the tight globe encasing their baby. Zoe closed her eyes and leaned back against him. Gabe had never seen her look more angelic. Inhaling, he took in the soft, subtle scent of her freshness. He could do nothing more than stare. What he had in his arms was precious.

She once again moved his hands to rest at what had

once been the curve of her hips. There was a small push against one of his palms. Gabe hissed. His heart swelled. Emotions too strong to comprehend grew in his chest and spread out to overtake him. This was territory he'd never been to before. "Zoe, thank you."

Zoe stood perfectly still. Gabe's voice was like a tender kiss upon her neck. She opened her eyes, meeting his intense, passionate gaze. He'd said he wouldn't touch her again unless she asked him to, so it was up to her to make the first move. Turning in his arms, she wrapped her arms around his neck and pushed up on her toes. Her lips lightly touched his. "No. Thank you."

Gabe's mouth pressed into hers, igniting that fire that only he could. He pulled her closer. His lips slid over hers, leaving sweet waves of sensation radiating out through her body. She put her fingers to the hair at the nape of his neck, ran them through it. Moments later, Gabe's gentle touch traveled over her back, grasping and releasing as his arms circled her, lifting her against him. She went willingly.

Where their previous kisses had been frantic, this one was loving and exploring, wondering and appreciating. Zoe moaned and melted further into him. She was sure she wasn't taking the most rational action, but she could no longer fight her emotions.

Gabe's mouth left hers to skim along her cheek, leaving small caresses that held more reverence than passion. He kissed her temple then the shell of her ear. "I want you. Just to hold you."

"I want that too," she purred against his lips.

Releasing her, Gabe lowered the gown covering her. He took her hand, leading her out of the bathroom and across the house toward his room. Zoe had resisted going into his space. Had even put off cleaning there. Something about it was just too intimate. Now she was being invited in. Wanted.

Gabe let go of her hand at the door, moving into the dark room alone. Seconds later, a small lamp on a bureau lit the space. Gabe's furniture was massive. It suited him. The king-size bed was the centerpiece with its dark green spread. On either side were two end tables. At one end of the room was a fireplace with enough space for a sitting area, but there was nothing there.

He returned to her, offering his hand. Zoe took it. She wanted this. Needed the closeness. Gabe led her to the bedside. His blue eyes seemed to glow with emotion. She was unable to identify which one before his lips found hers. His mouth touched hers gently, giving instead of taking. It was as if he was trying to convey his feelings without voicing them.

For the first time Zoe dared to hope that there might be a future for them.

When Gabe pulled away, he gave her another searching look. Going down on one knee, he took the hem of her gown and rolled it up. She sucked in a breath. With her heart in her throat, Zoe watched him lean in and place a kiss where their baby grew. Gabe turned his head, placing his cheek against her. Her hand cradled his head and held him close. Moisture filled her eyes.

He rose, bringing the gown up with him. Seconds later he stripped it off over her head. She shivered, her arms instantly covering her breasts.

"Please don't hide from me. You're stunning." Gabe knelt and slowly slipped her panties to her feet.

Zoe stepped out of them as he pulled the bedspread back. Gabe turned and swept her up against his chest. One of her arms went around his shoulders as she buried her face in his neck, her mouth finding heated skin. He worshipfully placed her between the sheets then stood gazing down at her as if memorizing each curve and dip.

"You're so beautiful. I just don't have the words."

Zoe's heart danced. She lifted her arms, inviting him to join her. Gabe sat beside her instead. Their gazes held as he placed a hand over the baby. Hers came to rest on his before he slowly leaned down to kiss her. His sweet, tender ways were her undoing. This was the affection that love was made of. In her heart she'd known it when she'd invited him into her hotel room that fateful stormy night. Cupping his face in both hands, she held his mouth to hers.

His kisses were easy, caring, loving. She was being cherished with each touch of his lips. He controlled their kiss, refusing when she wanted to take it deeper. Her soul played joyous notes as he lightly skimmed his mouth over hers.

Zoe sucked in a breath as his attention left her lips to travel over her cheek. His mouth found the sweet spot behind her ear, pressed and suckled. His fingertips trailed down along the length of her arm and up again. She shuddered. Every nerve in her body was alive where Gabe's next touch landed. He moved to her shoulder, leaving a kiss in the dip there before dropping more along a path to the rise of her breast.

Her breath hitched then caught when he cradled her in his hand. He shifted her breast, looked for a second before his mouth covered her nipple. Fireworks went off inside her, her breasts grew heavy, and her core tingled. Her fingers funneled into his hair as she relaxed on the pillow, closed her eyes and took in each precious nuance of his caresses.

"Gabe." She lifted her shoulders, tugging his head toward hers.

He resisted. "Shh. Just feel."

Could she take more? That was all she was doing—feeling. Her body was on fire with want. Her body throbbed, ached, begged for relief.

Gabe suckled then circled her nipple with his tongue. Her body clenched. As he continued to worship her with his mouth, his hand traveled tantalizingly slow over her hip then across her middle. A finger traced the circumference of her belly button before it glided downward. It brushed her curls and Zoe's hips flexed. Gabe kissed the baby once more before his mouth returned to cover hers.

He pulled away too soon and she groaned, reaching for him in protest. Gabe chuckled lightly as he shifted on the bed so that her calves lay across his lap. The firm bulge of his manhood was visible beneath his pants. A slight smile came to her lips. He hadn't remained unaffected by their kisses.

Zoe watched as he picked up her foot and began to massage it. When she pulled at a corner of the sheet in an effort to cover herself, he tugged it away.

"I want to admire you. Watch your body turn all rosy for me."

She'd never lain naked in front of a man, much less while he touched and kissed her all over. There was something titillating and erotic about it to be desired so.

Gabe paid special attention to each of her toes, pulling gently before moving to the next. When he was done, he brought her foot to his mouth and placed his lips to her arch. Zoe sighed. This was heaven. How it should be between a man and a woman. Their gazes met and held. She bit her bottom lip as Gabe slowly ran his hand from her ankle up to her thigh, slipped inside the crease of her legs and then moved down again.

How much longer could she take his ministrations?

His wicked smile was equally sexy as he picked up her other foot. Confidence covered his handsome face. He was aware of what he was making her feel, enjoying it. After giving that foot the same attention he had given the other, he grabbed a pillow, placed it beside her, then another and did the same before he said, "Turn over."

"Gabe, I don't think—"

"Trust me."

In spite of all her precautions, she'd found she could do just that. Gabe was so much more than she'd first given him credit for. Rolling not very gracefully onto her stomach, she allowed Gabe to help place the pillows so that any pressure was off the baby. She glanced back to see he had moved again so that he sat beside her hips. Over the next few minutes she concentrated on the provocative feel of his fingers as they teased their way up one leg, slipped between it and the other long enough for her center to burn with need, before moving away, leaving her wanting. Too soon his hand moved on to the other leg, teasing her to the point she quivered all over. When she believed Gabe could do nothing more to raise her arousal higher, his mouth found the curve of her back. His lips kissed their way up her back one vertebra at a time. At her neck, he pushed her hair away and gave her a sensual nip as his hand brushed the side of her breast. Zoe groaned.

"Roll to your back." Gabe's voice was gruff as if he were grasping for control. She couldn't have moved without his help. Gabe's magic hands had reduced her to nothing more than a lump of putty held together by bones. When she'd returned to her back, his attentions went directly to the V of her legs, touching, withdrawing and approaching to tease once again.

"I want to watch you find your pleasure." His voice was low, coaxing. His lips settled on hers as his finger slipped into her center. She jerked upward, eager for relief only Gabe could provide.

His mouth slowly released hers before his look captured hers, held. He moved his finger faster. Tension built in her, squeezed, pulsed, before the dam burst. Her eyes widened as she flew off into paradise. She saw the look of wonder on Gabe's face as she shuddered before her eyelids fluttered closed.

"Thank you," she murmured.

He kissed her forehead. "My pleasure, honey."

CHAPTER EIGHT

GABE'S FINGERS TRAILED across Zoe's shoulder as he pulled back and stood. He covered her. What he'd experienced with Zoe had never happened to him before. He had always thought of himself as a generous lover and seen to his partner's release, but he'd never given anyone the attention he had given her. He'd not worried about his own desires but hers instead, determined that Zoe understood all he felt.

She was special. Very. If she was willing, he wanted to work something out. Find a way they could stay together after the baby. When the time was right he would talk to her about it. See if she felt the same way. But still he worried he couldn't give her all she wanted. Could he be that present husband and father she dreamed of? Was he willing to find the balance in his life that would make it work?

He headed for the shower. It would be a cold one tonight. Sometime later he turned off the lamp and crawled under the bedcovers, pulling the warm, sleeping Zoe to him. With a sigh he drifted off to sleep. This was too right.

It was still dark when Zoe's warm bottom rubbed against him. In an instant his body responded.

"Mmm…" Zoe murmured, before she turned to face him, her hand resting on his chest.

Gabe wasn't sure she was awake but he certainly was.

Zoe slid her hand up his chest and behind his neck. When she kissed his chest he sucked in a breath.

"You awake?" Her sleep-laden voice sounded so sexy.

"Yes, honey. I'm awake." And in pain.

"Honey." She kissed his chest again. "I like it when you call me that."

Gabe brushed his hand over the lower part of her back. He'd never called a woman that before.

"I like it," Zoe mumbled. "And I like you."

"I like you too." His lips found hers.

She pulled closer, moving and shifting so the baby pressed more into his side than on his middle. Her mouth opened for him. Gabe took her invitation. His tongue found hers, performing an erotic dance that was theirs alone.

"If you continue that, I won't keep my promise to just hold you."

"I'd like being held but I like other things too." Her hand moved lower.

"Are you sure?" If she continued, he would do anything she asked.

Zoe pulled his face to hers, kissing his eyes, his cheek, his chin before her lips found his. She squirmed, brushing against his arousal. That was more than Gabe could take. He rolled Zoe to her back and braced himself over her on his hands.

Gently, he entered her. Zoe lifted her hips, helping him to settle deep in her. As he entered and withdrew in the age-old manner, Zoe hissed while her fingers gripped his shoulders as he moved. His lips found hers. He increased the pace. She squirmed beneath him as if trying to work closer. With uncertain control, he built their pleasure until Zoe moaned and the tension in her relaxed. Gabe thrust a few more times, before he groaned his release. He fell to Zoe's side and pulled her close, kissing her shoulder. Would life ever be this good again...?

The buzzing of his phone woke him. He was needed at the hospital. Only hazy sunlight was coming through the windows when he slid out of bed. Minutes later he was ready to leave when he leaned over and kissed the still sleeping Zoe. He wanted to climb back in beside her but he was being pulled away. He took a moment to watch her. Would it always be this way for him? Leaving her behind? What was he allowing to happen? If he could stop it, would he?

But what would he have missed if Zoe hadn't come into his life?

With the tip of his finger, he pushed a stray lock of hair off her cheek and forced himself to walk out of the room.

Zoe woke to cool sheets beside her, but the hot memories of the night before had her whole body still tingling. The room was bright with light. She jerked to a sitting position. Apparently she had overslept. She didn't ever do that. Making her way to her room for her phone, she called in and told the office she would be in soon.

She stepped into the bath and saw the bag sitting on the counter. Unable to resist, she peeked inside. A smile spread across her face. How like a man. Not wanting to spoil Gabe's surprise, she took the bag to the kitchen and placed it on the table. On the counter, she found a note.

Honey, I'll bring dinner home.

Honey. The word was like golden sunshine on a cloudy morning.

Zoe went through the day with a smile on her face. More than one person at her office commented on how happy she looked. She just smiled and kept her reason to herself. Saying why might make it disappear, and even if she did, what could she say? That she was in love with a man she wasn't sure was in love with her. Their relationship wasn't any more secure than it had been before. With her past, she'd learned the bitter lesson that not everything was always the way it appeared.

Gabe invaded her thoughts in every spare moment. Had they turned a corner where things would be different between them? Could they, would they find a future? Did Gabe want to? The baby was a life-changing event in their lives and she couldn't help but hope last night had been as well.

He'd given so completely, been so tender and caring during their lovemaking. There had been none of the frenzy of their first time, but the experience had been just as satisfying. The night had included passion but it had been wrapped in caring, sharing, getting to know each other on a level like never before. Had Gabe been expressing his feelings through his actions?

She could only hope. Yet a nagging fear remained that it might go away in the reality of everyday life. Zoe pushed away the negativity, determined to enjoy what they had shared and what she hoped would be between them in the future. She planned to make the most of Gabe's attentions for as long as they lasted, even if it was only for a few months. Her mother's illness and her father's defection had taught her not to take any day for granted. She would grasp all the happiness she could.

It was late afternoon when she arrived home. As she suspected, Gabe wasn't yet there. It was such a nice day and she'd been inside too much of it, so she planned to take a walk around the neighborhood. Zoe had reached the bottom of the driveway when Gabe pulled in.

Her heart fluttered just at the sight of him.

He stopped and rolled down the window. "Hi."

Zoe couldn't help feeling nervous and a little shy. "Hey."

He watched her too closely for her comfort. "What're you up to?"

"I was going for a walk." She shifted from one foot to the other.

Gabe smiled. "Give me a sec and I'll go with you."

She wasn't sure but she was afraid she might have looked at him as if he was from another planet. That had been the last thing she'd expected out of his mouth. "Won't dinner get cold?"

"It'll need to be warmed up anyway."

"Okay." Wasn't this the man who'd said he didn't have time for family? Now he was home early, with dinner in his hand, and he wanted to go for a walk? It was too good to be true.

He continued on up the drive. She walked behind him and waited at the porch while Gabe parked. Zoe watched as he strolled toward her with a sense of pride. Gabe was a tall, handsome male with a swagger of confidence that made him even sexier. The collar of the light blue shirt that matched his eyes was open and the sleeves were rolled up on his forearms. His pants were classic and fit him to perfection. All of this magnificence was hers. Gabe could be any woman's dream, but he was hers to enjoy.

When he reached her, he smiled and took her hand. "So how was your day?"

She was still uncertain around him. After all the emotion of the night before, he seemed so calm when she was still walking as if on clouds. "Good. I stopped by to see Mom on the way home. She's doing about the same. How about yours?"

"The usual—but I do have some news I think you'll like."

She looked at him. "What?"

"The committee agreed to list Mr. Luther."

She grabbed his arm, stopping him. "That's wonderful. Thank you!" She wrapped her arms around his waist and hugged him.

He pulled her close. "None of it was really my doing. The committee all voted yes after the social worker and psychiatrist had spoken to him. He assured them that he'd do what he needed to do."

"Still, you were the one who agreed to see him in the first place." If she had believed him wonderful before, he was her hero now.

"You're welcome."

Gabe was so humble about what he did for other people. Just another reason she was crazy about him.

They continued down the sidewalk, their hands clasped between them.

"You know, I've never taken you for a person who might enjoy a walk around the neighborhood. But I like it that you came with me."

"I can be full of surprises." Gabe squeezed her hand.

He was. Just a few weeks ago she would have sworn this day would never happen.

They walked a couple of blocks and turned around. As they did so, Gabe said, "I called my mother today. Told her we were having a boy. She was excited. Said she was looking forward to meeting you."

What did his mother think about their situation? "I look forward to meeting her too."

That worrying thought was interrupted by someone calling, "Hi."

Zoe looked to see an older couple standing near a manicured flower bed.

She and Gabe stopped.

The balding man, followed by his wife, stepped closer

to the walk. "You must be our newest neighbor. The one who moved into the brick house with the curved drive."

"Yes, sir, that's us," Gabe said, offering his hand to the man. The man took it and they shook. "I'm Gabriel Marks." He put his arm at her waist and said, "And this is Zoe."

The way he left the introduction implied that they were married. Zoe wasn't sure how she felt about that. Had Gabe just not wanted to go into the details of their relationship at a casual meeting?

"I'm Richard Mills, and this is my wife, Maggie."

"It's nice to meet you both," Gabe said.

Maggie stepped closer and smiled. "I see that you're expecting a little one."

Zoe placed her hand on her middle. "Yes. He's due in a couple of months."

"A little boy. How wonderful. We'll need to get the neighbors together and give y'all a baby shower."

"Oh, that's sweet but not necessary." Zoe didn't want to have to go into explaining her and Gabe's relationship. The bubble of happiness she'd had minutes before had popped.

"We could make it a block party and shower. It'd be a wonderful way for everyone to meet each other." Her enthusiasm made her voice higher. "It'd be a lot of fun."

Zoe just smiled.

Maggie continued, "A lot of us who live around here are grandparents but our grandkids are no longer small. To have small children around will be wonderful. Ooh, to get to buy one of those cute little outfits." She all but rubbed her hands together in glee.

Zoe felt like a fraud. This couple thought her and Gabe were a happy couple in the process of becoming a happy family. She wished it was true. But Gabe had said nothing about that happening.

Gabe's smile had turned tight. "We need to head home. We've supper waiting for us."

"Great to meet you," Richard said. "See you soon."

"You too," Gabe said, as they started down the sidewalk.

"They seemed like nice people," Zoe said quietly. "They think we're married."

"Yeah, I suspect they do." Gabe didn't look at her while matching his pace to hers.

What was he thinking? Some of the joy of the day had dimmed. They continued in silence until they were in front of his house. She wanted their earlier camaraderie back. "I enjoyed our walk."

"I did too."

Zoe gave him a suspicious look. "What's happening to you?"

"Uh?"

"I'd have never guessed the always-busy type A doctor would've ever said something like that."

He grinned. "Could be you're a good influence on me."

Did she really have that kind of effect on him?

As they entered the house through the carport door, Gabe said, "I brought us some of the best Italian in town. Or so I've been told. It's from a little restaurant close to the hospital. I'll get it warmed up."

"Then I'm on dish duty." Zoe headed for the kitchen. She'd forgotten about the bag waiting on the table. Picking it up, she held it out. "By the way, you left this in my bathroom last night."

He gave her a wolfish grin. "I had other things on my mind."

Heat warmed her cheeks. She'd had other things on her mind as well.

Gabe took it from her. "You didn't peek, did you?"

She shrugged and tried to look innocent. "Maybe a little."

"Why am I not surprised?" He dug into the bag. "What do you think?" Gabe proudly held up a ball and a tiny baseball glove.

She smiled. "I think it'll be a while before he can use them."

Gabe grinned. "Maybe so but he'll have them when he's ready."

"Yes, he will." But would Gabe be around to play with him? Go to the games?

They worked around each other for the next few minutes. During one of her passes by him, Gabe caught her hand and pulled her to him. "I haven't had one of these in too long." He gave her a tender yet searching kiss.

The insecurity of earlier disappeared, replaced by the bliss of being in his arms again.

His lips left hers. "I could do without a meal to have you again but you need to eat. You tempt me so much."

She tempted him? Had she ever received a more exciting compliment?

After dinner Zoé stood at the sink, washing up the few dishes they had used. Gabe came up behind her. The heat from his body warmed her from shoulders to hips. His arms circled her before he pushed her hair away from her neck and gave her a kiss.

She could get used to this attention. His change in attitude and all his actions were almost surreal but they were everything she had dreamed of having in a husband.

"Forget those and let's go outside and sit for a little while."

Her heart opened more. Even that simple statement made her melt. He wanted to spend time with her. The impression she'd had of him when they'd first met had been that he would never have slowed down long enough to enjoy anything as simple as sitting outside under the stars. Then his life had seemed to center on his career. "Almost done here. You go on and I'll be right there."

Minutes later she wiped her hands off on the dishrag and headed to the patio. Gabe was sitting on the settee with one foot propped on the table. He looked relaxed and content. With his stressful job, he needed downtime. She was glad he could find it.

She moved to take a chair but he grabbed her hand and tugged her toward him. "You'll be too far away if you sit there."

She sat next to him. His arm went around her shoulders, pulling her close.

"This is much better."

Zoe sighed softly. *Much.* The evening sounds of bugs and the occasional bark of a dog joined the sound of Gabe's soft breathing. Could life get better than this? Only if it could be like this forever.

"I've been thinking about a baby name now that we know what it's going to be." She sat so near she could feel the tension of anticipation in Gabe's body. Did he hope the baby would be named after him?

The calm of his voice didn't give anything away. "Have you decided on something?"

"I have."

"Will you tell me?"

"William. Call him Will. What do you think?"

"I like it." The hint of disappointment in his voice didn't escape her.

She couldn't help but tease him, prolonging saying more.

In a huff he asked, "What about the middle name?"

"Well…" She turned so she could see his face. "…I was thinking about Gabriel, after his father and grandfather. What do you think?"

"William Gabriel Marks. That's a fine, strong name."

"Avery. William Gabriel Avery."

He gave her a searching look. Would he argue? He couldn't expect the baby to have his last name if they weren't married. He nodded. Was it acceptance or appeasement?

"Tell me what you know about your daddy. I'd like to know something about Will's heritage."

Gabe didn't like the sour taste in his mouth that came with knowing his boy wouldn't carry his last name. Yet he didn't believe he could demand the name be different. He was well acquainted with Zoe's strong will and determination. She wouldn't easily change her mind. Neither probably should she.

He wasn't sure he was qualified to answer the question about his dad. This wasn't how he would have imagined their romantic moments on the patio going. But then, he'd have never guessed he'd be enjoying an evening like this.

Zoe wouldn't let the question about his father go either. He could only name a few people he'd ever share the story with. "I don't know a lot about him. Like I said, Mother never told me much. I think it's too painful even to this day. He was from Arizona and a teacher. He liked the outdoors. I think my parents had a good marriage but a too short one."

He'd never thought about how deeply his mother must have cared for his father. Had his mother never remarried because she'd missed his father so badly she couldn't bear the hurt of losing another? What would it be like to love that deeply? Could *he*? Did he already?

"That's a shame. It can be hard to find the right person, and when you do, to lose them so..." Zoe's voice trailed off, as though she'd said more than she wanted to.

She must know from experience. Her father had run out on her and she'd lost him, and now for all intents and purposes her mother was gone as well. She had to understand loss far better than he. Possibly love as well.

"Zoe, if you don't want to answer this I'll understand, but would you tell me about *your* father?"

She was close enough he felt her body stiffen.

He squeezed her shoulder. "You don't have to talk about it if you don't want to."

"It doesn't make the hurt any less by not talking about it. I was crazy about him. He could do no wrong. If he was at home I was under his feet. I don't know if I just didn't want to see his unhappiness or I couldn't, but it had to have been there."

She was too hard on herself. "You were a kid. You weren't supposed to see."

"I know, but it would have been easier than him just not coming home one day."

He hugged her again. It would have.

"I asked Mom what happened and all she could say was that he just wasn't happy. That he had to leave."

"You never saw him again?"

"No. We found out a few years later he had died of an overdose." The last few words were but a whisper.

Her pain must be at a level he'd never experienced, yet she still believed in and wanted a marriage, husband and family. Misery filled him. That wasn't something he felt he had the ability to give her, even if he wanted to. What if he failed her? He cared too much to have her hurt like that again.

It was time for a change in subject. Talk about something more pleasant. "Have you given any thought to decorating the nursery? Especially since you know the sex now."

"Not really…" Her voice trailed off as if she wasn't really listening.

"I wish you would. Will needs a place to come home to."

"Mmm…" Her head rested heavily against his shoulder.

Gabe just held her as she slept. A while later, he gently shook her. "Come on, sleepyhead. We need to go to bed."

"I didn't mean to go to sleep on you," she mumbled.

"Not a problem." He walked her inside.

Zoe headed toward her side of the house.

"Hey, where're you going?"

"To bed."

"Wrong way. You're with me." He extended his hand.

For a second he worried she might not take it. To his relief, her palm met his. She curled her fingers around his as they walked to his bedroom. There he led her into the bath and turned on the shower, adjusting the water temperature.

"Are you getting a shower?" Zoe asked, her voice drowsy.

"We're getting a shower." Gabe begin to remove her clothes. She put up no resistance.

"You and me?"

Gabe grinned. She really was out of it. "Yes, honey, you and me." He cupped her face with his hands and kissed her before he turned her and opened the door to the shower stall. "In you go." Gabe gave her a gentle nudge at her waist before she stepped under the water.

He quickly removed his clothes and joined her. Zoe was so tired she was just standing beneath the water, letting it fall on her shoulders. They'd had an intense night the night before with little sleep. He picked up the soap and started washing her. She purred as his hands slid over her. He was deeply aroused but Zoe needed rest more than he needed release.

When she shivered, Gabe increased the temperature of the hot water and put her further under it. He quickly soaped up and rinsed. Cutting off the shower, he opened the door and jerked a towel off the rack. He dried Zoe and wrapped her in a towel. A minute later he'd dried, dropped his towel on the floor and guided Zoe to the bed. He jerked the spread back then removed the towel from Zoe. "Climb in, honey, before you chill."

She did as he said. Seconds later he joined her, pulling her to him and the covers snugly over them. In no time Zoe relaxed against him and was softly sleeping.

Contentment settled over him and he joined her.

The next evening when Gabe arrived home Zoe wasn't there.

The security he'd found in having her waiting for him was suddenly gone. How had she, in such a short time, managed to become such an important part of his life? He looked forward to coming home to her. The house was empty—not just the space, but the life force that made it a home was gone. Could he survive if she moved out?

An hour went by and still Zoe hadn't come home. Then another. He should have stayed at work. Guilt crept in. He had plenty of policies and procedures to read before he could start making serious changes to improve the program. He'd been leaving the hospital early far too often as it was to come home to see her. Now he was here and she wasn't.

As time went by, guilt turned to anger then to worry, which grew like a virus in a lab tube to the point where Gabe kept checking his phone, thinking he'd missed her call. More than once he'd stopped himself from phoning her because he had promised not to question her movements or try to control her. This anxiety and the waste of his time was drama he didn't need.

He loved having Zoe in his bed, but the emotionally draining side of their relationship would soon eat at him.

Might even affect his job. He couldn't have that. But letting Zoe go was unthinkable.

Relief flooded him at the sound of the garage door opening. She was home. He was waiting at the house door before she could get out of the car. Gabe said, more casually than he felt, "I've been worried about you."

"I went by to see Mom for a few minutes. Told her about William Gabriel, then did a little shopping for the nursery."

"You did?" Any residue of concern completely disappeared with the sound of happiness in her voice. At least the joy over the baby was overcoming her despair about her mother's health.

"Come and help me bring these packages in." Her head disappeared inside the car.

Gabe moved to stand beside her. She handed him a couple of huge plastic bags filled with fluffy items. "You did do some shopping."

"You said you'd like me to fix up the nursery. I got off a few minutes early today, so I thought I'd pick up some things."

"This is a little more than some." He chuckled as he headed toward the door of the house. His pleasure at seeing her and his relief over her being home safe made any discord he'd felt earlier disappear.

"Babies need a lot." Her tone held a defensive note.

"Hey, I was just kidding." He put the bags down in the hallway and wrapped his arms around her waist. "You can buy twice as much, for all I care."

Her hands were full of bags but her arms came around him anyway. "It was so much fun. I can hardly wait to show you what I got. I'm going to need your help."

"You've got it. Have you eaten yet?"

"No."

"Then why don't I fix us some breakfast for supper? You can sit at the table with your feet up for a while and tell me about your day and how your visit with your mother went." Who had he turned into? Nothing about those suggestions sounded like the person he thought he was. Zoe was changing him.

"That sounds great. Let me put these in the baby's room." She held up the bags in her hands. "I'm going to change into something more comfortable too."

"Sounds like a plan. I'll get started on dinner. Just leave these bags here and I'll get them later."

After eating, they spent the next two hours working in the nursery, and now Zoe sat on the floor, pulling open another package. She was dressed in baggy sweatpants and a shirt she had asked to borrow from him. Her skin was glowing, her eyes sparkled and she giggled as she showed him each new item. He couldn't think of a time she'd looked more amazing. But didn't he think that daily?

During the last hour he'd hung curtains under her direction and helped her place a bed skirt on the crib. He wasn't sure it was particularly useful but he didn't voice that out loud. All the time she had been chattering about her decision to get this or that and opening bags. Gabe didn't care one way or the other about any of it but he was enjoying listening to Zoe. Her excitement was infectious.

"This is the last thing." She opened the clear package and pulled out some material with a triumphant look.

"I have no idea what that is." It wasn't the first time he'd thought that about some of the objects she'd bought.

"It's a crib sheet."

"Oh." He nodded sagely. "Should have known that right

away. Hand it here and I'll put it on and that way you don't have to get up."

"Are you saying I can't?" There was a teasing note in her voice.

"No. I was just trying to be helpful. That's all."

"You weren't implying I was fat."

He grinned. "I know better than to do that."

"You'd better not."

After a struggle with the mattress and sheet that had Zoe giggling, Gabe finally had it in place. Done, he sat behind Zoe, spread his legs wide and wrapped her around her middle to bring her back until she rested against his chest. She placed her hands over his. He rested his chin on the top of her head.

He scanned the room, looking at the yellow and gray plaid curtains whose panels hung straight on either side of the windows, to the gray pillow with the yellow polka-dot cover, to the crib with a yellow sheet and the same plaid as the curtains on the bed skirt. He would have never thought to put those combinations together. He liked Zoe's taste. "So, are you pleased?"

"Hmm... I am. I still need to get a mobile and I want to do his name above the crib."

Gabe smiled. Her mind was still racing with ideas. "For someone who I had to talk into fixing up a nursery, you sure have run with it."

"It's fun, and you were right. Will needs a nice place to come home to."

But not live. There was that sick feeling in his gut again. Zoe yawned.

"I think I need to get you to bed. You've had a long day." Gabe stood and then helped her up.

"I need to clean up this mess." She started to pick up a bag.

He took her hand. "Leave it until tomorrow." Gabe ushered her out of the room and turned off the light. He wanted her attention now.

Zoe was so tickled with the way the nursery had turned out. Gabe was a great help and even seemed to enjoy it. She hadn't even hesitated when he'd led her to his bedroom. In a few short nights she had started to think of it as hers. Sleeping without being in Gabe's arms would be impossible.

They were climbing into bed when he said, "I called my mother today. Told her what name we had decided on. I think she cried."

Zoe wasn't sure what to say to that. "She liked it, then?"

"She loved it. She said my father would be so proud." He gave Zoe a nudge to move further into the bed.

"What have you told your mother about me?"

"Nothing much really."

"She didn't ask any questions?" Zoe rolled to her side so she could see his face.

"I didn't say that."

Was he ashamed of her? Had he told his mother how easy Zoe had been to get into bed? She moved away from him. "Like what?"

"I told her your name. What you do for a living. That your mother is sick and you're wonderful with her. That sort of thing. Enough about her." He pulled Zoe toward him. "Let's think about us."

Zoe stopped his advance with a hand on his chest. Her look met his. She hated that she might ruin the happiness they had found together but she had to ask. "Gabe, what are we doing?"

"I don't know" was his soft reply. "Let's just see what happens."

For tonight she could accept that but for how long?

She was afraid that what happened would end up with her heart getting broken. Gabe drew her to him, giving her a deep kiss that had her thinking of nothing but what he made her body feel.

Their lovemaking had a desperate edge to it. As if what they had found they feared would soon disappear.

CHAPTER NINE

A WEEK LATER Zoe was on her way out of her office to make her weekly rounds to area hospitals. Her cell phone rang. Gabe's name showed on the screen.

She and Gabe had spent a blissful week together. They had taken walks, visited her mom, enjoyed the patio and spent precious moments in bed, many times just in each other's arms, talking. Yet there had been no more discussion of where their relationship was headed or what would happen after the baby was born. It was as if they were living in a bubble of happiness and they were the only ones who existed. They were pretending nothing would ever change, therefore no decisions needed to be made. Gabe's silence told her that he hadn't changed his mind about what his life would be. She couldn't accept less than what she wanted. They were living on borrowed time. Despite all that, her heart did a flip at the mere thought of him.

She touched the button.

"Hi, honey."

Would she ever get over the thrill of Gabe's voice calling her that? "Hey."

"I just received word there's a match for Mr. Luther."

"Really? That's wonderful." She couldn't believe it. So soon. The wait was usually much longer. The match must have been perfect.

"I've already made the call for him to come in. Hold

on a sec." Gabe spoke to someone else then said, "He should be on his way now. I expect to be in surgery late this evening."

"I'm on my way."

He hurriedly said, "I don't know if I'll have a chance to see you or not."

"I understand. I'll be busy with Mr. Luther anyway."

Gabe had been keeping exceptionally normal hours for the past week but she was sure that wouldn't always be the case. As often as possible, liver transplants were done during business hours, but there were always emergency situations. She worked in the medical field, understood that better than most. Tonight was an example.

Forty-five minutes later she arrived at the hospital and took the elevator up to the third floor, where the liver transplant unit was located. She went to the nurses' station and showed her credentials to the unit tech before requesting to look at Mr. Luther's chart. Zoe had just finished her review and was headed to his room when Gabe walked up.

He smiled. "Hey, I thought I'd miss you."

"Glad you didn't."

She glanced at the desk to find the unit clerk and a couple of nurses watching them.

"Come on. We'll go and see Mr. Luther." He put his hand on her back and directed her toward the other end of the hall.

At Mr. Luther's door she knocked. When there was no answer, she pushed the door open slightly. "Mr. Luther?"

The room was dark and the TV wasn't playing. Had the OR tech already come to get him? She moved further into the room with Gabe close behind. "Mr. Luther?"

A movement caught her attention. The man sat in a chair, looking out the window.

"Mr. Luther, it's Zoe. May I come in?"

"If you want."

It was as if all the blustery wind had gone out of the man. What was going on? "I needed to finalize some things before they come to take you to the OR. Dr. Marks is here too. May I turn the light on?"

"Please don't. I'm enjoying the sunset."

She knew that tone. It was the same one her father had used just before he'd left. The hopeless one. The one that said he had nothing to live for. Zoe wasn't going to let the same thing happen to Mr. Luther that had happened to her father.

She glanced back at Gabe then went to stand beside Mr. Luther. "Mind if I watch with you?"

"If you want to."

Gabe came to stand behind her. His hand came to rest on her waist. Would he have taken the time to do the same a few weeks ago?

The sky, already orange, slowly darkened to black. With the sun below the horizon, Gabe stepped back and she did too.

"I need to listen to you, Mr. Luther, before I have to go to the OR," Gabe said.

The man nodded and moved back to the bed. After he settled in, he focused on Gabe.

He pulled his stethoscope from around his neck. "You know, Mr. Luther, I'm good at what I do. I've done many liver transplants. I don't anticipate you having any problems."

"If you say so."

"I do. I want you to try not to worry." Gabe listened to Mr. Luther's heart.

"I thought if you didn't mind I'd stay right here with you," Zoe said as she stepped closer to the bed. "Maybe walk down to surgery with you. Would you mind?"

Mr. Luther, who had hardly had time for her when she'd visited, looked at her and smiled. "I'd like that."

"Zoe," Gabe said in a sharp voice and with a direct look. "It might run late."

She met his glare. "I know."

"You need to take care of yourself," Gabe insisted.

Mr. Luther nodded toward Gabe but looked at her and asked, "So what's the deal with you and the doctor here? That baby?"

Was their relationship that obvious? Apparently so. Under normal circumstances their conversation wouldn't have taken place in front of a patient. At least it had Mr. Luther thinking of something besides his impending surgery.

Zoe stared at Gabe. What should they say? How like Mr. Luther to ask such a direct personal question.

Gabe straightened. "Zoe is carrying my baby. We're having a boy."

She liked the pride she heard in his voice.

As if Gabe's statement had confirmed what he thought, Mr. Luther said, "Congratulations. Now, Doc, do you think you can put in that new liver?"

Zoe blinked at his change of attitude and subject.

"I can and I will. I'll see you in the OR." He looked at Zoe. "Can I speak to you in the hall?"

Zoe placed her hand on Mr. Luther's arm. "I'll be right back." She followed Gabe out the door.

"You shouldn't be spending long hours here," Gabe hissed before she could completely close the door. "I don't want to have to worry about you."

"I'll be fine. If I start feeling bad I'll get one of the security guards to walk me out if necessary. I'll just be in the waiting room." She glanced toward Mr. Luther's room. "He needs to know someone is here for him. I promise to only stay as long as I feel up to it."

"I guess there's no point in arguing with you." Gabe sounded resigned to the fact he couldn't fight her.

She smiled sweetly. "No, I don't think there is."

"Okay, but if you do leave, will you please text me and let me know you made it home?"

"I will. Thanks for caring."

Gabe's look captured hers. "I do, you know."

Joy flowed through her as hot as a beach in the summer. That was the closest Gabe had come to expressing his feelings. She smiled. "It's always nice to hear. I care about you too."

"Maybe we should talk about how much when I get home." He checked his watch. "I have to go. My team is waiting."

There was something about Gabe that hummed like electricity when he talked about doing surgery. His thoughts were already on the job ahead. He was in his element. Gabe knew how to save lives and did it well. She was proud of him. "I understand. I still have to do vitals on Mr. Luther."

He briefly touched her hand before walking away. Hope burned bright. Were her dreams coming true?

Gabe couldn't believe he had almost admitted to Zoe that he loved her in the middle of the hospital hallway. He had truly lost his mind where she was concerned. In his wildest dreams he would never have imagined opening his home to her would have also opened his heart. The last couple of weeks had been the most wonderful of his life. He'd never felt more content or cared for. Even going home had become more appealing than working late at the hospital. That had never entered his mind as a possibility or a desire before Zoe.

"Hello, ladies and gentlemen." He spoke to his transplant team less than an hour later. He was pleased with how they were slowly coming together to create an impressive group. "I appreciate all of you making it a late evening." With only their eyes visible over the masks they wore, they nodded. "This is our patient, Mr. Luther. He'll be getting a new liver today. Let's make sure he receives it in short order and with top care."

A couple of his staff gave him a questioning look. Gabe moved to stand beside the table. He said to the anesthesiologist, "Are we ready?"

"He's out and vitals stable," the woman answered.

"Scalpel," Gabe ordered.

His surgical nurse placed it in the palm of his hand. Seconds later Gabe went to work.

They were in the process of closing when the fellow, Dr. Webber, released a clamp.

"That needs to stay in place while we look for bleeders," Gabe said sharply.

"But this has been the process before," Dr. Webber replied.

"Not this time. I am trying a new procedure."

"Yes, sir." Dr. Webber replaced the clamp. "It's your patient and your call."

When Mr. Luther's incision had been closed, Gabe said, "Well done, everyone." He looked at the fellow. "Thank you. It's been nice working with you. I believe we have a world-class team here."

Despite the masks, he could see their smiles in their eyes. He left the OR and stepped into the next room to remove his surgical gown. A couple of the other staff followed.

"Nice job, Gabe," one of the team said.

"Thanks. I thought it went exceptionally smoothly." Gabe threw his gown in a basket.

"You were a little hard on the fellow in there, weren't you?" another said.

Gabe shrugged. "My OR, my call."

"Yeah, it was."

Gabe headed straight for the surgery waiting room to see if Zoe was still there. Hopefully she'd gone home, but if not, he could at least walk her to the car. He wasn't surprised to find she was still there.

Zoe stood and met him at the door. "Well, based on that smile on your face, everything went well."

"It did. There were no complications. Barring any infection, Mr. Luther should recover quickly and I anticipate him doing well with a much-improved quality of life."

She wrapped her arms around his waist and hugged him. "Thank you."

He pulled her close, not caring who might see them.

When Zoe eased away, he said, "Now it's time for you to go home. It's late. I have to stay a while longer, but I'm going to walk you to the car."

As they stood beside Zoe's car, Gabe pulled her into his arms and kissed her. Zoe gladly returned it. His kisses made her forget the noise of an ambulance approaching, cars on the nearby freeway whizzing along and the clang of a large truck going over a bump. There was nothing but Gabe.

There was a promise in his kiss. Something that hadn't been there before.

Gabe released her. "I'll be home as soon as I can. Now, in the car with you."

A little later, with a large yawn Zoe pulled into the carport and parked. It had been a long day. A few minutes later she climbed into what had become her and Gabe's bed. Tonight she missed his welcoming body next to hers.

Sometime later she was aware of the moment Gabe

slipped underneath the covers. The bed had gone from cool and lonely to warm and heavenly. He snuggled her in, just as he always did.

"What time is it?" she asked.

"Late."

"Mr. Luther?"

"In ICU and doing great. Now shush, go back to sleep." He kissed her forehead.

The next time Zoe woke, the morning sun was high and beaming into the bedroom windows. Gabe still snored softly next to her. She slowly slid out of his arms and from the bed. Picking up one of his shirts, she covered herself.

Knowing she would be out late, seeing about Mr. Luther, she had called the office and told them she wouldn't be in that day. She would go by the hospital and check on Mr. Luther later in the day. Zoe smiled. Since she lived with the transplant surgeon, she could get a personal update.

She'd just started the coffeepot so it would be ready when Gabe walked into the kitchen.

"Mornin'."

His voice was extra-low and gruff from sleep. Oh, so sexy.

She smiled. "Hey."

He took her in his arms. "Before you even ask, I just called the unit. Mr. Luther is doing great. They have already started weaning him off the respirator."

"I can't say thanks enough."

"Why don't you kiss me and we'll call it even." Gabe's head was already moving toward hers.

Her arms circled his neck and she eagerly went to him. She put all the love she felt into showing him how much.

As she pulled back, Gabe said, "You keep that up and I'll have to take you back to bed."

"I don't have a problem with that." She smiled at him.

He chuckled. "That's nice to hear but we should talk."

"Why don't we make breakfast first? Then we can talk while we eat." Zoe was already pulling a pan out of the cabinet.

"Sounds like a plan."

Half an hour later she and Gabe sat down at the table to what had turned into their favorite meal of eggs, bacon and toast.

Zoe had just picked up her fork when her phone rang. She looked at it. Shorecliffs. For them to be calling, something must be wrong with her mother. She answered.

"Ms. Avery, this is Ms. Marshall."

"Yes?"

"I'm sorry to have to tell you this but your mother is missing."

"What!" Panic shot through Zoe, mixed with disbelief and shock. She looked at Gabe, who had stopped eating and wore a concerned look.

"One of the new employees left a door propped open and she walked out. We have it on video. We're searching for her now. I have called the police. I wanted to let you know in case she comes to you."

No one would be at the apartment. Her mother wouldn't remember that Zoe now lived with Gabe.

Zoe stood. "I'll help look. Please keep me informed."

"We will. Again, I'm sorry about this."

Zoe ended the call. To Gabe she said, "Mom's missing. I have to go."

Before he could respond his phone buzzed. Zoe rushed to her bedroom, already stripping off Gabe's shirt as she went. Where could her mother be? What if she was hurt? Guilt assaulted Zoe. Her mother should be living with her. Instead, Zoe was busy playing "happy home" with Gabe.

He came to the door. "Tell me what happened."

As she pulled on clothes, she told him what the woman had said. "I'm going to the old apartment to see if she's there, even though I can't imagine how she would get there."

Gabe came closer. "That call was from the hospital. There's an emergency and I'm needed. I'm sorry but I can't go with you. I have to see about this."

Zoe glared at him. "What? My mother is missing. You aren't going to help me look for her?"

He gave her an imploring look. "I've got to go. It's my responsibility."

"Couldn't someone else fill in for you just for a little while?"

"I'm the head of the department. It's my job."

"Go. Do what you need to do. If you're needed, you're needed." She pulled on her pants. But she needed him too. Still, his job was important. It hurt that he couldn't be there for her. When had she last been this scared? When her father had left.

"You take care of yourself. Don't do anything crazy. She has to be near the home."

"You don't know that. She could be anywhere!" Zoe lashed back. She jerked her shoes on.

"Call me the second you find her."

Zoe pushed past him and hurried down the hall toward the garage. "Okay. I've got to go and find my mother."

Gabe shook his head. As nice as the day had started, with Zoe sharing his bed and the plans he'd had for them coming to an understanding about the future, it had all turn upside down and ugly with two quick calls. He had left the house with the thought he would clear up the problem at the hospital and join Zoe in the search, but it didn't work out that way.

When he arrived at the hospital, he soon learned the

patient would need surgery and he was the most qualified to perform it. Any hope he held of being at Zoe's side
slipped away.

Going into the OR, he told the unit tech, "Please let me
know if I get any messages."

She gave him a curious look but nodded. "Yes, Doctor."

Most of the time he left a "Do Not Disturb" request.
This time he was worried about not only Zoe but her
mother.

It was a couple of hours later while Gabe was busy su-
turing the vein that had been bleeding that the OR phone
rang. A nurse answered and relayed a message. "Dr.
Marks, the mother has been found. She is well."

Gabe didn't let himself falter as he continued to work,
but relief washed over him, along with sadness. He wasn't
there to support Zoe. She must be so relieved. Her desperation and fear had been written all over her face but
he had still left her in her time of need. It gnawed at him.
She'd needed him then and now, and he wasn't there for
her. Would be, if he truly cared. Zoe should be the number one thing in his life, always come first.

The very thing he'd feared the most and had tried to
avoid had happened. He'd proved he was right about himself. He had chosen his career over her. For him, his profession and a family didn't mix. He didn't know how to
make them mesh. Others could do it, he'd seen it, but he
just wasn't capable of doing it. He'd not even grown up
watching a marriage. And to think he had started to believe he could have one. Zoe had made him care enough
to want to try. But now...

On his way home he made a decision. He had to let her
go. For her sake, she needed to find a man who could give
her what she needed. Today had just been an example of
how he wasn't that person. Zoe deserved better than him.
He would be there for Will, but Zoe wanted more from

their relationship than he could give. It might kill him but he would have to let her go.

It was turning dark before he pulled into the drive. The lights shone brightly in the house. Zoe was waiting for him. He had no doubt of that. There would be a hot meal there as well. His chest ached for what had been and what he was about to do. Her day must have been emotionally exhausting yet she'd thought about him. Zoe had such a capacity to love. Her mother, he himself and Mr. Luther were all evidence of that, and soon Will would be.

Gabe pulled into the garage, cut off the engine but didn't get out immediately. He needed to gather his thoughts, think through what he was going to do. He couldn't continue to live in the house with Zoe. Having her so close and not being able to touch her would slowly drive him mad. He would have to move out. Go stay in a hotel. No way would he ask her to go. The baby was only weeks away. She wouldn't like the idea but he would make her accept it.

He slammed his hand down on the steering wheel. This was just the drama he wanted no part of. The kind that would steer him away from his goals. Made him think of other things besides his career.

The door to the house opened. Zoe was silhouetted there. Oh, heaven help him, he was going to miss her. He climbed out of the car.

"Hey, are you all right?" she called.

"Fine. Just on my way in." Gabe stepped closer to her. "Tell me about what happened with your mom."

She smiled and headed toward the kitchen as he closed the garage door. "Thank goodness it sounded worse than it was. She did leave the home but didn't get far. The door she went out of was the one to the garden area. They found her in the potting shed, filling pots with soil. You were right. She was close by. I'm sorry I acted so irrationally. I shouldn't have demanded you stay with me."

"They didn't look there before calling you or the police?" Anger filled Gabe at the distress they had caused Zoe.

"Someone had, but apparently my mother had stepped around to the back of the shed to look for something to dig with and they missed her. On the second pass, there she was."

"I'm sorry they scared you."

They continued into the kitchen.

"I have to admit all kinds of things were running through my head at what could go wrong." She stopped near the sink and turned to face him. "I fixed supper. Thought we could eat out on the patio tonight. You hungry?"

He was. For her more than anything. "Yeah."

"Then you go wash up while I get it on the table."

Gabe went to his room. Zoe had no idea what was coming. Her mother's successful return hadn't changed his mind. If something like that happened again, where would he be? Beside Zoe or off seeing to a stranger? No, he couldn't do that to her again.

When he returned to the kitchen, Zoe wasn't there. She waved to him from outside where she sat at the patio table, waiting for him.

"I just filled our plates. Simpler that way. I hope you don't mind."

"No." There was little he minded about Zoe. As far as he was concerned, she was near perfect.

The weight of what he was about to say made each of his steps feel as if he were wearing lead shoes. Nothing in his life had been more difficult. He would wait until they had eaten before he explained how it must be. At least they could share this last meal.

As he settled in his chair, Zoe asked, "So how's your patient doing?"

How like Zoe after the day she'd had to show concern for someone else. "She's stable and should recover without any issues."

"I'm sure that's due to your superior skills." She nibbled at a roll.

It didn't make what he had to do any easier, hearing her vote of confidence. "I have a good team." He took a bite of the chicken she had prepared. "This is good. Thanks for going to the trouble after the day you've had."

"Not a problem. After things were settled with Mother and I calmed down, it turned into a perfectly nice day."

Which he was getting ready to ruin. Suddenly his food had no taste. "What kind of arrangements did Shorecliffs make for what happened this morning not to occur again?"

Zoe took a sip of the hot tea she was having. "They were going to fire the guy that propped the door open but I told them that wasn't necessary. It had scared him enough that he won't do it again."

"You're a better person than I am." He had no doubt she was.

"I don't know about that."

When they finished their meal, Zoe stood and picked up their plates. "I made a pie as well. Want some?"

He'd put off what needed doing long enough. "Maybe later. Leave those. I'd like to talk to you for a minute."

Zoe put the plates down, sank into her chair and clasped her hands over her middle. He held her attention. "I know we promised to talk but—"

"Zoe, please..."

Confusion filled her eyes and she pursed her lips. "What's going on, Gabe?"

"This—" he waved a hand between them "—isn't working for me."

"What're you talking about?" Her voice was flat as fear replaced confusion in her eyes.

"I've been leading you to believe that our relationship is moving toward something more permanent. It can't."

"You said you care about me." She watched him closely, as if searching for the truth.

"I do."

"So what does that mean?" Zoe's eyes narrowed.

He shrugged both shoulders. "That I care about what happens to you. To the baby."

"I don't get it."

Gabe wasn't surprised. He wasn't making any sense. "I'm not who you need."

"Isn't that my choice?"

He wasn't sure how to answer that. "Yes," Gabe said with hesitation. "But I'm not going to let you."

Zoe straightened her shoulders, glared at him. The stubborn look he knew so well came over her face. She was no longer on the defensive; she was taking the offensive position. "For a man of your intelligence you aren't making any sense. Just what's the problem? Tell me."

"I can't be there for you like I should be. I've been pretending for the last couple of weeks. I had thought we could make a real go of it, but this morning just proved I'd been right all along."

"And just how's that?" Her tone had turned patronizing.

"My career, my choices would always go to my patients. Your mother was missing and I get a call from the hospital and choose them over being with you. A real relationship is about caring for the other person. I let you down."

"So you think I'm weak?"

His eyes narrowed. What was her point? "I didn't say that."

"I believe that's what you meant. You think I can't handle something like what happened today with Mother on my own. I've been doing that for years. Just because you came into my life, it doesn't mean I still can't. You had a patient who needed you today. I understand that." She pointed to her chest. "Remember, I work in the medical field too. I get it better than most women do."

"But I should have been there to support you."

"Next time you will be. Today you were needed elsewhere. You had a good reason."

"But you're the one who told me you wanted a husband and a family. Isn't that what someone does when they're a husband, be there for the other person?"

"Sure they do. When they can. As for what I want, mostly it's for someone to love me."

"I'm not that guy." The devastation that filled her eyes almost had him on his knees, begging her to forgive him. But he'd never be the man for her. "You expect a marriage to be perfect. I don't even know how to do marriage. Today proves it. I'd make a horrible husband."

"Sure seems like the last couple of weeks you've been doing a fine job of playing the part. Everything about our day-to-day lives looked like a marriage. The neighbors even thought so. Were you just playacting?"

Gabe didn't want to answer that question. He hadn't been, but if he told her that then he'd offer her hope. "Zoe, it's just not going to work."

"You didn't answer the question, Gabe."

He pushed back from the table. "No, I wasn't pretending." Why couldn't she just accept what he was telling her and let them move on? Zoe reached out but he pulled back. If he allowed her to touch him, she would melt his resolve.

"Gabe, forget all the shouldn'ts and let loose. We can make this work together. Let yourself feel. Trust me enough to love you. I do. I have for a long time."

He could hardly breathe. Was a truck running over his

chest? One slight woman had a hold on his heart and was squeezing. "I've let things get out of hand. I knew this would happen. I shouldn't be putting you through this. My patients will always come first. You don't deserve that."

"Don't I get to decide that too? I understand you're a doctor."

"You shouldn't have to. I want better for you."

"Do you really? Or is that the excuse you're using?" She paused then looked at him as if she'd realized something. "Oh, I get it. I've just been one in the long list of people you feel you need to help. Your patients, strangers in airports, your child. You took me in because you're a good guy. That's it. It has had nothing to do with loving me. It must be hard to carry all those needs of the world on your shoulders and still not let yourself feel. Such a burden." Her tone dripped sarcasm. "How noble, and unnecessary. The problem is you do care. You know, Gabe, I would've never have thought you, of all people, would be running scared."

Gabe jerked to his feet. He'd taken all he could. Right now he didn't like her and liked himself even less. It must be this way. He loved her too much to fail her like her father had, and he would if they continued down the road they were traveling. The sudden need to get away clawed at him.

He'd had enough. Of Zoe. Of what could have been.

"We're done here. I'm going to move to a hotel. I want you to stay here as planned until after the baby is born. Hell, keep the place, for all I care." He stalked off.

Zoe called to his back as tears spilled, "I don't need noble. I need your love."

She had told Gabe the truth when she'd said she understood about that morning. It wasn't as if he had chosen to watch a ball game over going with her. His surgical skills had been required. In her heart she'd known he would be there beside her if he could have been. Frustration rolled through her. Why couldn't he see that?

What was she going to do now? Chase after him and beg him to reconsider? She couldn't do that but she was living in his home. That couldn't continue. She would have to find a place sooner than she'd planned. What about her mother? She wouldn't survive a second move. Zoe would have to figure something out. To put Gabe out of his house would be wrong. Staying here without him would be just as impossible. The memories would be more than she could stand.

She picked up the dishes and carried them to the sink. The sound of the door to the carport opening and closing screamed that Gabe had left. Zoe's hands covered her face and she let the tears of misery flow.

CHAPTER TEN

IT HAD BEEN two weeks since Gabe had driven out of the driveway, his intention to only return for clothes later. His contact with Zoe would only have to do with the baby after it was born. He couldn't continue seeing her and keep his promise to stay away. He wasn't even sure it wouldn't be a good idea for him to sell the house when she moved out. Facing the memories might be more than he could manage. It would never be home again unless Zoe was there.

Just seeing her would make his resolve disappear like mist on a sunny day.

Gabe couldn't imagine being more miserable than he had been over the last couple of weeks. He'd missed everything about what his life had once been and it all hinged on Zoe. The way she looked when he called her honey. Or her laughter as he told her something that had happened at work, the joy in her eyes when she'd heard Mr. Luther was doing well. The unconscious way she'd put a protective hand over their baby when they'd talked about it.

Shoving the take-out paper bag away, he groaned. He missed her delicious meals and their simple conversations. She'd been what had been absent in his life, and now that he'd had her, he wanted her back. His personal life was in a shambles.

It was starting to affect his work. The lack of sleep because he was living in a hotel and didn't have Zoe was starting to take its toll. A couple of his coworkers had given him questioning looks when he said something too sharply. He tried to remember to think before he spoke but it didn't always work.

It was Tuesday and his clinic day. He wasn't looking forward to seeing the next patient. He lightly knocked on the door. A gruff voice called for him to come in. As he entered the small room, Gabe said, "Hello, Mr. Luther. How're you doing?"

"Better. The scar doesn't hurt as much as it uscd to."

Gabe nodded. "Good. That sounds like you're making progress."

The man had only stayed a few days in ICU and had been out of the hospital in less than a week. Gabe had seen Zoe's name beside notes on Mr. Luther's chart a few times but Gabe hadn't run into her. He couldn't keep dodging her but he needed a little more time to adjust to what his life was now.

"I feel better than I have in years. My neighbors are taking good care of me."

"I'm glad to hear that. I'm going to give you a good listen then look at the incision site." A few minutes later Gabe said, "Every day you should be improving and you're doing that. I'll see you back here in a couple of weeks. Is there anything you have questions about?"

"Yeah. I'd like to know what you did to Zoe. She looks sad all the time."

Gabe's chest ached. Of course, Mr. Luther would notice. "How is she?"

"Why don't you ask her yourself?"

"It's complicated." Gabe stepped toward the door.

"That's what she said. One thing I've learned through all this is that life can slip away before you know it. Think about it, Doc."

Gabe did regularly over the next few days. Still, he

couldn't see how things could be any different. For Zoe to find that man who could give her what she wanted, she couldn't have Gabe hanging around. Even the idea of Zoe being with another man made him feel physically sick. Surely with time it would get easier, but so far that didn't seem to be the case.

While in his office that evening, his phone rang. He looked at the ID. "Hi, Mom."

"Hey, Gabe. I've not heard from you in a few weeks."

"I'm sorry, Mom. I've been busy." He sounded so much like his mother used to when he was a child, never having enough time when he wanted to talk.

"So how's Zoe and the baby doing?"

"Fine."

There was a pause. "What's going on, Gabe?"

"Nothing I can't handle." He wished he felt as confident as he sounded.

"I'm here if you need me."

She might have worked a lot when he had been a kid, but he'd always known she was there to support him. With or without a father, his mother had been there when she could be. "Mom, why did you never remarry?"

Again there was a pause. This one was longer than the last. "I guess I never found the right man. Your father was a hard act to follow. Then I just got too busy. I worry that you're doing the same. I learned too late that you can't make more time. Don't let it slip by. Especially with the little guy coming."

"I heard you say once that you were worried I had no father figure to model myself on."

"I did?" Amazement was evident in her voice. "Single mothers worry about all kinds of things. Big and small. Gabe, you're one of the most intelligent, caring, giving men I know. I have no doubt that my grandson will have the best father ever."

A sense of relief came over Gabe. His mother believed in him. Hadn't Zoe said close to the same thing? So why couldn't he believe in himself?

"By the way, I'm planning to come for the birth," his mother added. "Help out. Is that okay?"

"I'll have to check with Zoe." He wasn't prepared to go into all the details about his and Zoe's relationship with his mother at that moment. He would have to sometime soon but he wasn't up to explaining it right now. Even if his mother came, she'd have to stay in a hotel and see the baby through a window.

How was he going to explain what had happened between him and Zoe? His mother had been so excited when he'd told her he'd found somcone special. When he told her he and Zoe were no longer together, his mother would be so disappointed. "It's great to talk to you, Mom. I'll see you soon."

Zoe wasn't sure her heart would ever completely recover. The pain she'd feared would come with the loss of Gabe was nowhere near as strong as that she was carrying now. Her days had become a foggy existence. Every night was a struggle without Gabe next to her and every morning an act of survival to meet the day. She had become reliant on him so quickly and now he wasn't there.

Going home daily to Gabe's house compounded the pain but she had no choice. She couldn't move her mother, and the only way Zoe could afford a new place was to move her mother. So she was stuck living at Gabe's. It seemed wrong that she was and he wasn't. Her life had become so twisted. At least she'd just have to endure for a few more months. The only bright spot in the mess her life had become was that Will would arrive soon. That she could get excited about.

Had Gabe changed his mind about his involvement with

Will? Had he broken it off not only with her but their child as well? He'd been so adamant about being involved, but with the change in their relationship, had he decided staying away was better? That decision was his. Gabe would have to approach her about it, not the other way around.

Because of Will, she and Gabe would always be connected. She would have to figure out some way to control her emotions when they had to meet. Even though she was certain a little bit of her would die each time they did, knowing the happiness she'd once shared with Gabe was gone.

At her obstetrician visit, the doctor was concerned about her weight loss. She promised to take better care of herself. Only with great effort did she make herself eat and do what was necessary for the baby's health.

She'd not heard or seen Gabe since he'd left. The day he'd come to pick up his clothes, she'd noticed his car in the drive and had driven around the neighborhood until it had gone. Now she'd do almost anything for a glimpse of him. Even when she visited Mr. Luther she'd not seen Gabe.

It didn't take Mr. Luther long to zoom in on her unhappiness. As she would have guessed, he commented on it.

"What's wrong with you?" he asked as she wrapped the blood-pressure cuff around his arm.

"Nothing."

"Yeah, there is. You've got that pitiful look. Usually you come in here with a smile on your face. I bet your face would break if you smiled right now."

"I think we should concentrate on how you're doing." She pumped the bulb attached to the cuff.

For once Zoe wished Mr. Luther would go back to being the sad, self-centered man she'd known before the transplant. At least he wouldn't be focused on her.

"You know, the doc doesn't look much happier when he comes in."

He didn't? Why did the idea make Zoe's heart beat a little fast? Maybe Gabe was as miserable as she was. Zoe continued to do vitals. "I'm sorry to hear that."

"You two have a fight or something?"

"Mr. Luther, I appreciate your concern, but Dr. Marks and I are fine."

He grunted. "Don't look fine to me. That baby deserves happy parents."

That statement Zoe couldn't argue with.

On the way home that afternoon, she stopped by to visit her mother. Now that Gabe wasn't at the house, Zoe had made a habit of going each afternoon. Going home to Gabe's house wasn't comforting for her. It was just a place to lay her head, no longer the place of dreams it had once been.

With the exception of the one escape episode, her mother seemed to have stabilized and was thriving since moving to Shorecliffs. She seemed more aware, and despite most of what she talked about being in the past, it at least made sense. With her confusion remaining at bay for the time being, Zoe's guilt had eased. Her mother was as happy as she could be.

Today her mom was well dressed and sitting in a cushioned chair in the lobby. There were a number of other residents there as well. Zoe took an empty chair beside her. "Hey, Mom, how're you today?"

Her mother smiled.

The tightness in Zoe's shoulders eased. Her mother was having a good day. There was a sparkle in her eyes, not the dull look of reality slipping away. "I'm fine. How're you?"

Zoe ran her hand over her extended middle. "Me too."

"Baby?" her mother asked.

"Yes, I'm having a baby." Zoe had to remind her almost every visit. Anything that had happened recently her mother couldn't remember, but she could recall almost anything in detail from her childhood. "He's growing."

"Your daddy and I had a big fight about you."

Was she making that up? Zoe had never heard this story. To her knowledge, they had never fought.

"He was mad when I told him I was going to have a baby. He didn't want a family." Her mother's face took on a faraway look.

"Mom, I've never heard you say anything like that before."

"That's not something you tell a child. A baby should be wanted. Loved."

A deep sadness filled her. "He didn't want me?"

"After you came he loved you dearly, but he never adjusted to family life. He was always looking for a way out."

Was she expecting Gabe to embrace an ideal he wanted nothing to do with? Was she asking the impossible from him? Was that why he had left? They had been happy together for two weeks without more commitment. Could she settle for that if it meant having Gabe in her life? Her child having a full-time father?

Was there some way she could convince Gabe she would take him any way she could get him? Make him feel like what he could give was plenty.

Gabe searched the patient's open abdomen. Something was wrong. He could feel it.

"Suction." He looked again. Nothing. The surgery was going by the textbook. So why the nagging feeling?

The phone on the OR wall rang. One of the nurses answered. "Dr. Marks." The nurse held out the receiver. "Do you know a Zoe Avery?"

"Yes. Why?" Was the baby coming? It was too early. It was at least another six weeks away.

"This is the ER calling."

Gabe's heart went into his throat.

The nurse continued, sounding perplexed. "They said they found your card in her purse. She'd had a bad car accident."

Zoe hurt! The baby?

Gabe looked at Dr. Webber standing on the other side of the surgery table. He was more than qualified to handle the rest of the operation. Gabe had to get out of there. See about Zoe. He spoke to the fellow. "You've got this. I gotta go." Gabe didn't wait for a response before he hurried out the doors, leaving them swinging. Zoe needed him and he would be there for her and Will this time.

He flipped his surgical headlamp up on his head and didn't bother to remove his gown as he raced toward the staff stairs that would get him the two flights down faster than the elevator. Less than a minute later he burst through the ER doors, one of them hitting the wall.

"Whoa," one of the techs said as he put his hand out to stop Gabe. "Can I help you, Doctor?"

Gabe pushed the man's arm away. "Where's Zoe Avery?"

"Let me check the board." The tech turned to the large whiteboard on the wall. "Trauma Six."

Gabe looked around wildly. "Where's that?"

"This way. You must be new here. Were you called in to consult?"

"No. She's my…uh…" What did he call Zoe? His friend, girlfriend, lover, the mother of his baby? Thankfully he didn't have to explain more before they reached the room. Gabe rushed inside.

His heart sank and his belly roiled. The stretcher was surrounded by people working on Zoe. Two different monitors beeped, one giving Zoe's heart rate and the other the baby's. Oxygen hissed as the doctor gave orders.

With his gut churning with fear at what he might see, Gabe stepped closer. "Zoe." Her name was barely a whisper over his lips.

The doctors and nurses were so busy they didn't even respond to him. Gabe looked over one of their shoulders. Zoe's eyes were closed and she wore an oxygen mask. Around it and beneath he could see her pale, bruised skin. Her right arm lay to her side with an air cast on it. The real focus was on Zoe's leg. There was a large gash on her thigh.

"We need to get her to surgery, stat. She's lost a lot of blood. Do we have a next of kin?"

"I'm it," Gabe said. "She's my girlfriend."

The ER doctor turned and looked up and down at Gabe. "Aren't you Dr. Marks?"

"I am."

"Okay. Let's get her up to the OR," the doctor ordered. To Gabe he said, "You take care of the paperwork and the surgeon will be out to speak to you in the waiting room."

"I'll see him in Recovery," Gabe shot back. He watched helplessly as Zoe was pushed away. The first chance he had to tell her how he felt about her he was going to. If she would have him, he'd promise to do whatever he could to make her happy.

Zoe worked at opening her eyes. Why were they so heavy? Someone held her hand. She shifted. That hurt.

"Don't move, honey."

That voice. She knew that voice. *Gabe.*

Dreaming, that was what she was doing. Her eyes fluttered closed.

Zoe woke again and blinked as the lights were so bright. Where was she?

"Honey, stay still."

There was Gabe again. He sounded worried. Why? "Gabe?"

"Right here." His hand squeezed hers as his face came into view.

"You're here." *He was here.*

"I am, and I'm never leaving you again." He kissed her forehead.

All the pain of the last few weeks washed away. Gabe was next to her. Touching her. Calling her honey. What had happened? Why did he look so scared?

A nurse moved around her bed, checking the IV lines and doing vitals. "Ms. Avery, we're getting ready to move you to your room."

When the nurse left, Zoe searched Gabe's face. "What happened?"

"You were in a car accident."

The haze started to clear. She'd been driving home and had been hit from behind. The next thing she'd known, she was being slammed into the car in front of her. Tears filled her eyes. Zoe reached for her middle with her un-injured hand. "Will?"

"Shh, honey. Our baby is just fine." Gabe's hand came to rest over hers.

Zoe drifted off again.

When she woke next, it was dark outside and she was in a hospital room. She looked around. Her eyes focused on Gabe, who was sitting in a chair facing her. His hand held hers as if it was a lifeline. "Gabe."

He straightened quickly. "Right here. Is something wrong? How are you feeling?"

"I ache all over."

Gabe stood, but didn't let go of her hand. "I'm not surprised. You're lucky it wasn't worse. I saw pictures of the accident." His voice hitched with emotion. "I could have lost you both."

She squeezed his fingers. "We're right here. My leg hurts."

Gabe's doctor persona returned. "You have a broken arm and had a deep laceration on your thigh. Both were taken care of in surgery."

Zoe looked at her arm, which was in a cast. Tears threatened to spill over. "I won't be able to take care of Will when he comes."

"With any luck, it'll be off before then. Either way, I'll be there to help."

"You will?" She watched him closely. Did he really mean it? But he'd never lied to her, only to himself.

"I can't wait any longer to say this. I'm sorry for how I treated you. You were right. I was just afraid. Still am. I know nothing more about being a husband or a father than I did before, but what I do know is that I can't live without you. I promise to put you and our family above anything else in my life. If you'll just have me. I love you, Zoe."

Gabe's plea squeezed her heart. "Of course I will have you. I love you."

His lips found hers. The kiss was tender but held a promise of many to come.

They were interrupted by a nurse entering the room. While she was seeing about Zoe, Gabe stepped out into the hallway. As soon as the nurse was finished, Gabe re-entered the room.

"Why're you wearing a surgical gown?" Zoe asked.

Gabe gave her a sheepish grin. "When they called me about you, I was in surgery. I left in the middle of the procedure and didn't stop to change."

He had? "You shouldn't have done that."

"Yes, I should. I'll always be there whenever you need me somehow or some way. I won't leave you again."

"Gabe, your work is important. It saves lives. I understand that." Zoe could only imagine the drama he'd caused.

"I left the patient in good hands. He's doing fine. I just checked in."

"I love you," Zoe mumbled.

"I love you more," she heard as she slipped off into sleep once more.

She had no idea how much time had passed when she woke again, but Gabe was still there beside her. He was leaning back in the chair with his eyes closed. His long legs were stretched out in front of him and his ankles crossed. Zoe couldn't take her eyes off him. He was such an amazing man with such a large capacity to love. And he'd chosen her. She was blessed.

"You're staring at me." Gabe opened his eyes and smiled at her. "How're you feeling?"

"Pain meds are a good thing."

"Yes, they can be." He stood.

Zoe didn't miss his professional habit of checking all the monitors and lines before his attention returned to her. "Gabe, you know you don't have to stay here with me. You need to go home and get some rest."

"My home is right here. You are it."

Her heart melted. If he hadn't already owned her heart, he would have after that statement.

"What made you change your mind about us?" She had to know. Believe that it wasn't just because of the accident.

"Honey, I've been miserable without you. Nothing has been right. It was even starting to be noticed at work. No hospital needs a lovesick surgeon heading a transplant program. And I spoke to my mother. When I was a kid I overheard her say something about me not having a role model for fatherhood. She didn't even remember saying it. That seed grew in my mind to the point I believed it."

"You have so many qualities that'll make you a great father."

"I think with you at my side I can be." He kissed her.

"Zoe, I know this isn't the best time to ask this but I need to know—will you marry me?"

Gabe was everything she'd ever wanted in a husband but she didn't need marriage to prove they loved each other. "You don't want to get married. I understand that. Accept it."

"Yes, I do. I want people to know you belong to me. I want my son and any more children we have to carry my name. I love you."

"My mother had a lucid moment and we had a conversation about Daddy. It seems he never wanted a family, felt strangled by one. I don't want you to ever feel that way. If not being married is what works for you, then I'll be satisfied just to be in your life."

Gabe leaned over until his face was near hers. "I love you and *want* to marry you. Now, will you please answer my question? I'll beg if I have to."

With effort and some discomfort, Zoe circled his neck with her good arm. "Yes, I will marry you. I love you." Her lips found his.

EPILOGUE

GABE LEFT HIS mother in his kitchen, fussing with dinner, and went to find Zoe. He stopped in the nursery doorway and looked at the picture Zoe and their baby made as they slowly rocked in the sunshine. A glow that could only be love radiated from Zoe as she looked down at the perfect baby boy in her arms. His family.

She must have heard him because she looked up with an angelic smile and met his gaze. The love he'd just seen for Will was now transferred to Gabe. It didn't waver. What he'd done to earn it, he had no idea. The thing he did know was he would spend the rest of his life honoring it.

"Hey, honey." Zoe's smile grew, just as it always did at his endearment.

"Come in and join us. Your son would like to say hi."

Gabe walked to them and gently kissed Zoe on the forehead. "You did well, Mrs. Marks."

"Thank you, Dr. Marks. I think we both did well." Gabe carefully took Will from her, cradling him against his chest. Zoe's cast had only been removed a few days earlier.

Gabe looked at the peachy chubby face and he worried his heart might burst from the amount of love filling it. "Hello, William Gabriel Marks."

Zoe rose to stand beside him.

He looked at her, at the tears filling her eyes. His lips found hers. "I love you."

"And I love you."

"Just think, in my stupidity I almost missed out on this."

She leaned her head against his shoulder. "But you didn't and that's what matters."

* * * * *

THE SURGEON'S
ONE-NIGHT BABY

CHARLOTTE HAWKES

To Monty & Bart.
You make me laugh louder and love deeper.
xxx

CHAPTER ONE

WITH MOUNTING HORROR, Archie stared out of the open aeroplane doors and three thousand five hundred feet down to the ground below her. As the penultimate static line jumper prepared to take his step out of the back of the plane, terror pinned her to the hard deck of the aircraft.

'You're up next, Archie.' Her instructor's words were more seen than heard as he yelled over the roar of the engines and the rushing wind.

'I can't. I can't do it,' she muttered desperately, but the sound was whipped away, unheard. Thankfully.

Throughout her entire life, those had been the only words her beloved air force father had ever flatly refused to hear... *I can't.* She glanced down at her colourful 'Make Cancer Jump' skydiving suit and felt a hot prickle in her eyes.

Guilt and regret; they had made terrible companions these last five years.

Whatever had happened to the bold, fun-loving, spirited Archana Coates of old? Even of six years ago? Back then she and her father would have jumped out of that door without a second thought. Now here she was, glued to the deck, unable to even inch her way forward.

She didn't dare look over her shoulder. She was the last of her group of static line jumpers but there was still half a planeload of tandem skydivers all ready to ascend to their required altitude of ten thousand feet. They were just waiting for her to go.

He was waiting for her to go.

Kaspar Athari.

She'd tried to ignore him from the moment she'd spotted him that morning across the vast chasm of the training hangar. Just as she'd ignored the way something had kicked in her chest, and if she hadn't already known it had died the same day her father had—almost five years ago to the day—she might have been fooled into believing it was her heart.

Kaspar. The boy who had burst into her family's life when she'd been six and he'd been almost eight, and had turned things upside down in the best way possible. For the seven years he hadn't just been her brother Robbie's best friend. He'd also been like a second brother to her, spending every school holiday from their boarding schools— thanks to Kaspar's money and her own father's career in the air force—with her family.

Or at least...mostly like a second brother. Even now, even here, she could feel the hot flush creep into her cheeks at the memory of childish crush she'd had on him that last year. She'd been thirteen and it had been the first year she'd been acutely aware that Kaspar wasn't a brother *at all*.

The same year his narcissist Hollywood royalty mother had finally tired of her latest husband and dragged herself and her son back to the States in the hope of kick-starting both their careers. But, though having once been one of the most heartbreaker child actors in Hollywood, thanks to a combination of his stunning blonde British mother and his striking, dark-haired Persian father, somewhere along the line Kaspar had turned his back on the industry.

Now he was a top surgeon who risked his life in former war zones and on the battlefield. Saving civilians and soldiers alike. Winning awards and medals at every turn, none of which he appeared to care a jot about. With the press hanging on his every choice.

'The Surgeon Prince of Persia', the press had dubbed him, as much for his bone-melting good looks as for his surgical skill.

And even though she'd devoured every last article, had known he split his time between the US and the UK, had seen the Christmas card and US Army antique he'd sent her avid collector father every year without fail, she'd never seen Kaspar again in person. Until now.

Not that he'd even recognised her after all these years.

'Archie. Are you ready?'

Snapping her gaze back up to her instructor, who was still smiling encouragingly, she shook her head, half-incredulous that, even now, even here, Kaspar Athari had managed to consume her thoughts so easily. Especially when she hadn't thought of him very much at all over the intervening years.

Yeah, a voice inside her scoffed. *Right.*

But right now wasn't the time to go there. This skydive wasn't about him. It wasn't about anyone. Just herself. Just the fact that she'd spent the last five years, ever since her beloved father's death, ricocheting from one disaster to another, and today that all stopped. It was time. She just needed to make that leap. Literally.

Edging forward she somehow, miraculously, managed to summon the strength to push herself off her seat onto the metal floor, closer to the open hatch, and peer nervously down again.

The wind ripped at her, as though it could pull in even more different directions.

'I ca...' She began to mutter the refusal again but this time something stopped her from completing it.

It was time to regain her dignity. The life she'd somehow put on hold for the past five years since her father's death. In fact, almost five years to the day since her fearlessness had seeped out of her like a punctured rubber dinghy in the middle of a wide, empty ocean.

'I can do this,' she told herself fiercely. Out loud. Safe in the knowledge that no one could hear her over the roar.

She wanted to make the jump. She *needed* to make it. Five years of mistakes and disappointments had to end today. From her marriage, which had been doomed from the start, to the baby daughter she had lost at eighteen weeks. Even the baby that her ex-husband and his new wife would bring into the world barely a month or so. It was time to stop being a victim. To erase this weak, pathetic shadow of a person that she'd somehow become and rediscover the fierce, happy woman she'd once been.

Sitting on the cold, metal floor, paralysed with fear, wasn't part of the plan. And she hated herself for it. She reached out her arms and tried to shuffle across the floor on her bottom, but despite her best efforts her body refused to comply.

'I *have* to do this,' she choked out, desperately willing herself to move.

She was letting people down. She was letting herself down. She felt exposed, vulnerable, worthless.

Her head snapped around at the movement in her peripheral vision to see Kaspar edging his way through the plane. As if he knew exactly what was going on. As if the last fifteen years were falling away and they were once again the teenagers they'd been when she'd last seen him. As if he was still every inch the superhero he'd always been to her, even when she'd been nothing more than the annoying kid sister.

She should be more shocked. Shouldn't she?

He couldn't be coming to her aid. He wasn't that boy any more.

So what was hammering in her chest harder than the vibration of the aircraft engines? Had he recognised her after all?

'Everything okay?' he yelled. Concerned but with no trace of recognition.

Archie stared helplessly, attempting to shake off the irrational hurt that needled her. Why *would* he recognise her? It had been fifteen years and she'd liked to think she no longer looked *quite* like the gangly kid she'd been when he'd last seen her. It wasn't even as though her name would mean much to him, even if he could hear it over the roar of the engines. Archie was a name she'd only settled on in her later teens, and she doubted he'd ever even realised her name was Archana. Like her family, he'd only ever called her 'Little Ant', in reference to the ant farm she'd had as a kid, and the way she'd been so proud of her undaunted, determined little pet colony.

He moved closer, his mouth nearer to her ear so that she imagined she could even feel his breath.

'You want to jump?'

'I *have* to jump, but…' she choked out quietly, not sure whether he could read her lips.

He nodded curtly in response, before turning to her instructor.

'She can come with me. I was doing a tandem jump but my guy didn't even make it onto the plane.'

So Kaspar was an instructor here? Of course he was. What did the press call him? *Playboy…surgeon…adrenalin junkie.*

Articles waxed lyrical about his trekking in the Amazon, skiing down avalanche-prone mountains, or diving off hundred-foot-high cliffs into sparkling tropical waters. Being a skydiving instructor on his weekends off would be a cake walk to someone like Kaspar.

'You need to change harness.'

'Sorry?'

She didn't mean to flinch as his hand brushed her shoulder. It was instinctive. Consuming.

Now that her instructor had closed the door for the plane to ascend another six thousand feet or so, it was possible to hear each other without having to shout so loudly over the engines or the wind.

'The tandem's easier than the static line, and I'll run you through the basics, but you'll need to change harness.'

And then Kaspar was addressing her, for the first time in fifteen years. She stared at him intently, as though willing up some spark of recognition, even if it was only to realise she was the kid sister who'd bugged him and Robbie. The one who had tried to get her brother to let her in when Robbie had far rather push her out. The one who had taught her little words in Persian, and chastised Robbie when he'd taught her swear words.

She gazed and, for a moment, she thought he stared back. Holding eye contact that fraction longer than necessary. It was as though the very blood was stilling in her veins, her body hanging for a split second. Everything seemed to tilt, to change colour.

But then he looked away, searching for the right harness, and she realised that moment had only existed in her own head. She could only watch in silence as Kaspar busied himself with the kit, slipping them both into the adult equivalent of a forward-facing baby carrier then sitting, with her perched on his lap, like the other tandem jumpers left in the plane.

It felt surreal. Nothing about this moment remotely resembled the hundreds of naïve fantasies she'd nurtured—for longer than she cared to admit—about how a conversation with him would go if she ever saw him again.

She'd envisaged beautiful clothes, perfect hair and make-up, and her sexiest smile. She'd imagined making

Kaspar gasp at what he'd failed to see, right under his nose, all those years ago. She'd dreamed about making him chase her, just a little, before inevitably giving in to some all-consuming desire. Her innocent, wholly unrequited teenage crush finally blossoming into some movie-perfect moment.

She had *not* imagined being in an aircraft in the most unflattering, unshapely skydiving suit, which bunched around the crotch thanks to her heavy harness, and, to cap it all off, too frightened to even make her jump.

Well, she'd be damned if she was going to bottle this one, too. She had to make this jump. From ten thousand feet. With Kaspar.

She absolutely was *not* thinking about how close they were going to be, strapped together in a harness, her back pressed against his front.

Her blood was absolutely not racing away in her body, leaving her feeling decidedly light-headed and clammy.

She was going to concentrate on the jump and be grateful for the second chance. She had to do this well.

For charity.

For her father.

For herself.

And not because Kaspar was going to be with her for every single spine-tingling nanosecond of it. *Truly.*

Abruptly, everything faded to a blur, from Kaspar sorting out her gear to going through rigorous checks that would ordinarily have been completed on the ground. And then they were ready. Waiting. Her back glued to his chest.

Somehow that inability to face him lent her confidence.

'Why are you doing this?' she asked suddenly, surprising even herself.

Kaspar frowned.

'Sorry?'

Despite the relative quiet of the plane now the hatch

door was closed, one still had to speak loudly and clearly to be heard and her murmur hadn't been nearly loud enough.

'Why are you doing this?' she repeated, grateful that no one else would stand a chance of hearing.

'Why am I doing this?' Kaspar repeated slowly, as if checking he'd heard right.

But she knew that cadence. Realised it meant he was choosing his words carefully. It felt like a tiny victory. She still knew him. Or a part of him anyway.

'Like a lot of people up here today, I'm doing it in memory of someone.'

'Who?' The question was out before she could swallow it back.

She could picture his face tightened, his jaw locked. So familiar even after all these years. The unexpectedness of it knotted in Archie's stomach and stopped her heart for a beat.

'We'll be at altitude soon.' He jerked his head to the door, clearly sidestepping her question, but she couldn't help it. She couldn't explain why but suddenly she needed to know.

'Who?' she insisted.

His jaw spasmed but, presumably because it was meant to be a charity jump and people had been sharing stories all day, he schooled his features into a neutral expression.

'His name was Peter. I knew him…a long time ago.'

He stopped curtly, as though it was more than he had intended to say. But it was more than enough for Archie.

Peter? Her father?

Archie shook her head, her lungs burning with the effort of continuing to breathe. He was doing this in memory of her own father? An odd sense of pride surged through her that even now, five years after his death, her big-hearted father still touched lives. And yet a sickening welling of emotion quickly snuffed out the pride. Kaspar clearly had absolutely no idea who she was. Despite all her earlier reasoning, that feeling of hurt, of rejection, coursed through her with all the power of a tsunami. She couldn't possibly hope to stop it, as illogical as she knew her reaction might be.

She opened her mouth, trying to find a way to tell him who she was. But at that moment the hatch door had re-opened and her words were sucked out and into the ether before Kaspar had heard them. And as she sat there, her body feeling like lead, she was semi-aware of the other skydivers making their jumps even as her eyes blurred to everything around her.

The next thing she knew, Kaspar was hauling her to her feet, carrying out the final procedures, and then they were moving to the door, exiting the plane, dropping for what seemed like for ever but was probably no more than thirty seconds or so.

And without warning every thought, every emotion seemed to fall from Archie's mind, leaving her strangely numb.

At some point, it had to have been quite quickly, Kaspar tapped her shoulder to remind her to spread out her arms and legs in the freefall position as they rushed towards the ground, although it was as though the ground was rushing to them, her back pressed to his solid, reassuring chest. There was no chance for conversation up here, they could shout and yell and the other one would never hear them, and to Archie there was something freeing in that. For all intents and purposes she was alone, even if she could feel Kaspar's rock-like mass securing her. As the adrenalin coursed through her veins, pumping along like nothing could hold it back, it was as though the wind not only blew away the stiffness from her body but the fog that had clouded her mind for so long.

Too long.

Kaspar opened the chute at what Archie knew would have been around five thousand feet, the loud *crack* ripping through her entire being as they were yanked up into a more upright position, as if breaking her open and allowing the first hints of fear and anger and regret to seep out.

And then absolute silence.

Peace.

Her heart, her whole chest swelled with emotion.

They were still descending but, with the parachute above them now slowing their rate of descent, if she didn't look at the ground, it almost felt as though they were floating. Suddenly time seemed to stand still.

Another thrill rippled through her.

She remembered what it had felt like on that first jump with her father. The life she'd intended to have. The strength of character that used to be hers. And for a moment she felt that again. Free of any responsibility for opening the parachute, steering them to the landing zone, or even having to land safely, she felt her body relax for the first time in years. And the more her body let go of some of the tension it had bottled inside for too long, the more her mind also opened up.

Lost in her thoughts, she was almost startled when a thumb appeared in front of her.

'Okay?' he yelled, his mouth by her ear.

Instinctively, she thrust both her hands out in a double thumbs-up, nodding her head as vigorously as she could, and then he was offering her the paddles to try controlling the chute for herself for a moment.

She was about to shake her head when something stopped her. For a split second she could almost hear her father's voice in her head encouraging her to do it. Tentatively, she reached up and took hold, changing direction slowly at first, surprised at just how comfortable and natural it felt. Even six years on, it was as though her muscles had retained the training her father had given her.

'Were you really going to do tandem jumps today?' She twisted her head so he could hear her easier.

Kaspar nodded. 'I was subbing for another instructor friend of mine who's unwell today. Originally, though, I was going to sky surf. Peter would have loved that.'

He stopped again, clearly catching himself.

Archie thought back to the surfboards she'd seen in the hangar on the ground and smiled into the expanse of blue. Of course a simple skydive wouldn't be enough for adrenalin junkie Kaspar, but he was right, her dad would have loved it.

Bolstered, she tried a slightly trickier turn, surprised and delighted at how comfortable and natural it felt, things that her father had taught her coming back quicker than she might have anticipated. Again and again she steered the chute, going further, trying things out, wishing she had the skill to really push her boundaries. All too soon it was time to release the paddles back to Kaspar.

Almost as though he could read her mind, Kaspar steered them into a high-speed turn, a gurgle of laughter that she hadn't heard from herself in years rumbling through her and spilling into the silent sky. She revelled in the sound as Kaspar led them both into a series of high-speed manoeuvres that thrilled her beyond anything she'd hoped for.

They held such echoes of what she'd loved until recently. For a moment it was as though she could almost reach in and touch the spirited, strong girl she'd once been.

It was transitory. Archie knew that. Soon Kaspar would have to stop and once they landed this moment, this connection to her old self, would be lost.

But this jump had done the one thing she'd desperately wanted it to do. It had finally reminded her of the girl she'd once been and—however deeply buried that part of her may be—today had helped her to begin her journey back to the old Archie.

The biggest shock of all was that it wouldn't have happened but for Kaspar Athari.

He might have no idea who she was, and once this jump was done he'd be out of her life again. Maybe for another fifteen years. Probably for good. But she was grateful to him nonetheless. Part of her longed to reveal her identity to him, but part of her was afraid of ruining the moment.

She was still gazing at the scenery spread out beneath them like the most vivid green screen image, trying to decide, when a small explosion by a truck in a layby below them snagged her attention. They were still a little too high up to see much detail but a dark shape lay on the ground. Archie opened her mouth to speak but Kaspar was already steering the parachute around for a better look.

'Is that a person?' she asked tentatively after a few moments. 'Or bins? Or bags?'

'I can't be sure. Possibly a person.'

His grim tone only confirmed her fears. If it was a body, they would likely have been caught in the blast.

'They have ambulance crews on the ground at the fete,' she shouted.

'That's true but the fete's some way away, they won't have seen the blast we saw. And I know that stretch of road, it's on the route from the hospital and Rick's Food Truck is parked in that layby six days a week, popular with both weekday truckers and with weekend walkers, all looking for a hot bacon and egg bap. For me, Rick's sausage and tomato toasties are more than welcome after a long night shift.'

'So what's the plan?' she asked, knowing neither she nor Kaspar would have mobile phones on the jump.

The decisive note in her tone was something she hadn't heard in all too long.

'There's about a mile over the fields, as the crow flies, between the truck and the fete. If we land as close as we can to the layby we can check it out. If it *is* a person, I'll stay on scene while you run back and alert the medical crews at the fete. Understood?'

'Understood,' she confirmed, caught off guard by an unexpected flashback to a time when Robbie had come off his bike, trying to do some somersault trick, and had been lying deathly still on the ground.

She'd been beside herself, but Kaspar had taken control then much as he was now. Assessing, verifying, trying to assimilate as much pertinent information as he could. Kaspar had taught her a lot, even as a kid.

Just like her father had.

Right now, she suddenly realised, she felt more like her old self than she had for years. Who would have thought she would owe Kaspar Athari part of the credit for that?

CHAPTER TWO

KASPAR VAULTED OVER the hedge and through the field. A part of him was glad to be getting away from the girl—*Archie*, her instructor had called her—with her expression-laden eyes that seemed to see altogether too much. It made no sense and yet even through her obvious fear up there in the plane, every time she had fixed that clear gaze on him he'd been unable to shake the impression that she could see past the façade he'd carefully crafted for a drooling press over the years, and read his very soul.

If he'd actually had a soul. But that had been long shattered. As much by his own terrible mistakes as anything else. Not least the one night that had altered the course of his life for ever.

And yet he couldn't seem to shake the notion that this one girl—woman—almost *knew* him. As though she was almost familiar.

He told himself it was just the emotion of the day. Five years since he'd heard Peter had passed away, the closest thing he'd ever had to a real, decent father figure. Who, even as a widower trying to hold down his air force career, had been more of a father *and* a mother to his son and daughter than either of Kaspar's own very much alive parents could or would ever have been.

Peter Coates had taught him that the volatile, physically

terrifying marriage of his own parents wasn't normal or right. He'd taught Kaspar to handle his emotions so that he didn't lose control the way his own father had. The way his own mother had, for that matter.

Hearing about Peter's death had winded him. Along with the rumour that Robbie had subsequently sold the old farmhouse and emigrated to Australia. Kaspar could understand why. With both parents dead, Robbie, only twenty-five, and with that kid sister of his to look after, it made sense to have a completely fresh start. And yet somehow, knowing the Coates family no longer lived in that cosy, old, sandstone place with its roaring open fires, it had felt like the end of an era.

'Rick? Mate, can you hear me?' Kaspar shook the memories off and called out with deliberate cheerfulness as he approached the figure lying on the ground, one eye half-closed and bloodied.

The extent of the blast damage made it almost impossible to recognise the man as Rick, but the man's build and clothing fitted. There was one way to tell for certain, though. Carefully, Kaspar ripped the man's shirt sleeve.

A clipper ship stared boldly back.

Rick. But he wasn't conscious. Pinching the man's side, Kaspar began a quick examination, surprised when Archie came running up not far behind him. Her intake of breath was the only acknowledgement that the dark shadow was indeed a person.

'Is it your friend Rick?'

'Yes. Get a medical crew,' he instructed.

'He might have a mobile,' she suggested hopefully, but Kaspar shook his head.

'He doesn't. Claims to hate them. So you'll just have to hoof it. Can you do that?'

'Yes.'

'Good. Tell them to alert the air ambulance and say

we've got an unresponsive adult male, around fifty, with severe maxillofacial blast injury, including tissue loss of the right eye and nose and unstable maxilla. GCS three and his airway is going to need to be secured immediately.'

She recited it back clearly and competently despite the slight quake in her voice then left. Kaspar turned back to Rick. By the looks of it, the man was mercifully beginning to regain some degree of consciousness.

'Rick? It's Kaspar. Can you hear me?'

At least the older guy was making vague groaning noises now, even if he didn't appear to recognise Kaspar at all. He certainly couldn't seem to speak, although that was hardly a surprise. Keeping up light, breezy conversation, Kaspar concentrated on the injuries and the potential damage to the man's airway. If that collapsed, things would spiral downwards pretty damned fast.

Occupied, it felt like it was only minutes later when the helicopter landed and the on-board trauma doctor came racing over.

'Kaspar Athari.' The doctor nodded in deference. 'Your partner said it was you. I'm Tom. What have we got?'

'Adult male, around fifty years old. Name is Rick.'

'Rick the food truck guy? You're sure?'

'Sure enough.' Briefly, Kaspar tapped a bold, unusual tattoo on the man's upper arm. 'Approximately fifteen minutes ago he was changing a gas bottle on his food truck when it exploded, no witnesses except myself and my skydiving partner but we were too far away to see clearly. He appears to have been projected by the force and hit his face and neck on something, I would guess the vehicle bracket. There's tissue loss of the right eye and of the nose, unstable maxilla and suspected crushed larynx. Initially unresponsive, he's now producing sounds in response to verbal stimuli. GCS was three, now four.'

'And he's breathing?'

'For now,' Kaspar said quietly. 'But with the soft tissue swelling and oedema there's still a risk of delayed airway compromise, while haemorrhage from vessels in the open wounds or severe nasal bleeding from complex blood supply could contribute to airway obstruction.'

'Okay, so the mask is out, given the damage to his face, supraglottic devices are out because of his jaw, and intubation is out because if the blast caused trauma to the larynx and trachea, any further swelling could potentially displace the epiglottis, the vocal cords and the arytenoid cartilage.'

The trauma doctor ran through the list quickly, efficiently. He was pretty good—something Kaspar always liked to see.

'One more thing,' Kaspar noted. 'There's a possible cervical injury.'

'One p.m. So we've got a high risk of a full stomach after lunch, which means increased risk of regurgitation and aspiration of gastric contents. I could insert a nasogastric tube or I could apply cricoid pressure, but either of those procedures could worsen his larynx and airway injuries.'

At least the guy was thinking.

'Yes,' Kaspar agreed slowly, not wanting to step on anyone's toes. Ultimately, this was the trauma doctor's scene. He himself might be a surgeon, but today he was a skydiver on his day off. 'Still, I'm not confident that his airway will hold without intervention.'

'Can't intubate, can't ventilate,' Tom mused. 'Which leaves a surgical airway option. Tracheotomy or cricothyroidotomy.'

'I'd say so,' Kaspar concurred, thrusting his hands in his pockets to keep from taking over. The doctor was actually good, but Kaspar knew he'd be faster, sharper. It was, after all, his field of expertise.

It was the one thing that gave him value in this world.

Every patient. Every procedure. They mattered. As though a part of him imagined that each successful outcome could somehow make up for his unthinking actions that one night with a couple of drunken idiots. As though it could somehow redress the balance. A hundred good deeds, a *thousand* of them, to make up for that one stupid, costly error of judgement.

But it never would.

Because it hadn't been merely a mistake. It had been a loss of control. The kind that was all too reminiscent of his volatile father.

The kind that Peter Coates had tried to teach him never to lose.

The memories burned brightly—too brightly—in his head. It must be why he was feeling so disorientated. He'd thought the jump would help, but jumping with that woman had somehow heightened it all.

A familiar anger wound its way inside him. Even now, all these years later. All his awards, his battlefield medals, the way the media lauded him meant nothing.

In many respects he was glad that Archie woman was gone. She was, for some inexplicable reason, far too unsettling. The way she'd looked at him on that plane. As though seeing past the playboy front and believing he would do the right thing and help her.

He couldn't explain it, but she didn't look at him the way almost everyone else in his life looked at him. She didn't look at him as though calculating what being with him would do for her career, or reputation, or fame. In fact, she'd looked at him with eyes so heavy with meaning he hadn't been able to stop himself from wondering what it was she'd seen. Why she made him feel more exposed than anyone had in long, long time.

It made no sense. And Kaspar hated things not making sense.

Just as he hated the part of him that had wondered whether, when this was over and the patient was safely on board the air ambulance, he might head back to the fete or the hangar and perhaps buy her a coffee. Or a celebratory drink that night.

For the first time in a long time the idea of a *date* actually made him feel...alive.

'Want to do the honours?'

Tom's voice broke into his thoughts.

'You're the on-duty trauma doctor.' Kaspar hesitated, fighting the compulsion to jump straight in, needing to be sure. Not to protect himself but to protect the hospital. He owed them that much. 'And you're good.'

'I am.' There was nothing boastful about the way the doctor said it. Simply factual. Exactly as Kaspar might have said it. 'But you're the oral and maxillofacial specialist, it's right up your street and this is a particularly complex patient. I can't afford to make a wrong move. If anyone is going to be able to stabilise him enough to survive the flight, it's going to be you.'

'Fine,' Kaspar acknowledged. It was all he needed to hear.

He bent his head to concentrate on the job he loved best, and pushed all other thoughts from his mind. He wouldn't think any more about Archie. He wouldn't be taking her for a drink that night. And he certainly wouldn't be attending the charity wrap party.

The party was in full swing and, predictably, people were crowding around him, from awed wannabe colleagues to seductive wannabe girlfriends.

But there was only one person from whom Kasper couldn't seem to drag his gaze.

It was ludicrous. So uncharacteristic. Yet it felt inexorable.

He hadn't been able to eject her from his thoughts since the skydive, however hard he'd tried. And he wasn't a man accustomed to failure—as a surgeon he had one of the highest success rates—which made it all the more incredible that banishing one woman from his thoughts was defeating him. If anything, with each day that passed she'd become more of a delicious enigma until he'd found himself powerless to resist coming here tonight.

Just on the off chance that he might see her again.

When was the last time a woman had done that to him?

Had *any* woman? Ever?

He tipped his head in consideration, finally allowing himself to give in to impulse.

Archie was stunning. Not necessarily in looks, although she was certainly very pretty, from her sexy pair of *look-at-me* heels to legs that seemed to go on for ever before they finally slipped beneath a short, Latin-inspired, tasselled dance dress number, showing off perhaps the shapeliest pair of legs he ever recalled seeing. He couldn't seem to help himself, but he practically imagined her wrapping them around his body as he sank into her, so deep that she wouldn't know where he ended and she began.

His body tightened just thinking about it.

Him. Kaspar Athari.

He had never wanted *any* woman quite like this.

He'd never *wanted* quite like this.

He'd had enough women throwing themselves at him on practically a weekly basis that he'd never had to lust after any woman quite so...*helplessly.* Not the most stunning supermodels, or the most worshipped Hollywood starlets. But he was lusting after this perfectly pretty, perfectly cheeky, perfectly ordinary woman. Who, it turned out, was to him most extraordinary.

A little like the woman who had been too frightened to do the static line jump but who, when steering the tandem jump chute with him, had displayed a skill and eagerness that had belied his initial conclusion that she was a novice.

Against all logic, Kaspar found himself fascinated.

There was a story there. *But what?* And why did he even care?

Sexual attraction was one thing. But this was something else. Something...*more*. Certainly more than the physical. She possessed a magnetism in the aura she gave off and the way people gravitated towards her. Especially—and Kaspar gritted his teeth at the thought—the other men on the dance floor. Was he the only one to notice how she danced and twirled, shaking and shimmying quite mesmerisingly, and yet all the while deftly kept her friend between herself and any would-be suitors?

As if the intensity of his stare had finally reached her, she lifted her head, met his gaze and froze. Even from this distance, in this light, he could see the sweetest bloom staining her cheeks and down the elegant line of her neck, her chest rising and falling rapidly in a way that had nothing to do with the fact she'd been dancing. Or perhaps it was just the vividness of his imagination. Remembering the way she'd flushed in the plane the other day.

Either way, he was certain she was consumed by the same greedy fire as he was. The fire that had brought him here tonight, against every shred of logic.

And then she moved, heading off the floor and away from him. His stomach lurched in a way that was all too alien to him and before Kaspar knew what he was doing, he had set his untouched drink down on the bar behind him and was shifting his feet, ready to move. Not prepared to lose her.

Abruptly, her friend caught her and pulled her back. He kept waiting for them to glance in his direction, maybe share a giggle, which he'd seen from women time and again. A part of him almost welcomed it. It might help to topple her from whatever invisible pedestal on which he'd set her, help remind him that she was a woman like any other.

But it didn't happen. If anything, Archie studiously avoided meeting his gaze again, and had clearly omitted to mention him to her friend, and her dignified discretion only seemed to add to her allure. Especially when she resumed dancing, only to be a little more self-conscious, a fraction stiffer than she had been before. It was the tell he needed, knowing now she was indeed equally attracted to him.

It should concern him more that it felt like such a victory.

Alarm bells were sounding but too faint, too distant to have the impact he suspected they should have had. To jolt him back to reality. To warn him that she didn't look like the kind of woman who did one-night stands. She looked like the kind of woman who did walks along beaches, and romantic meals, and talking until dawn. Relationships. *Love.* It was such bull.

He'd seen first-hand the toxic depths to which such emotions could plunge. His parents' explosive marriage had been equalled only by their acrimonious divorce. And him, in the middle of it all his life. Their pawn. The tool they'd used to goad and taunt each other. The burden they'd each tried to make the other one bear.

And not just his parents. What about his own explosiveness? That out-of-control side of him that had only had to emerge once to completely ruin someone's life. He'd sworn it would never happen again, and it hadn't. Some might call him emotionally detached, or unavailable. He wasn't. Where his patients were concerned he felt as much empathy as he could, for patient and family, without it impairing his ability to do his job. It was only in his personal life where he exerted such emotional...*discipline.*

So he did sex. He did fun. He did mutual gratification. He didn't do intimacy and he didn't do complications.

Something told him that this Archie woman was both, and the best thing he could do, for both of them, would be to stay away.

Turning back to the bar, Kaspar picked up his drink and tried not to be irritated by the group of preening, simpering women who had begun to cluster around his part of the bar. It was about as easy as pretending he wasn't searching out blonde hair and a metallic shimmer in the reflection of the mirror behind the glasses.

Apparently, his skydiving butterfly was now edging her way off the opposite side of the dance floor. About as far away from him as she could get.

He didn't give himself time for second-guessing. For the second time that evening, he set his untouched drink down and gave in to temptation.

CHAPTER THREE

'ARCHIE, WAIT. SLOW DOWN. Where are you going this time?'

'Relax,' Archie cast over her shoulder, a bright smile plastered to her lips at her friend's typically bossy tone. 'I'm just going for a drink.'

Still, she didn't slow down in her quest to get off the dance floor and around to the other side of an enormous pillar that would shield her from Kaspar's view. No easy feat in the ridiculously high heels Katie had insisted on lending her to go with the seriously sexy metallic number her friend had also talked her into buying this afternoon.

It was years since she'd been out so called *clubbing it*—not that she'd ever had the time or inclination to go out all that often, neither was this charity wrap party exactly *clubbing it*—but, still, she hoped she hadn't looked too awkward and robotic out there on the dance floor. She'd felt fine…right up until she'd seen him watching her.

The minute she'd spotted him, her body hadn't quite felt her own. As though it wasn't completely under her control. Even now the memory of his eyes scanning over her left her blood feeling as though it was effervescing through her veins, making her entire body hum.

It was an unfamiliar, but not altogether unpleasant sensation.

Ducking behind the pillar, Archie pressed her back

against the cool, smooth concrete and rested her hand underneath her breastbone. She could feel the tattoo her heart was drumming out, leaving her unable to even catch her breath. And it had nothing to do with the dancing. Oh, she'd tried to ignore him, especially when his usual harem had draped themselves around him and he'd barely had the decency to offer any of them the time of day.

But who could ignore Kaspar Athari?

'So, if you're getting a drink why are we the other side of the room from the bar?' Katie bobbed under her nose, her brow knitted.

'Hmm? Oh. I just…needed to catch my breath.'

It wasn't exactly a lie, but she might have known her old friend would see through it.

'Archie, you're about as jittery as a beachgoer trying to get across hot sand.'

'No, I'm not.'

Katie's eyes narrowed sharply.

'Is this about "the Surgeon Prince of Persia"?'

'I don't know what you're talking about,' she managed loftily, only for Katie to snort in derision.

'Yeah, sure you don't. He's been devouring you with his eyes all night and you've been lapping it up.'

'I have not,' Archie spluttered, her knotted stomach twisting and flipping. 'And it hasn't been all night. It has been half an hour at most.'

'Aha!' Katie declared triumphantly. 'So it is about the perennially sexy Kaspar Athari.'

'No…not at all…well, not really. That is… Why are you frowning? Aren't you the one who said I needed to get back out there and have fun, like we used to in uni? Like I did before my dad…died? Before I married Joe?'

She tailed off awkwardly as Katie pulled a face.

'I've said it before and I'll say it again, I always hated the way you changed when you married Joe. You went right into yourself. Nothing like the fun, sassy Archie I'd come to know.'

'It wasn't Joe who did that.' Archie wrinkled her nose. She'd tried a hundred times to explain it to Katie, but her friend had never quite understood. Still, she couldn't help feeling she owed it to Joe to try again. 'He was exactly what I needed at that time in my life.'

'I disagree.'

'I know you do. You remind me often enough.'

Still, there was no rancour in Archie's tone. In many respects it was buoying that her friend cared enough to do so. And Katie's wry smile of response revealed that she knew it, too.

'I just feel that, while he may not have intended to, Joe took advantage of the fact that you were young and naïve. You were grieving for your dad, and your brother and his new wife were half a world away.'

They were falling into a conversation they'd had a hundred times before, but it was impossible to stop.

'He didn't take advantage. It was mutually beneficial.'

Katie's eyebrows were practically lost in her hairline, but at least she had the tact not to bring up any painful reminders of more than three years of failed pregnancy attempts. The miscarriage at eighteen weeks.

Agony seared through her. Black, almost debilitating. *Faith*.

As though it didn't lacerate her from the inside out just *thinking* her unborn daughter's name.

She swayed dangerously.

Had it not been for the silent, supportive hand at her elbow, Archie was afraid she was about to tumble to the floor. She blinked at Katie gratefully. Unspoken, unequivocal support shone back at Archie. Bolstering her. Making her want to forget the fact that, barely a year after she'd lost her unborn daughter, Joe was expecting a baby with his new wife.

It hurt.

Though not, perhaps, in precisely the way Archie might have thought it would. She couldn't pinpoint it, but neither could she help suspecting that it had less to do with Joe than it ought to, and more to do with the simple pain that another woman seemed to find it so easy to have a baby while her own traitorous body hadn't been able to do the one thing she felt it had surely been designed to do.

'Fine, let's say it was mutually beneficial...' Katie conceded at length, though Archie could hear by her friend's tone that she didn't remotely believe that.

'You look like you've swallowed a bee.'

She couldn't help a chuckle, even it did sound half laugh, half choked-back sob. Katie valiantly attempted to ignore her.

'Mutually beneficial,' she repeated firmly. 'And you're right. Now is your time to get back the Archie I used to know. The one I admired so much that I used to wish I was more like you. The Archie who threw herself out of a plane today, for her father, for Faith, for a new start.'

'You make it sound so easy.' Archie smiled softly, the sadness she tried so hard to shake but couldn't still tiptoeing around inside her.

But she wanted to. And the jump today was the first time she'd felt she might actually be ready to do so.

Because of the jump? Or because of Kaspar?

Archie slammed away the unbidden thought in an instant but it was too late. It couldn't be *un*-thought. Instinctively, her eyes were drawn back to where Kaspar had been standing, staring at the pillar as though they could bore a path straight through it to see him.

It was pathetic.

But it was also the biggest vaguely positive reaction

she'd had to anything or anyone in a very long time. And that felt strangely compelling.

Kaspar Athari, back in her life after all these years. He'd been her first, only crush. Except back then he hadn't even noticed her and so she hadn't had the guts to do anything about it. Suddenly, here he was again and this time he had certainly noticed her. It was as though she was being offered a second chance. It couldn't be just a coincidence, surely? It had to be *fate*. Either way, it was making her want to…*do* something. Anything.

She turned to Katie with as firm a nod as she could manage.

'Fake it till you make it, right?'

'Absolutely.'

It was easier said than done, but what the heck.

'Fine.' Archie sucked in a deep, steadying breath. 'Then if I'm going to…what did you say earlier this evening? Get back on the horse? Then why not go all out with the infamous "Surgeon Prince of Persia"?'

Why did it feel easier to call him by his ridiculous nickname? Was it because it felt too close to home to call him Kaspar?

'Yes.' Katie didn't look remotely abashed. 'I did say that. But not with him. He'd gobble you up and spit you out. The man is pure danger.'

Seriously, how difficult could it be to dredge up a casual grin while simultaneously trying to stop her stomach from executing a perfect nose-dive?

'Maybe that's what I need?' she tried hopefully. 'A bit of danger.'

'Absolutely not.' Katie shook her head so vigorously her shiny halo of curls bobbed perfectly around her pretty face. 'No chance. There's absolutely no way I'm letting a guy like that get anywhere near you. Over my dead body. You can count on me for that.'

Archie frowned, confused.

'I've heard you drool over the Surgeon Prince a hundred times. Are you really saying you wouldn't go there after all?'

'Of course I would,' Katie scoffed loudly. 'Trust me, I'd be in there like a shot if the guy so much as squinted in my direction.'

'So he's okay for you, but not okay for me?'

Archie didn't know whether to feel insulted or honoured.

'He's not okay for you *right now*. If you were the old, fearsome Archie from back in uni, then I'd say go for it. *That* Archie could have handled a man like Athari.'

This was it. She could either go along with what her friend was saying, proving Katie right. Or she could show a little spirit. Like she had on that skydive. Not that she'd told Katie, who'd been occupied with her own charity water-polo match, about the tandem jump.

Archie blew out sharply.

'You know, I think I can handle one little prince.'

Katie opened her mouth, eyed her and closed her mouth again. A crooked smile that Archie knew so well hovered on her friend's lips.

'I do believe you mean it.'

'I do.'

Katie paused, considering.

'Then far be it from me to stop you. Okay, you know that sexy, dangerous scar across his jawline?' Archie nodded silently. 'Apparently it was the result of some big fight when he was younger.' Katie hugged her arm tightly and whispered in conspiratorial tones. 'You remember those massive Hollywood kung-fu, karate-style blockbusters he did as a seven-and eight-year-old?'

The Hollywood life he'd been only too desperate to

run away from, Archie remembered. Not that she could say anything.

'Yes, I think so,' she hedged instead.

'Of course you have to know them. They were _huge_, until his mother apparently demanded too much money or riders or whatever and he got kicked out and replaced.'

The rumours didn't come close to the damage his volatile mother had caused. But she couldn't say that either.

'So you heard he got the scar on those films?' Archie tactfully changed subject.

Katie's eyes sparkled with excitement.

'No, the rumour I actually read somewhere was that the fight was down some back alley when he was about seventeen or something, and wasted after a drinking session. Apparently he was outnumbered five to one but he still beat their collective backsides. Juicy, isn't it?'

'Juicy,' Archie agreed half-heartedly.

The idea of the quiet, controlled Kaspar of back then drinking, let alone fighting, was a complete anathema to her. No doubt a lie the press had spun to help them with their paper-shifting image of the playboy Kaspar. Not that he hadn't played his own stupid part to a T.

But the man in the media bore little resemblance to the boy she'd once known. And it was the latter who had stolen her adolescent heart.

Besides, she'd been there when he'd really got that scar, climbing the forty-foot oak tree outside Shady Sadie's house when he'd been fifteen. Or at least she'd been in the living room with her father when Robbie had raced back to say that a damaged limb had given way and Kaspar had fallen to the ground. He'd been carted off to the hospital with a few superficial cuts and bruises and that one deep gash. He'd worn it with all the pride of a battle scar, of course. Trust the media to come up with something far more dark and exotic to explain it.

But they couldn't have made up *everything*, could they? The playboy lifestyle? The dangerous reputation? It had been fifteen years since she'd last seen him so of course he wasn't going to be the same boy she'd known. As Katie gabbled on, Archie let her head drop back, the cool concrete of the pillar seeping into her brain, and tried to think a little more clearly. Maybe opening the Kaspar Athari can of worms really wasn't the best idea she'd ever had.

As Katie's hands grabbed her shoulders and hauled her off the pillar, Archie was tugged back to the present.

'This is your chance, here comes your Surgeon Prince.'

Before she could stop it, she was being swung around and thrust out around the column. The breath whooshed from her body. She didn't need to turn to know that Katie would have already gone.

'And there I was thinking you were hiding from me, Archie.'

The rich, slow drawl was laced with a kind of lazy amusement as every inch of Archie's skin prickled and got goosebumps. Not least the fact that he knew who she was after all. Her stomach spiralled like a helter-skelter in reverse.

Archie. He rolled her name on his tongue as though sampling it, tasting it. She imagined he was measuring it against the woman she was now, compared to the 'Little Ant' he'd always known her as.

She opened her mouth to speak just as Kaspar stepped closer to her. Everything in her head shut down as her body shifted into overdrive. Heady, and electrifying, and like nothing she'd ever known before.

He was dressed smart-casual, a vaguely lemony, leathery scent toying with her nostrils, and he practically *oozed* masculinity. Enough to eclipse every other male in the room most probably. Even every other male in the county. The world.

Even her childhood crush on him didn't compare. It made her feel physically winded and adrenalin-pumped all at once.

The indolent crook of his mouth, so sinful and enticing, gave the distinct impression that he could read her thoughts. Feed into her darkest desires. It made her very blood seem to slow in her veins. A sluggish trickle, which her thundering heart seemed to be working harder and harder to process.

He was simply intoxicating. She cast around for something, anything, that wouldn't betray how at sea she felt.

'How is the patient? Rick, wasn't it?'

Not exactly ideal, but it would have to do. Kaspar only hesitated for a moment.

'He's in pretty bad shape.'

'But you can help him?'

'Possibly.'

He didn't want to talk shop, she could understand that, but it was buying her some much-needed time. She had to settle down. Katie was right, she was like a beachgoer on hot sand.

'I think I read last year that you had a patient who'd had a firework go off in his face and you used some kind of layering technique?'

'You're in the medical profession?' Kaspar's stare intensified.

Archie swallowed. Hard.

'No, actually I'm in the construction industry. I build the hospitals, you work in them.'

'You build them?'

'Well, I work out layout, ease of movement so it isn't a rabbit warren; service routes such as for heating, lighting and medical gases especially for the operating rooms; whether to connect to the existing back-up generators, or build new ones; medical incinerators, that sort of thing.'

There was a lot more to it, and given how much she loved her job she could probably go on about it all night. Which would be a problem. It was hardly the most seductive of conversations.

'Are you part of the team building the new women's and children's wing for our hospital?'

Pride outweighed her need to change the subject.

'Yes.'

'I'm impressed. It's looking really good and I believe you're pretty much on time and on budget.'

She was powerless to prevent a grin so wide it might well crack her face in two.

'Thanks. It isn't going too badly. There are a few niggles but I built decent float into the programme so it shouldn't be too much of an issue. Once we've finished on the new wing we'll start on the new hospice facility across the site. We should be done within ten months, hopefully.'

'Even more impressive.'

'Dad always loved what I did,' she added suddenly.

Waiting, *hoping*, for Kaspar to add something he also remembered about her father. Then fighting the sense of discouragement when he barely even reacted.

'I can imagine.'

'Anyway,' she caught herself, 'we were talking about your firework patient.'

She didn't know why it felt so important that he should answer her. Perhaps because her dad had once told her and Robbie that getting Kaspar to open up about the things he loved was the key to knowing the boy. He kept everything that mattered to him so closely guarded, as though he feared the pleasure could be snatched from him at any time. The way his mother had often cruelly snatched away anything he'd shown an interest in as a kid, from toys, to hobbies, to his only decent stepfather.

According to her dad, Kaspar had never been a kid in

the strictest sense of the word. His parents' volatile relationship had caused him to grow up quickly, to distance himself from people, to distrust easily. But her own father had brought him round, treating him exactly as he'd treated Robbie, encouraging when he could, laying down the ground rules at other times. And she'd treated him like a brother while Robbie, of course, had just been Robbie, sweet, funny and easygoing.

Did Kaspar remember all that? If he did, did he care? Enough to answer her?

He hesitated and, for a moment, she thought he was going to sidestep it.

'The boy's jaw was shattered. He'd lost a chunk of it along with the teeth on the right side. He couldn't eat, couldn't even speak, so I needed to build a new jaw and simultaneously implant teeth. We layered pieces of titanium and then used a laser to harden the material. The lattice structure allowed us to really bend and form it so that it was the right size and shape for the kid, fitting perfectly and looking natural.'

Archie didn't realise she'd been holding her breath until he stopped speaking. He was looking directly at her, his eyes were dark, intense, like a moment of understanding. Of connection.

She didn't know whether it was a good or a bad thing that at that moment the music cranked up a notch and whatever else he was saying was lost, swallowed up by the thumping bass line.

'Say that again?' she shouted, but he shook his head.

The moment of opening up to her about his career was clearly over. She leaned in to speak into his ear, swaying slightly on her friend's heels, her body lurching against his as he put his arm around her to steady her. Her lips grazed his skin and she smelled the tantalising citrus scent.

It hit her again, that wall of primal need, stealing her

breath away as his touch seared every inch of her flesh. It was almost a relief when the music kicked down again and he released her.

'You want to get out of here?' she asked instead.

'Together?'

'Is that a problem?'

The words were out before she had even thought about them. Seductive, teasing, another flash of the old, adult Archie. Yet the way she could never have dreamed of being as a thirteen-year-old with a crush. It was exhilarating.

'Not for me,' he growled. 'But, then, I'm sure you've heard the endless scandals that seem synonymous with my name. This isn't a high-profile charity event, but it isn't a small gathering either. If any press spot us, your photo will be on the internet before we even get to my hotel.'

'Is that your attempt to warn me?' She deliberately rolled her eyes. 'Only I make it a point never to believe idle gossip. I don't think they know the old Kaspar.'

'The *old* Kaspar?' His brow furrowed and as two light indentations peeked out from between his eyebrows a wave of familiarity unexpectedly coursed through Archie, making her clench her fingers into a fist just to keep from reaching out and lightly skimming them even as her stomach executed another downward dive.

So he *didn't* know who she was. No wonder he hadn't reacted to her mention of her father. Sick disappointment welled in her, but instead of backing away, as she might have done, a flash of the daredevil Archie Katie had been talking about suddenly flared within her.

Maybe, just maybe she could jog his cobwebbed memory. She would rather he piece it together himself than simply hit him over the head with it. She didn't want to risk anything that might make him back away from her.

'You know, the pre-"Surgeon Prince of Persia" reputation,' she prompted. 'The kid who climbed trees, and built dens, and fought with his best friend.'

Another beat. Imperceptible to perhaps anyone else. She felt rather than saw the shift.

'There is no pre-"Surgeon Prince of Persia".' He winked.

It should have irritated her, being altogether too seductive, suggestive and downright overconfident. It didn't. She'd seen the façade sliding back into place as though he regretted his moment of perceived weakness. That *tell* she recognised from long ago. More polished now, but there nonetheless. Kaspar the playboy might be standing in front of her, but she'd seen the Kaspar she'd known, the one she'd wanted, was still in there. She could still unearth him. For a moment back there she had succeeded.

A thrill coursed its way through her, lending her the confidence she'd been lacking.

'I don't know whether to admire your confidence or deplore your arrogance.' She cocked her head to one side as if genuinely giving it serious consideration. 'I rather fear it's the latter.'

'Oh, I seriously doubt that.'

His wolfish smile did little to soothe her jangling nerves. It was as though he was enjoying the banter. Relishing the challenge. Maybe if she dropped the right prompts, he would finally realise who she was. Finally remember.

'Are you really the blasé Lothario the press paint you as? Bedding a different woman every other night?' she challenged.

'Well, if it's in the press, then it must be true.'

Which wasn't really, she couldn't help but notice, an answer at all. It begged the question of why, if he was more like the Kaspar she remembered than the Kaspar the media seemed to describe, he would ever have allowed this unfavourable reputation of his to slide?

'So you haven't slept with any of the hundreds of women you've been linked with over the years?'

'I didn't say that either.' His teeth almost gleamed and Archie shivered as she felt their sharp edges as surely as if he had them against her skin.

Grazing her. Nipping her. An intimacy she'd read in books or experienced in her fantasies. Never in real life. Certainly not with Joe. She held his gaze, steady and sure, until eventually—incredibly—he broke his gaze.

Archie wasn't sure who was more surprised, her or Kaspar himself.

'I confess that I'm always impressed how I have the time to date quite so many women. Although I won't deny that when I get chance I do enjoy the company of the fairer sex.'

Something kicked hard, low in her stomach.

'Of course you do.'

'I am, after all, a man.' He took a step closer to her and she found herself backing up to the pillar, her entire body fizzing with anticipation. 'Or are you going to pretend that you haven't noticed?'

'And if I said I hadn't?'

'I'd say that, public perceptions and exaggerations aside, I know women well enough to read that such an assertion would be a lie.'

'Is that so?' She barely recognised the husky voice coming out of her mouth. And Kaspar only cranked that sinful smile up all the higher.

'That's so. You noticed me. What's more, you want me. Almost as much as I want you.'

'There's that hubris again.'

'Perhaps it is hubris.' He took another step closer, not looking remotely remorseful. 'But it doesn't make it any less true. Shall we put it to the test?'

Suddenly, she was caged. The pillar at her back and Kaspar on the other three sides. Huge, and powerful, and heady. He wasn't actually touching her, and yet she felt the weight of him pressing in on her. Holding her immobile.

Not that she felt remotely like trying to escape.

'You really are altogether too sure of yourself.' She had no idea how she managed to sound so breezy.

Especially considering the frenzy into which her body currently seemed hell-bent on working itself. Lust and longing stabbed through her.

'Imagine how disappointing it would be if you fell short.'

He actually looked affronted just for a split second, before his eyes crinkled and a warm laugh escaped his lips. It was as though all the air in the room—in the world—went into that laugh. As though she didn't need it to breathe and could exist on that laugh alone. As though there was nothing else but Kaspar.

'I can assure you, Archie, I do not...*fall short*. In any respect.'

Her name on his lips again. If only she had the guts to reach up and kiss him, to discover whether his mouth tasted just as good as she imagined. She tried to but her body wouldn't move, probably due to this overriding need for him to recognise her properly. So in the end she simply stared back into eyes, which were all too familiar. In colour if not in expression.

'Well, of course, you would think that.'

'It isn't a matter of what I think.' His dark, indolent tone spiralled through her. Every inch of her body felt it wrapping around her. Pulling tighter. Drawing her closer. 'It's a matter of what I know.'

It was all she could do to offer a nonchalant eye-roll.

'Let me guess. A hundred women hailing you as a deity in the throes of passion?'

She didn't want to think of those stories the papers loved to run with. The fact that his sexual prowess was lauded quite as much by quite so many. Although, now he'd mentioned it, it didn't add up that he should be quite such a driven, dedicated surgeon and yet have so much time for personal indulgences.

'Bit of an exaggeration. Although, frankly, I wasn't thinking of a single other woman. I was only interested in one. And she's standing right in front of me.'

'Oh, you *are* good,' she conceded, hoping against hope she didn't look half as flushed as she felt.

Hoping he couldn't hear the drumming of her heart or the roaring of blood in her ears. Hoping he couldn't read the lust pouring through her and making her nipples ache they were so tight. Hoping he couldn't feel the heavy heat pooling at the apex of her legs the way no man had ever made her feel before. At least not quite so wantonly.

She had a terrible fear that perhaps no other man would make her feel that ever again.

'Care to confirm that conclusion?' he murmured, his voice pouring over her just the way she would imagine warm, melted chocolate would do.

If she'd ever been that sexually adventurous, of course. Which she never had been. She imagined this version of Kaspar was, though, and the thought made her pulse leap in her wrists, at her throat.

What was the matter with her?

Kaspar didn't miss a thing. His eyes dropped to watch the accelerated beat, his face so close she could almost draw her breath as he exhaled his. His eyes never left hers, their intentions unmistakeable.

What wouldn't she have given for Kaspar to look at her like this when they'd been kids and she'd been besotted with him? And now he was.

Before she could stop herself, she reached out to trace the scar Katie had mentioned earlier.

'Is this really the result of some drunken bar brawl?'

'What else could it be?' His voice rasped over her as though his very fingers were inching down her spine. It was all she could do not to give in to a delicious shiver.

'I don't know, something more banal.' Archie had no idea how she managed to execute such an atypically graceful and nonchalant shrug. 'Like a childhood accident. Falling off a bike? Charging into a table? Tumbling from a tree?'

His eyes sharpened for a moment.

Something hanging there. Teetering between them.

'You have brothers?'

Her breath caught in her chest. A tight ball of air. Was Kaspar finally remembering?

A slew of emotions rushed her. Feelings she'd thought long since dead and buried. Idealistic, romantic, intense fantasies she'd cherished as an adolescent fancying herself in love with the oblivious Kaspar.

He'd ruined her, without ever touching her. Archie was sure of it. His mother had hauled him back to America right at the peak of her crush on him. If that hadn't happened, no doubt the infatuation would have run its course, as it did with most young girls. Instead, for years, she'd imagined she and Kaspar to be some kind of modern-day star-crossed Romeo and Juliet, torn away from each other before Kaspar had even had a chance to open his eyes and see what had been in front of him all along. She'd carried the ridiculous dream with her long after she should have let it die.

It was the reason she'd never had a serious boyfriend, always holding a part of herself back in her relationships. Until Joe, of course. But that had been tainted with other issues.

Now, suddenly, she had the chance to be with Kaspar. Only for one night, perhaps, but why not? They were both adults. She might never have imagined herself having a one-night stand before—she probably wouldn't with anyone else in the world—but Kaspar wasn't just anybody. Forget the wicked playboy everyone else knew. She wanted one night with the first and only boy she'd ever had a crush on. It might not be who Kaspar was any more, but at least it would help her to finally let go of her unrealistic, romantic, adolescent ideals.

Too late, she realised that his last words hadn't been a question as he'd pieced together who she was but more about explaining her accuracy away as if she was any girl with a brother.

'Nice guess. Most boys have fallen out of tree at one time or another,' he muttered. 'Still, it's refreshing to meet someone who would prefer to see the good in someone rather than simply believe all the media scandal.'

'No one can be quite as two-dimensional as the press seem to like to paint your Surgeon Prince alter-ego,' she breathed, willing the shutters to stop rolling down over his eyes.

'You'd think,' he offered flatly. 'But they're right about me. The bar brawl, the women, the flashy lifestyle. All things a girl like you would be best staying away from.'

It was impossible not to bristle, even as her entire body lamented the way he was pulling back from her.

'I'm twenty-eight, hardly a mere *girl*.'

'But too nice to get chewed up and spat out by the press, which, I can assure you, would happen if I kissed you the way I want to.'

It purred through her, starting at her toes and gaining speed and strength, until by the time it reached her head the roar was so loud in her ears that Archie was almost shocked the entire party couldn't hear it.

He wanted to kiss her. *Kaspar* wanted *her*.

'Let me get this straight.' She had no idea how her vocal cords even remembered how to speak. 'On one hand the infamous playboy Kaspar Athari is telling me that he lives up to his depraved reputation and on the other he's trying to protect mine by not sleeping with me?'

'Call it a Christmas miracle.'

'You're quite a few months out,' she pointed out shakily. 'What *would* people say if I told them you weren't quite the bad boy they think you are?'

'They wouldn't believe you,' he answered simply.

It felt like a sad fact.

Worse was the fact that he was pulling away from her. Ironic that she'd been right about him being the old, good Kaspar deep down, and that it was exactly *that* Kaspar who was trying to protect her now. Even though he still didn't recognise her.

She couldn't let that happen.

She couldn't allow this one opportunity to slip away from her because she'd let the last few years beat her down. She'd promised Katie she was getting back to her old self. She'd sworn to herself on that skydive that it was the moment she finally stepped away from the mess of the last five years or so.

If she wanted Kaspar, she was going to have to prove it. And she was going to have to tell him who she really was.

Leaning forward before she could second-guess herself, Archie fitted her mouth to Kaspar's. And she kissed him.

CHAPTER FOUR

IT WAS ONE of the most extreme, adrenalin-fuelled rushes of Kaspar's life. Like nothing he'd experienced before. Ever.

And it was only a kiss.

What would it be like to touch every millimetre of her? Taste her? Bury himself inside her? He'd never wanted a woman with such fierce intensity. Fighting the need to possess her with his body in exactly the way he was now possessing her with his mouth. Claiming her and stamping her as his.

He angled his head, the fit becoming tighter, snugger, and when his tongue scraped against hers, she answered it so perfectly that he felt it through every inch of his being. Her body surged against his as though she couldn't get close enough and her arms looped around his neck as though she couldn't trust her legs to stand up on their own.

Kaspar wasn't sure that his own could.

What was it about this woman?

A few minutes ago he'd been priding himself—not to mention surprising himself—on the urge to protect her by staying the hell away from her. Then she'd kissed him and he'd lost the tight sense of self-control he'd honed to perfection over the last fifteen years. Despite what the press said about him.

The urge to press her to the pillar and shut out the rest

of the partygoers was almost overwhelming. But if he did that, he was afraid he would lose himself completely. Here, in a dark corner of a club. He couldn't even think straight. He would never know how he found the strength to pull away.

She looked startled, then embarrassed, but before he could say anything she was already pulling herself together.

'Tell me that wasn't all you've got?' Teasing him again. But he didn't miss the undertone, the hint of uncertainty.

Somehow it only made him want her more.

Ignoring the alarm bells going off in his head, Kaspar forced himself to step away from her. The sense of loss was as shocking as it was nonsensical. He placed his hand at her elbow, telling himself it was only to guide her away from their current position, but he knew that wasn't entirely true. It was an excuse to touch her again.

'You mentioned getting out of here?' he muttered. A statement disguised as a question.

'Yes. *Hell, yes.*' She started forward, then stopped abruptly and placed her hand on his chest, the shake of her fingers betraying how much effort it was taking her. 'Before we do, there's something I need to tell you.'

Kaspar fought the bizarre urge to throw her over his shoulder and carry her out.

'Can it wait?'

Talking was pretty much the last thing on his mind right now.

'I guess.'

He couldn't decipher her expression. Guilt? Or relief?

In that instant, it didn't matter to him. His fingers closed around hers and he couldn't seem to lead her away fast enough. Anticipation made him feel drunk even though he hadn't touched a drop all night—rarely did, despite what the press loved to report—but no alcohol had ever made him feel like this. Like Archie made him feel. He made a brief call to his chauffeur to bring the car around. He just wanted to be alone with her. He *needed* to be, like the hormone-ravaged teen he'd never been.

Ducking down the stairs and past the few photographers milling around was easier than he'd expected, and his car was waiting right outside the door, Still, it was all he could do not to bundle her inside.

'Mine or yours?' he asked, wanting her to feel in control.

'Mine.' She didn't hesitate. 'I don't want to run another gauntlet of photographers.'

She probably wouldn't, but he didn't intend to argue.

'Come here.' His voice was raw, aching.

Obediently, she shuffled across the back seat towards him, having given the driver her address, but he could see her mind still whirring, and knew she was going to try that *talking* stuff again. It was a complication he could do without. Scooping her up, he hauled her into the air before settling her on his lap. His body tautened with approval.

'Much better.'

'Much,' she managed.

And then his mouth was claiming hers again, his hands roaming her body as she straddled him, the way he'd so urgently wanted to do in the club. From the exquisite curve of her calves to toy at the back of her knees, and then up those impossibly long thighs. But instead of going higher, he toyed with the hem of her short dress, then traced a path up her body instead, over the top of the metallic tassels. The material remained a barrier between them, the halter neck almost taunting him as it concealed her breasts from his gaze.

He cupped her chin with one hand, allowing the other to slide into her mass of blonde hair and cradle the back of her head. And for her part Archie met him stroke for stroke, making an exploratory journey of her own over his shoulders, his arms, his torso. She traced every curve and muscle and sinew, and let her head fall back as he scorched a trail of kisses from her mouth, down the elegant line of her neck and to the hollow by her clavicle. Her intoxicating scent filled his nostrils and heightened his senses.

With every sweep of her tongue and graze of her nails, she was driving him wilder and wilder. The fact that her fingers trembled as they undid the buttons of his dress shirt only added to the delicious tension. He yearned to know every inch of her. Intimately and completely. Reaching up, he unhooked the clasp at the back of her neck and allowed the two sides to fall down, exposing the most incredible breasts and hard, pinkish-brown nipples, which seemed to call out to him.

Kaspar couldn't resist. He bent his head and took one perfect bud in his mouth, his tongue swirling around it before he tugged on it. Just the right side of rough.

Her sharp gasp was like a caress against the hottest, hardest part of him. And then she offered the other breast for the same and as he obliged he couldn't stop a groan of desire slipping from his lips. He liked this bold, demanding side of her. He didn't know why, but he got the impression it wasn't a side of her that everyone got to see.

The idea appealed to him far more than it should have.

Lifting his hand, Kaspar lavished attention on one breast as he lowered his mouth to the other. Sucking on the nipple and then drawing back to watch her shiver as the cool air did the rest. He tried it again. And then again as he swapped sides. Until she wriggled on his lap, unmistakeable heat against the most sensitive part of his body. He reacted. Already hard, he was now so solid it was almost painful. Aching to touch her wet heat, to slide inside her.

But not here. Not in the car. With anyone else maybe

he wouldn't have cared, but no one else had ever turned him on with quite the feverish quality that Archie had. He only knew he wanted more with her, and not on the back seat of a car.

'What's wrong?' she asked, sensing his change of attitude immediately.

Moving his hands to her hips, Kaspar shifted her backwards slightly. Enough so that every tiny movement of her hips didn't make his body throb quite so tightly.

It damn near killed him.

'Not here. Not the first time,' he managed hoarsely.

'The first time?' She arched one eyebrow as though that would distract him from the way her body quivered on his lap. Her pent-up tension equal to his. 'You're optimistic.'

'Once isn't going to be enough,' he bit out, the rawness in his own voice catching even himself by surprise. When had *that* become a fact? 'You must know that.'

The distinct hitch of her breath didn't help. But whatever answer she might or might not have been about to give was cut short when the driver pressed the intercom to let them know they'd arrived, moments before the car pulled up.

He could barely believe the ridiculous way he couldn't seem to think straight with this woman. She made him lose his head.

Worse, a part of him *liked* it.

Archie opened the door to her apartment and reached for the lights.

Her skin still sizzled at the mere memory of his touch. It was impossible to shake the presentiment that she would never again be able to quash this shiver that ran so deep inside her. She had absolutely no idea how she managed to keep her voice so calm.

'So here we are.' She licked her lips anxiously. This was the first time she'd ever had a man back to *her* home.

In fact, this was the first home she'd ever had by herself. 'In my apartment.'

Kaspar looked around.

'Nice place. Been here long?'

She shifted her weight from one leg to the other. This was her chance to tell him.

'Ten months. Since my marriage fell apart.' She shrugged, as though it hadn't felt like yet another catastrophic failure on her part, in her litany of mistakes over the last five years.

'You were married?' He made no attempt to hide his shock.

'For almost four years.'

'What happened?'

'I thought I loved him. I thought he loved me.' Another shrug as she desperately tried to keep the evening light. 'In hindsight, we rushed into it. My father had just died and my brother had emigrated. I was looking for something to fill a void, and Joe was it. He was kind and he cared for me. It was a mistake.'

She couldn't tell him about Faith. She wouldn't be able to dismiss that loss as lightly. Besides, he was still processing the bombshell she had just dropped.

But what choice had she had? He'd rebuffed her attempts to talk to him. To tell him.

'Your father had died, and your brother had emigrated?'

He raked his hand through his hair. A nostalgia-inducing young-boy action she hadn't seen in any press photograph of him for years. Perhaps ever.

She swallowed, her tongue feeling too thick for her shrinking mouth. Then she raised a shaking hand to a small cluster of photos on the wall. They could say all the things she couldn't.

He peered at them. Stepped closer. Stared harder.

She imagined she could see his eyes moving from one

to the other. Photos of Robbie, of her father, of herself. And even the one with Kaspar himself.

The growing look of shock on his face twisted in her gut. He honestly hadn't had any idea. The knowledge clawed at her insides. The silence crowded in on them. Sucking every bit of air from the room, making it impossible for her to breathe. It was an eternity before Kaspar spoke, the words hissing out of his mouth like some kind of accusation.

'Little Ant?'

Despite his incredulity there was also a tenderness in the way he said her old nickname that pulled at her in a way she hadn't been prepared for. And he'd addressed her as an individual in her own right, not simply as *Robbie's sister*, which had to mean something, didn't it?

Even so, he was already physically backing away, heading towards the door. And she hated it. Now, more than ever, she wanted that connection with him. The moment they had never had.

Abruptly, desperation lent her an outward strength. Her voice carried an easy quality that she hadn't felt for years, even though her internal organs were working as hard as if they were completing some marathon or other.

'It's Archie now,' she offered redundantly. Awkwardly.

'God! I kissed you.'

Whether he was more disgusted at himself or at the kiss, she couldn't be sure. Either way, it was everything she'd feared.

'We kissed each other,' she corrected, madly trying to slow her thundering pulse. 'Oh, don't tell me you're suddenly getting all funny about it.'

'Of course I am,' he snarled, his eyes glittering. Dark, and hard, and cold...and something else. Something she couldn't identify. 'You used to be the closest thing to a little sister.'

He headed for the door, unable to sound more disgusted if he'd tried.

'Exactly. *Used* to be,' Archie echoed, refusing to cow at his tone, however it might claw at her. 'It has been fifteen years, Kaspar, and you didn't even recognise me. To all intents and purposes I'm no different from many other women at that party.'

'You aren't any other woman at that party. You're Little Ant. You're far more innocent than any of them.' He reached for the door, opened it, and she'd never felt more powerless. 'Certainly for someone like me. I have to get out of here. Now.'

And suddenly everything slowed down for Archie. She could read the anger and anguish at war on his face, and she realised what was going on. It bolstered her. A rush of confidence warmed her.

'You're not angry with me for not telling you so much as being angry at yourself that you still want me.' Her voice held wonder. 'You *really* want me.'

He didn't stop, didn't even falter. He just continued walking right out of the door.

'I'm exactly the kind of guy you should stay away from, Little Ant.'

'I'm not Little Ant, Kaspar. I haven't been that girl for over ten years. I'm a woman now, with a career, and my own home, and a failed marriage.'

He hesitated in the hallway, just as she'd hoped he would, and turned to face her. He was still fighting temptation, she could tell, but he knew his arguments were holding less and less sway. Deliberately she swept her tongue over her lips, as if to wet them.

His eyes slid down and watched the movement with a darkening expression. A thrill coursed through her. He wanted to do what he thought was the morally right thing, he was *trying* to do it. But things had gone too far in the car. They'd been too intimate. And now he was having a difficult time turning the attraction off just like that.

'I thought you were in Australia.'

He was stalling, she realised incredulously. No one would ever believe it. Not the press, not the public, certainly not the broken-hearted women who flailed in his wake.

'Robbie went after Dad died because his then girlfriend, now wife, was from there. My life was here. I'd just finished my degree, I had a new job...'

'You'd met your husband.'

She couldn't place the edge to his tone, but she did know the moment she'd been imagining was slipping away from her. Too fast.

She needed to salvage the evening, convince Kaspar that she wasn't that kid any more. She was the woman he'd been kissing, holding, touching in the car.

'As nice as this little catch-up might be, we didn't come back here to my flat to shoot the breeze, did we, Kaspar?'

She couldn't decide whether he admired her forthrightness, or if it merely caught him off guard. Either way, she didn't care. She had a small window in which to press her advantage. If she missed it, that would be it.

She stepped forward boldly and flashed him a cheeky grin, disarming him.

'Good, so now we've aired our concerns, can we get back to the fun we were having in the car?'

'Archie, are you listening to me?' he bit out, but he didn't move away.

She stepped forward again.

'I'm trying not to. It's hardly the greatest foreplay conversation. Certainly not worthy of the great Surgeon Prince of Persia.'

'This isn't going to happen,' he warned, his voice gritty. Not entirely as forceful as she imagined he could be.

'I'm pretty sure it already has. Or have you forgotten just how intimate we were on the car journey here?'

She heard the low growl, which reverberated around her. She knew the image of his mouth on her nipples, making her moan and writhe on his knee, was as imprinted in his head as it was in hers. He was close to giving in to her. To this attraction. She just needed to give him that nudge over the edge.

'I'm leaving now, Archie.' He reached his hand out to grab the door handle and close the door behind him.

She had one last chance to stop him.

'Are you sure?' she asked evenly, even as she reached up to the back of her neck, undid the clasp and let the dress drop to the floor, past the flimsy scrap of electric-blue lace, to pool around the skyscraper heels, which she suddenly didn't remotely feel silly wearing.

She felt sexy and powerful and wicked.

But Kaspar wasn't moving. And she had absolutely no idea what he was thinking.

He couldn't move.

Frozen to the spot, his eyes riveted to the vision in front of him, for the first time in his life Kaspar felt powerless. He should leave. Turn around and walk away. But he couldn't bear to.

She was sublime. So completely and utterly perfect. The tasselled Latin-dance-style dress might have looked good on her, but they hadn't flattered the sexy, voluptuous curves of her body anywhere near as generously as they should have. They should have worshipped her...the way he ached to do right at this moment.

The pictures were still on the wall, a mere few feet away, but he couldn't reconcile the kid in those photos with the woman standing in front him. This one was a *siren*.

From the long line of her neck, down to glorious breasts,

which he hungered to cup, caress, kiss, down to the indent of her waist and the belly button around which he could imagine swirling patterns with his tongue. His eyes dropped lower, appreciative and unhurried, to take in the soft swell of her belly and the sensational flare of her hips, and then the incredible V of her legs where the scrap of blue lace, barely concealing her modesty, only seemed all the more titillating.

'Tell me you don't want me, Kasper,' she murmured. The faintest hint of a quiver in her voice, a moment of uncertainty, only making her all the more irresistible.

His entire body pulled taut. Unequivocal male approbation. God, how he wanted to be where that lace was. With his fingers, his mouth, his sex. He couldn't recall ever having ached to be with a woman before. Not like this.

'You know I want you,' he rasped, unable to keep the admission from spilling from his lips.

'Then claim me,' she breathed, offering herself to him.

But now it was about more than just sex. Perhaps it always had been. Perhaps a part of him had known he knew her, even if he hadn't recognised her. It certainly explained the connection he felt.

And that in itself posed the greatest threat. Archie knew him in a way no one else did. Not the press, and not his previous lovers. And that made her dangerous. Hadn't she already told him that she knew the playboy image wasn't really him?

She saw too much. She knew him too well. And that enabled her to slip under his skin every time he wasn't paying full attention. He certainly couldn't afford to spend the night with her.

He hadn't turned himself into the press's idea of the Surgeon Prince of Persia because he'd wanted to be a playboy. He'd turned himself into that two-dimensional version of himself because, ultimately, it was all he deserved. Because his bad-boy image was the only thing that stopped them painting him out as some kind of surgeon hero. And he wasn't a hero.

Just ask the family of that kid whose life he'd changed that night in the bar. But the press had never run with that story. They, like the judge, had vindicated him, Kaspar, of all blame. No matter that he had been the one able to walk out of the hospital that night while the other kid hadn't.

It was why he'd deserved his bad-boy reputation all these years. It was why Archie should stay away from him. And it was why he should walk out of her door now.

But, then, who in their right mind could walk away from someone like her?

Not just because she looked quite like...*that*. But because there was something more than just the physical, more than the undeniable sexual attraction that crackled between them. There was a connection. He'd felt it on the plane, although it had taken him until now to recognise it for what it was.

Archie knew him in a way that no one else did.

Despite the media's potted history of his less-than-enviable childhood, pushed and pulled between two parents who had seen him more as a pawn in their sick game than as a flesh-and-blood boy who either of them loved or wanted, it had nevertheless always been somewhat sanitised and glamorised. Entertainment channels ran specials on his actress mother and himself but they had never, ever even come close to how miserable it had actually been.

In many ways he was grateful for that. But Archie wouldn't be fooled by it. Her father had been the one to save him. She had been there through enough of his childhood to know the truth. Not all of it. No one but him knew all of it. But certainly closer to the truth than anyone else ever could. Or would.

And that was the problem.

He allowed people to paint him as the cad, the woman-iser, because that ensured that no one really knew him, un-derstood him, could get close to him. And if they couldn't do that then they couldn't get under his skin. He couldn't bear the idea that anyone could break through his mental armour and make him feel…something…*anything* be-cause then he'd have to feel all those terrible childhood emotions all over again.

It wasn't just that he was a danger to Archie…she was a danger to *him*. To his sanity. And yet he still stood mo-tionless. Powerless to resist her.

'Come and claim me, Kaspar,' she repeated, her voice cracking through the command.

He was sure it was the sexiest sound he'd ever heard.

Logic and sense flooded from his brain, something far more base and primal flooding the rest of his body.

'This can't lead anywhere, Archie. I fly back to the States next week. I don't know when I'll be back.'

'So you'd better make this the best night of your stay, hadn't you?'

So damn sassy. So damn sexy.

He heard the deep growl that seemed to come from the vicinity of his throat, was barely conscious of kicking the door closed behind him with an accurate jab of his foot, and found himself striding across the room towards her.

Towards Archie.

Some madness had taken hold of him, he was sure of it. And then Kaspar wasn't thinking of anything any more. He was dragging her into his arms, moulding her mouth-watering, practically naked body to his, and plundering her too temptingly carnal mouth. And his seductive siren wasn't remotely shy in her sudden state of undress.

Archie wound her arms around his neck, pressing her-self so tightly against him he could almost imagine there wasn't a barrier of clothes between them at all, and lifted her legs to wrap around his body as he willingly cupped her firm, neat backside.

He kissed her mouth, her neck, every trembling inch of her collarbone, and she matched him. Kissing his jaw, tugging at his ear lobe and rocking her body against his sex until he feared he might not be able to hold on much longer.

'Which way?' he managed gruffly, scarcely ripping his mouth from hers.

Her reply wasn't much clearer.

'Behind me.'

Obligingly, Kaspar navigated his way to the door, shouldering it open and carrying Archie into the room, smiling at the queen-size bed with its overabundance of scatter cushions.

He lowered her down, less gently than he might have liked, holding himself still while she reached for the buttons on his shirt, undoing them with painstaking care, kissing her way over his chest and abdomen with each new section of bare flesh she exposed. It felt like an eternity before she finally undid the last button and he could shuck off the shirt, but it seemed Archie wasn't done. She reached for his belt, the crack of leather reverberating around the room as she unbuckled the clasp, followed by the unmistakeable sound of the zip opening.

Kaspar circled her wrist with his fingers and pulled away from her as she protested. He couldn't afford to let this go any further. He'd never felt such a lack of control, as if he might explode like a hormone-ravaged teenager. This was as much about Archie's pleasure as his.

He pressed her lightly back onto the bed and covered her body with his, bracing himself as he looked down at her, drinking her in. Marvelling. Every inch of his skin was on fire as Archie ran her fingertips over him, tracing the muscles on his shoulders and down his body.

Heady, and exhilarating, and addictive.

When he cupped her breast, his thumb grazing deliberately against one straining nipple, she gasped, her back arching slightly. Repeating it offered the same glorious result. Then Kaspar lowered his mouth and tasted her as he had in the car, his tongue tracing out an intricate whorl as Archie slid her fingers in his hair and gave herself over to pleasure. He took his time learning every last contour of her breasts, then her abdomen and her hips. Slowly. Thoroughly. Ignoring the almost painful, needy ache of his sex.

Finally, when her soft moans became more urgent, he laid a trail of hot kisses from her navel straight down over her belly and over the top of the flimsiest blue lace panties, which he pulled off in one swift movement. Then he dropped back down to press his mouth to the hottest, slickest, sweetest part of her, making her cry out.

She tasted of fire, and honey, and *need*. Her hips were moving, dancing with him, as he licked his way into her. Her hands cradled his head, the most beautiful, wanton sounds escaping her mouth almost against her will. It spoke to something utterly primal inside Kaspar. As if he would never get enough.

He kissed, licked, sucked until her hands slid from his hair to clutch the cover of the bed, her hips moving erratically, trying to jerk away.

'Please, Kaspar...' She reached for him, but despite the hunger in her voice he had no intention of taking his pleasure yet. This was about Archie.

'There's no rush,' he murmured. 'We've got all night.'

Then, slipping one hand underneath her to hold her in place, he lowered his mouth back down to her intoxicating heat and slid his finger inside her, deep and sure.

Archie shattered, crying out his name as she arched her back and fragmented all around him like some victory he couldn't identify. He kept it going long after she would have pulled away, making her shudder over and over, murmuring against her and making her come apart again.

And when she finally begged him to release her, he let her go, a satisfaction he couldn't explain seeping through to his very bones. As well as a slow, deep ache.

'That was...' She floundered for the words to describe the incredible way she felt. Like nothing she'd ever experienced before. Not even close. 'I feel... You were...'

'We're not done yet.'

His voice was gravelly, raw, and still it felt to Archie as though she was taking a lifetime to refocus. Her body felt exhausted, contented. She struggled to lift herself up onto her elbows.

'We aren't?'

'Not by a long stretch.'

She wasn't sure if it was an avowal or a warning, but the sight of Kaspar standing up, shedding himself of the rest of his clothes until he was naked before her, stole her breath away all over again. His solid physique and utterly male beauty, waiting there just for her, went beyond even her wildest fantasies. Archie let her eyes drop to take in his length, straight and flat against his lower abdomen, as taut and unyielding as a steel blade. Though she would have thought it impossible a moment before, her body gave a fresh kick of lust.

How could it be, after all that, that she wanted him again so instantly?

'That's a relief,' she tried to tease him, but the quake in her voice betrayed her. 'I was beginning to think that was all you had. After talking yourself up earlier tonight, I was expecting a lot more.'

'Is that so?' He arched one eyebrow and she couldn't contain the gurgle of laughter that rumbled in her chest.

'It was a...concern.'

Then he was moving back over her, nestling himself between her legs as his hands moved under her shoulders and he rested on his forearms above her.

'Then let me put your mind at ease. We have a long, long night ahead of us.'

Whatever witty response she might have come out with was chased from her head as he nudged against her hot, wet core. It was too much, and at the same time not enough. She sucked in a deep breath, her legs parting slightly further as his amused eyes caught hers.

'You were saying?'

She shook her head and bit her lip, unable to speak. And then he thrust into her. Hard and strong and deep, stretching her in a way that felt more delicious than uncomfortable. As though she'd been made for him; they'd been made for each other. She shifted instinctively and he groaned, making her feel sexy and powerful all over again. Archie watched him in fascination, his face pulled tight as though he was trying to control himself, as though *she* made him feel unrestrained.

She couldn't help it, this wanton side of her that seemed to be taking over tonight. Lifting her legs, she wrapped them around his waist, locking her heels at his back, drawing him even deeper into her slick, welcoming heat. He groaned again and it pulled at something low in her, and then his eyes caught hers, smoky and strong, the colour of richest brandy, his intent undisguised. Archie's breath hitched somewhere in her chest. All she could do was dig into his arms, his shoulders, as he began to move. A dance as old as time and a pace equally as steady. Her body was helpless to do anything but match it, stroke after stroke, thrust after thrust, his eyes never leaving hers.

She had no idea how long they moved together. A lifetime. Maybe longer. As though she had never been meant to be anywhere else but here. With Kaspar. Better than any of her dreams if only for the simple fact that this was real.

At some point he swept his hand down her side, her already sensitive body shivering at the feather-light touch, and then he was touching her at the centre of her need and there was nothing *feather-light* about it at all. He knew exactly what he was doing. And how much pressure he needed to exert.

Archie gasped and arched her back, her hips, her neck. She wanted to tell him to slow down, not because she didn't want this but because a tiny part of her couldn't stand the thought that he might leave as soon as this was all over, but her tongue refused to work. At least as far as talking was concerned. Instead, she slid her hands down his back, her nails leaving their own exquisite trail, and he shuddered and growled, plunging into her more deeply. So desperate and demanding and *right*. It threw her straight back over the cliff edge until she was tumbling and tumbling, and she didn't care where she landed so long as it was with Kaspar.

And as she called out his name, surrendering herself completely to him, this time Kaspar followed.

CHAPTER FIVE

'FOURTEEN HOURS OF surgery and it all comes down to this.' Kaspar grinned with satisfaction at his team. A reconstruction and rehabilitation procedure on a patient who had lost almost all of his upper jaw and teeth almost a decade earlier, following oral cancer surgery.

'Yeah, rebuilding a man's jaw and bone palate using advanced osteointegration and three-dimensional computerised design. It's awesome.'

Kaspar glanced at the young surgeon. Rich, arrogant, the son of a renowned surgeon, he came across entitled and lacking in empathy, but he was a solid surgeon, if only Kaspar could find a way to steer him.

'More than the medical kudos, it's going to be life-changing for our patient. He'd become almost hermit-like, unable to venture out without people pointing and staring.'

'I guess. But, still, we're, like, in ground-breaking territory here.'

Normally, today's surgery was exactly the kind of challenge on which Kaspar thrived. Had always thrived.

But despite his triumph, Kaspar was preoccupied. He had been ever since that stolen time with Archie almost five months ago.

Five months in which he hadn't been able to get her out of his head. The way she sounded, smelt, tasted. Night after night his body ached for her, in a way it never had for any other woman. He told himself it was just the sex, that he didn't recall the walks, the laughter, the shared memories with such clarity. He refused to admit to whatever alchemy went on in his hollow, astringent chest. Even so, one night hadn't been enough. He'd had to eke out the weekend, then an extra day. Even that hadn't sated the yearning he had for her.

Yearning.

Him.

Every day had been a battle not to contact her. Even whether or not to send her flowers when he'd seen the date a couple of months earlier and had realised it was her birthday. Every day he'd prayed for challenges like this one to walk into his consultation room, if only to have somewhere else to pin his focus.

But it always came back to Archie. And whether, if he took up the offer to return to the UK next month, he should contact her or not.

'I mean, think of it this way,' the younger man enthused, pulling Kaspar back to the present, 'using implant bone to live and grow around a titanium plate, being able to create the bone and tissue to support an implant of a whole new set of teeth. Traditionally we'd have had to use plates and grafts and cadavers.'

'And our patient,' Kaspar continued firmly. 'Being able to speak and be understood, or to eat food or have a drink without fluid spilling from his sinuses and mouth.'

But the young surgeon was only interested in the surgery, and Kaspar didn't have the inclination to lecture as he might otherwise have done. His head was too full of Archie.

He'd told himself he was too damaged. Too selfish. Too destructive. Especially for someone as bright and vibrant as Archie Coates was. He'd kept an ocean between them with the excuse that he was protecting her. But the truth was that he was concerned about her. The longer they'd spent together, the more he'd noticed that she'd seemed to have lost a little of the special lustre he remembered about her. As though life had somehow scratched at her when it shouldn't have. Her father's death, the idiot husband she'd mentioned, maybe even Robbie emigrating.

Whatever it was, something in him ached to be the one to take her pain away.

Ridiculous.

He was the last person to take *anyone's* pain away. It was better to keep his distance.

She was going to be sick.

Archie let her hand fall from the door for the third time in as many minutes, her legs threatening to collapse beneath her. Around six hours ago she'd still been somewhere across the Atlantic. And twelve hours before that she'd been to have a twenty-week ultrasound to determine that her baby was all right.

Their baby.

Hers and Kasper's.

She'd had months to get used to this but it had made little difference, it still felt utterly surreal to her. So how was it going to feel for Kaspar?

Perhaps she should have thought this through better. Yesterday she'd only been grateful that her work and her life to date meant she had three years remaining on her visa which allowed her multiple visits to the States, for up to six months.

Foolishly, she'd taken it as some kind of sign.

The push she'd needed to go and find Kaspar. To tell him about their baby.

Now Archie stopped, one hand reaching out to lean on the wall, the other hand running tenderly over the slight swelling in her abdomen. It was incredible. A miracle. At least to her. Nothing would ever make up for losing her first baby, Faith, at eighteen weeks gestation, and no baby could ever replace her, but in some ways this new tiny human growing inside her went some way to healing those still-raw wounds.

She hovered outside the door, the small cabin bag and work laptop at her feet, trying to summon the courage to knock. It had to be the last thing he would want to hear. Might even prefer not to know. The Surgeon Prince of Persia a father? The press would have a field day.

Nevertheless, deep down she knew she owed it to this baby, and to herself, to at least tell him. To let him make that decision for herself. Still, it was turning out to be a lot harder than she'd hoped it would be.

The old Archie would probably have blurted it out, however awkwardly or untimely. The Archie of the last few years might have shamefully buried her head for as long as she could.

But which Archie was she now? She was more confused than ever. Swinging wildly from the daredevil Archie of old, right over to the reticent woman of recent years, and then back again.

The skydive, then that night with Kaspar when she'd stripped—*stripped*—to seduce him, emboldened in a way she hadn't been for years. For weeks afterwards she'd strutted around feeling ten feet tall and even her friend, Katie, had been forced to admit Kaspar hadn't been such a bad influence after all.

When she'd discovered she was pregnant, it had been a moment of sheer joy and disbelief that her body had effortlessly achieved the one thing it had been struggling to do throughout her entire marriage to Joe. And then she'd been catapulted right back into the dark, cold prison of her mind.

The fear of losing this baby the way she'd lost Faith

overrode everything else. With it, the uncertainty, the confusion, the regression to the hesitant Archie of the previous five years. And so she'd spent the past few months bouncing between the two polar opposite versions of herself.

It was how she'd had the confidence to fly halfway around the world to confront Kaspar, and yet now she was here she couldn't bring herself to lift her arm and knock on that door. She could make that final move or she could turn around, head straight back to the airport and be on a plane, with him none the wiser. The most shocking part about it was that Archie had absolutely no idea which way she was going to jump.

Who was she? Really?

And then the decision was taken out of her hands. The door suddenly opened and he was striding out. Stopping dead the instant he saw her.

'Archie.'

'Kaspar.'

There was a beat as his eyes seemed to take her in. Scanning her face, then dropping down. Another beat as they hovered around the evident swell of her belly.

Her whole world pinpointed around him, her breath seeming to slow and then stop in her chest. Time had done little to diminish the impact he had on her. Maybe it had even amplified it. She had the oddest sensation of falling. Plummeting.

The question was, *How painful was the landing going to be?*

'You'd better come in,' he managed at last. The unusually hoarse tone to his voice only made her nerves jangle all the more.

Then he picked up her bags and was gone. Walking back into his office with as little surprise, as little emotion as if she'd been his next patient he'd been waiting to see.

Still, it took her several long moments before she was able to follow him.

She was barely through the door before he was speaking.

'You're pregnant.'

His voice seemed palpably colder now. More forbidding. Or perhaps it was just her nerves. Behind her the door closed with a soft *click*. It might as well have been the clang of prison gates but somehow it offered her the strength she needed.

'*Clearly* pregnant,' he added.

Had her hand wandered to the obvious swell of her abdomen before or after his observation? Lifting her head, Archie met his eyes, not allowing her voice to falter for a second. Though how she managed it, she would never know.

'Yes.'

'We used protection,' he stated flatly.

A statement but not a defence. As though he didn't exactly disbelieve her. She was grateful for that much, at least. It allowed her to soften her voice somewhat.

'Not that first time.'

'So he or she really is mine?'

It felt like a slap across her face, although she supposed it was a reasonable enough question. Still, she couldn't seem to prise her jaws apart, answering him through gritted teeth.

'Who else's would it be, Kaspar? The invisible man's? I'm not in the habit of picking up random men or sleeping around. Yes, it's your baby. *Our* baby.'

It was impossible to follow the flurry of emotions that passed across his face. But, then, he had always been the poster-boy for denial. Pretending that he was happy, that his family life was fine, to his friends, his school, the world, when her family had seen first-hand how broken he'd been inside. How he'd spent every school holiday with them, along with his nanny, Maggie, just to avoid being dragged into yet another of his parents' twisted games against each other.

'He or she,' he bit out flatly.

'Sorry?'

'Say *he* or say *she*. Don't call the baby an *it*.'

She frowned, confused.

'I don't know whether it's a boy or a girl. I didn't find out. I didn't want to.'

'I don't care,' he growled, the unexpectedly menacing quality to his tone making her skin prickle. 'This baby is not an *it*. Pick *he* or *she*, interchange them, or I'll call her a *she* while you call him a *he*, for all I care. Just don't ever use the term *it* again.'

Fury swirled in his words, but it was the look of torment behind his eyes that really clutched at her, squeezing at her heart. A torment that made her wonder about the childhood she'd pieced together from things she remembered, things her father had said, things she'd read.

'Okay.' She dipped her head. 'I'll say *he*, you can say *she*.'

He didn't reply, but his lips curled in what she took to be a silent thank you.

'So you're...'

'Twenty weeks,' she cut in, barely able to help herself. Although he wouldn't have any idea how significant that was to her.

'You should have told me,' Kaspar bit out, and she had to protect herself against the kick of emotion. The irrational fear that by talking about it she was somehow jinxing things.

'Would you really have wanted to know?'

'That has nothing to do with it,' he almost snarled. 'You've had five months to tell me.'

He hadn't denied it. And even though she'd known the answer before she'd even asked the question, it still hurt.

But she couldn't let him see that. It took everything she had to keep her voice even.

'I'm telling you now.'

'That isn't good enough.'

'It will have to be.' She jutted her chin out, trying not to let him intimidate her.

He narrowed his eyes as if he could see straight through her. As if he knew there was something she was hiding.

'Why not?' he demanded abruptly.

Archie flinched.

'It's...irrelevant.'

'I don't believe that for a moment,' Kaspar barked, folding his arms across his chest.

She tried not to notice how it made his already wide shoulders seem all the bigger, his strong chest all the more unyielding. And she tried not to notice the long fingers that had done such...*things* to her. Over and over that night. That weekend.

When they'd made a baby.

What was she playing at? They were kids and this wasn't a game. She owed him an explanation.

'I didn't tell you because I was scared. I was pregnant once before.' She heard her voice crack but she pushed on, pretending it hadn't. A part of her had known this subject would come up. That it was inevitable. She was ready for it. 'Eighteen months ago. But I lost that baby at eighteen weeks.'

She stopped abruptly, pain ripping through her. Lacerating her from the inside out. Dizzying and unforgiving.

'I'm sorry,' he said simply.

'Her name was Faith.'

She didn't even realise she'd spoken until she heard the words. The agony that had haunted her ever since with *what ifs* and *if onlys*. The self-recriminations. She'd thought she'd been mentally prepared. She'd been dealing with the pain every single day, and each day it had felt just that tiny, minuscule bit easier. But hearing the words aloud, for the first time since it had happened...nothing could have prepared her for that.

She only realised he'd caught her from crumpling on the spot as she found herself in a seat she didn't recall moving to, and Kaspar coming back into the room, a steaming plastic cup in hand.

'Sweet tea.' He thrust it at her. 'Drink it. All of it.'

She didn't dare disobey.

Bit by bit, she sipped at the cup until it was empty. And Kaspar just sat opposite her. Waiting. Wordlessly. While the minutes ticked by. As if he had nowhere else to be but right here. With her.

Tears pricked her eyes and she blinked them back. She shouldn't read anything into that. It didn't mean anything. She couldn't afford to think it did.

'I...needed to get past that point...the eighteen weeks. And then I thought that when I had my twenty-week scan, if it...' What had they agreed, that she would call the baby *he*, and Kaspar would say *she*? 'If *he* was okay, I would tell you. So...here I am.'

She trailed off. Not quite sure how to articulate the storm that roiled around her entire body, constantly up-ending everything.

His eyes never moved from her. Clear and unblinking.

'So the scan was fine?'

'Yes. But these things are always fine until...until they're suddenly not.'

It was all she could do to keep her voice even and sound calm. There was no point in letting the dark fear that lurked deep inside her take a hold. No point in imagining scenarios that might never happen. The doctors didn't think there was anything they needed to worry about or do, so she had to trust them. They were the medical professionals. Not her.

'What are you doing?' She frowned as Kaspar stalked around his desk, snatched up the phone and stabbed a couple of numbers on the pad.

He didn't answer her, too intent on the call.

'Dr Jarvis, please, it's Dr Athari.' There was a brief pause. 'Catherine? It's Kaspar. I have a patient I need you to examine. It's urgent. Archana Coates, twenty-nine-year-old, approximately twenty weeks pregnant.'

Too shocked to speak, Archie listened as he described her in completely dispassionate terms. Like a third person. *Like a patient.*

'She has a past history of spontaneous second-trimester abortion.' Archie flinched. It was the same terminology the doctors had used around her and she'd never hated a medical term so much in her life. It sounded so wrong, as if she'd had any choice in the matter whatsoever. Kaspar continued, oblivious. 'No, not a referral. It's personal.'

Within moments he had replaced the handset.

'What…what are you doing?'

'Catherine Jarvis is one of the best perinatologists in the world.' He paused as Archie stared at him in confusion, then clarified. 'Maternal-foetal specialist. She has a patient with her now but she'll see you in half an hour.'

'I don't… *No!*' Archie shook her head at the implications of what he was saying, the suggestion that the pregnancy wasn't as low-risk as she'd believed hitting her altogether too hard. 'I've had a scan. I've been checked. They know my history. If something was wrong, if it was going to happen again, they would have known.'

'Shh,' he soothed. 'I'm not saying they're wrong. I'm just… I want to be sure.'

But the expression in his eyes didn't exactly fit.

'Is the loss of the baby...of Faith why your marriage fell apart?'

She knew he was distracting her, but the very fact that he'd remembered her daughter's name cut through everything else. It was more than Joe had done. He hadn't even cared enough to want to name her.

'Yes,' she managed quietly. 'And no.'

'Meaning?' There was a slight curl to his lip, as though he couldn't help but sneer. As though he knew what kind a man Joe had been.

But he didn't know anything at all.

'He got the job opportunity of a lifetime in Switzerland. I didn't want to go with him.'

'Why not? He was your husband.'

'My life was in the UK, plus I'd just lost my baby, and I didn't love him,' she began hesitantly.

'You married a man you didn't love?' His censure made her bristle.

'I thought I loved him. I told him I loved him. But, with hindsight, I don't know if I ever did or if I was more grateful to him. He was there after Dad died. I was falling apart and Joe looked after me. He was kind to me. He took care of me. He loved me. I thought I loved him, too.'

'Enough to marry him?' Kaspar didn't even try to keep the scorn from his voice.

'He was twelve years older than me. He was like a rock. Stable, emotionally secure, knew what he wanted, including a family. That all appealed to me. Now I know I was just trying to fill the void left by Dad's death and Robbie going to Australia.'

'It sounds like this bloke took advantage of you.'

'No.' She shook her head. 'At least, not like you're thinking.'

'He knew you were grieving and vulnerable and he seduced you into marriage by pretending to love you,' Kaspar accused.

'No, it wasn't like that.'

Archie shifted on her seat, splaying her hands out as though that could somehow help her articulate the words that were in her head but which she couldn't seem to get out.

'I think it was. You were lost and grieving while he should have known better. I think when you finally see it for what it is, you'll stop making excuses for him.'

'I think the sooner you get your head out of your backside the sooner you'll stop trying to tell me exactly what I do or don't feel,' Archie snapped suddenly, taking both herself and Kaspar by surprise. A welcome flash of the vibrant, no-nonsense side of herself.

Still, she didn't expect Kaspar to drop his head back and let out a laugh.

'What's so funny?' she demanded coldly.

'You are. Welcome back, Little Ant.'

A small smile played on her lips, despite herself. He was right, and it felt good to see the re-emergence of her old feisty self.

Every time she was around him, it seemed.

Hastily, she bit her tongue before she could utter *that* particular nonsense aloud.

'I'm sorry for judging. For criticising.'

Kaspar's tone was surprisingly tender. Even…nostalgic? It elicited another smile from her, albeit this time a wry one.

'You and Robbie may have called me Little Ant, but Dad used to call me his Little Tardigrade.'

The throaty laugh rippled through her, doing things to her it had no business doing. Rushing straight through her body and to her very core, where she was, shamefully, in danger of melting all over again.

'I think I remember that. You always were little but hardy.'

'Yet also, sometimes, more fragile than people thought,' she heard herself replying, too late to clamp down on her words, to swallow them back.

She'd never admitted that to anyone but her father before. Why on earth would she say it now? And to Kaspar, of all people.

'I never realised.' His face sharpened. Hard, angular lines that signified his disapproval. 'I always thought you were such a tough little thing. So strong.'

Archie took in his almost contemptuous expression. It left her feeling as though she'd let him down, let herself down, and she told herself that her heart wasn't being squeezed, right there, in her splintering chest. She gritted her teeth.

'Kaspar, I didn't come here to talk about my ex-husband or my historical mistakes. I just felt I owed it to you to tell you I was expecting a baby, *your* baby, and I didn't think it was something that I should do over the telephone.'

'And then what? You expected me to fall on one knee and propose? To play happy families?'

Actually, she hadn't thought past this awful meeting. But now he looked so dark, so forbidding, so cold, it was like being plunged into an icy, glacial milk flow. She got the sense that no amount of shivering would ever be able to warm her up while his eyes bored into her like this.

It occurred to her that her best form of defence right now was attack. She folded her arms, tilting her chin up and out as she forced herself to stare him down. Refusing to cower, however he might make her feel.

'No, Kaspar. I've been there, I've done that. Marriage isn't a mistake I intend to make again.'

'So then what? You thought you'd drop the bombshell and then hop on the next plane back to the UK?'

He was goading her, his scepticism unmistakeable. It was a struggle not to bristle. She had no idea how she forced herself to her feet. Took her first few steps across the room as though she was in complete control of herself.

'I don't know what I expected you to do. Any more than, I suspect, you know what to do right now. But I just felt I owed it to you to at least tell you I was pregnant.' It was a hauteur she hadn't even known she possessed. 'Now that I have, I think it's time for me to leave.'

Kaspar, apparently, wasn't as impressed as she was.

'Sit back down, Archie,' he ground out furiously. 'You're mad if you think I'm letting you go anywhere with my baby.'

CHAPTER SIX

WHAT THE HELL was he playing at?

Pacing silently on the other side of the curtain as Catherine conducted a thorough examination of Archie, he struggled to quell the out-of-control fear that was spiralling inside him.

He wasn't ready to be a father. He'd never thought he ever would be. And that was another of the reasons why he'd always avoided romantic entanglements. He could never, ever risk being the kind of parent his father had been. Worse, being the kind of parent his mother had been. He remembered how it had felt to feel insignificant, unworthy, not...*enough*. Pain and grief poured through him, like the boilermakers he'd drunk as an unhappy, lost, late-teen; a shot of whisky chased down by a strong beer.

But now his life and Archie's were bound together. For ever. He'd known that after the first few moments of blind panic had cleared, back in his office. He would never allow a child to grow up the way he had, feeling unwanted or unloved.

He had to be the kind of father to his child that Archie's father had been to his own kids. The closest thing Kaspar had ever had to a father himself. He owed it to Archie. The woman whose door he suspected he would have been banging down months ago had he not kept the expanse of the Atlantic between them.

Which made no sense. Because that absolutely wasn't him. He didn't know what had come over him. The ghosts she had been resurrecting ever since that first night together when he'd realised who she was. When he hadn't been able to help himself from claiming her anyway.

It was all he could do to stay this side of the screen and not march around that blue curtain and demand to know exactly what was going on. But staying here was as much about trying not to crowd or frighten Archie as it was about stopping himself from trying to tell Catherine Jarvis how to do her job. As much as she might like and respect him, Catherine wouldn't think twice about calling him out for interfering where one of her patients was concerned.

'Right,' Catherine addressed Archie. 'Let's clean you up and then you can sort yourself out. When you're ready, come back around and we can all have a bit of a chat.'

His stomach lurched. It was exactly the professional, calm tone he used when he suspected a serious issue but didn't want to worry anyone. Or perhaps it was his imagination.

It was strange, being this side of the proverbial table. He felt ill at ease, *lost*, and he didn't like it at all.

So how must Archie feel?

An unexpected wave of...*something* flooded through him. He'd told her that he wasn't about to play happy families. And that was true, he didn't want that. But there was something else there, too.

Had any other woman walked back into his life and declared herself pregnant with his child he might have expected to feel anger, resentment, and maybe there was a little of that with Archie. But there was something more. Like it was his duty to look after her. *To protect her?*

It was like a physical blow. For a moment all he could

do was fight to maintain his balance, rocking on the balls of his feet. His whole career he'd fought for his patients. To the last moment and without exception. Because it was his duty, and because they mattered.

He'd felt a kind of protectiveness towards her as a kid, but that had been completely different. Certainly never in his entire adult life had he felt the urge to protect someone because he cared about *them*, on some…emotional level. He hadn't even thought he was capable of such an impulse.

What was he even to do with such sentimentality?

Unnerved, Kaspar thrust the plethora of questions from his head. He would concentrate on the medicine. That, at least, would make more sense. Sitting down, he forced himself to engage in polite conversation with his colleague, none of which he could recall even a minute later, and waited for Archie to appear.

The sight of her wan, nervous face twisted inside him. Instantly, he switched into cool surgeon mode.

'What did you find, Catherine?'

'Right. So, I did a full examination of you, Archana, and I would concur that you are approximately twenty weeks pregnant.'

'What is the issue?' Kaspar prompted sharply. This might not be his field of expertise but he wasn't considered a top surgeon for being oblivious to other fields. The way his colleague's examination had progressed, and the comments and questions she'd been asking didn't fit with a smooth, non-complicated pregnancy. Sure enough, she turned to him with an almost imperceptible nod. One colleague to another.

'I did see faint evidence of funnelling but I stress it *is* faint. I could send you for an MRI but I'd prefer to concentrate on the cervix length before making any firm decisions.' She turned back to Archie. 'However, I don't have a baseline length without calling your doctors and requesting your notes.'

Kaspar nodded, turning expectantly to Archie, whose expression was even more pinched and white. Instinctively, he reached out to take her icy-cold hand in his.

'Archie,' he prompted gently.

Slowly, so slowly, she turned her head to him, her eyes taking a little longer to focus.

'Archie, we need your doctors' details so that Catherine can contact them.'

'No one told me there was a problem.' Her voice was so quiet they had to strain to hear her.

'Archana.' Catherine's voice was gentle, coaxing. The way his usually was with other patients. But this wasn't *other patients*, this was Archie. 'Would you like me to explain this in more detail?'

Archie nodded stiffly. She didn't look at him but her fingers gripped his surprisingly tightly. Something shot through him, a powerful but fleeting sensation. He couldn't identify it. He wasn't even sure he wanted to.

'All right, during pregnancy the cervix, or the neck of your womb, normally remains closed and long, rather like a tube. As the pregnancy progresses and you get ready to give birth, the cervix begins to soften, shortening in length and opening up.'

Catherine paused, waiting for confirmation as Archie jerked her head in a semblance of a nod.

He bit back his own questions. He couldn't take over, he had to let Archie go at her own pace.

'However,' Catherine continued gently as Archie mumbled a vague acknowledgement, 'in your instance, there is evidence to suggest that the neck of your womb might be shortening. It's very faint and without knowing what the measurements were at the start of your pregnancy I can't be sure. It isn't, at this point in time, less than twenty-five millimetres, which is the point at which I would usually advise having an emergency, or rescue, cervical suture. However, with your past history of miscarriage I would suggest that there is a high enough risk of premature delivery for me to consider performing the suture on you.'

'So...? We...wait?' Archie managed, frowning as if she was having trouble processing it all.

'For right now, yes. But we don't want to wait too much longer.' Catherine shook her head. 'After twenty-four weeks we don't usually perform cervical sutures either here in the US or back at your home in the UK. The standard of care for preemies is of such a high standard that it's generally considered that the risks of being born early is less than the risk to the baby of attempting to delay labour with an emergency suture.'

'So there are risks?'

For the first time, Archie's head snapped up, as though she was hauling herself back to reality by her very fingernails.

Kaspar felt a sliver of pride slip through him, and he clasped her hand tighter as if that could somehow lend her strength.

'There are risks with any procedure,' his colleague answered, 'but particularly in an emergency procedure where the cervix has already shortened and is partly dilated. There's a risk of waters breaking and of infection developing. In your case, there's only faint evidence of effacement and no dilation.'

'But if I'm going to have it, it has to be now?' Archie asked tightly.

'As I said, I'd like a baseline measurement first, and we'll go from there.'

'Why didn't my doctor pick up on it?'

Her pained expression tugged and twisted at something inside him. He wasn't prepared for it. It was a strange, inner tussle not to jump in and grill Catherine on a much more detailed, medical level. Instead, he forced himself to continue sitting quietly, allowing Archie to go at her pace. The kind of questions he wanted to ask would only frighten her unnecessarily. They would deal with any other issues if and when they had to. Still, he would be calling Catherine as soon as he got a moment alone.

'As I said, it's very faint. This is my area of expertise...'

'They're supposed to be experts too...' Archie cut in, panicked, and, with an instinct he hadn't known he possessed, Kaspar found himself drawing her to him, making her meet his gaze. His voice quiet, level, as one might use to a frightened, cornered animal.

'Catherine is a highly specialised, world-class neonatal and maternal-foetal surgeon,' he soothed. 'We will deal with this. *She* will deal with it.'

'But if we miss it. If I don't have the...the...'

'Cervical suture,' he supplied evenly, wondering if this raging storm inside him was how every patient felt when they were sitting opposite him and *he* was the one delivering their diagnoses or prognoses.

'Right. If I don't have that then I lose this baby like I did before?'

'There's no way to know,' continued Catherine. 'You're past the point at which the previous miscarriage occurred. However, there is some evidence that your cervix *might* be beginning to efface. It's possible you could go to term like this, without any intervention. I can't be sure. I need more information. In cases like yours, where it isn't clear, the suture is usually only put in if there's a history of two or more late miscarriages or premature births.'

'Lose two babies?' Archie gasped, horrified. 'Before they will do anything? No. No, I can't lose another baby. I can't.'

'I know it's hard, I'm sorry. But sometimes we have to

be sure,' Catherine was saying, but he couldn't sit quietly any longer.

'If Archie doesn't have the cervical suture and then after that twenty-four-week mark begins to go into labour, you'll do what?' he asked his colleague sharply. 'Pessaries?'

'Yes.' She nodded, turning her focus back to Archie. 'If that is the case, then we would probably offer you progesterone or pessaries instead. As you mentioned during the examination, they tried an Arabin pessary with your first baby.'

'Which didn't work,' Archie choked out as Catherine bobbed her head, again softly.

'And that's why I'd like to request your medical records from your doctor to determine whether a cervical suture might be a sensible precaution.'

'And it will stop me from losing my baby?'

'There's no guarantee. Research into how well cervical sutures stop preterm birth is always ongoing, but it is thought to reduce the risk of early delivery by significant percentages. Once I have more information, I'll bring you back for a further examination and we'll discuss things in greater depth if we feel we might go ahead.'

'But...'

The pleading in her tone twisted at Kapar's gut, but he couldn't indulge it. He had to be the strong one.

'Archie, give Catherine your doctors' contact details. Once she has your full notes she can make a more informed decision and, I promise you, we'll answer every single one of your questions then.'

'Right.' Catherine shot him a grateful look. 'You have full insurance?'

'No...' She froze, as if she hadn't really thought that far ahead.

'The medical expenses will be covered,' Kaspar cut in firmly.

He'd pay for it out of his own pocket if necessary.

'And she's staying with you?'

'Yes.'

He ignored Archie as she glowered at him.

'Good.' Catherine nodded, holding out a form for Archie's medical contact details.

Grimly he took it, coaxing the information out of Archie, line by line. And when it was finally done, he helped her up, sorted out her scant belongings, and led her out of his colleague's office with a word of thanks.

She looked dazed, thrown. The exact way he felt. But he refused to give in to it. He couldn't afford to. If it sucked him in, he'd be no use to Archie, and right now he knew she needed him more than ever.

'I didn't come here for your money,' Archie muttered as she found herself being ushered out of the office. Her mind was grappling for some diversion, however banal, from the bone-gripping terror that she might lose this baby the way she'd lost Faith.

'Or for you to house me,' she added absently.

She had given Dr Jarvis the right name, hadn't she? The right address for her doctor's surgery?

'What should I have said, Archie? That you jumped on a plane and came out here wholly unprepared?'

She pursed her lips, his tone exactly what she'd feared when she'd been halfway across the Atlantic. The accusation out before she could stop it.

'You'd rather I hadn't told you about the baby.'

'That isn't what I said.' He blew out an angry breath and, for one moment, if she hadn't known it to be impossible she would have thought he was as confused as she was.

'I'll stay in a hotel.' It was hard to summon some semblance of pride when all she wanted to do was break down on his shoulder and howl.

Kaspar let out a scornful snort.

'You're pregnant. With my baby. You will remain with me. For the duration. It isn't up for debate, Archana.'

'There is no *duration*. What you and Catherine seem to be forgetting is that I don't come from here, and besides I can't afford medical care. I need to go back home and I need to speak to my own doctors.'

'You can't just run away,' Kaspar snapped. 'And as for medical costs, I will deal with that. You won't be going back to the UK while you're pregnant. In fact, you won't be going back at all.'

'Sorry? What?' she asked. Very calmly. Very deliberately.

She couldn't possibly have heard that correctly.

Did it make it better, or worse, that he looked equally stupefied?

'You won't be returning to the UK,' he said slowly, as if he wasn't really sure of the words coming out of his own mouth.

It was disconcerting to see the famously focussed Kaspar Athari uncertain about anything.

'I... I...' Archie was aware that, for a moment, she opened and closed her mouth feeling much like the fish in the calming tank in the luxurious waiting area outside. Finally, her voice came back. 'I can assure you that is *exactly* what I'll be doing. It's where my flat is, my career, my *life*.'

'Except that now you're carrying my baby.'

'I had noticed.' Her heart pounded so loudly she was afraid it was ready to slam its way right out of her chest. 'But you told me we wouldn't be playing happy families.'

'That was before.'

The conversation was all too similar to the one she'd had when her ex-husband had told her about his job opportunity in Zurich. She'd known then that there was no way she wanted to leave the UK, that her life *was* there. This time she heard the words but she didn't feel the same passion.

She told herself the difference was the baby. Not Kaspar.

It couldn't be him. She couldn't afford to let it be. She turned on him.

'Before what?'

'Just…before,' he ground out. 'I don't know, Archie. You need to give me time. You've had months to get your head around this pregnancy. I've barely had a couple of hours. You'll stay here until I have a plan.'

She could see what it cost him to admit to her that he, Kaspar Athari, had no idea what to do right at this moment. She could more than relate. But she couldn't afford to crumble right now, much as she might want to. Much as the weaker Archie wanted to lean on him, even cling to him. She forced her head up.

'I can't stay here forever. I think Immigration might have something to say about that.'

Far from throwing Kaspar, her words seemed to galvanise him. The powerful, authoritative man the world knew was coming back. Shutting out once and for all that tiny glimpse she'd seen of a remotely vulnerable side to him.

'We'll sort that out.' His disdainful rebuttal was aggravating. 'We'll have to. You're carrying my baby. My blood. Which means, whether I like it or not, you're now my family. And I'll do whatever I need to in order to keep my family with me. I won't allow this baby to grow up thinking she wasn't wanted. Feeling she doesn't have a home.'

'It…*he* will have a home,' she bit out, remembering at the last moment their agreement not to call the baby *it*. Surely there was no doubt that Kaspar's current autocratic attitude stemmed as much from whatever horrors lay in his childhood as that *it* label had been?

'His home is with me. The mother.'

'And with me. The father,' he said, narrowing his eyes

at her. 'I will not be an absent father. You can't push me out of this, Archie.'

'I'm not.' Her voice was too loud, too fractured, but at least she now knew she was right about Kaspar's past dictating his actions now. 'You're the father. I wanted you to know. I felt I owed it to you, to the baby, to give you the choice of being part of its life. But... I can't give up my whole life just to stay in the States with you. I can't even work out here, for one thing.'

'I can take care of you.'

'Out of what? A sense of duty?' she challenged. 'Not because you *want* me. Or our baby.'

'What difference does it make?' And it was only at that instant that she realised just how desperately she wished he could tell her otherwise. 'I *will* take care of you. Both of you.'

'I don't want to be taken care of.'

'Make your mind up, Archie.' His barbed tone pierced its way through her, lodging inside her, twisting painfully. 'An hour or so ago when I said you'd always been a strong kid, you were telling me how fragile you were. Now you're telling me you can handle everything yourself?'

'That isn't what I said.' Archie threw her hands up. He was distorting things, confusing her. Or was he right? Was *she* confusing things? She tried again. 'I want to be...cared for. Not cosseted.'

'And I will be a part of my child's life.'

'I'm not saying you can't be...'

It was infuriating. And yet, somehow, it was also re-assuring. The fact that he was planning for the baby's— *their* baby's—future. As though it had one. As though the fact that she might lose it the way she'd lost Faith wasn't even a possibility for him. It was what she'd needed. He made her feel strong again. Just like he had a hundred—

a thousand—times before. As a kid. Even if he didn't remember it.

Suddenly she was tired of fighting. And scared. And it was making it harder and harder for her to think straight. Words began floating around her head. The risks she hadn't even known about a few hours ago were now threatening to overwhelm her.

She really could lose this baby the way she'd lost *Faith*. Having her suspicions had been one thing, but to hear it so unequivocally was another.

She longed for him to fold his strong arms around her and pull her to his huge chest, comforting her and caring for her, as though he really wanted to. Not just out of some sense of moral decency. But he didn't. They simply stood there, pretending they weren't squaring off against each other.

'I want you to be a part of our baby's life, Kaspar,' she said softly. 'A big part. But I can't stay here. Your life is here and that's fine. But mine isn't. And for what it's worth, I don't see you offering to give up *your* life and *your* work to follow me permanently to the UK, where you could also be with your child on a daily basis.'

Kaspar sighed. 'We both know that your work is more relocatable than mine is. I have teams here that depend on me, patients that trust me to be there throughout their care.'

Archie scowled, though she knew he had a point. As much as she loved her job, it was fairly flexible, and unlike his it wasn't a matter of life or death. 'You just think your life is more important than mine,' she finished petulantly, in spite of herself.

His dismissive shrug didn't help.

'There is no *your* life and *my* life. Not now. You're carrying my baby so whatever our individual lives were like in the past, that's all gone now. Like it or not, it's *our* lives. I will not be apart from my child.' Misery was etched into every line, every contour on his unfairly handsome face. 'I won't have her growing up the way I did, pulled between one parent and the other.'

His unexpectedly searing admission ate at her.

Archie began to speak, then hesitated. She had to choose her words very, very carefully. She reached out to touch his chest, steeling herself for the jolt of awareness that charged through her even before she made contact. Even prepared for it, even now, she couldn't make herself immune to him.

That was another thing she was going to work on.

'We're not your parents. If we both want to be with this baby, we'll find a solution. It...*he*...will know he's wanted. We don't have to be in the same country but we do have to work it out carefully and fairly.'

'I want to be in my child's life. Every day.' He covered her hand with his, but didn't even seem to notice what he was doing. Still, it stole her breath away.

'It doesn't have to be that way,' she began, but he cut her off.

'You'll move in with me, Archie. For all intents and purposes, this child will have a proper family.'

Without warning, her heart flip-flopped in her chest. It was worrying how much the notion appealed to her. How close she was to agreeing to such a ridiculous idea. But as much as she tried to back up both physically and mentally, she could no more remove her hand from the compelling heat of his body than she could refuse outright.

'But we won't be a proper family, will we?' It was meant to be a demand, but her voice was far breathier than she would have liked. Sadness and regret still lined his face.

'Of course not,' he scoffed, oblivious to the fact that he found it so easy to slam all her pitiable dreams away with those three words. 'But our child will at least have a mother and father around who don't want to kill each other on a daily basis. And that's more than I ever had.'

'I don't want to settle for that.' She barely recognised her own shaky voice. 'I want so much more. I want love. I want to be cherished. I want what my father always told me he and my mother had before she died, but which I was too young to remember.'

He shut her down, clearly not listening to her.

'This subject isn't up for discussion, Archana. You're coming home with me and we'll work out the rest from there.'

And before she could respond any further Kaspar was gone and she was alone. In the middle of an empty corridor.

CHAPTER SEVEN

Kaspar's home was everything she should have expected and so much…well, *less*.

It was stunning. Modern glass, sleek design and cool granite perched atop a slight hillside overlooking a private, tantalising beach. As if he was showing her all he could offer their child that she never could.

Archie stared up into the double-height ceiling space of the main living area. All gleaming white and black metal, framing enormous windows that offered breathtaking views across the sea and off into the horizon.

Gorgeous.

It was also completely and utterly soulless. As if no one lived here at all. The perfect show home. Which only proved to her that it wasn't all about money. She cradled her belly protectively. It was about love, and stability, both of which she could provide.

Strong foundations. Dependable.

Could Kaspar?

She doubted it. Or perhaps that was just her own bias since everything he did left her wound too tightly to even think straight. It hadn't escaped her that ever since he had walked out into that corridor when she'd been trying to pluck up the courage to knock on the door, her body had filled with a low, faint humming. Desire. Need.

One afternoon with the man was all it had taken to convince her that she wasn't over anything. That a part of her still hankered for him. Even now. That realisation alone should have told her that she needed to stay as far away from Kaspar as possible. Certainly not spend even one night at his home.

But he'd terrified her by taking her to see Dr Jarvis. Reinforcing every last fear she'd spent five months telling herself was simply in her head. That what had happened with Faith wouldn't happen again.

For all her earlier arguing, the car journey home had given her time to calm down. Time to acknowledge that she would stay with Kaspar as long as she needed to if it meant her baby would be all right. In many ways she was more grateful to Kaspar than she could ever have anticipated. He didn't have to help her, there'd been nothing compelling him to get her in to see his colleague. He'd always made it clear to the media that he didn't have any intention of settling down or having a family. He could have thanked her for telling him and let her return to the UK.

But that wasn't Kaspar.

It was reassuring to know she hadn't misjudged him five months ago.

'There's a guest suite through those doors over there.' Kaspar cut across her thoughts as he headed back down across the hallway to a different set of doors. 'I'll be through that way.'

She gripped the large, rather masculine-looking, leather wingback chair in front of her.

'You're going?'

'I have to get showered and changed.' He frowned. 'I've got a charity dinner event tonight. I'm a guest speaker.'

'Okay.'

'Do you need me to stay?'

A part of her wanted to say yes. A bigger part of her

knew the time to herself would be welcome. She forced a bright smile.

'No. I could do with the evening to myself. Besides, you can't let people down.'

He nodded, unsmiling.

'I would prefer not to. But if I wasn't speaking, I wouldn't go.'

'Should I...? Do I...come with you?'

He looked entirely unimpressed. She tried not to let it get to her.

'I hardly think that's the best idea. Aside from the fact that you're meant to be resting, tonight is a high-profile event and being photographed out with me—especially looking like...*that*...' he gestured to her baby bump '... is the quickest way to get people nosing into every single facet of our lives. I can't imagine you want to see yourself splashed across the entertainment news headlines tomorrow morning, do you?'

'No, of course not.' Archie blinked, attempting to command her faithless heart not to read so much into the way he'd said *our lives*.

As if it implied some form of...togetherness.

'Good.' He nodded, satisfied, although she thought he might have had the decency not to look quite so smug. 'Then you'll stay here, keeping a low profile.'

He was gone before she could answer, leaving Archie alone to explore her new surroundings at her apparent leisure. Instead, she could only stare at the closed door and wonder where they were supposed to go from here.

She needed a distraction. Something to take her fears off the idea of losing this baby, something to ground her and remind her of the strong woman she was in other arenas of her life.

Like in the workplace. Yes, that was it. She could work, she'd brought her laptop. She was lucky that the nature of her job meant she could work from any number of sites or offices—emails and video conferencing were practically *de rigueur*. Certainly at this stage of the project. And she was lucky that she'd worked with the commercial manager on so many projects before over the years that he knew how reliable and fastidious she'd always been. Still, hopping on a plane to different country wasn't exactly usual practice. If she was going to keep her job then she would need to do some work for as long as she was out here.

And she would need a job to get back to once the baby was born. How else was she supposed to keep a roof over their heads? Because no matter what Kaspar had said back in the hospital, it wasn't practical for them to live together and pretend to be some kind of family, even for the sake of their baby.

She booted up her laptop, the waiting emails a welcome diversion as she fired off a handful of easy responses before working on a couple of more carefully worded letters to contractors and the client. But after a few hours the words began to swim before her eyes, the grid patterns of the spreadsheets all merging into each other. And, instead, Kaspar's face began to creep back into her head.

It couldn't be a good thing that all she could think about was him. And their baby. He was insisting on taking control, the way he always had seemed to do, but what kind of a *real* father would he allow himself to be?

The realisation clung to her mind.

She'd never appreciated, growing up, just how badly his parents' volatile relationship had damaged Kaspar. What if he couldn't get past that? What if he carried it into any relationship with their own baby? With her?

It was as though in asking herself that first question, she'd opened the floodgates for a hundred more to rush into her brain.

She'd never realised just how deeply his parents had influenced him before. She'd known a bit, growing up, but her father had shielded her from a lot. Had she been completely naïve in clinging to her memory of the sweet, sensitive young boy she had once known, who had looked to her own father as more of a role model than anyone else?

She couldn't bear the idea that, in time, Kaspar might come to resent her if she and the baby impacted too heavily on his life.

What if he dated other women?

Something spiked inside her, like the stinging slice of a razor-sharp blade, even as she told herself that it didn't matter to her either way. She told herself that what he did in his personal life was no more her business now than it ever had been. It wouldn't make any difference to her. She would have him to thank for the most precious gift he could ever have given her.

Archie slammed the laptop lid down without even thinking about what she was doing. She could tell herself she didn't care all she liked. She didn't buy a word of it. Not even for a second.

What Kaspar did mattered to her. It shouldn't, but it did. And the longer she stayed in his company the more hurt she was going to wind up getting. It was inevitable. Inexorable.

And yet there was no way she could leave. Not to go to a hotel, and certainly not to return to the UK. Not after what she'd discovered today. The very life of her unborn baby now depended on Kaspar, and how he could help her, and she'd walk over coals searing enough to melt the soles of her feet if it meant not going through the agony of another hateful miscarriage.

She'd just have to find a way to seal her heart, her mind off from Kaspar. Think of him as a business deal. The father of her baby but, ultimately, nothing to do with her.

That couldn't be too hard. Could it?

* * *

Kaspar dodged yet another nameless woman—he'd lost count of how many had tried to corner him this evening—and glowered at the auctioneer who was delighting the crowd as he chaired the charity auction.

It was a successful evening, even pleasant, but he couldn't enjoy a moment of it. His thoughts were centred around Archie, their baby and the unwelcome news Catherine had delivered.

He wondered what Archie was doing now. Still working on her laptop, as she'd been when he'd left her? So focussed and wrapped up in her work that she hadn't even noticed him leaving. It was ironic, the one thing he strived for in himself, admired in others, was the thing he was already beginning to resent in Archie.

Because he didn't need her to tell him what that driven expression on her face meant. He recognised it. It told him she was determined to maintain her job, and therefore her life, back in the UK. That she intended to return with his baby as soon as she could, despite everything he'd said to her about not wanting to be an absent father.

He hadn't even realised how strongly he'd felt when he'd first uttered those words. But the fact of it was that it was true. The idea of losing them was unimaginable. *No.* Kaspar pulled himself up short. It was *unacceptable.*

The temptation to go home and tell Archie exactly that was almost overwhelming. There was only one thing stopping him. He needed something more compelling than words. He needed to prove to her that he would do anything for this baby. He needed to prove to her that he *wanted* this baby.

No easy feat when, if anyone had asked him twelve hours ago how he felt about having a baby, he would have laughed in their face. He'd never wanted children, or a family, or a wife. He'd been content to play the genius surgeon, perennial bad boy, who would never inflict himself on anyone the way his parents had inflicted their distasteful, damaging vitriol on either their son or themselves.

For decades he'd told himself that the best thing he could ever do for any child was to ensure that he wasn't their father. No child should ever have to endure the upbringing of his own youth. Pushed from one volatile parent to the other, a pawn in their explosive games. Unwanted and in the way, even when his mother had suddenly realised that it might help his father's career, and hurt hers, if she didn't drag her unhappy fifteen-year-old with her.

And then Archie had knocked on his door and his whole world had shifted on its axis.

He was going to be a father.

Possibly.

Without warning a terrible tightness coiled through him, as unfamiliar as it was uncomfortable. For a moment he couldn't identify it at all, and then it dawned on him. It was fear. And powerlessness.

Everything that Catherine had said this afternoon had made sense to him *medically*. But now that the initial shock was wearing off, his brain was finally locking onto the fact that this wasn't any baby they were discussing, this was *his* baby. His and Archie's.

He wanted this baby to be safe and he wanted to provide the loving family he had never had.

The fact that Archie had made it abundantly clear that she would rather cross the Atlantic, swimming the entire way if she had to, than have him be a daily part of her baby's life cut him deeper than he would prefer to acknowledge. It scraped at him like nothing else ever had.

He'd thought he'd long since got over the pain of not being wanted. By his mother, his father and, to some extent, his best friend Robbie when they'd fallen out over some girl whose name he couldn't even remember any more. *Sarah* perhaps? *Suki? Sadie?* Not that it even mattered.

But Archie's rejection of him ate into him far, far deeper. She'd done her duty by telling him she was pregnant, but she evidently now wanted to be as far away from him as she possibly could get. And he didn't want to let her go. Not just, he suspected, as an image of her breathtaking smile and dancing eyes filled his head while his insides hitched, for the health of their baby. The restlessness he felt whenever he was around her was like an ache of desire.

It made no sense. He was losing his mind and Archie was the one making him lose it. She threatened the order he had created around himself, blurred his clearly set-out parameters, and blasted away his peace of mind.

He could pretend he had been strong all afternoon for Archie's sake, but he was terribly suspicious that the truth was that he needed to stay strong for himself just as much. What he really needed was a plan. Something that would keep his unexpected family around him, allow him to be the father his baby deserved.

Something with which Archie couldn't possibly argue.

'Do you promise to love, honour, cherish and protect...?'

Archie stared at the registrar as though her soul was wholly disconnected from her body. As though she was one of the witnesses, who she didn't even know but apparently Kaspar did, watching the brief ceremony, rather than the not-so-blushing bride standing opposite a grim-faced Kaspar and clutching a small bouquet that was so jaunty and bright it seemed to mock her.

She felt numb. As numb as she'd felt when Kaspar had returned home from the fundraiser early the other night and issued his edict.

Even now she could recall exactly how her body had felt, as though it had been too small to contain her, squeezing her until every last breath had been crushed out of her. And yet Kaspar had looked, for all the world, as though he was relaying something as banal as the weather.

'Marriage?' she had whispered, a lump of something that was halfway between desolation and fury, or perhaps a combination of the two, lodged in her throat. 'We'll never get a license.'

'This is California, there's no waiting time. A long line could mean a two hour wait, but that's about it.' He brushed her concern aside with a sweep of his arm. 'Then we have ninety days to actually get married before the license expires, so unless you're planning on some elaborate ceremony somewhere, I know a couple of ministers who can perform marriages. Either one of them would be happy to step in at such short notice for us. I'm sure we can even go to the beach if you'd prefer something more...romantic.'

He pulled a face which wasn't exactly encouraging. She tried again.

'I'm not Californian. I'm not even American.'

'You don't have to be a resident.' Again, he dismissed her with apparent ease. 'And there's no restriction against foreigners marrying here either. You just need the correct documentation which you have. I've already checked. '

'Kaspar...'

'There's no other way.' His crisp response had been damning. 'But if you need another reason, then how about this; you need to be here where you can be seen by Catherine and my health insurance will cover you only if you are my wife.'

She had savings. Money she'd set aside year in and year out as her rainy-day fund. But nothing that might cover something like this. She'd hated to put it to Kaspar, but she'd had little choice.

'What if you paid?' She could actually remember running her tongue over her teeth in an effort to free them from her top lip. 'I would pay you back. Every penny...or at least every cent...in time, of course.'

'No.'

'Please, Kaspar?' It wasn't like he wasn't wealthy enough to afford it. Although she hadn't been able to say that, it would have sounded so cold-blooded, and that wasn't how she would have intended it. Her voice had dropped to a whisper. 'Why not?'

'Why should I pay out of my pocket just so you can run back to England and take my child away from me at the first chance you get?' he had ground out, and if she hadn't known better she might have thought he sounded almost urgent. But then his commanding tone had come back and she'd known she'd just imagined it. 'I told you, this baby will be brought up knowing her father.'

Archie blinked as she realised that, back in the present, the minister was looking at her expectantly. She clutched the flowers tighter and prayed her subconscious was paying enough attention to know what stage of the ceremony they were up to.

'I do,' she choked out, relieved when he bobbed his head, turning back to Kaspar. 'Repeat after me. I, Kaspar Athari...'

She tried to concentrate, but it was too much. Her head still swam with memories of that night. She had assured him that their baby would know him. Promised him. But he had been intransigent, his cool, level responses only heightening her agitation.

She hadn't known why the idea of marriage had disconcerted her so much. She'd told herself it was because the idea was ludicrous, but feared it was more because a part of her actually longed to say yes. To take the easy solution that he was offering. To accept the safe stability of a marriage. A unit.

But how long would that safe stability last? Especially

with a man like Kaspar, who had spent his life vigorously avoiding ties of any kind.

As if he could read her thoughts, he had thrust his hands into his pockets, looking, for all the world, like the conversation bored him.

'I don't work on promises, Archie. I never promise my patients or their families anything that I can't one hundred percent guarantee. I prefer to put in place assurances.'

'And marrying me is an assurance?'

'The closest I can get, yes.' He'd given a light shrug. 'You can't deny me, or the baby, that way.'

She'd told herself that it couldn't be happening. That it wasn't fair. She'd resisted the urge to run from the room, knowing that it might offer her relief for a moment or two but that ultimately she couldn't escape Kaspar. Or the conversation.

'Please. I'll give you any other assurances you want. Sign any contract you put in front of me.'

'Of course you will. It will be called a marriage contract.'

'No.' Her vehemence had turned Kaspar's eyes to hard, opal gleams. As though she'd hurt him. But such a notion was ludicrous.

'If the idea of marrying me is that abhorrent to you, Archana, then surely you can see how I might think you'd leave with our baby the first chance you get.'

But wasn't that exactly what the problem was? That she *didn't* find the idea of marriage to Kaspar so abhorrent. Or at least she only abhorred the idea of a loveless marriage to him. She could tell herself it was because she'd been there and done that. She'd made the mistake of thinking the way she and Joe had cared for each other had been enough. But it hadn't, and she didn't want to go through that again. Certainly not with Kaspar.

Because the truth, as much as she'd tried to deny it

until now, was that a part of her—a small, childish rem-
nant from her youth, no doubt—was in love with him. And
being married to him, without him loving her back in any
way, would be too much to bear. How could she stand the
fact that he would never be *hers*? Even if she married him?

Kaspar Athari was his own man. He would never belong to any one. And she wanted so much more than that
from him.

Archie paused as the celebrant turned to her now. Her
turn to repeat the vows. She didn't even recognise her
own voice. The ceremony could have been happening to
someone else. She was still stuck there, in her own head,
stuck back in that night.

In her urgency, she'd even asked him exactly what marriage to him would look like. She didn't know what she'd
hoped he would say. It certainly hadn't been the casual
shoulder hunch he'd offered. The nonchalant, *'Why don't
we cross that bridge when we come to it?'*

There certainly hadn't been any words of love, or even
affection. There and then she'd promised herself that she
would never settle for half-measures, with Kaspar or with
anyone else. If she couldn't have all of him, she wanted
none. She'd done half-measures before and look where that
had got her. She refused to do it again.

In her mind's eye, Archie could see herself heading
resolutely across the room. But it was no good. By the
time she'd reached the door she'd stopped, her hand on
the handle but still not turning around.

'I can't marry you, Kaspar. I've made that mistake
before. And I can't make you help me,' she'd whispered
again, desperately summoning the strength to turn the
door handle. 'But I'm begging you to do so.'

He had crossed the room, the heat of his body like a

wall behind her, searing her as his hand had covered hers and drawn it from the cold metal.

'Are you so sure it would be a mistake?' The rawness in his voice had been like a rasp against her heart.

Archie had wanted to tell him that of course it would be a mistake. She'd known she shouldn't cave. But his question had sounded so skinned, like an exposed wound, his hand had still been holding hers and she could still *feel* his body so close to her. She remembered dropping her head, then in defiance of all logic she'd turned and faced him.

The pinched expression on his face had taken her aback. As though she'd wounded him. As though he actually cared. She'd wondered if she could be wrong about him. If he could really want her in his life. As his wife.

She'd averted her eyes but his other hand had slid instantly beneath her chin, his fingers had tilted her head up and forced her to look at him.

'My baby will want for nothing,' he'd stated firmly, fiercely. 'I'll make sure of that. Neither will you, but your lives are here now. With me. I'm not your idiot ex-husband who let you walk away from him. I suggest you don't make the blunder of mistaking me for him.'

She hadn't been about to tell him that was hardly likely. That no one could mistake Kaspar for anyone but himself. His utter certainty had been mesmerising. No wonder people rarely refused him. Including her. *Especially* her.

'Love should be the core of your marriage.' The registrar smiled benevolently now. 'Love is the reason you are here. But it also will take trust to know in your hearts that you want the best for each other.'

She tuned out again. Joe might never have been enough to compel her to leave her life for Zurich. But Kaspar was so much she wondered if she might even leave her life to follow him to the very bowels of hell.

The notion had terrified her. Kaspar didn't love her or want her, he only wanted their baby. Abruptly she'd heard herself lashing out. Wanting to wind Kaspar the way he had done to her.

'I should never have come here,' she'd blurted out, hugging her laptop in front of her chest like it had been some form of body armour against Kaspar's words. 'I should never have told you about the baby. You ruin everything.'

She hadn't been even remotely prepared for the look of absolute pain and devastation that had tugged at his features. She'd opened her mouth to apologise, to find some way to take it back, but then it was as though he'd sucked all the misery back in and instead a wave of fury had smashed over her, emanating from him like a thick, black, lethal cloud.

'You won't take my baby away, Archie.' His ferocity had been unmistakeable. 'You won't shut me out of my child's life, or leave her thinking for a single moment that I didn't want to be there for her. This is my baby, too. I will be a part of every aspect of things. Not some weekend or holiday father but a proper dad, who is there for the first word, the first step, the first dry night.'

She'd tried to take it back. Guilt and regret had almost overwhelmed her. She'd opened her mouth to tell him she had never meant those words that had tumbled, so cruelly, out of her mouth. But the apology hadn't come, and anyway Kaspar wouldn't have let her.

'This isn't about you or me, it's about the life of this baby,' he'd hissed out, his voice lethal. 'You need medical supervision, which is here, with me. This is non-negotiable.'

And that had been the end of it. Those words, uttered in what felt like a lifetime ago.

Now, a few days later, they were here, and Archie was

gazing at a grim Kaspar. She gaped as the registrar beamed his widest smile yet.

'I now declare you to be husband and wife.'

The worst thing was that a part of her was only too eager to comply.

CHAPTER EIGHT

'DID YOU CALL that a kiss?' Kaspar demanded as they stepped back into his...*their* home a scant few hours later.

He didn't know why he was trying to tease her. Perhaps because now they were married he knew they finally needed to get past the animosity that had settled on them. Black, heavy and cold. They had to move on from it.

It was one of the reasons he'd arranged for them to have their wedding breakfast at a private, fine dining experience in one of LA's most exclusive restaurants. It was his attempt at an olive branch, but he hadn't accounted for how entrenched they had become.

The silence at their table, the scrape of metal against fine china, the hollow clink of crystal wine glasses, both filled with water, had only emphasised the emptiness of the day, until finally Kaspar was able to bear it no more.

'I know you're not sure about this marriage,' he sighed, covering her hand lightly with his across the table, 'and I'm sorry if you feel I pushed you into it. Seeing you in front of the minister looking so sad...well, that isn't what I want. Please,' he implored her, and in his eyes she saw an unexpected flash of the vulnerable, proud boy she had once known. 'Let's try to make this thing work, let's try to make our home a pleasant one, if nothing else. The baby deserves that much.'

Archie's heart sank a little. Of course it was the baby he was really worried about, but she nodded anyway, and in a small, tight voice agreed. 'I can be pleasant.'

'Thank you.'

Now, though, as they walked down the hallway of the beach house, Kaspar tried for a little more levity. 'I know you can kiss far better than you showed me today.'

Archie tilted her chin up at him, utterly elegant and poised. It gave him an unmistakeable kick to realise that he could see straight through her. He could read her in a way he'd never expected to be able to.

'It may shock you to know this, Kaspar, but I don't want to kiss you again. I certainly don't want to sleep with you.'

He grinned unexpectedly. The first in days.

'I was talking about a kiss. Who said anything about sleeping together?'

'I surmised it was where you were going with the conversation.' She flushed, struggling hard not to sound so prim. Too hard.

'I hadn't been. Interesting it was where *your* mind went, though.'

'My mind went nowhere untoward, I can assure you.'

Something like relief skittered across her face and Kaspar realised it was a game. One designed to speak to his basest instincts. She was wriggling under his skin, the way she'd always been able to as a kid. Only there was nothing childlike about the attraction that now fizzed between them.

'Is that so?'

'That's so,' she confirmed, but her voice quivered.

'Are you sure?'

She didn't answer and his gaze held hers, missing nothing. Not her quick, shallow breathing, or the flush creeping up her neck, or the way she tried to swallow so discreetly.

For a moment there was nothing. No sound, no movement. Then, suddenly, without even thinking, he closed the gap between them and hauled her body to his and wrapped his hand around her hair to tip her head backwards until she was staring up at him.

She didn't speak. He suspected she couldn't, and that send a shot of pure triumph jolting through him. And then he was crushing her mouth to his and a thousand glorious, dazzling fireworks were going off in his head all at once. Greedy and demanding, he feasted on her and she responded willingly. Wantonly. Her body, bump and all, pressed to him, her tongue dancing to his tune, her hands reaching for his powerful shoulders. And when she moaned against his lips his whole body tightened in response, everything shining that much brighter in his mind.

If he didn't stop this now, he feared he would never be able to do so. She was too damned intoxicating. Still, he didn't know how he succeeded to drop his arm or move away from her. He had no idea how he managed to hold his ground as she stood there, swaying and confused. It was a battle to talk as though he wasn't every bit as affected by the kiss as she clearly was.

'You're right, your disinclination to have sex with me again is abundantly clear,' he taunted softly, feeling bizarrely exhilarated as the oddest sense of calm seemed to permeate his body.

It didn't matter that Archie was staring at him as though he had lost his mind, and it didn't matter that even though he could see the jumble of thoughts that were barging through her head, he felt oddly detached. Confident. *Right*. A whisper of euphoria curled inexplicably through him.

'You had no right to do that,' she choked out eventually. 'I don't want you to do that.'

'Then you shouldn't kiss me back so willingly,' he responded, offering no room for argument.

Not another. Not when he was already feeling so rattled. And yet so triumphant. He felt another chunk of ice fall away.

'Marriage isn't what you wanted when you came here,' he told her quietly. 'I know that. Just as I know you gave me a thousand reasons why it was insane. But we're married now and those reasons don't matter. *You* don't matter. I don't matter. All that matters is our baby. And that he or she has the childhood, the life that you had. Not the one that I had.'

'How would I know that much about your childhood?' she bit back. 'I saw a little but my father kept his confidences. Mostly, I know the rumours from the press. Now I'm your wife. But how can I begin to really understand?'

He had no intention of answering, certainly not in a way that invited investigation of his life, but suddenly he heard himself speaking.

'What do you want to know?'

'You would tell me?' Wide, round eyes pinned him down. It was all he could to get a response out.

'Ask.'

She visibly deflated. Her anger seeped out of her and into the ether so suddenly it was though it had never existed. Still, he wasn't prepared for her fingers to suddenly reach out and skim his cheek.

'What happened, Kaspar?' she murmured. 'I know your mother was volatile, selfish. I know both your parents were. But what is it that I *don't* know?'

She was asking him to trust her enough to open up with the one thing he'd never told anyone. Not ever. His entire life.

He drew in one deep, steadying breath. Then another. And all the while she stood there, her eyes locked with his and her fingers resting on his cheek, so lightly that he wasn't sure if he could feel them or merely sense them.

Everything in him railed at the mere thought of revisiting those hateful memories, let alone voicing them aloud, reliving them. But he'd offered. He couldn't renege now.

Wordlessly, he led her into the living room. It took an eternity for them both to settle. And then she sat, staring at him. Half expectant, half just waiting for him to shut her out instead.

He wasn't sure where to even start. As if she could read his mind, Archie tried to prompt him.

'Robbie met your parents once. Or at least saw them dropping you off once at boarding school. He...said they wasn't exactly...loving.'

He swallowed a bark of bitter laughter. Let it burn the back of his throat. Used it to propel him forward the way he always had done.

'They wouldn't have been remotely loving.' His voice was more clipped than he might have liked, but that couldn't be helped. 'Love didn't exist in our home. At least not towards me. Which I think was a step up from my parents' twisted version of *love*.'

'But you were their son.' She looked dazed.

'I wasn't wanted. Not like you and Robbie. I was a mistake.'

'That's how you felt?'

'That's what they called me.' He let out a humourless laugh. 'It was one of their more restrained names for me. The only time they really referred to me was to call me names or to fight about whose turn it was to take responsibility for me. I was rarely a *he*, I was most often an *it*.'

Cold realisation flowed through her.

'Which is why you got so mad when I called our baby *it*.'

'I couldn't stand it,' he admitted. 'The memories were so strong when you did that, that a sense of worthlessness that ran through me, even all these years later.'

'Were they…as volatile as the press makes out?' she pressed cautiously.

How could she already have grown to hate that expression that clouded his face? To detest his parents for putting it there? It occurred to her that she'd seen it once before. The first summer Robbie had invited him to stay at their house. Too late, she remembered the introverted, awkward seven-year-old he'd been back then.

'You don't have to answer that,' she blurted out suddenly.

Her entire body felt like it was combusting as he cupped her chin gently as if to reassure her.

'You know when Hollywood make films and they're horrific and poignant and the world says how it makes them think, and yet the truth is that it doesn't even come close to how appalling the real truth actually was? Well, that's what the media have reported my life and parents' marriage to be versus the reality.'

'They've always called it explosive.' She frowned.

'And then they've dressed it up to be something sensationalist and implied that such uncontrolled passion was somehow romantic and dramatic,' he ground out. 'But the truth was that there was nothing romantic or sensational about it. It was ugly and twisted and destructive. What's your first memory, Archie?'

It was a fight to keep his voice even, not to let the bitterness creep in. Nonetheless, Archie bit her lip as she slowly bobbed her head.

'It's probably not a real memory, just a memory I've cobbled together from photos and the stories my father told me. But it's of my mother helping me to paint a wooden race cart my father had made for me. It was just before she died so I was probably about six. Then we went out onto the dirt track behind our house and Robbie and I raced each other while my mother refereed and my father pushed me to help me keep up with Robbie.'

His chest cracked even as he knew that such special memories were exactly what he wanted for his child. For the baby Archie was now carrying.

'Mine is of my parents screaming at each other as my mother accused my father of not wanting her to succeed in Hollywood because he wouldn't give her another tummy tuck. I was standing in the kitchen doorway as they went at it the way they always did. She was throwing pots and pans and he was grabbing her and pushing her. I think I shouted out because my parents turned to the door and my mother roared at me to get out because her sagging figure was all my fault anyway. Only her words weren't that restrained. Neither was their fight.'

But he didn't want to scare Archie away. To make her fear that he was *too* damaged.

'Kaspar!' Her cry tugged at something he couldn't identify. 'How old were you?'

'Who knows?' He shrugged. 'It wouldn't have been a unique occurrence. I ran for the phone, I don't know who I was going to call. Anybody, I guess. Then I recall his footsteps thundering behind me, cuffing me across the back of the head and telling me to mind my own business. Then he picked me up, opened the front door and threw me outside, telling me to go and play in the garden or the sandpit or something. Only no one was as polite as that.'

He had a hundred memories like that locked away in some dark, deep pit of his mind. In many of them he'd copped a lot more of the blame, verbally and physically.

'Didn't anybody know?'

'There was a woman who lived down the road. Her husband was some high-flying guy in the city. She'd been the stay-at-home wife, and also his punch-bag. Her kids had grown up and moved out and she took me in often enough, gave me milk and a cookie. Somewhere to lick my wounds. She made me feel cared for. Like I wasn't alone.' He shrugged again, not able to put into words how much she had helped him, in her own way.

'That's appalling,' Archie uttered in disbelief. 'I never really understood.'

'Why would you? Your childhood was so different. And that can only be a good thing.'

She shook her head at him.

'How can you be so blasé?'

Kaspar wasn't sure how to answer that. 'I don't know. It was just…how things were. It was normal to me. It could have been worse, I guess. A lot of the time they didn't really take much notice of me at all. If I stayed out of their way I could pretend the shouting and screaming and fighting was some bad movie on a TV in another room. I used to pretend I was somewhere else. Someone else.'

'Is that why you used to love school so much? Because it made it easier to pretend?'

'I guess. I never really thought about it.' Actually, that wasn't true. He'd thought about it from time to time. 'I don't think it was personal, Archie, as odd as you might think that sounds. I don't think it was ever about me. It was always about them. That was the point.'

'Is that what you think?' She shook her head.

'I guess. It's what your father once said to me.'

'I remember Dad used to take us into his workshop and help us make a wooden toy, or later a metal one on his lathe, and weave long stories that you couldn't help but find yourself caught up in.' Archie laughed softly. 'The next thing you'd be pouring your heart out to him about whatever was wrong. At least, *I* would be.'

He smiled, bowing his head so that she couldn't read his expression. He suspected it was suddenly a fraction too wistful. Of all the people he'd felt he'd let down when he'd lost his cool that night in the bar, it was Archie's father. To this day, he had no idea whether the man ever knew about the monumental mistake he'd made that night.

Suddenly Kaspar felt too full of sorrow for all he had lost over the years but never previously allowed himself to mourn. He swallowed, breathed, waiting until he felt less emotional.

Him. Emotional?

'Your father helped me to realise that it wasn't my fault. Whatever they said there was nothing that I did or didn't do that influenced them. I was an easy target, but they would have followed the same path with each other whether I'd been around or not.'

'You sound so…rational about it all.' A hint of wonderment coloured her tone. 'So logical. I can't imagine how I could handle it the way you do.'

A laugh escaped him. A hollow, empty sound that seemed to bounce off every hard, flat surface.

'You have no idea. I don't handle it, Archie. I never have. I ignore it, hiding it away somewhere and pretending it doesn't exist. I did it successfully for years, but in the end it all bubbled over. I physically hurt someone, Archie. Why do you think I've let the press portray me as this ridiculous "Surgeon Prince of Persia"? Because it's what I deserve.'

'You don't deserve anything of the sort.'

'Yes. I do. Why do you think I avoid relationships? Why do you think I avoid emotional connections of any kind? Why do you think that until you came along I didn't want to settle down and have a family of my own? I couldn't bear the idea that I might do to them even a fraction of what was done to me.'

'You could never do that,' Archie asserted fiercely, the certainty in her voice surprising him as much as it warmed him. 'You aren't them. You're nothing like them.'

'I was never sure of that before. Not until you turned up, carrying my child. Not until that moment when I knew I *would* be a part of my baby's life. A full, complete part, not some part-time dad. I won't accept that, Archie. And I won't let you relegate me to that. That's why we had to marry.'

He couldn't tell her that he was becoming more and more suspicious that it was only part of it.

She watched him intently, her eyes never leaving his face.

'And what about love?' she challenged, so quietly he had to strain to hear her.

There was no reason for his heart to suddenly hang a beat. He didn't like what it might mean. What it might be trying to tell him. Kaspar forced himself to regain control.

'I can't tell you about love,' he informed her steadily. 'But I can tell you about chemistry.'

'Five months ago?' She let out a nervous laugh.

'It wasn't just that night, Archie. You know it as well as I do. That kiss before proves it.'

She wanted to argue. But she didn't. She couldn't. And he felt that was a good start.

She was still riding on the unexpected high of Kaspar opening up to her the following day when they were back in Dr Jarvis's office. Wondering if marriage to Kaspar would be so bad after all. Her marriage to Joe might have gone wrong, but they hadn't had a fraction of the chemistry Kaspar had mentioned. Not to mention the fact that she was carrying Kaspar's baby.

Could it really be that easy? Fitting together so neatly? It almost felt too good to be true.

'Right.' Dr Jarvis strode across the room to them, snagging Archie's attention as she advanced.

The woman's expression was too careful. Something dark, and terrifying, churned inside her.

'So I've spoken to your doctor and got your records, as you know, and I've carried out another examination today. I believe that there is funnelling taking place. However, it's no more advanced than when I examined you last week.'

Kaspar's arm unexpectedly moved around her back, and instinctively she leaned into it, drawing strength from his solid body.

'So what happens next?' he asked clearly, calmly, like he knew her vocal cords were too paralysed to even try to speak.

He probably knew already, of course. He was asking for her benefit. But that only made her all the more grateful.

'It means it's your call, Archana. There's no need to become alarmed but, given your history I would be prepared to do a cerclage in the expectation that it might help to ensure this baby stays in there where it needs to be.'

'What would that entail?' She swallowed a wave of nausea, trying to focus, to understand.

'I would place a band of strong thread around the neck of your womb, under spinal anaesthetic. I could do it this afternoon and it should take around twenty-five minutes. Antibiotics will help to reduce the risk of infection but I would want to keep you in for at least twenty-four hours anyway to ensure that the procedure hadn't induced labour. After that you should be able to go home provided you take things very easy.'

'Bed rest?' Kaspar sounded gravelly compared to his usual voice, but Archie couldn't process it. She didn't know what it meant.

'For a few days if possible.' Dr Jarvis nodded. 'Then you can slowly start to resume light movements, graduating to normal. With some emergency cerclage, we recommend no sexual intercourse for the duration of the pregnancy, but with Archana the funnelling is so faint that I'm anticipating you can resume sex in a week or two as long as it's light and infrequent, say once or twice a week.'

Later, much later, she would flush at the memory at the rather one-way conversation, and the fact that neither she nor Kaspar had refuted the idea that they were enjoying a healthy sexual relationship.

Later. Not now.

'But you should wear a condom, Kaspar,' Dr Jarvis was continuing blithely. 'Obviously that's more about reducing the risk of infection rather than concern about conception.'

On some vague level Archie was aware that the woman had been making a joke. No doubt one she made to all her patients to try to elevate the mood a fraction. But Archie couldn't laugh, she barely even cracked a smile. She wasn't sure if Kaspar did any better.

'We won't be having sex,' came Kaspar's tight, rasping admission eventually. But when Dr Jarvis continued, it wasn't clear if she had misunderstood or was simply being discreet.

'That's probably wise until I have chance to do a two-week post-op check-up. Then I'll have a better idea of how your body is reacting to the cerclage, Archana. Often orgasms can soften the already compromised cervix, which can also lead to premature birth. Although, again, in your case, I don't believe that will be the case. This is more a precaution due to your history along with the fact that there is faint funnelling. If it was just one of those factors then I wouldn't be considering the procedure.'

And if Kaspar hadn't been the one pulling the strings, would anyone have done anything at all? Her doctors had dismissed it, if they'd even noticed it, just as they had done when she'd been carrying Faith.

She couldn't lose another baby. She *wouldn't*.

She didn't need to look at Kaspar to know what she

wanted to do. Somehow, him just being here, his arm around her, gave her the confidence she needed to make her own decision.

'Schedule the procedure, please.' Her voice cracked but she didn't care. 'I'll have it done as soon as possible.'

CHAPTER NINE

THE SUN BEAT DOWN, seeping into Archie's skin and melting into her very bones, its warmth heating the poolside
paving slabs under her feet. Archie relaxed in the shade
and tried not to stare too obviously at the sight of Kaspar
cutting through the water as he executed perfect length
after perfect length.

The past few weeks since the cerclage had seemed surreal. Like she'd woken up in a parallel life where she lived
in pleasant domesticity with Kaspar. He'd been attentive,
and patient, and easy company.

But they'd never mentioned his childhood again. Or
their marriage.

They never really talked about anything of substance.
Not even the cerclage. Their conversations were light,
sometimes funny, always friendly, but they verged on the
superficial, and it galled Archie more than she cared to
admit. As though their moment of breakthrough had never
happened.

Even when Dr Jarvis had expressed her satisfaction that
Archie's body seemed to have accepted the intervention
well with bed rest slipping into house rest then into gentle
activities, but not yet sexual activity.

Archie had no doubt that her searing cheeks had raised
the temperature of the consultation room by several de-

grees, mortified that she'd instantly thought back to that weekend together and had not been able to get the incredible X-rated images from her head. Yet Kaspar had schooled his features as though the conversation hadn't bothered him in the least.

It had somehow felt demoralising, making her wonder why he hadn't even touched her since the kiss that wedding night. Had it simply been about proving a point? Why did it even bother her?

Archie stood up abruptly. The need to get away from the house—something she hadn't been able to do in the last few days—more overwhelming than ever.

That one moment of openness, of almost vulnerability on Kaspar's part those weeks ago had been gone even by the following morning when she'd awoken. She could remember it as vividly as if it had only been hours ago.

Not even a trace of their temporary connection had remained as he'd presented her with a freshly squeezed orange juice courtesy of the juice-maker on his sparkling kitchen island, scrambled eggs with asparagus on wholemeal toast courtesy of the pan on the pristine cooker, and rich herbal tea courtesy of the instant hot-water tap at the plush sink.

She had plastered a beatific smile to her lips and pretended not to notice that the vulnerable Kaspar had disappeared as abruptly as he'd appeared. Pretended not to care that he hadn't dipped his head and kissed her the way she'd so ardently wished he would as they'd stood in that room, her hand over his heart, trying to feel whether it was beating as loudly and as quickly as hers had been.

But he'd remained as shut off to her as he always had been. A closed book.

'So you do actually use this kitchen for cooking?' It had been an effort to keep her tone upbeat at first. To tease him. 'I'm impressed.'

'You should be. It was your father who taught me how.'

'His only real signature was all-day breakfasts,' Archie had corrected him, this time striving for a laugh. Surprised when it was actually more genuine than she'd expected. 'He was useless at most other cooking.'

'You're right.' Kaspar had nodded after a moment's consideration. 'I've been making his famous all-day breakfast since I was fourteen.'

'Ah, yes. You and Robbie would cook it every single Sunday of every single holiday.'

'I seem to remember you wolfing it down as fast as anybody.'

'I had to.' Archie had feigned indignation. 'I had to keep up with you two. You didn't exactly want a twelve-year-old following you around. You both always tried to ditch me.'

'Yeah.' Kaspar had chuckled. 'And you've no idea the rollicking your father gave us whenever we were successful.'

They'd laughed and, for a moment, it had felt good again. Until she'd realised that all Kaspar's light-hearted banter was a way of keeping her at arm's length. Even as she lived in his home as his wife, carrying his child.

Shaking off her thoughts as she reached the expansive glass sliders that led from the poolside to the cool lounge, Archie sensed, rather than saw, Kaspar coming up behind her as she entered the house.

'Archie? Is everything okay?'

She wanted to shout and rail and vent all her frustrations. Instead, she simply turned to greet him with a pleasant, if rather flat smile plastered onto her lips.

She should be grateful he cared.

She should be.

'I'm fine. The baby's fine. I just wanted to head in for a while.'

He didn't believe her for a moment. His gaze pierced through her, making her blood fizz in her veins in a way that even the hot sun hadn't managed.

Dammit, when was she ever going to get a grip of herself around this man?

'What's wrong?' he demanded. 'You've been more and more jittery with each passing day.'

Fear that he could read her so easily, that he might guess the embarrassing truth, lent her voice a frustration she hadn't intended.

'I'm sick of being cooped up in this house, unable to even go out, when you refuse to talk to me about anything remotely important. I can't take it any more. I'm getting my trainers and I'm going for a walk along the beach.'

He eyed her again, the same intensity, the same knowing expression in those unfathomable depths. How was it that he seemed to find it so easy to read her while she had no idea what he was thinking, most of the time? It was hardly fair.

And now she sounded like the kind of petulant teen she liked to pride herself that she'd never been.

'Have I upset you in some way, Archie?' Evenly. A little too calmly.

'No.' She gritted her teeth.

'Have I treated you badly and not been aware of it?'

'Of course not.'

'Then perhaps you would care to tell me why I suddenly seem to have become your enemy.' His eyebrows shot up. 'Only here was I thinking I was looking after you.'

He had been. That was the problem. He was looking after her for the baby, which was right and proper, but not because he also wanted to look after *her*. The difference was subtle, but it was there. And it hurt.

Logic, it seemed, stood little chance against a heart that

yearned for something else. Especially when that something else was Kaspar Athari's love.

Archie balked at the realisation.

Surely she wasn't still imagining herself *in love* with
Kaspar? No, that had to be the baby mushing up her head.

'You're right.' She backed down abruptly. 'Sorry. Maybe
I just need to get out of the sun.'

The last thing she needed right now was to engage in
a bit of verbal back and forth with him. Or stir up more
emotions in her that her hormone-riddled head might mistake for *love*. It was all she could manage not to squirm beneath his unrelenting gaze. Assessing her, as he always did.

'Get changed,' he bit out unexpectedly. 'I'm taking you
out for the afternoon.'

Flitting around the city, playing the tourist with Archie
and doing the sightseeing thing was certainly not the way
he'd been expecting this day to turn out. Yet here they were
in downtown Los Angeles, soaking up the atmosphere.

To his surprise, he found himself enjoying it, even forgetting his concerns for Archie, and for their baby, for a
while.

Over the last week he'd become more and more aware
of the beatific yet simultaneously false smile that she'd
flashed him from time to time. He was aware that, to a
greater extent, it was his own fault. After opening up to
her that one night he'd not so much regretted it but, more,
had had his misgivings. At loading something like that
onto Archie when she already had enough to worry about.
And, yes, about opening up so easily, so naturally. As if it
hadn't been the greatest secret he'd lugged around for his
entire life, which had defined him, driven him, moulded
him. And as though it didn't even matter any more. Not
when he had Archie.

Because the truth was, he didn't have Archie. She may

have married him, but only because she'd been pregnant with his baby and he'd insisted on it. He would do well to remember that before he risked letting himself get carried away with this sham marriage of theirs. The marriage he was altogether too happy to accept. So he'd managed to shut himself off to her as he always had. A closed book.

But always aware that Archie could so easily take him off the shelf, blow the cobwebs away and open him up if she took it into her head. Encouraging him to give up his stories, his secrets when they were better left unread.

Unseen.

'The Walt Disney Concert Hall?' she breathed, a look of quiet awe on her face as she dragged him back to the present.

'Yeah, well, I figured with your background in construction this might be of particular interest.'

'It is.' Archie nodded, taking in the iconic structure in front of them. 'The way it looks and, I believe, the sound are incredible.'

He dipped his head in confirmation.

'The LA Philharmonic are performing next month. I have tickets. Accompany me.'

It was meant to be an invitation but he knew it sounded more like a command. Even more unexpectedly, however, Archie merely looked up at him in surprise and then smiled. A genuine, sweet smile that he felt everywhere, as if she were running her hands over his bare flesh the way he knew her eyes had been doing—albeit against her will—earlier in the afternoon at the pool.

She made him feel so good. Perhaps too good. He didn't have any right to still want her the way he did. As wrong as he knew it was—she was the mother of his child, after all, and he was supposed to be caring for her, protecting her—he couldn't seem to stop it. She preyed on his waking thoughts. And most definitely his sleeping thoughts.

'Come on.' He forced one leg in front of the other, but his hand still reached for hers as he led her around the building he'd somehow *known* she would love to see.

The tour should have been a welcome distraction, allowing him to clear his head, but Kaspar was too preoccupied to enjoy it. He was just grateful that Archie seemed happy, throwing herself into the history and the story as though nothing was more important to her.

After that, they toured the MAK Center for Art and Architecture, the gardens at the exposition centre and another museum whose name he couldn't remember afterwards. Yet each time she barely seemed to notice he was even accompanying her while, for Kaspar, the drive in the back of the chauffeured car was becoming a little harder with each journey. He couldn't shake an irrational urge to jolt her, to remind her that he wasn't just the guy who'd got her pregnant, he was her husband. Whatever that meant.

'Where now?' Archie asked as she glanced out the window as if she had any idea where they were.

'Home.'

It was ridiculous how those words rippled through him, but it was only when Archie shivered that he realised she wasn't quite as immune to him as he'd let himself believe. With mounting curiosity he watched her force herself not to react, grasping instead at the first thing to come into her head.

'You mean that incredible house you own with the stunning views? Though I couldn't describe it as a *home*.'

'By which you mean…?' he prompted when she stopped talking with a strangled sound.

'Forget I said anything.'

He knew he should do precisely that. Let it go. It wouldn't do any good to encourage the kind of conversation they'd had the other night. Yet he couldn't just stay silent. He wanted to know what she thought. It *mattered* to him.

He didn't care how dangerous that sounded. At least it was something more than the trivial conversations they'd been having recently. He told himself he was being foolish. But *that* didn't seem to matter at all.

For her part, despite all the biting of her lip, which he was fast recalling meant that Archie was trying to bite back words she knew she shouldn't say, Archie swivelled her head to look at him.

'It's hardly a home, Kaspar. It doesn't have an ounce of heart. It doesn't tell a visitor the slightest thing about the person who owns it. It's a beautiful building but it's soulless. There's nothing of *you* in it.'

She was right, of course. Because that was exactly how he'd wanted it. At some point he'd come to equate being unreadable with being invulnerable. Not that he would ever have admitted that before now, of course.

'So change it.' He shrugged as though it was no big deal but his eyes never left hers.

As if somehow that way he could convey all the thing he couldn't, *shouldn't*, say. He told himself it was part of the plan. A necessity. To break down the barriers in order that they could grow close enough to be the kind of parents their child would need. It wasn't about *wanting* to break down barriers with Archie.

He wasn't sure even he believed himself.

What the hell was wrong with him?

'Sorry? Change what?' she pushed tentatively.

'Change the house.' He waved a hand that he was glad to see didn't look as leaden as it felt. 'We're married and we're having a baby. That place is your house too now, so make it a home. The family home of your dreams.'

'What, to match the marriage of my dreams? I can

change anything, but without your input it will just be *my* home in *your* house. It still won't reflect you at all.'

The tone verged on hysterical. Out of nowhere, or so it felt. The words cracked out like a whip slicing through the air. He had to fight not to flinch.

'So?' he replied coldly, not trusting himself to say any more.

The silence was so stark that he could hear the almost silent hum of tyres on tarmac. Archie blew out a deep breath.

'I just don't understand you, Kaspar.' She splayed her hands out on her knees. 'It's like we take one step forward only to take a giant leap back.'

'I disagree.'

'Really? One minute you're telling me we won't be playing happy families, the next you're hauling me off to the registrar. You kiss me like we're in some kind of epic movie, but then you don't even look sideways at me. You open up to me finally about something that actually *matters*, and then you shut me out as though I have no right to know anything about you. Now you're telling me we can redecorate your house like a real couple but you barely react when I challenge you about this not being a real marriage. Which version of *Kaspar* should I believe in?'

'The movie version sounds good. This is Hollywood after all.' He didn't know how he managed to sound appropriately dry. Even amused. 'This place loves a good "Girl Next Door Tames Playboy" love story after all.'

'This isn't a movie,' she snapped, a little shakily. 'This is my life.'

'Now it's both.'

She exhaled again. Even deeper this time, and more forcefully.

'If this really were a movie, Kaspar, you wouldn't be shutting me out.'

He really didn't like the way his blood suddenly rushed through his body at her accusation.

'I haven't shut you out,' he managed, although even on his lips the words sounded hollow. 'I opened up to you.'

'One conversation? One night?' She was incredulous. 'That's your idea of opening up? You cracked the portcullis a fraction and then the next morning you'd not only slammed it back down but you'd dug a moat, filled it and set me squarely on the other side.'

His jaw locked so tightly he thought his bones might crack, but he couldn't refute her accusation. More to the point, *why did he find he even wanted to*?

'What did you expect me to do?' he demanded. 'Rage and roar and gnash my teeth? That isn't who I am, Archie. I thought you knew that.'

She flinched, just as he'd expected she would. But then she rallied. Quickly.

'I didn't expect you to treat me like the enemy because you regretted even that tiny show of vulnerability from yourself. I didn't expect you to push me even further away. I didn't expect you to shoot down any conversations that involved anything real.'

'You saw a bike with stabilisers in a shop and asked what colour we would for buy our baby,' he stated in disbelief. 'The baby isn't even born yet.'

'It was hypothetical. And it wasn't just that. It was about getting an opinion from you on anything at all. You know exactly what I mean. Every conversation. Every time.'

He shot her a deliberately disparaging look.

'I don't know anything of the sort. You're being overly dramatic.'

He did know, though. That was the issue. For a moment she didn't answer, but when she did it wasn't to say what he might have expected.

'Please, Kaspar. I know you *do* understand.'

Her soft plea scraped away inside him. Raw. Guilt-inducing. He tried to ignore it. Turned his head to watch the LA landscape as it sped past the window, the sights and smells as clear to him as if he'd been able to taste then, feel them, without the thick glass and metal in the way.

Abruptly he hit the intercom, instructing his driver to change direction.

'What's Hector's?' Archie asked, despite herself, and, incredibly, a smile began toying with his lips.

How did she change the mood so easily? Bring him around when he'd thought things too dour?

'You'll see,' he replied, only half-surprised when the hint of teasing didn't satisfy her. 'Fine, it's a crazy golf course. I used to go there all the time when we first moved out here and I was sixteen.'

She eyed him, a little too knowingly.

'Do you remember the course we used to sneak onto as kids? When it was closed for the day and the guy who ran it knew we didn't have enough pocket money to pay full price but he let us give him whatever money we could scrape together?'

'And then he'd leave us whatever pastries hadn't been sold that day and were going to get chucked out anyway?' Kaspar added.

Archie laughed, her face flushing with pleasure.

'You were really good at crazy golf. Robbie used to hate it because sometimes you'd hit the shots backwards just to give him a chance.'

'Considering how co-ordinated he was at other sports, he really was remarkably bad at the game. So were you, for that matter. The athletic Coates kids, foiled by a crazy golf course.'

'I wasn't that bad,' she objected.

'You weren't that good either.'

'Now wait a minute…' She paused, then jabbed her

finger at the tinted glass with barely disguised delight. 'There. Is that Hector's?'

He knew the drive without even looking.

'That's Hector's.'

'Come on, then.' She was out of the door the minute the car pulled up. 'I reckon today might be the day for a little payback.'

He vaulted after her.

'Payback, huh? Care to wager?'

'How much?'

'Not money. A forfeit.'

She wrinkled her nose.

'What kind of forfeit?'

'Winner gets to choose.' He shrugged, striding ahead and slapping the money on the counter of a rather disinterested-looking young man.

'Surely that's not Hector?' Archie whispered as they ducked through the paint-chipped turnstile.

He wasn't fooled.

'Changing the subject, Coates. Are you that doubtful about your crazy golf abilities?'

'I am not.' She selected her club and thrust her chin in the air. 'Fine. A forfeit. Winner's choice.'

In the event, the game was more fun than he had anticipated. Light relief after the tension. He'd never thought that revisiting any element of his past could ever be anything but painful, but he was beginning to understand that in his need to bury his childhood he had lost many happier times. Almost always concerning the Coates family, the way her father had taught him to be a man, or the way Robbie had shared everything with him, or the way Archie had treated him like another annoying big brother. They had made him feel like any other normal boy. A person, not an *it*.

All too soon, they were at the final obstacle, their game

almost over, and Archie hadn't been quite as appalling as he'd remembered.

Still, Kasper knew it was a mistake the moment he moved behind her, her back against his chest, his arms skating down the length of hers, her delicate hands under his, all under the pretext of holding the golf club with her and allowing her to help him make his winning shot.

Until that moment it had been a good game. Simple, uncomplicated fun, a round of crazy golf on a balmy afternoon. They had exchanged banter and laughed and she had teased him, coughing and doing funny dances to try to put him off his shots, like a grown-up version of the Little Ant he had known. Her ploy hadn't worked, his shots had been true each time. But occasionally he'd pretended her antics had put him off, making some melodramatic mishit that had only made her laugh all the more.

A genuine, throw-her-head-back laugh, which was surpassed only by the vivid sparkle in her glorious eyes. The more she did so, the more he yearned to make her do it more. The intense pleasure it gave him to be the person making her so outwardly happy had taken him back, made him forget who or where he was. It seduced him into focussing on Archie and himself together, simply playing crazy golf. Like when they'd been young, carefree, their whole lives ahead of them.

She'd played well but he'd played better. Of course he had. Because everything in life was a competition for him. And yet, right at that moment, he'd wanted them both to take that winning shot. He'd invited her to join him and she, without even thinking about it, had skipped almost girlishly to comply.

The moment his body had touched hers everything changed. The innocence of the moment was gone, replaced instead by something far more charged. Far more sensual.

Only then did Kaspar admit it had been there all afternoon. Simmering quietly. Just waiting to catch them unawares.

He should move back. But he couldn't. He could barely even breathe. His head was over her shoulder, his cheek brushing her ear as they both stared at the ball. Archie's own breathing was shallow, fast, although he knew she was trying to fight it, desperately struggling to control it. He could take the shot, pretend he didn't feel what she felt. But he was powerless to move. Rooted where he stood.

He turned his head, so very, very slightly it should have been imperceptible. But Archie noticed. She knew. Her head mirrored his, and now their mouths were an inch apart and the beast inside him was roaring with the compulsion to close the gap. His body wanting her with the same ferocity it had all those months ago.

He had to walk away.

Now.

CHAPTER TEN

KASPAR DROPPED HIS head but misjudged it. Or rather he judged it perfectly, his lips skimming the bare skin just above the neckline of her T-shirt. Archie shivered and he was lost.

Before he could think once, let alone twice, Kaspar tilted his head and then they were kissing as she pressed her back into him, their hands still holding the grip of the golf club and his feet still positioned on either side of hers.

He drank her in, her taste, her feel, her scent every bit as perfect as the recollection imprinted on his brain, and yet also a hundred times better. He remembered kissing every inch of her skin, tracing it with his fingertip, his mouth, his tongue, and as his body tightened against Archie's perfect bottom, she pushed back against him, then gentlest of moans reaching his ears.

He almost lost it, there and then. A lifetime of being in complete control gone because no one else had ever got under his skin like this. No one but Archie. He would never know how he managed to pull his brain into focus, to remember where they were, or that he was meant to be easing Archie's stress, not adding to it.

It took everything he had to wrench his mouth away. This was pure physical desire, nothing more. *Nothing more.* But if that was true then why was he still behind her, why were his arms still around hers, her hands still held under his?

If he didn't stop now, he wasn't sure he ever would. Somehow he found the strength to pull away.

The loss of contact was almost painful.

'What was that for?' Archie whispered, turning slowly to face him, her fingers hovering over her lips.

He wondered if her mouth burned for him as his did for her.

'Call it my victory kiss.' His attempt to sound casual fell far short of the mark. 'Your forfeit.'

'You didn't win.'

Half teasing, half shaky, and entirely shocked. He knew exactly how she felt.

'You'd better finish the game to prove it.'

'I don't give a damn about the game.'

He just gave a damn about her.

'The game, Athari.' She emitted a delicious growl.

All he really wanted was to haul her back into his arms and finish kissing her, thoroughly and completely. Even though it made absolutely no sense.

'Right,' he muttered eventually, stepping forward and taking the proffered club.

Stepping to the mark, he swung and hit. He barely even waited to see if it reached its mark. He knew it would.

'Let's go.' He spun around and begun walking away, but he couldn't help extending his arm behind him. Felt triumphant when she took his hand without a word.

He told himself it meant nothing, the way his chest constricted as her fingers entwined with his. He promised himself he'd let go as soon as they were back in the car.

But now they were back in the vehicle and he still hadn't let go of her hand. He still couldn't take his gaze off her sparkling eyes as he instructed his driver to finally take them home. He couldn't shake the fact that the word *home* sounded somehow right, and natural, and easy, and perfect.

Archie stared right back at him, her gaze never leaving his for a moment, but he saw the hesitation on her face. Watched the way her tongue flicked out nervously to wet her lips.

'Why are you looking at me like that?'

Uncertainty in her tone mingled with raw need. Kaspar gritted his teeth. It was a heady combination.

'You realise that we kissed out there. Like a proper married couple.'

'Imagine that,' she tried to tease him, but her breathy tone belied her confidence.

Another Archie quality that he apparently found sexy as hell. Especially after the overly cocky women of his past. *What had he ever seen in them?* The answer was clear now. He hadn't. They'd been the perfect choice for a man looking to keep himself emotionally unavailable because they'd never threatened to unravel his carefully crafted design. The construct that Archie had picked apart in a matter of months. Or, indeed, one heady weekend.

'If people see us, recognise me with a woman looking as unambiguously pregnant as you look, your photo will be all over the papers. The internet. We might have kept things out of the media for now, but they will find out eventually and it *will* fire up their interest.'

'So you'll control it.' She schooled her features. But it was too late, he'd seen that flash of contempt in her eyes. 'You control anything you want to. You're Kaspar Athari.'

Until a few months ago he might have believed her.

'Not anything,' he muttered. 'I can't control how I am when I'm with you.'

The words were out before he could swallow them back. Archie paused, as though momentarily unable to answer. Then her hand reached out, slowly, tentatively, giving him plenty of time to draw away. Had he wanted to. Her fingertips brushed his jaw. Gentle. Careful. But it fired him up nonetheless.

Before he could stop himself, he was lifting her through the air to settle her on his lap and her soft, startled cry even as she leaned instinctively into him, her arms slipping around his neck and her bottom nudging against the hottest, hardest part of him, only acted as an accelerant to the fire.

He closed the gap and allowed himself to taste her all over again, light and deep, languid and demanding. Indulging in the feel, the scent, the breathy sounds of pleasure that were so essentially Archie when he plundered her mouth and pressed kisses into the creases at either corner. She quivered deliciously as he scorched a trail down her neck to the sensitive hollow where his lips, his tongue, his teeth all worked in harmony until she was breathing hard and wriggling on his lap. And he was aching, *physically* aching, for her.

His hands found their way to the hem of her T-shirt, hauling it over her head in one fluid movement, and as her hair tumbled back down and over her shoulders, he couldn't help lifting one hand to wind it around his fist, pulling just the wrong side of gently to tilt her mouth back up to his and claim her all over again.

Archie pressed her chest to him. Hard nipples scraped urgently against him, even through his own thin shirt. She fumbled with the buttons, tugging them open and rubbing against him as though the skin-to-skin contact might somehow alleviate her longing. And Kaspar loved it. The way she acted out of pure desire. The feel and the taste, and what she wanted. The kind of women he'd been with before her had been too busy trying to show him how good they were and too hung up on the aesthetics of it.

He let his thumb graze one swollen peak with deliberate nonchalance, moving quickly away when she arched her back in order to repeat the action. She groaned softly.

'Kaspar...'

'What is it, Archie?'

He was amazed that he could managed to sound even a fraction as in control as he did.

'You know what,' she whispered, pushing her chest to his again.

'Tell me,' he rasped. 'I want to hear it.'

She flushed slightly, but met his eyes boldly.

'Touch me.'

It was like some exquisite torture, keeping his hands to himself. But he wanted to hear her say it. He thirsted to hear the longing in her tone, knowing that it was a need only he could sate for her.

For both of them.

'Where?' he demanded.

'Anywhere,' she whispered. 'Everywhere.'

He couldn't stand it any longer. Dropping his head back to the hollow, he kissed and teased.

'Here?'

'There,' she agreed, tilting her head to one side to allow him better access. Taking his time, he made his way down her body, his fingertips hooking down the lace of her bra to free one perfect nipple.

'Here?'

She gasped, and nodded, her head falling back slightly as he licked, sucked. And with every stroke of his tongue he stoked the fire and revelled in the way the flames roared within him. It was all he could do to stay where he was, lavishing attention on first one rosy peak and then the other. Then back again, as her breathing grew ever more shallow, catching in her throat.

And then he was sliding his hand up the bare skin of her thigh, the summery skirt puddling around her bottom as though only too happy to fall away for him. Archie moaned, a low, soft, long sound that seemed to wind its way through him and coil around his sex as potently as if it were her delicate hand. He reached the top of one thigh and then, his knuckles barely brushing her hot, molten core, he skimmed his way slowly down the other thigh.

'You're teasing me again,' she moaned, burying her head in his shoulder.

Half a gasp, half a growl, but wholly frustration. Another shot fired through him.

'I am,' he managed, shocked at how difficult it suddenly seemed to speak.

Kaspar could stand it no longer. He ached for her. Physically *ached*. He wanted her. And she was his. He lifted his hand and slid it beneath the silky triangle of material.

Hot. Wet. So very ready for him.

He had never wanted anything more than he wanted her right now. It was time to claim her. Brand her as his. He would never want anyone the way he wanted Archie.

She froze at exactly the same moment he did.

What the hell was he thinking? She was pregnant. With his baby. And Catherine had said there could potentially be an issue. They couldn't risk it. They couldn't take that chance. Allowing himself to be driven by his desire, his emotion was exactly the kind of selfishness that his parents had exhibited time and again. He would not repeat their mistakes.

He would not let the fact that he shared their DNA make him like them.

'This can't happen,' he growled, lifting her bodily of his lap and placing her as far across the back seat as he possibly could. Never more grateful for the privacy glass which concealed them from both the driver and the outside world.

She made a sound. It might have been a mutter of agreement but he didn't care. He busied himself locating her clothes. Fastening his shirt.

'That should never have started.' He was aware that he was directing the fury he felt at himself towards Archie, but he couldn't seem to stop himself. 'You have the baby to consider.'

What the hell was wrong with him?

'Dr Jarvis said occasional light sex is acceptable,' she parroted. 'It's not as if we're going at it every day.'

A flush raced up her cheek as though she could scarcely believe her own audacity. It was more of a turn-on than he was prepared to admit.

'This can never happen again.' Determined, Kaspar cut her off. 'This *will* never happen again.'

But she was becoming emboldened.

'Really? Because it seems that the more time we spend together, the more it's inevitable.'

For a moment she actually sounded like it wasn't such a bad thing. And he wanted too much to believe her. If he stayed, he was sure that he'd wind up letting her talk him into things when he ought to know better.

'Then it seems clear to me that the only solution is to spend *less* time together.'

'You're going to stay at the hospital,' she guessed, cutting in.

'One of us has to take responsibility for this...*thing* between us.'

To his shock, she swung around, her eyes flashing with a fury he hadn't seen in her since she'd been a little kid shut out of the more daring exploits he and Robbie had egged each other onto.

'That's not taking responsibility, Kaspar. That's running away. It's not something I thought I'd ever see you do.'

* * *

It was only when the car pulled into the drive of Kaspar's oceanside home that Archie felt she could finally breathe again, let alone speak. Ever since her uncontrolled outburst the atmosphere in the car had pulsed with barely suppressed fury, but Kaspar hadn't uttered a word to her.

If he had, she feared she might have melted from their molten ire. The urge to run inside and bolt the door was almost overwhelming, but if she did that then Kaspar would leave. She didn't want him to.

So instead she folded her arms across her chest and summoned one last ounce of strength.

'Don't go, Kaspar. Not tonight.'

For a moment she thought he was going to ignore her, but then he turned his head, his eyes pinning her to the seat.

'I have to.'

'Please.' She couldn't say what passed between them, or what it meant, but she knew instinctively that he was going to stay. 'Take me for a walk along the beach?'

Carefully, with his arm under her elbow, she made her way down the hillside to the beach, slipping her sandals off and spreading her toes in the soft sand. She tilted her face towards the warm setting sun and realised that in spite of everything she wasn't unhappy, or lonely, or wishing she'd never got on that damned plane to America.

To Kaspar.

Because if she hadn't got on that plane then she wouldn't be here now, walking along the beach and realising that even if he never loved her the way she wanted him to, he would always love their child. Always fight for him or her.

'Why are you so determined to fight your feelings for me, Kaspar? Whatever they amount to. This isn't just about the risk to the baby, is it? You're scared to let go with me. Why?'

'It's for your benefit,' he bit out.

'What is it you think I need protecting from? You? In case you've forgotten, I know the other side of you. That kid who I think is more of the real you than you've ever allowed anyone else to see. A good, kind kid.'

'Then your memory isn't what you think it is,' he mocked derisively.

'It's exactly what I think it is. Why haven't you met someone before now, Kaspar? Had a family? You really will make a strong, good, supportive father.'

It took a little while for him to answer and, for several long moments, she wondered if he was ever going to answer her.

'My mother is, in polite terms, an oxygen thief,' he stated. 'She always has been. My father was no better. So what does that make me? Their son. Their blood. The lethal mix of the worst of the both of them.'

'I've said it before—you aren't like them, Kaspar.'

'You don't know what I really am like.'

'Maybe, but I don't think you do either.'

It was a silent challenge and he could either ignore her or talk to her. She knew what she wanted him to do, but she tried not to let herself get too carried away.

'I...don't *do* emotion, Archie,' he managed, at length. 'I don't connect with people. I'm not built that way. I know how destructive so-called relationships might be. How intense and violent and toxic. You say I'm not like them, but I'm still a product of them. I share their DNA and even if it wasn't about nature, I was certainly around them long enough for it to be nurture.'

'Is that why you've made a point, all these years, of never allowing yourself to get caught up with any one woman?'

'It's easier that way.'

'It's lonely,' she refuted. 'And it doesn't suit you. You're a decent guy, underneath all the playboy rubbish.'

'Did you know that as a teenager I stole a girl from under Robbie's nose? Not because I liked her or particularly wanted to date her but because Robbie did and I didn't want him ditching me to spend time to with her. That was when I realised I wasn't rounded and *normal*. I wasn't the decent human being your father tried to teach me to be. I was a product of my own parents, already on the way to becoming damaged and twisted.'

'You can't be serious.' Archie swing around to gawk at him. *'That's* what you're basing part of your argument on? *Shady Sadie?* Because I can tell you plenty of mean things my brother and I did to each other and so-called friends as we were growing up. It's called a part of being a kid. And a teenager who thinks the world revolves around them.'

'No, Archie. It's not just that. You don't want to know the things I did when I came out here. They weren't part of growing up, they were out of control. Harmful.'

His face twisted painfully but she couldn't believe it. Not of Kaspar.

'You mean after your mother dragged you out here? Ripped you away from the tiniest bit of security you'd ever had? You played up? But look at you now. You turned your back on the Hollywood scene she'd mapped out for you and instead became a skilled surgeon, a decent person. You volunteer your time to make surgical trips to war zones to help people who really need you.'

He looked frustrated, and angry, and drained. But most of all he looked torn. She'd never seen him look that way before. Her whole body ached for him.

'It's not as altruistic as you think. Did you ever stop to wonder why I went from acting to surgery? Did you think that out of nowhere I developed a driving need to take after my volatile, unpredictable plastic surgeon father?'

'Becoming a surgeon like him doesn't also make you as…unhinged as him,' she cried.

'That's where you're wrong. I'm every bit as out of control as he was. That's *exactly* why I turned my back on acting and suddenly worked to get into a good school, gain a good degree, get into med school.'

'You got into top universities, Kaspar. Not just good schools.'

'You're missing the point. I wasn't doing it because I was a good person, I did it because it was the only way I could think of to make amends for…something I did. So bad that even you couldn't make excuses for me if you knew, Archie.'

'Isn't that the definition of *good*? How long are you going to punish yourself, though?' she whispered. 'What did you do that was so bad?'

The quiet was almost oppressive.

'I fought someone, Archie. I put them in hospital because they looked at me the wrong way in a bar one night.'

Her chest stretched and ached. So that was how that story Katie had told her that night at the charity wrap party had got started. Still, she knew there had to be more to it than that.

'How old were you?'

'Old enough to know better.'

'How old?' she demanded.

'Seventeen.'

'And the other guy?'

'Twenty-five, though I didn't know that at the time. I saw them in court.'

Her stomach lifted and dropped.

'Them?'

'There was another lad.' Kaspar lifted his shoulders. 'But he was almost too drunk to walk. He'd just been swinging a piece of wood around.'

'A piece of wood in a bar? And no one did anything?'

'We were outside by then, in a back alley.'

'And all because they looked at you the wrong way? I
don't understand.'

Kaspar gritted his teeth, obviously hating every moment of the story but determined to tell her, to make her
understand why he was so *damaged*.

'We were in a bar, a bit of a dive. As they passed me,
one of them tripped over my bar stool. He pushed me off
it and told me to apologise. I refused and they suggested
taking it outside and I didn't have the sense to say no.'

'So there were two of them and one of them was wield-
ing a plank of wood. My God, Kaspar, you could have been
killed. Surely you were just defending yourself?'

'No, I wasn't drunk. They were. I could have walked
away. I should have.'

'You were seventeen,' she cried. 'It was a mistake.'

'I hospitalised the guy. They were both swinging at me
and I saw red. I made a kick—*one* kick, Archie—and I
broke his jaw. He needed reconstructive surgery.'

'God, Kaspar.' Her fingers were pressed to her mouth.

'In one stupid, drunken, angry moment I'd changed
some stranger's life.'

'It…it was one kick, Kaspar.'

'Exactly. What if I'd really lost control and not been
able to stop even there?'

For a moment she couldn't respond and then, suddenly,
it was easy.

'But you *didn't* lose control. You stopped. One kick,
unfortunately well placed but hardly premeditated or un-
provoked. What did the judge say?'

'It doesn't matter what he said. It's what I know that
counts.'

'So he said it was self-defence?' she guessed.

'The guy was wasted, he probably couldn't have hurt
me, but still the judge dismissed the case,' Kaspar said
contemptuously.

'Because even a drunken guy could get lucky if he'd, say, picked up a bar stool, or a glass ashtray, or who knows what else,' she argued. 'What did the judge say?'

He eyed her reluctantly.

'That there were too many witnesses who had told him how those men were acting up all night, were always in there, acting that way. He said *I* was the innocent party and he let me walk away scot-free.'

'Only you didn't walk away scot-free, did you? You changed your whole life because of that one incident. Your whole new career choice was based on that moment, wasn't it? Because of the surgeons who repaired that lad's face? They're who you wanted to become?'

'It was a hell of a lot better than the out-of-touch, diva-like actor that I was becoming.'

'It was self-sacrificing.'

'Hardly,' he snorted. 'I knew if I turned my back on the lucrative deal my mother had just made with a major studio, she'd never forgive me. Two birds, one stone.'

It was pointless arguing. She knew the truth and she felt sure Kaspar did, too, deep down. Instead, she reached her hand out, placing her palm on his chest, feeling the heat and thrumming of his heartbeat.

Drawing strength from it.

'You didn't just become an average doctor, Kaspar, you became one of the top surgeons in the world. A pioneer in your field. You're even more famous than some of Hollywood's best A-listers. And what's more, you save lives. Do you really believe you're still damaged? Out of control? Just like your parents?'

'It isn't what I believe, Archie,' he bit out, remorse etched into every contour of his face. 'It's what I know.'

'You're wrong.' She shook her head vigorously but she already knew Kaspar wasn't listening.

She'd lost him. Again.

CHAPTER ELEVEN

'THIRTY-TWO WEEKS.' CATHERINE, as Archie had finally come to know her, smiled as she finished up the examination. 'And you're doing really well.'

'The cerclage is okay?'

'It's fine. If anything, it appears to have lengthened the cervix and reversed the funnelling that we were seeing before. It's a great sign but it can be temporary so don't think it's a green light to start running marathons or anything.'

'So I keep limiting the physical activity.' Archie nodded. 'Got it.'

'And I understand it must be difficult, but you're keeping the sexual activity gentle and less frequent? No more than a couple of times a week?'

She nodded, but couldn't bring herself to look at Kaspar, her face feeling like it probably resembled some kid's rosy-cheeked doll. They'd both agreed it would raise fewer questions if they didn't try to explain the situation.

'Again, use protection,' Catherine continued blithely. 'More to reduce risk of infection than as contraception.'

Archie forced a laugh. The same joke as last time and just as awkward.

'So now that we're getting closer to the due date—' it felt incredible good saying that '—what can I expect?'

Catherine glanced at Kaspar as if assessing how much

he might have told the concerned mum-to-be, then continued professionally as if Archie were any other patient and not one with a renowned OMS sitting next to her.

'If your baby was born right now, barring any health troubles in the womb, it would have a very good chance of surviving and of continuing life with no long-term health problems. One of the most common concerns would be under-development of the respiratory system.'

'Which is one of the reasons we previously considered steroid injections?' Archie prompted.

'Right. However, your body seemed to have been adjusting well to the cerclage so we decided not to go ahead. I think that decision has proved correct given how good it all looks now.'

'So if I go into labour now?'

'If you go into labour now we would still try progesterone or pessaries to try to delay the birth. Every additional day the baby is in there now, he or she is gaining that all-important weight and strengthening internal systems. But as I say, birth at thirty-two weeks has a very good survival rate. Depending on the baby, he or she may spend as little as a week in NICU if feeding and breathing are going OK.'

'And if he can't?'

'If he or she can't—' Catherine's continued care not to give the gender away continued to delight Archie '—then he or she will remain in the NICU with a feeding tube and a respirator for as many weeks or even months as might be necessary. But we'll cross that bridge if and when we come to it.'

'Right.' Archie nodded, her eyes sliding across to Kaspar, who looked remarkably stiff in his chair. She couldn't stop a smile. *Expectant father* mode, not *skilled surgeon* mode. It was so very endearing. She might even say he looked…*content*.

'There's a medical charity event this weekend...' she began, as Catherine nodded in recognition.

'Kaspar's the patron, I know. You want to know if I recommend going?'

'Yes.'

'I don't see why not, depending on how you feel on the day. As long as you take it easy, aren't planning on running around madly getting ready or dancing a jive.'

'Definitely not.' Archie laughed, although maybe it was time for her to show Kaspar a flash of the old, confident Archie.

The one she'd felt returning over recent months. Thanks, ironically, to Kaspar. She'd spent so many years putting him on a pedestal and thinking, somehow, that his lack of interest in her had been because she wasn't pretty, feminine, sexy enough. Especially given Shady Sadie's maturing fifteen-year-old body compared to her thirteen-year-old one. But from that first charity wrap party when he'd homed in on her to the golf course the other day when he hadn't been able to keep from kissing her, Archie was beginning to realise that she had more allure, more dynamism, more *power* than she'd realised.

If Kaspar could resist her then perhaps it was simply because she wasn't trying hard enough to be his undoing. And that sounded like the kind of fun challenge she was more than willing to take up. Perhaps tonight she could remind him what he was missing. That she wasn't just the mother of his baby but a woman in her own right, too.

'Then I'll probably see you there,' said Catherine with a smile.

Archie adopted her most beatific smile, not willing to give Kaspar any forewarning of what was to come.

'I look forward to it.'

* * *

Leaning on the bar, an untouched tumbler of some of the most expensive brandy money could buy in hand, Kaspar leaned back against the bar and watched Archie from across the room.

It was a scene that seemed all too familiar to him. An echo of the charity wrap party that had started all of this.

Only this time, instead of having to watch her fend off a couple of admirers on the dance floor and being able to glower in peace, he was forced to pin a smile on his face as she sparkled and floated, as though she was on some kind of mission.

She charmed every single person who stopped to talk to her, particularly the men despite, or perhaps because of, her pregnancy radiance.

And all the while she made sure she was absolutely anywhere but by his side.

It was his own fault, of course. He had no idea what had happened the other day in Catherine's office but Archie had walked out a very different woman. And yet, in many ways, altogether too familiar. More confident, more vivacious, a grown-up version of the Little Ant he'd known. She'd been adamant about accompanying him to this party, and hadn't let any of his, albeit half-hearted, objections deter her.

He was letting her dictate to him. Worse, he was comfortable with it.

To a degree anyway.

Kaspar refused to accept it was because a part of him secretly wanted the world to know the truth. That he was about to become a father. That he, the feckless Surgeon Prince, was quietly content being married to the mother of his baby.

It made no sense.

Archie had even begun to tease him and galled by his constant inability to master his desire around her, he'd determined that tonight he would keep his distance. Allow her to weave her magic of the people in his social circle and the press alike, without his physical presence, which inevitably meant him placing a guarding hand on her here and there. And he knew exactly where that always led to.

Perhaps a part of him had expected her to fail, even hoped she would. Just so that he could finally have a reason to tell himself that this perfect image he'd had of Archie was flawed. That she couldn't possibly be as perfect for him as his mind—and body—seemed to want to believe, and thus she might stop invading his dreams every night. Stop making his body react in ways it had no business reacting when he saw her.

So there she was, working the room and channelling more and more the spirit and boldness he'd begun to remember. And he, for his part, was standing here staring at her like some lovesick puppy.

It would not do.

In a minute he would turn around. He would find a decent medical conversation and he would throw himself into it, as he always did.

In a minute.

The only thing tempering his immense frustration was that at least the distance afforded him the pleasure of observing, and appreciating, Archie at his leisure. And there was certainly plenty to appreciate in her stunning blue, floor-length ballgown with silver straps that hooked over silky smooth shoulders to cross over beneath her breasts and frame her burgeoning baby bump. Radiant and beautiful. And his.

But she couldn't be.

He could only bring her trouble. His parents' miserable marriage wasn't something he ever wanted to risk inflicting on any woman, but certainly not Archie. And not their child. He had spent too many years terrified, lonely, numb, before he'd met Robbie. Before the Coates family had welcomed him into their safe fold.

They could have seen him as an unwanted entanglement. Yet they had welcomed him. Because he'd wanted to be there. Because he'd craved that life, that stability. And now Archie had returned to him. The fact that she was pregnant with his baby after a one-night stand should have been the greatest unwanted complication of all. Instead, he'd welcomed her. Wanted to be with her. Craved her.

Another man had crossed the room now to greet her, her obvious state of pregnancy apparently not putting him off in the slightest as he leaned in a little too closely to whisper in Archie's ear. *As though the guy didn't care for the fact that Archie was his.* And Archie tipped back her head so that the glorious long line of her elegant neck was exposed, and laughed unashamedly.

Kaspar didn't recall moving from the bar, but suddenly he was across the room in an instant, the blood bubbling and *popping* in his veins. The man didn't even stay long enough to introduce himself, although Kaspar supposed the baring of his teeth in what wouldn't have passed for a smile might have had something to do with it.

'Shall we dance?'

'Are you intending to chase off any male who dares to talk to me, as though you're some dog peeing on a post to mark its territory?' she enquired archly.

He shrugged, unrepentant.

'If I need to.'

'I see.'

Half amusement, half chastisement. Still, Kaspar merely held out his hand. A command rather than a request.

She eyed him, a touch incredulously.

'I'm pregnant.'

'Funnily enough, I hadn't forgotten.'

'Don't be facetious.' She bit her lip. 'I have a bump. The press will photograph us. It will look silly.'

His bump. *His* baby.

'It would never look silly,' he ground out fiercely. 'Besides, isn't this why you insisted we come here tonight? Why else put yourself through this ordeal if not to show the world?'

Without waiting for her to agree, he took her hand and led her to the dance floor. People moved out of their way, one pair of curious eyes after another locking onto them, wondering if this was where he was going to make his unspoken statement to the world. Necks craning to see how his Hollywood royalty mother was taking it.

But he ignored them. No one else mattered anyway. It all simply fell away until there was nothing but the feel of Archie in his arms. At last. Her fingers curled into his, her delicate scent filling his nostrils, their baby cradled in her belly and pressed against him.

They moved together so sinuously, so harmoniously that it felt as though they were melding, just as they had done before. It felt comfortable, and good, and *right.* They danced until the meal was served, a sumptuous feast, which he couldn't remember tasting a morsel of, and some polite, inane conversation that flowed out of his head instantly. He could only remember the feel of Archie's bare skin as his hand rested on her back, or the way she leaned slightly against him, or her hand within his.

And then something changed, so quickly, so suddenly that there was no chance to pre-empt it.

Photographers were crowding in on them, their manner not quite that of the ball's official photographers and Kaspar tensed instinctively. He glanced around, but the security team seemed relaxed and comfortable, and not wanting to make a scene he forced himself to stand down.

Ordered himself not to let his imagination, or his worst fears, run riot.

Kaspar had no doubt a hundred cellphones had been capturing them all night, in order to post on the various crude forms of social media so many of the so-called charity supporters favoured. But it didn't bother him.

He only cared about Archie.

And then...

He thrust her back, gently but firmly, shock pulsing through him.

'Was that...?'

'The baby kicking,' she whispered, nodding, her eyes locked onto his as though, like him, she could barely register the other people in around them, the music, the noise.

Tentatively, he reached his arm out and then stopped. Only for Archie to take his hand and place it over her stomach. The kick bounced against him almost immediately. Hard, strong, playful.

Until this point, he'd appreciated everything in the abstract. Whatever other buttons being with Archie had pressed, the baby had always been something he'd known within context. Logically.

Suddenly, there was nothing reasoned or logical about it. Emotions coursed through him and he had absolutely no control over them. But instead of terrifying him, or worrying him, it was almost...*freeing*.

Right up until the throng crowded around them, jostling as they vied for position. Kaspar looked up and saw Archie's face turn from elation to panic. Watched helplessly as she stumbled back a step, a hair's breadth out of his reach so that he couldn't catch her.

And he lost it.

He didn't know what happened next but he had a vague recollection of trying to protect Archie, of grabbing a camera that was so close to her face she squealed and fell back, of it somehow smashing. Not what he'd intended but he didn't care right now. At some point he managed to haul Archie into the safety of his arms. The way her hands clutched at him as though she trusted him, and only him, to protect her, only heightened the wild, savage possessiveness with which he was already fighting a losing battle.

She was his. No one else's. *His.*

He had no idea how he didn't just scoop her into his arms and carry her out of the room. Probably because he knew that might have made her feel undermined and overly fragile, but, still, he recalled bundling her out of the ball and into his car. Throwing himself to the other side of the back seat just so that he didn't give in to this rushing, roaring urge to claim her as his, right there and then in the back of the car.

It was a lethal combination of anger, and fear, and that flicker of helplessness when he'd seen her stumbling and had been unable to get to her in time. Watching it all happen in sickening slow motion. Just like that night when he'd lost control in that back alley fight, doing the only thing that had come into his mind to save himself. Realising too late that if he hadn't been who he was—Kaspar Athari—the thug would probably never have bothered to have a go in the first place.

And if Archie was any other pregnant woman, would the press have crowded in on her like they had? Or was it because of him? Because she was carrying his child?

Kaspar already knew the answer. Of course he did. He should have known better than to risk Archie like this. He should have kept her well away from here.

The car ride couldn't end soon enough. He was out of the door before the vehicle had even come to a stop. Racing around, he snatched open Archie's door and, this time he didn't fight the impulse to lift her into his arms and carry her, still trembling, through the house and to her rooms. Only once he was sure she was settled and okay did he leave, stalking through the corridors until he came to his suite, hauling his clothes over his head, slamming the shower on and stepping inside.

Icy-cold water spilled over his body, biting and unforgiving. But it still couldn't assuage the fire inside him that raged so fiercely it felt as though it was devouring him from the inside out. As it had been all evening, when they'd been so close, so intimate on that dance floor, oblivious to anyone and everyone around them.

There had only been Archie. In perfect, crystal-clear, vibrant detail. Her hand folded into his, her fragile body standing side by side with him. All night. And he had beaten back every single urge to drag her off somewhere more private and haul her onto his lap. Had intended to when he finally got her home.

And then the incident with the photographers had occurred. He'd lost control. Smashed a camera, though he couldn't even remember how. It was all such a blur but it rammed home, in no uncertain terms, that Archie was much better off without him.

And still Kaspar could barely restrain himself from slamming the shower off and pounding down that corridor to Archie's room. Every fibre of his being wanted to drag her back into his arms, lower her onto that bed and drive so deep inside her than he didn't know where he ended and she began.

Pressing his hands to the travertine tiles, Kaspar forced himself to stay where he was, rooting himself to the huge porcelain shower tray. Chill water still coursed off his shoulders, down his chest, his back.

He didn't hear the click of the door but instantly he knew she was in the room. His entire body knew.

Slowly, very slowly, he lifted his head and turned.

She didn't speak but she actually braced herself. The move was almost imperceptible but for the fact that it caused the lapels of her silken nightgown to fall open, exposing the creamy valley of exposed skin and a tantalising glimpse of her breasts, which he'd been imagining kissing, tasting only a few minutes earlier.

It was more than his body could take and as though he was some kind of adolescent kid all over again, Kaspar found his body reacting in the most primitive way it could. He could turn away or he could stand there and ride it out.

His muscles spasmed and clenched as she let her eyes drop down over his body, as surely as if it were her fingers scorching a trail over his skin instead. And then the slight widening of her gaze, the way she sucked in a deep breath, the way her chest swelled that little bit more.

He tightened, so hard it was almost painful. The way only Archie seemed to be able to do to him.

'Stop pushing me away,' she whispered, the longing in her tone twisting inside him worse than any knife or scalpel could have.

'You saw what happened tonight. It's better for you if I keep my distance.'

His voice rasped, raw and unfamiliar.

'Why? Because you protected me from the kind of gutter photographers who, unlike their welcome, wanted, respectful, carefully selected press colleagues, had never been invited in the first instance? Who had snuck in for the very purpose of causing trouble; pushing me and shoving their cameras into my face and against my stomach? They acted like animals.'

'Exactly like I acted.'

'Nothing like you acted,' she exploded. 'You were defending me. Anyone could see that. I was scared and you saved me. Besides, it was nothing compared to the way the security guards rough-housed them out of there, or didn't you see that?'

'I know what happened,' he lied. All he could recall was Archie's pinched expression, the fear in her eyes. 'I smashed that guy's camera. I lost control. Just like I lost control in the alley with that kid that night.'

She looked at him like he was crazy. It almost made him want to laugh. Almost.

'Firstly, that *man* in the alley was eight years older than you and looking for trouble. Secondly, you did not break any camera.'

'I grabbed it, it smashed.'

'You took it out of my face. That's all. The photographer tried to snatch it back and some security guy punched it out of his hands and into the post behind him. So forget that one, tainted moment, and remember the rest of the evening,' she whispered. 'Remember how good it was. And don't pull away from me now.'

He wanted so much to believe her. To take what she was offering him. But he couldn't.

If he stood here, enduring the icy waterfall still on his body, then maybe he could withstand the unfamiliar sensations that zipped around his chest. Which made him... feel. And wonder. And yearn.

'I have to. Because if I don't, if we start things, I don't know if I can stop myself around you. And we have to think of the baby.'

'That's an excuse. It might be a factor, even though I've told you I feel ready, and even though you've heard what the doctor has said in every check-up I've had, but it isn't the real reason you push me away.'

'Then what is?'

'That's the part I don't know.' She bit her lip. 'I don't think even you know for sure.'

He just about managed not to flinch. Her words cut

closer to the bone than he ever could have imagined. She knew him so well. Maybe too well.

'So,' he bit out, his tongue feeling too big for his mouth, 'if we're done here, perhaps you'd care to leave me to have the rest of my shower in peace?'

The pause stretched out between them.

'Not a chance,' she eventually muttered thickly.

Before he could move, Archie had untied the satin belt and let the dressing gown slide off her shoulders and down over her bump in one easy movement. Far from detracting from the moment, the fact that she was swollen with their baby—with *his* baby—only made her all the sexier.

Still, he should stop this, stop *her*, but she was walking into the shower enclosure with the air of a woman who knew exactly what she was doing and he found it utterly mesmerising.

Worse, though, was that gleam in her eyes. As though she saw a man the rest of the world had missed. As though she saw him the way no one else ever had—a better man. And when she looked at him that way, he so desperately wanted to *be* that man.

Suddenly, she was there, and Kaspar barely had time to turn the temperature up as she closed the last bit of distance separating them. The tips of her fingers grazed over his torso so feather-light he couldn't be sure if she'd actually touched him or if it was just the movement of air, and the wickedest of smiles toyed at the corners of her ridiculously carnal mouth.

What the hell was he meant to do with this woman?

And then her lustrous eyes not leaving his for even a second, Archie dropped to her knees, curled her fingers around his sex, and licked the droplet on the tip, which had nothing to do with the water cascading over him.

He was so nearly lost it took him a moment to move.

He tried to step backwards but she was still holding onto him and, honestly, he didn't try very hard.

'Let go, Kaspar,' she murmured. 'Stop trying to control everything and let me take the reins. Just for once.'

And then she took him into her mouth, hot and libidinous. So good it might well have also been immoral. He'd had this done to him before. Many times. A perfect sexual release.

But it had never, ever felt like this. Watching Archie move over him, feeling her hands, her tongue, even the graze of her teeth on him, and also experiencing these complicated emotions swirling around his chest.

Nothing had ever felt so like...*this*.

He gave up trying to think and finally tried to do what she'd instructed. Leaning back on the tiles, because his legs suddenly felt absurdly weak, he buried his hands into her hair and allowed her to take charge.

He wanted her. *Needed* her, even. And whatever he tried to tell himself, he knew it wasn't just the sex. It wasn't just the way she sucked on his head and then slowly drew his thick, solid length deep into her mouth.

It was *her*.

He wanted everything with her. No one else could ever possibly have convinced him to give up the reins like Archie had. And yet here he was, completely at her command. And a part of him thrilled in it.

She started slowly. Deliberately. Setting an unhurried pace as though she was intent on savouring every last moment. She licked him, and sucked him, swirling her tongue over him and using her fingers to apply just the right amount of pressure exactly where he needed it.

He heard himself groan, but he was no more in command of his voice than he was of his body. Instead he was completely and utterly at Archie's mercy and, as though she understood just how much she held the power at this second, she teased him until he thought he was going to die.

And then, suddenly, he was all too shamefully close. As though he was the kind of overexcited adolescent he'd never actually been.

Wrenching himself from her touch, Kaspar ignored her cry of protestation and scooped her up into his arms even as he shut the water off with a flick of his wrist.

'I wasn't finished.'

'I nearly was,' he growled, which only seemed to elicit an exceptionally cheeky grin from Archie.

'That's why I wasn't done. So where are we going instead?'

'Where do you think?' Kaspar demanded, carrying her through to his bedroom and depositing her carefully on the enormous bed.

He'd never wanted anyone the way he wanted Archie. In some dark recess, a voice asked whether he thought he'd ever get enough of her, and alarm bells jangled so loudly there might as well have been a belfry in there.

But he refused to heed them. Instead he muffled the sound.

Still, even as he moved over the bed next to Archie, his hands cradling the beautiful swell to her body, he couldn't help checking.

'Are you sure about this?'

'I've been ready for months,' she groaned, but it was softened with a smile.

The tremble of her body almost sent him over the edge again.

Dropping his head, his lips sought hers, demanding, claiming her as if her mouth was his to take, tilting his head until the fit was perfection itself. As though he could kiss her for ever and never tire of it. Archie looped her arms around his neck, pressing her body, her bump, against him. Not too tight, just enough, as his hands caressed her belly. The fire between them was hotter than ever, threatening to burn out of control at any moment.

Ignoring the deep, heavy throb still clutching at his sex, Kaspar lavished attention on her. When he'd finished kissing her mouth, he moved to her jaw, her ear, her neck, inching his way down her body until she was arching into him and wordlessly begging him for more. When his lips finally alighted on her breast, pulling one exquisite nipple into his mouth as she gasped in pleasure, he at last allowed his hand to wander lower.

She groaned again, her voice an insubstantial whisper. 'Kaspar, I need you to...'

'To what?' he demanded mercilessly, his mouth still full of her soft flesh, his fingers tracing an intricate pattern over her hips.

'To...touch me.'

'I am touching you.' He switched his attentions to her other breast, half enjoying himself, half fighting the urge to pull her on top of him and slide inside her. Finally branding her as his.

Just like he had that first night.

'Not there,' she managed hoarsely.

'Ah.' He allowed his fingers to wander to the top of her thigh, repeating the pattern on the outer side. 'Here?'

'Kaspar,' she moaned, shifting on the bed, subconsciously parting her legs for him, drawing him in.

'Here?' he teased, moving his hand back up until it was stroking her abdomen again.

He lifted his head and she caught his gaze. But this time, instead of the needy sound that threatened to undo him, she pursed her lips into a sinful grin, her hooded eyes were loaded with wanton need.

'Perhaps *you* need a little reminder,' she murmured,

moving her own hand down to flutter over him, his body reacting instantly.

He heard the guttural sound, but it took a moment to realise it was him. Her touch was like some exquisite torture. He'd never known it was possible to ache quite like this. Too incredible to be bad yet too painful to be good.

He sought out her core. So slick, and hot, and ready. His fingers played with her, moving over her at a pace that was faster than he would have liked but he couldn't seem to stop himself, especially at Archie's soft, urgent moans. And then he didn't know who moved first, him or her, but Archie was astride him, one of his hands on her belly and one cupping a heavy, perfect breast.

'Condoms?' she muttered.

'Top drawer.' He jerked his head towards the nightstand, before adding unnecessarily, 'The pack Catherine gave you.'

As though he needed her to know he hadn't bought them for anyone else. In actual fact, he had never brought anyone else into this space.

He watched her open the foil packet, fumbling slightly with her shaking fingers, rolling it down his length with excruciating care. And then Archie was moving over him, guiding him inside as he watched her face for any sign of discomfort. When he finally, *finally* slid inside her wet heat, felt her stretching around him, gripping him tightly despite the slightly shallower depth, he wasn't sure he would last at all. Experimentally, she began to move.

'Okay?' he checked.

She nodded, tentatively increasing the pace, and it was all Kaspar could do not to move inside her the way his body longed to do. He wanted to move faster, thrust into her deeper and harder until she shattered around him. But he couldn't. Not yet. He tensed with the effort, only realising it when she stroked his jawline, a soft laugh escaping her lips.

'Relax, I'm fine.'

'Sure?'

She nodded again and Kaspar let his hands trail over her body until his thumbs were circling in the soft hair between her legs, her head slumping slightly forward, her breath coming shallow and quick. He dipped lower, playing with her even as he moved inside her, her body thrilling to his touch, tightening around him, moving faster on top of him.

He was so close. So incredibly close. Everything about Archie turned him on in a way he hadn't previously known was possible. And as they moved together in flawless harmony, the initial soft shudders of her body giving way to something far more urgent, and unrelenting, he imagined that this, here now, her, would be all he would ever need.

It was the last thought he had as she finally came apart around him. Her body arched as she surrendered to him, crying out, rocking over him and against his fingers and her hands braced against his chest as though she thought she might otherwise collapse. And just as Archie seemed to start coming down, he changed his rhythm and hurled her over the edge all over again.

This time, when she cried his name, Kaspar couldn't contain himself any longer. He tumbled off the cliff edge with her, better than leaping out of any plane. He released himself into her, and the flames roared and surged through him and he feared they could never be quenched.

Dangerous, even lethal. Yet blissful perfection.

He might have known it could never last.

CHAPTER TWELVE

ARCHIE AWOKE THE next morning to the sun streaming through the curtains, the call of early morning seabirds. And the fact that she was alone. Again.

But this time she didn't worry. Instead she stretched languorously as rarely used muscles lazily grunted their objections, and recalled an hour earlier when she'd awoken to the feel of a warm, solid body behind her.

Kaspar, pressed to her back and his hand cradling her bump. She'd snuggled back, his reaction even in sleep unmistakeable, and tried to drift back off into slumber. As much as they might want to make love again and again, they couldn't. Light and infrequent, that was what Catherine had advised.

At some point, she could just about remember him mentioning going for a run. His attempt to distract his urgent body. And now here she was finally awake, what had to be several hours later. Her ears strained for the sound of the shower or for him in the kitchen, but she heard nothing.

Then again, marathons weren't unusual for Kaspar.

Abruptly she realised what had woken her.

The low, insistent humming of her phone tumbled through the room and though there was no reason at all for the sense of foreboding that flooded through her, she nevertheless shivered under the sheets, despite the warmth of the sunlit room. At this hour, what were the chances it would be the press? Especially after last night's little scene? Kaspar had wordlessly unplugged the phone last night and turned his own cell off, but it wouldn't have taken them much to get her number. She knew what they were like.

So Archie sat, her knees hugged tightly under her chest, waiting. Only breathing again once the drumming finally fell silent.

In.

Out.

In.

Out.

Throwing off the sheets, she crossed the room to look out of the window, seeing the golden beach spread out below her like the most luxurious picnic mat in the world. The sight of Kaspar racing powerfully along the sand, the only figure on the private beach, an unexpected but welcome sight.

Her fingers pressed against the glass as her eyes drank him in, from his muscled thighs to the wide, bare, olive chest that glistened from the exertion, all sending images of last night hurtling around her feverish mind.

But then she caught sight of the expression on his face. Dark, brooding, even angry. And her stomach flip-flopped.

Slowly she backed up, across the room, so that by the time he had powered up the hillside to vault over the small balcony and to the picture-height glass doors, she was already edging to the door. As though, somehow, the distance could silence whatever words he was about to utter. Words, she already knew, she didn't want to hear.

And then he was in the room, stopping dead as he saw her. For one moment she thought she could read frustration, regret in those chocolate depths. And then they were cold, and dark, and forbidding, shutting her out as effectively as anything he could say.

'Kaspar...'

'Have you seen the papers?'

He cut across her and it was almost too much to bear, the way his tone devastated her so easily. So completely.

'How could I have?' She swallowed hard, as if it could buy her more time. 'I've only just woken up.'

'Then allow me to show you.'

His harsh voice sliced her like a hundred scalpel blades, the barely contained fury in no doubt as he stalked past her, flinging the door open and striding down the hallway with all the ire that could have parted the ocean behind them had he changed direction.

It was all Archie could do to scurry behind him, her mind racing too fast for the rest of her thoughts to catch up. Later, she would wonder how she'd had the presence of mind to grab a dressing gown as she left. Short and flimsy as it was, she had no idea at that point how grateful she would be to pull it around her near-naked form in some semblance of self-pride.

'They're emblazoned with ugly photos of the scene from last night,' he continued bitingly, as he entered the study and powered up the laptop, which still sat quietly on the side from his latest round of research. 'Headlines detailing exactly what kind of a volatile, out-of-control man I am. Screaming it for the world to know.'

'They don't know you.' Her breath came out in a whoosh as she moved, actually took a step towards him. 'I do.'

She didn't realise how foolish it was until he snatched his arm away from her outstretched fingers, his eyes darkening with a dangerous glint, the spat-out word a Persian curse that she only now recalled from her youth.

'I do not want your sympathy, Archana.'

She flinched but he barely seemed to notice.

Or perhaps he was deliberately trying to hurt her. To push her away.

'This is exactly who I told you I was; who I told you I wanted to spare our baby from seeing. But you wouldn't listen. You, in your arrogance, thought you could change me.'

'This isn't who you are,' she faltered, but he shot her down.

'This is exactly who I am. I knew it before. It was only my own ego that let me believe your naïve, rose-tinted view of me. You insisted on making us a spectacle, but I was the one who should have known better. Now they have uncovered the story from my past. And so we must both pay the penalty.'

Archie opened her mouth to speak, but then she caught sight of some of the photos he'd been talking about and her lips became too dry, her throat too cracked to form any kind of coherent words. Even if she could have, her heart was clattering in her chest so wildly that she couldn't hope to think straight, couldn't organise the words that jumbled in her head.

One thing leaped out of her more than anything else. One sad, shameful, truth. The expression in her eyes as she stared at Kaspar. The pathetic, unadulterated adoration in her expression.

He was right. She was naïve, and a fool. Nothing more than the silly little girl she'd always been. She'd fallen in love with him. It was there on her face, mocking her, just as Kaspar was mocking her. Once again, she'd fooled herself into believing he'd let her in and here he was reminding her that he never truly would. Perhaps he simply wasn't capable of it.

Kaspar could never be hers. He could never be anyone's. She was a fool for even considering for a moment that he could be.

I deserve better, she chanted desperately, as if repeating it wildly in her head would be enough to convince her. *I deserve someone who truly* loves *me*.

And one day, maybe, she might believe that.

So much for the bold, sophisticated Archie she'd tried to kid herself that she was. It was time to grow up and take responsibility. And that meant putting Kaspar Athari into her past once and for all. Or at least the idea of any relationship with him. The truth was that he was her baby's father, she could never truly escape him for the rest of her life.

It was embarrassing how much that thought gave as much comfort as it did torment.

But she didn't have to show it. Lifting her head, Archie forced herself to look him directly in the eyes, her voice conveying a breeziness she hadn't known she possessed.

'You're right.' *Where did that hint of a tight, cold smile come from?* 'I see that now. This marriage was a foolish idea and I apologise for anything I did to make you feel you had little choice but to suggest it.'

Her entire chest wrenched at the words, splitting her apart from her insides out with such force that she had no idea how she managed to stay standing, let alone talking. It was torture not to be able to read a single expression on his face, not that any expression even flickered over Kaspar's unrelenting features. The only reaction at all was the clenched jaw and steady, clear pulse. But even that told her nothing of what was running through his head.

How had she failed to realise before how little she knew him?

'It's the most logical solution.' He offered a curt nod. 'Once the baby is born, we'll get divorced. Blame it on my playboy reputation. The press will be expecting that anyway. You can return to the UK. I'll make the financial arrangements to provide for my child. Once all the furore has died down, which I'm sure won't take too long, we'll decide how I can have contact without turning your life, or our baby's, into a circus.'

She wanted to answer him but she couldn't speak. Her tongue, like her body, was going numb. She could feel herself shutting down.

'I'm going for a run,' he bit out, as if her silence was answer enough. Neither of them mentioned the fact that he'd only just returned from his last one. 'You should pack. I'll let my driver know to pick you up and take you to a hotel near the hospital. It's five-star, and you'll have my suite.'

'No...' she blurted out, but he silenced her with a brief wave of his arm.

'I'll cover the costs.'

As if that was her only objection. Still, it was enough to silence her. Clearly he thought so little of her, what was the point in trying to defend herself?

'Understood.' Her tone sounded nothing like herself.

For a start it didn't betray any of the howling pain that raged inside her.

But then she clutched the flimsy dressing gown around her and was grateful she didn't have nakedness to add to her tearing sense of vulnerability right now.

Too late, Archie realised her mistake. Her action pulled Kaspar up sharply and he raked his hand uncomfortably through his hair.

'Archie...' His voice faltered, something so unfamiliar that for a moment she didn't recognise it for what it was.

And then suddenly she did.

It was *pity*.

Pride slammed into her. He could reject her, and distance himself, that was his right and there was nothing she could do about it.

But she *could* make damned sure that, on top of everything else, he didn't pity her for her pain.

'What about the press?' she asked.

'What? Does it matter?' He blew out a deep breath. 'Fine, we'll tell them it was the safest option. Closer to hospital, and people would always be around if anything… happened while I was away at work.'

So that was it, she realised as her heart actually seemed to slump inside her drooping ribcage. He had an answer for everything, and she had no more excuses.

She had to be strong. She had a baby to consider now. A future in which someone else was counting on her to make the responsible decisions, and she couldn't ignore that fact. Especially with the way the atmosphere had changed within the room. Heavy. Strained. Foreboding. Even the sunlight getting in on the act since it didn't quite reach this part of the house, and so the shadow left her standing, quite literally, in the cold.

It took more than she could have imagined to shake off the ridiculous notion.

'You're right.' The words sounded thick, heavy, gungy. She forced herself to say them anyway. 'It's best if you go.'

'Then you agree?' he bit out, his gaze boring into her until every fibre of her being trembled under its onslaught.

No, I don't agree, a part of her wanted to scream. But what was the use in arguing?

None of this was enough for her any more. Kaspar was right. Their marriage was a pointless sham. She'd almost convinced herself that if she'd married Joe for practical reasons, then she could certainly stay married to Kaspar. For the sake of their baby. Yet deep down she'd always known it was an entirely different scenario. She'd never *craved* Joe the way she craved Kaspar. Why spend her life watching him, yearning for more, aching for something that could never be?

'I agree.' She thought the words might choke her.

She didn't know whether it was a relief or a disappoint-ment that they didn't. Then, with an offhand dip of his head, Kaspar dismissed her. And she let him. She backed out of the door and walked down the hallway on legs that had no business holding her upright.

Just like that, she'd walked out of another marriage. Or Kaspar had pushed her out. Either way, there was no doubt in her mind that *this* time there would be no getting over it.

He was doing the right thing.

Pounding down the beach, his legs burning from their fight against the soft sand, Kaspar wondered if any amount of beating his body could ever assuage this agony that ripped through his chest.

The sense of failure. Of treachery. Of absolute loss. And it was all his own doing.

The moment he'd seen that photo, the murderous look in his eyes as he'd slammed away that photographer's camera, he'd realised that as much as he might pretend to be a different man—one worthy of someone as innocent and delicate as Archie, one who deserved the way she looked at him, as though he was something special, someone good—he wasn't.

He wasn't special and he wasn't good. He wasn't at all the man she seemed to have convinced herself that he was. He was still the arrogant, out-of-control, emotionally bankrupt teenager he'd been who'd destroyed a man's life all those years ago. All for the sake of a row over an up-turned bar stool.

He should have known better that night, just as he should have known better with the photographer at the ball. The press were animals. They'd had no right to jostle Archie as they had, especially not when she was so clearly pregnant. But that didn't mean he could be equally savage and uncontrolled.

And Archie had agreed.

The whole thing only proved that he was as toxic and dangerous as his father had been.

And, for that matter, as manipulative as his mother. Hadn't he pretty much blackmailed Archie into marrying him in the first instance? What kind of a man did that? What sort of an example could that ever set for their child?

Letting her walk away from their marriage was the only honourable thing he could do right now. Set her free. It was shameful that he was having to will himself so hard to keep running. Not turn around and race back up that beach, back to the house, and tell her that she couldn't leave after all.

All the while, a voice inside him grew. A whisper at first. Kaspar could barely hear it even as he pretended not to know what it was saying. It grew in volume, more insistent, more triumphant. He thundered along the beach as though he could outrun it, but the faster he moved the louder it grew. Until, at last, it was a bellow. A roar. It stopped him in his tracks, and it made him swing back round until the only thing he could see—the only thing his eyes would look at—was his beach house, in the distance.

Or, more accurately, the house that had become a *home* ever since Archie had set foot inside. He planted his feet firmly, as though willing himself to ground himself into the sand the way a tree bedded itself into soil. Anything to stop him racing back there and charging in. Telling Archie she couldn't leave. She could never leave. And not just because she was carrying his child. For a long, self-indulgent moment he allowed himself to imagine what she might say. What she might do.

And then he wasn't indulging himself any more because he knew exactly what she would say. She would ask if he loved her. The way she'd wanted to do so many times before, whether she realised it or not. He'd seen it for the first time one morning a few weeks ago. She'd been hovering by the pool, waiting for something, although he suspected she hadn't even realised it herself. It had taken him days to figure out she'd been waiting for him to tell her that he loved her.

And he did.

Unconditionally. Irrevocably.

It was the reason he needed her to leave now. From the instant he'd discovered she was pregnant he'd known he would be there for his child the way his parents had never been there for him. He wanted to give his baby the childhood the Coates family had given to him.

But there had always been something more to it than that. There'd had to be. He would never have proposed such a marriage to any other woman. Only Archie.

Because he wanted her. He wanted *to be with* her.

And if it hadn't been for his ruinous behaviour last night, he might have told her so. Now he knew he owed it to her to let her go. Before the press tainted her with the same poisonous brush with which they were so clearly intending to paint him.

It was only what he deserved.

Just as Archie deserved better. If he really loved her, as he claimed to, then he would let her go, no matter how painful it was to him. Wasn't that what love was supposed to be about? Selfless acts for another person?

All of which ensured that him returning to the house to declare his love for her was the one thing he absolutely *couldn't* do. Kaspar snarled, but only the crashing sea and the squawking gulls bore the brunt of his frustration. And then, with what felt like a superhuman effort, he whirled around and ran, sinking furiously into the sand as though he might leave his footprints there for ever.

He had no idea how long he kept running, or how far he went. But when he finally lifted his head he was no longer on the beach, he wasn't even anywhere near the ocean, and the morning sun was on the other side of the sky as people began to emerge for their early evening revelries.

He'd been running all day. Around in circles. Just as his head was doing.

Only then did Kaspar finally turn back and head for the house which would no longer ever be a home to him.

CHAPTER THIRTEEN

FOR THREE DAYS she had stayed cooped up in the hotel room, wallowing in her misery, which wasn't easy as she wasn't a person generally accustomed to self-pity. She hadn't wallowed when her marriage to Joe had ended, or when she'd lost the baby, or even when her father had died. She'd tried to be strong, and stoic, and soldier on.

And look where that had got her.

She hadn't actually pushed through all the grief and the heartache, at all. She'd simply been sucked even deeper down into it. The more she'd struggled to pretend she was fine, the faster she'd sunk, a little like trying to fight when the quicksand already had an unbreakable hold.

So Archie had decided that maybe if she wallowed this time, gave in to the wealth of misery that swirled around her, she could exhaust all her sorrow and make it out the other side.

It wasn't working. Because the more she indulged her sadness, the more her brain started whirring again, wondering if she wasn't perhaps missing something. Second-guessing herself.

Her mobile phone rang for the umpteenth time. An unknown number every time. She'd learned not to answer it after the first few times, when the media's questions had been fired at her before she'd even finished saying hello. But this number had a Swiss code in front of it.

'Archana?'

Archie stopped, any response lodged in her throat.

'It's me,' he faltered uncertainly. 'Joe?'

'Yes.' She bit back the additional, *I know who you are.*

'I just thought I should...' He cleared his throat and she could imagine him, rigid and upright.

A neat shirt and tie under a round-necked wool jumper. She couldn't imagine why he was calling. She couldn't imagine it was to revel in her public humiliation. Of all her ex-husband's flaws, taking delight in someone else's misfortune had never been one of them.

Archie sucked in a breath, waiting for him to continue. Not wanting to reveal her confusion.

'I saw your photo in the paper. I...wanted to call and congratulate you.'

'Sorry?' The word escaped before she could stop it. A squeak of shock.

'The baby. And that you look...happy,' he continued awkwardly, clearly mistaking her response. 'In love.'

The words didn't come easily to him. They never had. But she knew him well enough to know the sentiment was genuine.

'No...' she managed, her tongue struggling to wrap itself around any form of coherent response. 'You've got it wrong.'

'Archana.' He silenced her quickly, and she could hear the rueful smile in his voice. 'Please don't do me the disservice of trying to spare my feelings, however well intentioned.'

'I—'

'You love him. That's plain to see from the photos. Had you once, ever, looked at me in that way...' He tailed off, clearing his throat again. 'Well, perhaps if I had treated you to the same...passion as Kaspar Athari does, maybe you *would* have looked at me in that way. It's clear that he loves you in a way that I never did. Or could. The way you deserve to be loved.'

Archie wasn't sure what he said after that. She heard him speaking, as far from his usual reserved manner as she thought she'd probably ever heard him, but she was too busy hurrying across the suite to retrieve her laptop, to fire it up and find those images she'd refused to look at since that morning in Kaspar's study.

By the time Joe ended the short conversation, she was sinking down on the dining chair, staring at the truth, which had been there all along—only she'd been too caught up in the puppy-dog expression on her own face to see it.

Only this time that wasn't what she saw. It was as though all the scales had dropped from her eyes, taking with them all the preconceived notions she'd been carrying around. Suddenly, she could see what Joe could see. What he'd been trying, in his typically restrained way, to say. What the rest of the world could see.

A couple so patently in love with each other that it shone out from the page.

She didn't look like a pathetic, lost puppy. She looked like a woman—an expectant mother—very much in control of her feelings. And it showed a man who, even as he dealt efficiently and necessarily with the unmistakeable threat to her well-being, never once let his hot, possessive gaze leave her. As though she was the only important thing in the room. In the entire world.

How had she failed to see it before?

It was time to go and claim her husband. The father of her unborn baby. She wanted a life with him, as a proper family. It was the reason why she'd jumped on that plane to the States those brief few months before, whether she'd realised it or not.

Archie stood with more purpose than she'd felt in a long time, striding across the expansive space to snatch up the phone and call Reception.

'It's Archana Athari, from the Princess Suite,' she began unnecessarily. 'I would like a taxi, please. To take me to me...home.'

It was done. In that instant she felt lighter, and more optimistic.

She could call Kaspar's driver, of course, but he might call Kaspar, and she didn't want to alert her husband to her change of plans.

He loved her. She knew that with a bone-deep certainty that she'd never realised existed in her before now. But she also knew that Kaspar was proud, and stubborn. He had pushed her away because he truly, incredibly, believed that her life was better without him in it. He couldn't be more wrong, which was exactly what she intended to tell him. He wouldn't want to hear it at first, but she didn't care. She could convince him, however long it took. Still, it wouldn't hurt to stack the deck in her favour as much as possible, and that included giving herself the element of surprise. If he knew she was at his house, he might suddenly decide he had more pressing matters and stay at the hospital, but if he got home to find her already there, he could hardly just walk out.

She threw everything into her suitcases with lightning speed. It wasn't really difficult since she hadn't unpacked the bags Kaspar had sent over that first day. Possibly that should tell her everything she needed to know. And then she opened the door to the hallway ready for the bellhop.

As Archie checked the room over for anything she might have forgotten, she wasn't prepared for the first contraction that gripped her with almost no warning. Neither was she prepared for her husband to walk through the door as though she'd summoned him by her very thoughts.

'Kaspar...?' She gaped, her mind struggling to work.

Thirty-five weeks? She still had a month to go. They had to be Braxton-Hicks, right?

'There are probably a million ways I could do this that would make the moment romantic, and meaningful, and everything you could want,' Kaspar plunged on, oblivious. 'But right now I can't think of a single one of them. So I'll just say it as simply and as clearly as I can. I love you, Archie. Not as the mother of my child, but for *you*. I love, and I'm in love with, you.

'I thought I was broken, and beyond repair, but you found a way to put me back together, and although I may not always show it in the right way, I promise you that I'm learning and if you give me another chance I'll ensure you never regret it. Not for the rest of time.'

The pain was spreading through her abdomen even as her heart felt as though it was sprouting wings ready to take flight. Whoever knew it was possible to feel so frightened and yet so elated all in the same moment?

'Archie...'

'I love you too, you idiot,' she managed. A combination of clenched teeth and a joyful sob. 'But do you...do you think we could do this later? Only... I think the baby is on his way.'

One day, she knew, she would remember the look of marvel on his face. She would remember this feeling that she was ready for anything, and she would remember this moment as the perfect start to the new chapter of her life.

'Of course our baby is on its way.' The smile was wide, his eyes gleaming, and a look of almost triumph was in his gaze, making her feel very powerful. 'She clearly approves of the moment and can't wait another few weeks to join us in our new future.'

EPILOGUE

SHUFFLING FORWARD ON her bottom, Archana Athari took the hook from the front of her harness and fitted her static line through the eye on the floor of the tiny light aircraft, pulling hard to ensure it was locked securely in place before Kaspar double-checked the line for her.

'Are you ready?' Kaspar called over the roar of the engines and the wind. 'Remember, aside from our one tandem jump together four years ago, you haven't jumped in a decade. And a three-year-old and a one-year-old make the most critical audiences ever.'

'I know.' She grinned at the thought of her son and daughter down on the ground, waiting for them both. 'According to your eldest, those go-carts you made them last week are ruined because you put pictures of the wrong animated films on the side.'

She had no idea whether Kasper heard her or not but it didn't matter. He understood anyway, and his lazy, sexy grin of response sent a wave of adrenalin coursing through her, just like it always did.

Sliding forward, still on her bottom, to the door of the plane, Archie stuck her feet out and leaned forward. The blur of the ground rushing by a few thousand feet below snatched her breath away. For a moment she froze.

'*Go!*' he bellowed.

And then she offered Kaspar a cheeky wink, yelling against the rushing wind, 'Race you to the bottom!'

Grasping the doorframe with one hand and the metal spar with the other, Archie pulled herself out of the aircraft, twisted and let go. Gravity took over.

Every single thought went from her head.

Spread-eagled in the air, her back arched as she fought for stability, the plane seemed to disappear in seconds, its increasing height above her the only indication that she was falling. And then the jolt of the ripcord opened her chute and reminded her of where she was and what she was supposed to be doing.

One-one-thousand.

Two-one-thousand.

Three-one-thousand.

Archie looked up and her heart slammed into her chest. The canopy hadn't fully deployed.

I probably counted too quickly. I hope I counted too quickly. What did they say about cutting away? I don't want to have to do that. I'll count again and then I'll act.

Her mouth parched and her chest hammering, Archie reached up for the guides that would help her steer for landing. And when she looked again, even before she had chance to count a second time, the parachute opened fully with an ear-splitting *crack!*

And then the complete, utter silence.

She felt weightless. Perhaps not *being in space* weightlessness, but certainly as though she was just floating down, the sky going on for ever around her.

She'd finally done it. Not just for her young son, and younger daughter—who were waiting down on the ground with a very pregnant Katie, and who had been going on about wanting to see her skydive ever since they'd seen the photo of that first tandem jump of their mummy and daddy—but also for herself and for her father.

'Here's to you, Dad,' she whispered. 'I finally got everything I ever dreamed of.'

Peace flowed through her. Her life was so very different from the last time she'd tried this and it was all thanks to Kaspar, and Darius and baby Yasmin. She felt more complete than she had ever imagined possible.

For what felt like an eternity she simply drank it in.

Without warning, a figure dropped in front of her, arms and legs outstretched to slow their fall but, without an open chute, they were still dropping considerably faster than her. He might be too far away to impede her jump but she didn't need to see his face to know who it was.

Kaspar.

And, by his thumbs-up gestures, he was clearly taking her challenge seriously. Her stomach knotted with a kind of anticipation, a thrill, then he was gone, his legs straightening back and his arms pinned to his sides as he tipped his body to dive lower.

But he knew what he was doing and Archie knew he would be safe. The adrenalin junkie at his extreme was long gone. Replaced instead by a fun-loving, proud husband and father, although still—always—her Surgeon Prince of Persia.

Archie laughed into the silence. A rich, happy sound. Then she let the wind carry her gently down to earth.

She should have known that Kaspar would beat her. By the time she'd gathered up her parachute and made her way across the field, he was already heading back with a feverishly clapping three-year-old on his shoulders and a one-year-old glued to his chest.

'Wow, Mummy.' The awestruck voice carried easily with its childish lilt. 'It was good? Yes or no?'

'Yes, baby. It was very good. But being back here with you is even better.'

And it was true. Her little family was perfect. Everything she could have ever dreamed of having.

Her past, her present and her future, all rolled into one.

* * * * *

REDEEMING
HER BROODING
SURGEON

SUE MacKAY

This book is dedicated to all those amazing people who give their time and skills to helping those less fortunate. You rock.

PROLOGUE

SCREECH. THUNK. METAL hitting concrete.

Men shouting.

'Accident!'

'Quelqu'un est blessé!'

'Aidez-moi!'

Bang!

A swinging metal chain swiped the crane it was attached to, swinging outward.

More shouts and yells.

'Cherchez le médecin!'

Kristina Morton spun around and began running towards the noise, her heavy pack bouncing on her back, aggravating damaged muscles.

'I'm a doctor,' she shouted to the security guard standing at the steel gate accessing the wharf where a freight ship was being loaded. Tapping her chest, she said, 'Doctor. Me.'

The man shook his head. *'Non.'* He pointed to another ship. *'Docteur.'*

'Oui.' Pointing in the same direction, Kristina uttered one of about five French words she knew. 'Yes, I'm a doctor joining that ship. *Doctor.*'

Rolling her shoulders back, she slid out of the straps of her pack and dug into a side pocket, handed over her wharf pass. Written in French, it did say she was a doctor. Didn't it? She hadn't taken a lot of notice when she'd received it along with other documents at the hotel reception desk where she'd stayed in central Marseilles last night.

The lock clanged open and the gate swung wide, allowing a man in fluorescent overalls to run frantically towards the *SOS Poseidon*, the *Medicine For All* charity ship Kristina had been bound for.

The guard called after him with urgency and Kristina took the opportunity to slip into the sealed-off area, her pack knocking against her good leg. It wasn't hard to see what'd happened. Seventy metres along the wharf pieces of a metal cage were spread across a wide area, and from under what looked like a side of the crate protruded a pair of legs, while the man's helmet-encased head was under the edge bar. Men were clustering around, waving their hands and yelling at each other.

'Oh, hell.' She ran faster, reached the men and dropped to her knees with a hard thump. Ignoring the pain that set off in her injured thigh, she shouted, 'I'm a doctor.' 'Doctor' sounded similar to the French version; surely they'd get the message? Too bad if they didn't, she was already observing the man crushed under the steel strops meant to hold the side of the cage together, except they'd sprung apart on impact. 'What's his name?' she asked without thinking, and got a surprise when someone replied.

'Antoine. Is he unconscious?'

'I'm not sure.' Reaching under the metal for his wrist proved impossible, it was too far in, so she pressed a finger on his carotid. 'Antoine, can you hear me?' Damn. He wouldn't understand her. 'Can you talk to him, see if he's responsive?' she asked the man who spoke English, before focusing on the pulse rate. Normal. So far so good, but still a long way to go.

She couldn't understand what he said to Antoine but

she recognised the flickering eyelids. The helmet had done its job. A quick appraisal showed blood seeping through Antoine's trousers from his groin where a metal shaft had lodged. Her heart stuttered as the memory of a similar injury swamped her. Automatically her hand went to her thigh and rubbed down the ridge of scar tissue.

'I told him you're a doctor. I'll get some men to lift this.' The man now squatting next to her knocked the cage.

'Get them ready, but don't move it yet. Antoine's bleeding. Removing the pressure could cause a haemorrhage.' Bleeding out wasn't an option on her watch. Not again. The guilt at not being able to prevent Corporal Higgs dying had not dissipated so much that this didn't unnerve her. Not that she'd been in any position to help the soldier, being disabled herself, but doctors were meant to save people, no matter what. 'I need something to make a wad to press over the bleeding.'

Moments later Kristina was handed a small bundle of shirt pieces folded into squares, while another man was tearing his shirt into strips to tie the wads in place. She wouldn't think about the hygiene aspect, containing the bleeding was the priority.

'Thank you. *Merci*.' The odd angle of Antoine's left leg indicated a fracture above the knee. 'Be careful, don't hit this when you take the grill away.' She pointed to the rod.

'It's attached. It'll pull out.'

She hadn't noticed that. Now she'd prefer the man unconscious. He needed morphine, fast. 'Can you send someone to the *Poseidon* and get a doctor to bring drugs for pain and some oxygen?'

The man looked along the wharf. 'Someone's coming. He's got a bag and a small tank. Is that what you want?'

'I hope so.'

The man was there in an instant, barely puffing despite

his sprint. 'I'm a doctor.' He hunkered down on the opposite side of Antoine's legs.

'Me, too,' Kristina told him. 'I was headed for the *Poseidon* when this happened. Kristina Morton.' She held her hand out.

His hand gripped hers briefly, firm *and* electric.

Shock ripped through Kristina. Rubbing her arm, she stared at him. What just happened? He'd sent fire through her veins with a handshake? Unreal. She was supposed to be focused on a man in distress, not this one with the most intriguing face she'd ever encountered.

A startled look was reflected in the dark depths of his eyes, too. Had he felt that spark? 'Chase Barrington, SARCO.'

Shock of another kind rocked her. This was Chase? The man who caused his family heartache on a regular basis? No one had told her he was hot! 'I met your sister when I was a locum at Merrywood Medical Centre. I finished a fortnight ago.' His brother-in-law, Jarrod, was one of the partners there.

'Libby told me.' He gave her a sharp look. 'Bring me up to speed.' Chase was taking charge.

Typical. She'd worked with enough male doctors in masculine environments to know the signs. 'There's a rod intruding into Antoine's groin that's attached to the grill. I'm hoping you've got morphine in your pack.'

'Yes, and compression pads.' Chase nudged the kit with his foot, and focused on the man needing his attention.

Leaving Kristina to get her breath back and stop feeling flustered by Doc Barrington's touch. She could tell him to get the pads himself, but time was of the essence, not her pride. Finding the morphine, she read the date out loud, gave the vial to her counterpart to cross-reference before drawing up a dose. Once administered, she opened packs of compression pads, ready for the grill to be lifted away.

SUE MACKAY 11

Chase was methodically checking for further injuries on Antoine's body without jarring the grill. No wasted movements, his lean body muscular without being heavy. Picture perfect. So not good for her pulse. Deep breath, concentrate—on Antoine, not the SARCO. But he was so distracting. She closed her eyes, opened them and watched.

Without stopping those long fingers moving over Antoine, he told her, 'Ribs staved in, fractured femur and arm, blood loss from where the humerus protrudes, and I don't like the look of his mouth. It's possible he's bitten his tongue.' He was good, and thorough. Impressive in more ways than that magnificent body.

She nodded. 'Let's do this. The sooner we can get to him the better.' It was hard not to glance at Chase for another take on those muscles shaping his loose T-shirt but she managed. Looking behind to the men waiting to help, she said, 'On the count of three lift the grill—very slowly.'

The moment their patient was free she was pressing a pad onto the wound in his groin. 'The femoral artery's torn. Is there a catheter in your kit I can put in to keep the blood flow in the artery?'

'Unfortunately not.' Chase was gently removing the man's helmet in preparation for putting a facemask on Antoine for the oxygen. 'I haven't got a neck brace either.'

Kristina continued working on the haemorrhaging, making do with what was on hand, but the sooner help arrived in the form of a well-equipped ambulance the better. 'Has anyone called the emergency services?'

'Oui,' replied a man hovering in the background.

Like magic, the sound of a siren filled the air.

Kristina didn't relax. Antoine wasn't out of trouble by a long way.

A quick glance showed Chase working as hard, diagnosing all the injuries while keeping an eye on the man's breathing. There was a determined look on his face that said, I am not letting you die, Antoine. Something they had in common.

But anything else? She doubted it. The little she'd heard from Libby and Jarrod indicated she and Chase were like north and south. She was looking for a place to settle down and feel as though she belonged, a place where she wouldn't be thrown aside at anyone's behest, while this man apparently did not have the time or inclination for stopping still. He was driven. Not that she'd been told by what.

The ambulance squealed to a halt beside them. Instantly paramedics were moving in, asking questions in rapid French she didn't understand. Continuing monitoring their man, she left Chase to answer them.

'How's that bleeding?' he asked her moments later. 'Still bad?'

'Yes.' She nodded around the relief that getting Antoine to hospital fast was now happening, as long as the paramedics didn't take too long preparing him for the trip there.

'We've done all we can. The paramedics are taking charge,' Chase said, his hands clenched on his thighs, his jaw tight, and his eyes fixed on the two men as they put a cardboard splint on the broken leg and a brace around their patient's neck. He wanted to remain in control, was itching to continue working on Antoine.

Kristina knew that feeling but moved back, knowing she would not be thanked for doing anything else. The paramedics knew what they were doing, and were used to working without the luxury of all the equipment an emergency department came with, but couldn't they get a hurry along? Glancing at Chase again, the same thought was reflected in his steady green gaze.

When Antoine was finally loaded into the ambulance, relief loosened the tension gripping Kristina and she was free to walk away, if only her feet would move. Staring across the now quiet wharf, her gaze fell on the ship she'd be working on for the next three months, sharing the space with a man who had her hormones in a lather already. She'd be toast by the end of her time on board.

It had been Jarrod who'd suggested she do a spell with *Medicine For All*, instead of taking on the locum job in the far north of Scotland she'd been half-heartedly considering.

Watching men and women walking up the gangway laden with heavy packs for the start of the next three-week stint, tiredness enveloped her. She was weary of constantly moving from place to place, locum position to locum position, and not having somewhere of her own to return to after each contract finished. MFA was merely another diversion. It was harder this time because she'd finally found what she'd been looking for.

The quaint town of Merrywood and its friendly folk had sucked her in, made her welcome and comfortable in a way she hadn't known since she was ten and her family had imploded, leaving her bewildered and alone. She'd wanted to stay on, continue working at the medical centre and buy a cottage on the riverbank, only there was no job once the doctor she'd been covering for returned. However, Jarrod had told her to stay in touch and drop in when her time with MFA was up as he might know of a position for her. She planned on doing exactly that, fingers crossed and expectations high.

'Time to go aboard and meet everyone.' Chase stood beside her, legs tense, his eyes constantly on the move.

'I'm looking forward to this.' The organisation did amazing work with refugees and other people in need of medical attention in horrific parts of the world, and to be a part of it was awesome. And in case Jarrod didn't come up with the goods, she'd have time to research small towns and medical centres in the south of England in the hope of finding that same enticing family-orientated atmosphere she'd found in Merrywood.

Why did she look to the man beside her? He wasn't the answer to her need to settle down. From what she'd heard, Chase Barrington could no more stop in one place than he could knit a blanket for a baby.

'What made you decide to give *Medicine For All* a go?' Chase asked as they walked out of the secure area.

'I'm getting tired of locum work. I start to feel settled and then have to pack up and leave again. Jarrod suggested MFA and how I might fit in. Once I started delving into the organisation I knew I had to give it a go and contacted Liam.' The director had been effusive when she'd volunteered. Though again she'd be moving on afterwards.

Fit in. Chase studied the slender woman before him. Get under his skin, more like. His brother-in-law had been chuckling when he'd told Chase how Kristina Morton was perfect for the summer operation in the Mediterranean. Yes, he'd known who'd put her up to signing up and until now had had no problem with it. All doctors were welcome any time. But now Chase had to question what fates had put *this* doctor on *this* mission. 'You want to get away from GP work?'

Her laughter was soft and sweet, and stirred him. Not that he wanted to be stirred by a beautiful woman. Or any woman. He'd put her where he put any female who managed to tweak his interest—out of his mind.

'Not at all.' Her shrug was tight. 'It's just that I would like something permanent, somewhere to get to know people beyond their headaches and high blood pressures.'

Good. The complete opposite from him. 'You like ships? Being at sea, getting tossed around in storms?'

Another shrug. 'Wouldn't have a clue, but I'm about to find out.'

There was more to this. For someone who wanted permanence she seemed to move around as much as he did. Not that he was about to ask her about it. That spoke of being interested and getting involved. Not his thing. 'Liam's a great advocate for our organisation. Without him we wouldn't get half the volunteers that sign up.' If not for Liam, who knew where *he'd* be working right now? For all he knew, it could've been in Africa, Asia, New Guinea, anywhere there were lives that needed to be saved. That was his mission in life. Not that he'd ever make up for the loss of his best friend, Nick, but he would keep trying. One day the guilt might run out. Might.

'I didn't stand a chance once he started in on me,' the woman matching his strides admitted. Then her eyes went a bit sad.

He wasn't asking about that either. They'd reached the security gate. 'Yours?' He nodded at a pack and roll mat the guard held out.

'Thanks.' She stretched for them.

'I'll take those.' Chase reached out at the same time. His fingers skimmed across hers before wrapping around a shoulder strap on the pack. A jolt of heat caught at him. Spinning sideways, he swung the pack over one shoulder and hooked the mat under his arm then headed for the ship, ignoring Kristina and the inferno in his blood. That was the second time he'd felt the heat around her.

Unfortunately she kept up with him. 'I don't expect you to carry my gear.'

Chase stopped as quickly as he'd taken off. 'I'm not trying to show you up as incapable. I'm exercising the manners I was taught as a lad.' If not in the polite way his father expected.

'It's just…' She hesitated, seemed to be thinking how to say whatever was bothering her. 'I'm ex-army. No one ever carries your pack there.'

He'd read in her CV about Kristina being ex-military. And the evidence was in front of him in her upright, controlled deportment—and apparently in her determination to carry her own pack. Because she'd heated his blood and stirred him with her soft laugh, he was going to rock her boat. 'You're not in the army now. I'll carry these to the ship.'

'Fine.' Her mouth drifted up into a lazy smile, stirring him tighter. He should've walked right past the blasted gear and its owner. It was as though she was poking him with sharp pins to wake him up from a long, deep sleep. But he wasn't asleep and as far as he could tell Kristina hadn't come armed with anything sharp, except maybe her tongue.

Chase pulled on his co-ordinator's hat; only way to go. 'I saw in your CV that you've worked in quite a few different medical jobs.'

The smile slipped away slowly, painfully. The light that had begun shining in her eyes faded. 'I have.'

Again, there was more to this than the simplicity the words suggested. If she wasn't saying anything else it had to be that something had happened to affect her badly. He'd respect that, because he understood too well about keeping fears close, and pain closer. Suddenly he wanted her smile to return. 'On board we tend to treat one another kindly, no ordering anyone to do anything.'

Her nod was abrupt. 'Good.'

Try again. 'The refugees are going to love that calm manner you showed with Antoine.'

'That's me. Calm throughout a crisis, a bit rocky afterwards.'

'No one would know that from helping Antoine.' There. A subtle lifting of those lips he'd have missed if he hadn't been watching for it. His heart lightened. Then her perfume wafted across his nose and he pictured pine cones on the fire at home. Pine and roses. Yes, the strange mix that was home was this woman's scent. A scent he was not going to get out of his senses in a hurry. They'd just met, and she'd found a way to get under his skin already.

It didn't bode well for his sanity when they'd be crammed together for weeks with all the other medical staff in the small spaces that were the ship's medical facilities. They'd probably end up hating the sight of each other. It happened. There was little privacy, no space to think without being interrupted. Having no alone time did a number on everyone, especially on those used to their own company; like himself. Something about how Kristina held herself, self-contained, suggested she'd fit into that group.

Chase began striding towards the ship again. 'I think most people have arrived.' He automatically scanned the people at the gangway. And tripped. Ethan Reid stood at the bottom of the gangway, looking directly at him.

Chase's heart began a low thump, thump. So much of who he'd become was tied up in that man. And Nick.

The past charged at him in waves, winding him, curdling his stomach, raising the fear of not being able to save those he loved, bringing ice and snow pushing away the warm summer air, suffocating him. Death. Not his. Nick's. The crippling guilt.

I can't do this.

Yes, he could. He had no choice. He'd been the one to put out the feelers, asking Ethan to step up to the promise he'd made way back then. *If ever you need me, call.*

Right now Chase rued that phone call, even though it had been about helping others. But it was done. He needed to start moving forward, towards Ethan, the man he had saved instead of Nick, and the hideous past they needed to dispel, or at least subdue so they could work together. Would they be able to talk about what had happened that fateful day in the Alps? About why certain people had survived when others hadn't? Why Nick had died, and Ethan had survived? Why he'd had to make that choice about who to save even when there really was no choice? Turning his back on Nick as the last breaths left his body had haunted him ever since, and made him go over it again and again looking for a way to change the outcome.

'Chase? Are you all right?' Kristina's question seemed to come from miles away. Her hand gripped his arm, shaking him, soft and endearing in her touch.

'Yes,' he lied, stunned at how easily she saw past his barriers, how she was there with him. No one did that. No one. He shrugged free of her hand, his eyes firmly locked on Reid. *Don't think* you're *getting the chance either.* His past rose higher, flared, threatening to overwhelm him. Bile soured his tongue. 'I've got to talk to that man.' It was that or charge past him to shut himself away in his cabin and not come out for six weeks. *Six weeks.* Why had he made that blasted phone call?

Ethan was walking towards him like they did this every day, but as he got closer Chase saw the tight lines around his mouth, the rigidness in his shoulders. Chase's heart was still drumming that slow, heavy rhythm as he nudged his feet forward. 'I'd have known you anywhere.' Even after sixteen years.

'Same.' Ethan did the unexpected. He embraced Chase, tight, strong, hard.

Tears sprang to Chase's eyes. He refused to let them out. Refused. And won, by a scratch. Stepping back, he stared at the other man who'd haunted him for so long. Thump, thump, in his chest. This was relief over finally meeting up. It was time. Not that he had any expectations of this being an easy ride. No, the coming weeks were going to test patience and forgiveness on both their parts.

'I'll take my gear,' came the voice of female reason from behind him.

He barely noticed Kristina lifting the weight from his shoulder, although as she began walking away and he was watching Ethan, she slipped into his mind, sitting on the edge, like she was not going to be easy to ignore. Right now that was about the only thing he was certain of.

Hell, Nick, what have I done?

CHAPTER ONE

Six weeks later

'KRIS, GOT A MINUTE? I'd like you to look at my patient.'

Kristina Morton ignored the man, even when his voice was like fingers picking at keys on a piano. Only that morning everyone had returned on board from a three-day break, and she'd missed him way too much for someone she wasn't involved with.

'Kris, over here,' Chase called again, a little less friendly and a lot louder.

She continued walking through the overcrowded cabin towards the steps leading out on deck. About once a week he used the abridged version of her name, winding her up something awful. He hadn't a clue to the depth of anger and hurt being called Kris caused her—neither was he about to.

'Kristina, your attention now.'

Kristina's back straightened, her chin jutted forward and her arm began lifting in a salute. *Stop. You're not in the army now.* Being the person in charge of personnel on this ship didn't give Chase the right to shout at her. Or shorten her name. But, she sighed, he had finally used the name she answered to. Slowly turning, she asked calmly, 'Which patient do you want me to see?'

Determination radiated out of eyes that reminded her

of an English forest on a damp day. Chase wasn't used to being ignored. Everyone complied with his requests no questions asked, but then they weren't usually delivered as abruptly. So it was *her* that got his boxers in a twist. Good. Because he certainly kept her panties in a knot. Those sparks she'd experienced on day one of this adventure hadn't died down one bit. Instead, they'd got brighter, sharper, hotter during the weeks of working together. Neither of them had made a move to explore where that raw attraction might lead. She did her best not to be alone with Chase, and suspected he did the same, but the relentless ache was getting to her, and she spoke more abruptly than she'd intended. 'Is it the pregnant lady needing help?'

'Sorry I yelled,' he growled around a wary smile. 'You didn't seem to be hearing me.'

'Really?' She tipped her head sideways, locked her gaze with his and tried to deny the surge of longing those eyes brought on. Another six weeks of working alongside him. Keep this up and she'd either dislike him intensely or have gone raving mad with desire by the time she left the ship for good. Somehow she doubted dislike would make it onto the ladder.

Chase blinked and his face relaxed some more. 'Yes, that lady. She won't let me near. No doubt because I'm male.'

'You know that's not uncommon.' The pregnant women who arrived on the ship via the rescue efforts weren't used to men pressing their bellies and listening to their unborn babies through stethoscopes.

'I keep hoping for a different outcome.' Chase smiled ruefully. She knew he ached for these people like she did. 'This woman doesn't speak English.'

'I'll find Zala and ask her to explain what we're doing and if it's all right to continue.'

Chase's chin lifted a notch. 'Zala?'

Kristina smiled to herself. Chase wasn't the only one who got onside with the refugees effortlessly. He just thought he was. 'She arrived yesterday. I overheard her asking for water in English.' Not that it had been easy to understand her mangled pronunciation, but when she'd handed the girl a bottle of water she'd received the most beautiful smile imaginable and a garbled thank you. 'I don't know how much she understands but any is better than none.'

'Agreed. Bring her in and see if we get any further with our patient.'

Kristina gasped. Why hadn't her senses warned her Chase had moved closer? Suddenly her body was getting up to speed with the fact that this man was too near, sharing the same air as her. Damn the attraction for those arms and legs, for the flat stomach and strong jawline nailing her feet to the floor. She'd spent six long weeks trying to kill off the annoying magnetism Chase's body had for her. Her mind had it worked out—he was not a man to get close to. He was self-contained in every aspect, appeared to work every hour day and night, was on a life mission to save people no matter where that took him—or so the gossip went. Gossip that fitted with what Libby had told her. She couldn't risk falling for someone who couldn't settle down in a place for more than one Christmas in a row. Because, while she wasn't any better, she was at least working on it.

Time to try some other tactic for moving past the unusual longing to get to know this man who dominated her mind so much. He was all wrong for her, as she was for him. He didn't have time for anyone who wasn't a patient in need of his extraordinary medical skills, so she had to stop thinking about him in any role other than the director from whom she took orders. *Instructions, not orders.* Whichever.

Dreaming about his body and what she'd like to do

with it didn't change the fact she had no room for people who didn't have time for her. There'd been enough already, starting with her parents. Adding someone else to the list was a recipe for disaster, especially when she had an uneasy feeling that she could get a weeny bit too intrigued by Chase.

Out on deck Kristina made her way through the hordes of people waiting patiently in the shade provided by tarpaulins strung from bulkheads to railings to be seen by the medical staff. Her heart ached for them and made her grateful she could help with their untreated deep-tissue injuries, burns from fuel, malnourishment, infections. Thank goodness Claire had left the ship. Her pregnancy made her vulnerable to illnesses she wasn't prepared for. Now, there was someone whose life had changed since coming on board the ship. Claire had found love and a wonderful future to look forward to with Ethan.

Kristina shoved aside her envy and focused on reality. 'Zala,' she called.

'Hello?' The girl glanced at her from under lowered eyebrows.

'How are you?' She spoke slowly in order to be understood.

'All right.'

'Good. You had food?'

'Yes.'

Kristina again looked around at the people sprawled on the hard deck, hunger, fear, worry in every pair of eyes watching her. If only she could fix everything for all of them. Back to Zala. 'Can you help me talk to a woman who needs a doctor to examine…? To look at her baby.'

'I…' Zala tapped her chest. 'I say what you say my way?'

'Yes.' Kristina nodded. 'I'll keep it simple.'

'I don't know what you mean.'

'That's all right.' She reached for the girl's hand, hesitated. Touching didn't always mean the same thing to people from the Sudan as it did to Westerners. Retracting her hand, she said, 'Come with me.'

Back in the treatment room, persistent Chase had returned to his pregnant patient, holding out a water bottle and talking softly, even though not a word was being understood. Around here it was all about the tone of voice and not the words. 'I think we're in labour,' he told Kristina.

'How do you know?'

'The way her body stiffens every three minutes.'

Yea, she got her first smile of the morning. He should do that more often, it lightened the green of his eyes to that of a summer's day in the fields. And set her heart dancing. Damn.

'She's not going to want you here.' Kristina focused on the woman, avoiding getting tangled up in Chase's searching looks and that blood-warming smile. 'Do we know of any problems that could make delivery difficult?'

The woman caught her breath and pushed around the tightening in her extended belly.

'Minor fever. Exhaustion that's probably due to the pregnancy.'

'Fingers crossed the baby hasn't been infected with anything.' Kristina indicated to Zala to move closer. 'This woman's having a baby.'

Zala nodded as if to say, So what? Seeing a birth was probably part of everyday life for her. There'd be no racing off to a hospital or calling out the midwife where she came from.

'I'm clearing all male staff to the other side of the room,' Chase said. 'Call me if you need anything.'

'I don't think I've got much of a role here either,' she said, before turning to the woman Zala said was called Marjali. Light stretch marks on the skin covering the extended abdomen confirmed this was not her first pregnancy. 'She'll know what to do as much as I do.' *More than I do.*

Sweat shone on the woman's forehead as she pushed and groaned. Zala sat at her other side and chattered in short, sharp sentences before telling Kristina, 'Four babies. Two alive. On boat with her and father.'

'Are they all right?' What had happened to the other children? Kristina's heart squeezed. She'd never get used to the despair these people faced daily. There were times she felt so inadequate she wondered if it would be better to leave them to what they were used to and not offer promises through medicine. But she hadn't become a doctor only to turn her back on anyone needing her skills.

When her twelve weeks with *Medicine For All* were up she'd head back to England. She wouldn't do another stint on the ship. It was too distressing. Many of the medical people who worked in the organisation coped well with—or managed to hide—their emotions. She struggled to do either.

A sharp cry brought Kristina back to the marvel that lay before her. The baby's head was crowning while Zala chattered, excitement filling her dark eyes.

Kristina smiled as she watched the baby inching its way into the world. What was it like to give birth? To have a baby of your own? To hold him or her in your arms for the first time? She never gave much thought to it, afraid she wasn't capable of being a good mother. Her own mother had taken her to Los Angeles when she'd left her father, but had been quick to hand her back when the new man in her life said he'd marry her as long as *Kris* wasn't part of the package.

The man's wealth spoke strongly to her mother's life-long fear of ever being poor again, and Kristina had been returned to England and her other parent, who'd immediately deposited her in boarding school because he'd been too busy to be there for her.

A sharp cry from Marjali and a tiny new life with the cutest face and a smattering of tight curls was delivered with one final push.

'Oh, he's beautiful.' Kristina's eyes moistened as she cut the cord and took the baby to check his temperature and general appearance before placing him on the scales attached to the nearby wall. Back home, with a weight of two kilograms, he'd have been admitted to the neonatal unit. Here all they could do was get nutrients into him so he might put on a gram or two before leaving. It could've been worse given the circumstances. Laying baby across his mother's tummy, she said, 'You made it look easy.'

Zala looked perplexed. 'Women have babies. It's normal.'

'You're right.' Again she wondered about the odds of having her own baby. Strange how she was thinking about this. She hadn't found a man to love her no matter what, let alone have a baby with, a man who wouldn't leave her to fend for herself while he went off to follow his own dreams. That should be enough to knock her attraction to Chase out of the paddock. Since joining this ship she'd seen him playing with some of the youngsters who came on board, laughing with them, chasing a football and making sure each kid had a turn at scoring a goal. He understood them, enjoyed them, so why not want a family?

Crossing to a cupboard for cloths to clean Marjali, she passed Chase. 'All done. One new little man has arrived in the world.'

'That was fast. Does the baby appear healthy? In as much as you can tell without doing tests?'

'A bit underweight.'

'We'll keep an eye on him while he's with us.' That was Chase-speak for making sure there were extra rations for

Marjali over the coming days. What happened after she left the ship was out of their hands. Their job was to deal with these people for the time they were in their care, and then move on to the next intake.

'Life's so complex, yet Marjali makes this seem simple,' she sighed, watching the woman cradling her son. Zala sat cross-legged, still talking non-stop, reaching out to touch the tiny bundle pushing into his mother's breast, not knowing what to do when he found a nipple. But his mother did. Soon he was suckling. Whether he was getting anything nutritious was unlikely given Marjali's malnourished condition.

'Very unlucky for some,' Chase said. Then looked directly at her, stealing her breath. 'Sorry if that sounds simplistic.'

'A lot of how our lives turn out comes down to where we are born, doesn't it?' There were the wild cards that life dealt when a person wasn't looking but luck did contribute to how and where he or she sorted out those problems.

'You think?' His eyes sparkled and his mouth lifted into a weary smile.

'I do.' She smiled back, enjoying the connection without her hormones doing their dance. Then her back gave a stab of pain, and she tightened up, held still.

'Hey, you okay?' His instant concern could undo her resolve not to give in to the attraction between them. 'You seem to be hurting more than usual.'

He noticed that pain struck her sometimes? 'I'm good. An injury I received in the army is playing up, that's all.' She gasped. She never, ever mentioned that, not even lightheartedly.

His concern deepened. 'Are you serious? Is that why you got out?'

She shook her head, wanting to deny the truth. But she couldn't lie. 'I took an honourable discharge. My back acquired a dislike to humping around overweight packs and war gear.' She'd tried for light and friendly, thought she'd succeeded until she saw something in Chase's steady gaze that said he wasn't fooled. Something that drew her to tell him, 'I took a severe wound to my thigh and twisted my back. It's taking time but I'm coming right.' She turned towards her patient, needing to shut down this conversation.

Chase said softly, 'Glad to hear that, Kris.'

Her eyes closed and her head dipped. 'Kristina.'

He chuckled. 'Kristina.'

'You…' she spluttered as she turned back to him. 'You're deliberately winding me up.' She laughed, for real this time.

'Worth it to see your eyes widen as though I'd swiped one of your chocolate biscuits when you weren't looking.'

Which he had a penchant for.

As Kristina absorbed Chase's presence, her feet once again glued to the floor, the sparks that had flickered on and off between them since they'd met over Antoine suddenly became a raging fire in her veins. Worse, Chase was recognising her reaction.

Definitely time to put any dumb ideas about letting this attraction rule her head into the recycle bin. The only way to do that was to front up and explain she wasn't interested. In other words, lie her heart out. Tonight she'd do something about it, despite Chase never acknowledging the magnetism hovering between them. There were moments when he looked at her as though he wanted her. That was when her body really hummed; and her mind argued with it. Tonight she would not go to her bunk the moment she'd eaten dinner to get some sleep before the next draining shift began. No, she'd face up to Chase and deal with this annoying interference that crossed her day too often, sending her into an uncontrollable tailspin.

* * *

'Hey, Reid, how's things?' Chase settled his butt against the bulkhead of his private corner and stared out to sea, the phone hard against his ear.

'I'm good. You?'

Chase let out a long, satisfying breath. 'Another day almost done; more people helped, saved, fixed.' The relief was immense. He could rest easy—until the next day got under way. Ethan would understand where he was coming from. 'Not sure you're aware you left your tablet on board. I can send it out on the helicopter and have them courier it to you.'

'Keep it there till I come back. I don't need it for the next couple of weeks. Claire doesn't leave me time for reading.' Ethan chuckled.

'Glad to hear she's keeping you on your toes.' Chase grinned, and couldn't deny the envy sweeping through him. 'You decided where you're going to look for work after you finish with us?'

'I've been talking to the local refugee centre. If there's a vacancy coming up in Marseille then I want my name on it.' Ethan filled him in on what he'd been doing since he and Claire had left *SOS Poseidon*.

Chase listened avidly, enjoying the camaraderie— something he hadn't known since he'd withdrawn from getting close to people after the loss of Nick. He was still hesitant about letting loose and talking about anything and everything, but every day over the past six weeks when Ethan had worked on board they'd inched closer and the tension had eased somewhat. He still wasn't ready to let go the guilt about not saving Nick. And until he did that Reid would never get close.

For a span of time, standing here in his own small zone, letting Reid in, he could almost accept he'd made up for the past, could almost believe he deserved a chance at a future. Almost. Until he hit the pillow and the memories came knocking, and Nick appeared in his head. Then he'd have to get out of bed to start over.

'Anyone special in your life?' Ethan asked. When Chase growled, he added sadly, 'Just learning about you. You know?'

Yeah, he knew. There was so much between them, and yet even more they hadn't a clue about. 'The answer to that should be obvious. There's no one for a very good reason.' Chase ignored the flare of pain. And the image of Kristina Morton that flashed into his mind. *She* might be as sexy as anything, but there was something about her that said don't touch unless you're serious. He was serious about having sex with her, but nothing more.

'So you're not interested in Kristina?'

Silence. He couldn't lie. Neither would he give Reid ammunition to give him a hard time.

Ethan sighed. 'She makes you laugh when no one else does. As for the sparks between the two of you, they had me looking for the fire extinguisher.'

Again Chase ignored him. Those comments were too close for comfort. If this was what having a friend was like, he didn't need one. Except over the previous six weeks he had begun to look forward to moments talking with Ethan. 'Nothing's going to come of those sparks. I'm all work and no play.' He already had parents and a sister who loved him and who he couldn't risk letting down—like he believed he had Nick even knowing he couldn't have changed a thing. The guilt did that to him. This getting a little friendlier with Reid didn't mean he was capable of allowing a woman close.

The breeze moved around him, fanning his face. 'Got to go. Talk to you again.'

Kristina slipped up beside him. Apparently she had no qualms about intruding into his private spot out here.

From the first trip of the summer it had got around that this particular corner was his, and no one encroached. No one until tonight. Sure, he'd rung Ethan, and been relaxed about talking to him here, because it had been his choice. But… 'Kristina?'

The breeze also held that scent of pine and flowers. That sweet and spicy aroma went with her all over the ship. Sometimes it followed him into sleep at night. Those were the times he woke restless and in need of a cold shower.

Why did she invade his privacy like she had a right to? Funny how he couldn't find it in him to care. Instead, he felt unusually happy she'd joined him, a feeling he couldn't explain, neither was he about to try. It didn't mean he was letting her close. He hadn't lost all his faculties. They might've locked eyes over breakfast, sending the temperature in the room off the scale, but he'd had to deny the need boiling in his gut. Had to. How they'd walked away from each other was a mystery. *So send her away before it happened again.*

'Please, don't call me Kris.'

'Kristina. Got it.' That morning he'd kept crossing paths with her as they'd gone about their patients, and the tension in his body had wound tighter and tighter. Calling her Kris had been a deliberate wind-up. He'd thought she'd be angry, but instead she'd made him laugh.

'Good.'

'Other people must shorten your name.' There had to be a reason *Kris* upset her. She wasn't the type to be precious about her name. She carried herself with confidence and the upright stance common to military personnel. That poise kept everyone on their toes, including him, until one day on the last trip he'd seen a wealth of pain glittering in her eyes as they'd watched a child being buried at sea. Her tiny heart had given up within hours of coming on board—lack of food, too much sun, and who knew what else had taken the ultimate toll. It had been personally painful for him. Failing to save that girl despite doing everything possible and then some to bring her back to life had pained him.

He hadn't asked Kristina what was behind her agony. Things like that were too private to share. Hell, he was still getting used to the idea of him and Reid talking about the avalanche that had altered their lives for ever, and how Ethan had said they both had to learn to let go and move on. As if it was that easy. *It could be.* Oh, sure.

Leaning her elbows on the rail, Kristina stared out over the moonlit Mediterranean and breathed deeply, saying nothing.

A female who didn't talk the lid off a pot? Nothing like Libby, then. His sister never knew when to stop gabbing at him about why he should stop wandering the world and return home to be near the family. Chase sighed. He came out here for solitude while he went through his day and gave himself a pat on the back if he'd saved anyone. But right now he craved to hear Kristina's voice, couldn't bear this silence between them. He went with something innocuous. 'So you and Libby got on okay?'

'She makes the best blueberry muffins ever.' Kristina's head bobbed, and hair fell across her cheek. It was rare for her to let it free from the severe ponytail that was her signature style. Army style?

Many times over the past weeks he'd itched to flick the thick rope that fell down her back, pull away the band holding it in place to run his fingers through the golden waves. Shoving his fists deep into his pockets, he trawled his mind for something safe to say. 'What did you think of Merrywood?'

Kristina turned so the small of her back rested against the rail and a soft chuckle winded him with its warmth. 'I loved it. Everyone was so friendly and welcoming, I wanted to stay on.' Her fingers intertwined across her belly, tightening his gut further.

So much for playing safe. 'It can become claustrophobic, though. Especially when you're a teenager and don't want your parents finding out you've been smoking down by the river with your pals.'

There was a wistfulness in her eyes as she said, 'Surely that's part of belonging somewhere?'

Yep, and it tied a person to everyone so that when things went wrong they all were affected. Chase watched her hands making slow circular movements over her abdomen. Was she aware she did that whenever she went all thoughtful?

This time the urge to make her talk, to break down her barriers didn't bat him around the ears. Instead he relaxed, leaned against the rail, and went with being beside her, trying to accept this was as intimate as they should get. He had nothing to offer her other than a quick romp in the sack and they weren't doing that. He didn't trust this *thing* gripping him to let him go afterwards.

But Kristina was unlike any other woman who'd pressed his buttons. *She* pressed them hard. Could that be the reason for his restlessness? He wasn't in the market for a partner. Not when he had to be finding more people to save, trying to redeem himself for Nick. How many more lives would it take to be free of the guilt?

Chase pushed the past aside, took a deep breath. The air was soft and warm, not cooling as the sun dropped below the horizon. Summer warmed his skin and his soul. There'd been a year when he'd followed summer around the world, working in countries where snow and ice were alien, because he'd known how snow could destroy a person and he would never put himself in that position again.

But it hadn't been enough so he'd enrolled in med school to learn in earnest how to save people. London winters

were cold but his heart had coped, had borne the pain that
came with memories of a colder, icier, crueller place he'd
never returned to. Not once. Never would. He couldn't. It
wasn't in him to go there and bury the ghosts. They would
never let him get away a second time. Except these past
weeks, spending time with Reid, tentatively touching on
what had happened, he'd begun looking at things in a different light. Would it be possible to put it all behind him
one day?

Kristina's soft voice snagged him. 'I was called Kris in
the army. When I wasn't sir or captain.' A tightness had
crept into her tone.

'You let them?'

'Regardless of what the recruitment officers say, the
military is still a masculine world. To fit in I was Kris. But
I've objected to being called it since I was ten.'

'Am I allowed to ask why?'

'No big deal,' she answered in a harsh tone, suggesting
it was. 'When my parents split up, my mother took me to
LA with her where she met a man she was very keen on.
When he proposed he told her in no uncertain terms that
Kris was not part of the deal. The way he called me Kris
was derogatory. I loathed it.'

Chase leaned closer, breathed deeply of her scent. He'd
never call her Kris again. Not even as a tease. 'Did your
mother tell him where to go?'

'No. I returned to England soon after.'

'To live with your father?'

'Dad was working twenty-four, seven trying to recoup
the fortune he'd lost. I was sent to boarding school.'

'Geez.' She hadn't known the loving family environment he'd grown up with, had taken for granted, and now
struggled not to put in danger by being near them. Lightly
dropping his arm over her shoulders, Chase tucked her
close. 'That's lousy.' A damned sight worse. His parents

had stood by him through the days and years following the avalanche and still did. There'd been times they'd been so near he'd not been able to breathe, but he wouldn't have swapped that for what Kristina had missed out on. Yes, he was incredibly lucky to have such a loving, caring family.

'Yeah, it was.'

He daren't delve deeper, afraid she might sprint away, regret telling him in the first place. He didn't want her leaving his side, not until the tension in her stance softened and a smile returned to her eyes.

The silence returned, comfortable in an intimate way. Another first for him. The more he learned about this strong woman the more he wanted to know. Things like why she'd joined the army in the first place. Had she needed to belong to something, somewhere, to replace the lack of having a loving family around her? 'Were you ever deployed overseas?' He hadn't been going to ask any more questions so his words surprised him.

'I served in Brunei, where there are jungle warfare courses going on all the time.'

'I can't imagine being a soldier, charging around learning to kill people.' He shuddered. 'Not when my whole focus is on saving them.' Hell, she had *him* talking, wanting to tell her what made him tick. This was his time out, yet Kristina had sauntered into his space and *he* started gabbing on like he'd been on a desert island for months.

'It's not quite like that. I was a medic first and foremost. But sometimes I found myself questioning why I was there.'

'I'd be hopeless. Can't take orders from anyone.' Not since the day his skiing coach had dropped the ball when he'd been needed most. Coach Wheeler had phoned parents, tried to keep him from returning into the wrecked chalet, but he hadn't rushed in to help pull Nick free.

She turned under his arm and smiled up at him. 'Now, there's a surprise.'

He laughed, a belly-deep reaction that spread throughout his psyche. 'I know. Pig-headed is another term for the way I get things done.' Studying the sea, he asked, 'Do you miss the military life?'

'Not at all.' Her smile switched off. 'It wasn't what I wanted after all.' A little shiver and, 'See you in the morning.' Then she was gone, striding across the deck in that sharp, exact way of hers, heading for the hub of what went on day after day. Her leg left pulled a fraction higher on the upward movement. He'd noticed weeks ago how some days were worse than others, and how she sometimes winced or rubbed her lower back when she thought no one was looking. She wasn't one to complain or talk about her aches and pains.

She was back, a light smile on her face that heartened him. 'By the way, you'd make a lousy commanding officer.' Straightening, she mimicked him. 'Kristina, your attention—now.' This time she did leave him, flipping her hand over her shoulder on the way.

She left him chuckling yet bereft of company when he'd never before wanted anyone sharing this precious hour away from the cries and arguments and chatter that filled the ship twenty-four seven. Sometimes his head would be splitting apart with everyone's pain, his own grief and guilt working its way into the centre of it all, reminding him why he was there, and stressing that he'd never be able to escape to a normal life back in England close to his family. He had to continue moving, keep finding more people to save. Working for MFA did that by bringing him and those people together. Day after day, week after week. There was no end to it. And not likely to be for the rest of his life. Which suited him perfectly.

Except Kristina didn't recognise his barriers, or ignored

them, relentlessly chipping away, making him feel a little happier with life. Hell, he'd put his arm around her to give her warmth and support. Something more than her beauty, her confidence, her quietness, her heat-provoking body got to him—come on, it was a combination of all those.

Yeah, but there was an indefinable something else he couldn't put his finger on. When she'd told him about her name he'd known instantly she didn't talk about that to anyone, yet she'd told him. Not to shut him up, or at least not to let him think it was on a whim, but because she'd wanted him to understand there were heartfelt reasons behind her need to be called Kristina. She'd even told him those. Information he didn't want because it made him care. From now on he was done talking to her about anything deep. He had to be or he was doomed.

Chase tried to connect the dots between the doctor and her role as a soldier. Though the circumstances were poles apart, the requirements for patience and tolerance would be the same, yet he couldn't quite imagine Kristina issuing orders. Around here other medics did her bidding without question, her manner friendly and relaxed while underscored with determination, but a military officer would have to be sharp and firm. Bet she filled out the uniform perfectly.

Hell, he was in need of some diversion. Last time he'd got like this a nurse had spent a night with him on their three-day leave from the ship. Eight months ago, at the end of last summer. That was the last time he'd had sex? So it wasn't sleep he needed, was it?

CHAPTER TWO

SO MUCH FOR confronting Chase about the frustrating attraction going on between them. Kristina stared at the bunk above her. Damn, but she was tired, kept awake by the shock that she'd wanted to take a risk and throw herself at him as they'd stood in the quiet of his corner. That she'd so nearly thrown aside her protective barriers and plastered herself against that sexy body, known every last inch of him, felt him take her deep. So, so close.

How could that happen when she'd gone to tell him they had to get past whatever it was between them? She hadn't gone to make it worse, stronger, *real*.

Because Chase had got her talking about herself. That was almost sexy, being something she didn't do. Like laying herself out naked in front of him, telling him personal stuff was as intimate. At least she hadn't mentioned her guilt, how a man had died on her watch. That would've been a passion killer—exactly what she'd gone to him to do. Damn, but her head space was a mess.

She'd nearly thrown herself at him. But it was all right. She hadn't. Somehow she'd managed to step away, with a smile even. But she had turned back, fighting the need to leave and the greater need to stay. To risk everything. It was that risk that had caught up with her at the last moment and made her come out with the nonsense about him not making a good officer.

If only she hadn't. Glad she had. How had she done it? When her feet had been aimed in his direction, her blood thickening with desire, her fingers tense with the need to touch his skin? Guess looking out for herself was so ingrained it worked regardless of where her body wanted to go.

Kristina swallowed her confusion and rolled off the bottom bunk to stand hunched over, biting her bottom lip as pain jarred her back.

'You all right?' Jane, her cabin mate, asked from above.

'These bunks must've been designed by a sadist.' Knuckling her lower back, she began the ritual of straightening up, slowly easing tension from the muscles, not giving in to their stabbing protests. Then her left thigh got in on the act, shooting pain up into her butt.

'I wouldn't know. When my head hits the pillow I'm gone.'

Kristina's laugh was tight. 'I heard.' There'd been a lot of snoring going on during the night.

A pair of legs swung over the side of the bunk and Jane sat up, rubbing her eyes. 'What's with your back anyway? I often see you pummelling it.'

She gave her usual answer, not the one she'd told Chase. *Gave too much away there.* 'I haven't been doing the yoga exercises that keep me nimble.' No time or unpopulated space for those.

'Borrow Chase's bolthole when he's not around.'

Right, and be on guard in case he turned up? That would negate the purpose of yoga. He went there at some point every night. The plan was to turn Chase back into a man she could talk to about everyday things, not the deep or ugly, then walk away without a backward glance. Not a man to get hot and edgy around. 'There's little room for stretching.'

'That's a shame.'

No, it was a relief. 'Isn't it?' Getting into Downward Facing Dog with Chase watching would have her heart going ballistic. And who knew what the sight of her backside poking skywards would do for him? He might be disgusted, but she doubted it. The physical friction between them that she'd done nothing to stop screamed attraction, intense and exciting and getting stronger; the mental not so much. He liked to be in control of everything around him, probably had to be since he was SARCO.

Would he be like that in bed? His guard had dropped while they'd talked last night. That hour had been comfortable in a way she'd not known with any man. As though the friction had been on hold, allowing room for getting to know each other on a different level. He'd been understanding about why she didn't want to be called Kris, and she'd swear he'd nearly laughed when she'd taken the mickey out of him over calling her to attention.

There was more to the man than she'd discovered so far. Lots more, and what she wouldn't do to learn it all. Perhaps she should've gone the other way last night and dragged him along to his cabin and put these feelings to rest in the only way possible.

Oh, no, you don't. House and job in the burbs, remember?

Jane's feet hit the floor with a thud. 'I need a long, hot shower, then I'm going to try for some more sleep.' All she'd get was short, wet and cool in the shower box.

'Me, too, for the shower.' Kristina tugged clean underwear and a white T-shirt with the MFA logo and shorts from her pack. The simple dress code was a bonus. Dressing for the locum role wasn't so bad, but as for the army uniform, she never wanted to see another, let alone wear one. That'd taken her desire to fit in and belong to a whole new level. She hadn't belonged, she'd been submerged.

The knee-length shorts she shook out hid the scar running down her thigh to avoid the questions that'd invariably come when someone got an eyeful. Explaining that being thrown through the air by a bomb blast to land on a steel girder that had rendered her incapacitated wasn't happening. Not when it had meant she'd been unable to save Corporal Higgs from bleeding out, though it was unlikely he'd have survived anyway. She'd cried with frustration and despair until medics back at HQ had administered drugs that had taken her under. Unfortunately the drugs hadn't conquered her guilt.

A training exercise had gone hideously wrong that day, changing her for ever, altering the direction she'd been taking in an attempt to find the equivalent of family. The military wasn't it. People within the units were close, caring, and always had each other's backs, but something had been missing, something she'd spent most of her life looking for. Boarding school hadn't been able to make up for the loving family environment she'd known for the first decade of her life, neither had med school. Now she knew better, had grown up some, and understood she had to be comfortable in her own skin before anyone could share her life. She'd touched on that at Merrywood, enough to start believing it was possible.

Jane appeared in her misty line of vision. 'The showers are empty at the moment. Just saying, you know?'

'Thanks.'

When she arrived at breakfast, Chase was the only person there. 'Hey, where is everyone?' she asked.

'It's not six yet.'

Then they'd have a few minutes to themselves. That filled her with warmth when she should be taking her breakfast out onto the deck—alone. With a plate of scrambled eggs and toast cook had just put up, Kristina strolled across to sit at a table with him instead, unable to resist spending a few minutes alone with him. 'Have you done a round of our patients yet?'

'I've seen the earache boy this morning. Dad slept the night on the floor beside him and was very amenable towards me, all thanks to you, I reckon.'

The father of a young boy had been having trouble letting anyone near his son, mainly because he'd been exhausted and struggling to cope with where he was. 'Guess I got lucky.' She wouldn't mind getting lucky with this man. *Thought I was supposed to get over him.* 'Or the father was tiring and needed someone to indicate what to do next.'

'You don't accept compliments easily, do you?'

She shrugged. 'Wasn't aware of it.'

'I'll have to give you some more.' He laughed. He was doing that a lot lately around her.

More warmth flowed over her skin. How was she supposed to walk away from this? Forking food into her mouth, she tried to make sense of what was happening to her. The eggs were dry and the toast soft. But her mind was on high alert. So she was admitting she felt something for Chase? Chew, swallow. Try some more, wash it down with tea. She couldn't feel anything for Chase. Mustn't. Wanted to.

Chase asked, 'What did you do in Barcelona, by the way? I hardly ever saw you at our hotel.'

Like he'd been hanging around, joining in with everyone. And she'd been looking. 'It was Barcelona.' She gave a strangled laugh. 'Shopping, tapas, shopping, wine. I was with Collette and Rani, and they made my shopping attempts look pathetic.' At the end of the three days the two nurses had come back to the ship laden with bags. 'I also took a day trip to the Pyrenees, driving through stunning countryside along the way. It was all a bit rushed so I'd like to go there again for longer.' It had taken her away from the city and stopped her incessant scanning for this man.

'Spain's spectacular. I spent time there before I started my training. Surfing, jet-skiing, diving. All good fun.'

So he hadn't always been focused on nothing but patients and helping people. 'Time off before the real world took over.'

His hand tightened around his fork, and his face took on a strained look. 'Something like that.'

Wanting his smile back, she leaned over and stole a piece of his bacon. 'You emptied the dish, you've got to share.'

'Hey, first in and all that.' The strain disappeared.

Feeling so much happier, she stabbed another piece on his plate, held it at her mouth as she said, 'Pierre can't have cooked much if you got the last of it.'

'Keep this up and I'll hardly taste bacon.'

'Now you come to mention it.' She held her fork over his plate again.

Chase whipped his breakfast out of reach. 'I don't think so.'

'You want tea?' She rose from the table. 'Or coffee?'

'Coffee. Milk and one.' Then he glinted at her through eyes that seemed to see right inside her. 'Sugar, not salt.'

'Spoilsport.' She put the salt shaker back on the counter, and spooned sugar into a mug. 'Wonder how high the temperature's going to reach today. Yesterday was a scorcher.' A dollop of ice would help right now, tipped down the front of her T-shirt. Her body was steaming, all because of Chase, sitting there looking hot and yummy.

'The forecast's saying low thirties.' Chase looked happy. Not an ice man, then? 'I like the heat,' he added before she could ask.

Placing his coffee on the table, she sipped her tea and studied him, in particular those muscles shaping the front of his loose T-shirt. Those dark curls falling all over his head needed shaping, too—with her fingers. She gripped her mug with both hands. Lowered her gaze to the light stubble darkening his chin. Tightened her grip further. Rubbing her palm over his face would really quieten the thrumming of her blood. 'Just as well considering the countries MFA takes you to.'

'I guess.' He was watching her. What did he see? Not the guilt, the pain, the need to be settled, please. Try happy, fun, lovable.

'Seems you two were up early.' Calvin strolled into the room. 'Pierre, can we have some more eggs and bacon out here?' he called through the hatch into the galley. 'These two haven't left anything.'

Kristina felt her smile shifting, away from Chase and into a general one. Their brief moment alone together was over for the day.

'I've scheduled you with me this morning,' Chase told her. 'There're a number of patients with fuel burns that require debridement. There's one young man whose injuries are particularly disturbing.' He placed his mug back on the table and turned it round and round between his fingers, his gaze now fixed on the depths of milky coffee, his meal forgotten.

She nudged him, ignored the force of heat where her elbow contacted his arm. 'Eat up. You've got a full day to get through.'

'You're right.' Picking up his fork, he took a mouthful of egg and swallowed it without chewing.

'Food is a tool to keep going, no matter what's thrown at us.' The eggs weren't wonderful. Not even a heavy dousing of salt helped, and probably only aggravated their BPs. 'What time's the first patient scheduled?'

'As soon as we're done here.' There he went again, tilting his mouth into that fascinating smile. As though he'd shoved away whatever was bothering him and wanted to continue enjoying this break between patients and more patients without worrying about how to help them.

'Why me and not Abdul?'

'You're saying you don't want to help me?' A tightness entered his voice and turned his face into a scowl.

'Chase.' She tapped the back of his hand. No heat this time. 'That's not what I asked. But think about it. I'm a GP. Abdul might be insulted if I do his work.'

The tightness backed off, the scowl smoothed into a small smile. 'He's catching up on sleep after a long night doing minor ops. The last boatload we picked up came with a list of minor surgeries as long as my leg.'

Her gaze immediately dropped to his long, muscular legs with their tanned skin. She drank in the sight. *Get over yourself. They're legs. Everyone has them.* Yeah, but— She gulped her tea.

This was ridiculous. Chase's focus was firmly on helping those less fortunate, not on her. He was a man about whom no one on board had any grizzles. A regular guy doing extraordinary things to make life more comfortable for others. This attraction must've come from spending so much time in confined quarters surrounded by too many people. Like in the army when soldiers were jam-packed into bunkers for endless hours, watching for the enemy. Those times had always tested her patience. This growing need to get intimate with the most breathtakingly good-looking man she'd ever known would evaporate as soon as her contract was over—in a little over five weeks. An eternity.

What would it be like to leave the ship with him and go home? She wasn't going to know. She didn't have a place to call home, and when she did Chase would still be trotting around the globe.

How could her mind wander when Chase was still talking? But she'd been thinking about him, not the medical arena he was discussing. Time to focus on the practical, not the impossible. 'Right, I'll get ready for surgery.'

Surely the attraction vibes would shut up in the medical room where concentration on the operation and the patient was paramount?

Her hormones didn't get that message, sending heat zipping around her veins as she stood in the medical corner where they were working, listening to Chase explain which wounds they were to debride and which to leave.

'I'm concerned about infection, and working on every little wound will make him very vulnerable to bacteria.' Those strong hands described in fluid movements what they'd soon be doing to their patients. What would they feel like on her breasts? 'The larger wounds are going to be trouble enough.'

'Will you send him off with plenty of antibiotics and painkillers?' Chase dressed in blue, baggy cotton scrubs did nothing to quieten the excitement going on over her skin, in her moist places.

'Enough to get him through this crisis.'

In the meantime they'd do their best to counteract infection while the man was with them. She reached for the gloves and winced as her back protested. Definitely time to find somewhere to do a few stretches. Not on the open deck at the front when Chase could appear at any moment she was in her zen zone.

Chase peered at her. 'Back bothering you?'

About to die of embarrassment if he'd read her mind, she snapped, 'Just a twinge.' It was better when he hadn't noticed. Until Chase had asked yesterday she'd never men-

tioned her injuries to anyone on board, not even when filling in her application to work for MFA. So she'd fudged
the truth, but it wasn't as though it caused problems for
others, such as covering her shifts. Besides, the injuries
were improving, though slower than she would have liked.

'Right, we'll get started.' The shoulder he turned in her
direction wasn't cold, neither was it warm and friendly.

She'd let him down by not sharing. 'I'm okay, truly.'

He glanced across. 'I have some massage experience
if that'd help.' Then he straightened, shock registering in
his face. 'I mean…'

Chase lost for words? It would've been funny if she
wasn't feeling equally flustered. 'It's fine.' She shoved
her hand into a glove with such force it split. 'I'll do some
yoga later.'

'Here.' Chase held out the box of gloves. 'The offer
stands if you change your mind.' He'd obviously got a grip
on himself faster than she had.

'Thanks,' she muttered, turning to the table where their
man lay, mouth open, snoring softly. Thank goodness for
patients. Kristina picked up a scalpel and began cutting
away the infected skin around a large wound on the right
leg.

'Yoga, eh?' There he went again. Grinning like she
amused him.

'Don't laugh until you've tried it,' she retorted through
a smile.

Nearly an hour later Kristina stood back from the table.
'He is going hurt when he wakes up.'

'Morphine will help for a while, followed by strong
painkillers. Hopefully those wounds will be healing before he leaves us.' Chase dropped the scalpel he'd used
into a metal dish. The clatter was sharp in the stuffy room.

The next patient was wheeled across and they were away again.

'The air-conditioning gone on the blink?' Kristina wondered aloud as they finished debriding their fourth patient. Over the last thirty minutes the room had become hot enough to keep a mug of tea warm.

'Seems like it.' Chase snapped off his gloves and tossed them in the direction of the hazardous waste bin. 'Anyone for a quick coffee on the outer deck before lunch?'

'Definitely,' the anaesthetist said.

'Not me. I'll check how the vaccinations are going.' It'd take all day and half the night to get all one hundred and something people inoculated. Chase would have it covered, but she had to get away from him, breathe clear air into her lungs and not the kind that was tainted with Chase scent. Male, sharp, sometimes abrasive, sometimes seductive. Definitely mind-blowing. And disruptive.

'See you at lunch,' Chase grumped.

'Maybe,' she gave back.

In the end, Kristina decided to avoid Chase and took some sandwiches back to her cabin where she squashed her yoga mat in the narrow gap between the bunk and the wall. Sitting with her legs crossed at the ankles and her hands on her knees, she tried not to bang her elbows and closed her eyes to begin clearing her mind of everything. Taking slow breaths deep into her belly, holding, relaxing, gradually the tension in her aching muscles let go, and she was able move freely. She began a workout of simple positions, allowing her mind to drift and her body to mend.

Placing her hands on the floor and pushing her butt upward, keeping her legs straight, Kristina hung her head between her arms. So relaxing, so freeing. When no one was staring at her butt, that was, and in here she could be sure of that.

Chase Barrington strolled through her head like he had every right to be there.

Forget relaxed. Her body became a temple to tension. Every last muscle tightened. Dropping to her knees, she stared at the mat under her hands. Damn him. Why couldn't he leave her alone for once? All the good work had come undone in a flash. There wasn't time for any more. She should've been in the clinic ten minutes ago. Hauling herself upright, she dumped the mat on her bunk and headed out the door. At least her back and thigh felt better.

The same couldn't be said for her head space. Chase had settled in, and wasn't taking a blind bit of notice of her need for a clear mind.

He also had ideas about her next job. 'Kristina, could you examine Marjali? Zala says there's blood between her legs.'

Back up to speed, she answered, 'Hopefully it's normal post-partum bleeding. Zala mightn't know about that.' Slipping on gloves, she looked around. 'I'll talk to them, see if I am allowed to do an examination.'

'You will be.' Chase sounded so certain she turned to stare at him.

'There's no guarantee. We're the strangers in this situation.'

The shade of Chase's eyes lightened to summer and the corners of his mouth lifted. 'I wouldn't place a bet on this. I'd hate to take advantage of you.'

His belief in her ability to get along with a woman who lived such a different life startled her. It also lightened her heart, made her feel good. 'I promise not to deliberately skew the outcome of my discussion with Marjali just to prove you wrong.'

Wow. When Chase put a bit of effort into it his smile could light up the world. It certainly brightened hers, and she forgave him for crowding her head space. But she left him before she got carried away with this feeling of wonder and said or did something they'd both regret.

'Zala, help me pull these curtains around Marjali, will you?'

Zala grabbed a handful of curtain to tug along the metal rail. 'Is this right?'

'Yes. Now I have questions for you to ask Marjali.' Kristina drew a breath as she thought about how to word them in a way Zala would understand clearly to translate, and how Marjali would understand her intentions. 'Tell her I need to look at where the blood is coming from.'

'It's where the baby was,' Zala looked at her as though she was stupid.

'You are right, but sometimes after a baby there can be too much. Do you understand?' She had to or this wasn't going any further.

Zala gave an abrupt nod before talking to the other woman in a low, urgent voice, pointing at Kristina and then at the top of Marjali's legs.

Marjali regarded Kristina with a surprising intensity, her almost black eyes drilling right into her. Finally she nodded.

'You can look,' Zala informed her with satisfaction. 'I told her you are nice.'

Blink, blink. Really? Lifting her arms, she made to hug Zala, hesitated. Again she wasn't sure if it was acceptable. 'Thank you.'

Zala leaned in and put her hand on Kristina's wrist. 'It is good, yes?'

'Yes, it's good. Please tell Marjali everything I say.' Explaining in simple terms what she was doing, Kristina quickly found the source of bleeding. A tear had occurred since the birth. 'I am going to give her an injection.' Then she'd stitch the tear.

'Injection?'

'A needle to stop it hurting.'

Collecting the suture kit and drawing up a small dose of local painkiller, Kristina returned to the bed. Zala's explanation had gone down well. Within a short time everything was done and Marjali was sitting up.

'Slowly,' Kristina warned. 'What have you been doing since baby was born?'

'She's been carrying buckets of water to the men.'

'She's not to do that. That's why she was bleeding. There are other people to lift the buckets.' If any of the medics had seen Marjali hauling water around they'd have intervened, not that they'd necessarily be taken notice of. 'Tell her it's important to rest.' There might've been previous babies, but the woman wasn't in top health.

'I tell her.'

'What was Marjali's problem?' Chase asked as Kristina dumped her gloves, the used syringe and cotton pads in the waste.

'She's been hauling water containers around the deck when I thought she was resting with her baby.'

'Not any more she's not,' Chase growled. 'I'll talk to the man overseeing this group.'

'Maybe don't use Zala to translate that one. It might be seen as a female stepping into the men's shoes.'

'Good point.' Chase touched her lightly on the shoulder. A gesture that made her heart squeeze.

How could she close down these feelings for him? They were growing into more than attraction, more than the need to just have sex with him. But making love would be a great start.

Kristina put her plate in the dishwasher. 'That's it. I'll go and see Marjali and the baby then head to my bunk,' she said to the room in general. It was after nine. Dinner had been quiet, everyone lost in their own exhaustion.

'You're not going topside, then?' Jane asked quietly.

'No need. I did a few yoga moves in our cabin earlier.'

'I wasn't thinking about yoga.' The woman had the cheek to wink.

Jane knew she'd been up there with Chase last night? Why was she surprised? The gossip mill spun well in the confined places crowded with people having nothing better to occupy their minds. Everyone required a diversion from their work at one time or another. If only it wasn't her. 'I'll be in our cabin.'

Marjali was asleep, her baby swathed in a cotton sheet in a crib beside her. Reluctant to disturb either of them, Kristina stood watching over them for a few minutes. Such an unimaginable place to be, and yet the woman had had a baby and was getting on with being a mother. Not that she had any choice, Kristina sighed. At least *she* did. Starting with finding her next job—preferably in another Merrywood, if not the real deal. The more she thought about the quaint town the more she wanted to be a part of it. Merrywood had firmly lodged in her heart.

Stepping outside into fresh air and the light breeze that had come up, she wandered around the crowded space. The noise was continuous and blocked her thinking. The idea of retreating to the stuffy cabin no longer appealed. Which left only one place that might be quiet, cool and empty. Except for one person, and he knew how to be silent without creating a strain on her.

'I wondered if you'd come,' Chase said as she slipped in beside him and propped her elbows on the railing, making sure there was a gap between them.

Touching him was not an option. It wouldn't shut down the lure of his body. 'I needed some quiet time.'

'Then I won't ask what you're thinking about,' he said around one of those devastating smiles she'd started looking out for, and seemed to find more and more often.

'Work, as in where to next,' she told him, because he was far too easy to talk to.

'You want to return home.'

'Yes.' They weren't meant to be talking. Even if it was what she needed after all. He'd send her away. He'd started it, though.

'Pity.' He moved sideways a little, away from her, leaving her feeling she'd made a blunder. 'You're just what we need around here.'

As SARCO Chase gave more than most. Not everyone could be expected to do the same. 'If one percent of the medical profession gave six or twelve weeks out of their careers to work for *Medicine For All* there'd be an over-supply of staff.'

'Unfortunately it doesn't work like that,' Chase answered. 'What are you looking for this time?'

'I'd prefer a permanent position in a small town medical centre. But it's not as easy as I'd hoped,' she sighed. 'Merrywood spoiled me for choice. All the staff were welcoming and friendly. It was the same with the townsfolk.' Going to the pub for a drink on a Saturday had been relaxing and enjoyable, with people coming up to talk to her like she was a local. Now all she had to do was find something similar to make permanent and she was home and settled.

What about the love interest she'd started longing for? A man to come home to at the end of the day to share a drink and meal with while talking about what they'd done was a dream that slotted into the picture of family she'd waited for since her real family had fallen apart. The hazy memories of being hugged after school, taken out for a walk with the dog, being helped with her homework never quite disappeared, and always tugged at her, filled her with longing for another chance at that life.

Kristina's eyes moved sideways, towards Chase. Damn but he was gorgeous. Dragging her gaze forward again, she stared at the waters below. Dark and dangerous. Her gaze returned to the man beside her. His head was tipped slightly back and his eyes were closed. His hands lightly held the railing and his legs were splayed to counteract the rolling of the ship on the low swell. Dark and dangerous? Maybe. Intriguing and exciting, for sure. Was this what she wanted in a man?

CHAPTER THREE

'REID, I'M CHECKING you're joining us aboard the *Poseidon* for the three weeks.' The man was busy with planning a wedding and finding a house to buy, Chase allowed.

'I gave you my word.' The underlying note in Ethan's tone told him that when he promised something he didn't go back on it.

'Sorry,' Chase admitted. He'd said that a lot lately. Ethan and Kristina had a knack of making him say things without thinking them through first. 'It's not you I'm worried about. People are pulling out of contracts and others getting ill so the roster I worked out before summer has gone to pieces.'

'Afraid I can't do more time or Claire will hang me out to rot. Though I'm really over choosing between lace or satin. And that's for the place settings at the wedding party we're having later on.'

Chase relaxed and laughed. 'I like it that Claire can wind you up.' His laughter died. He'd never have that. There was no one to blame but himself. He'd chosen the solitary road.

Yet lately there'd been occasions, especially since he and Ethan had begun burying the hatchet, when he'd give anything to forget the past and move on to something exciting and loving that could span his whole future. A relationship, a marriage with rock-solid foundations, so that there were kids and a home to be proud of and go back to at the end of every day.

Kristina came to mind. He shoved her away. First he had to stop holding onto his guilt over having to let Nick die alone. It had taken a crane to lift the beam from Nick's chest the day after the avalanche had struck. While in Chase's head he knew what that meant, in his heart he couldn't quite reconcile himself with the truth. What would happen if he did relax on the guilt? Would the sky fall in? *Nick? Would you think I'd deserted you again?*

Ethan was muttering something.

Chase refocused. 'What did you say?'

'Being with Claire's taking some getting used to.' Ethan laughed. 'But I wouldn't change a thing.'

'Thank goodness she's stronger than you. She turned your head when you thought you had everything under control.'

'Don't get too wise, friend. The same could happen to you when you're least expecting it. How is Kristina, by the way?'

Chase winced. That was getting a little too close to the mark. 'She's good, as are Freja, Pierre, Mike, and Angel.'

'You might be fooling yourself, Chase, but you're not fooling me. The pair of you need your heads banged together. Six weeks and all that tiptoeing around as though you weren't remotely interested in each other, the air pulsing with electricity. Damned dangerous for anyone getting near. Kristina gets under your skin and you're not liking it.'

'Time I got back to sorting out the roster. I'll mark you as definite for the next three-week stint.' He already had. This call really had nothing to do with that and all to do with talking with this man who was rapidly becoming a friend—if he stopped giving him crap about Kristina. All part of letting go of the past, surely?

'You know the routine. I'll email the exact date for embarking. Catch you.' There were volunteers doing three-, six-, nine- and twelve-week hauls. It would be a lot easier if everyone signed up for the same length of time, but that wasn't how the system worked.

'Chase, don't hang up,' Ethan shouted. 'Forget your bloody roster. What's this call really about?'

About to hit 'off', Chase hesitated. It had taken too many years for them to start burying the things they'd said on that mountain for him to be stirring up more trouble. Losing ground wasn't an option. He had stopped blaming Reid for something he'd had no choice about—a huge step forward. Ethan now accepted Chase didn't hate him for surviving when Nick hadn't. Chase also understood the guilt he'd put on Ethan by letting him believe he'd made a choice between the two guys. Nick had never been coming out of there alive. *Nick, help me here.* Nothing but silence. The laden quiet he'd learned to live with, that crippled him.

Fill the hush. Try answering Reid honestly. Take a deep lungful and just say it. 'I wanted to touch base.' Reid would understand how big that was. They'd both admitted they'd avoided close friendships since that horrendous night, and that they weren't used to having someone to call just for the hell of it.

'You don't have to make up excuses to get in touch,' the man on the other end of the phone growled.

Chase grimaced. 'I'm still getting used to this.'

'You and me both.'

'Bet Claire doesn't let you go quiet on her.'

'Not a chance.'

How did that feel? Good? Frightening? Exciting? Kristina came to mind. Again. She did that way too often. What would it be like to give up this life and make a new one? With her? *Go away.* 'How are you finding this no more disappearing over the horizon at any moment thing?' He needed to know. For future reference, in case he ever decided to take a chance on a relationship. *Go away, Kristina.*

'There are moments when the fear grabs me and I start to tap into sites for jobs in the heat.' Ethan went quiet.

And this was summer, no snow and ice. But Ethan was in France. Where he'd sworn never to return. Chase waited. The last thing he wanted was to say something glib. They were better than that now.

Finally Ethan continued in a subdued voice. 'Then I look at Claire and know I don't want to go. That staying here, with her, is all I want, need, look forward to every morning in that split second between waking and opening my eyes to find her beside me. She's worth everything. Including being at the bottom of a mountain.'

Chase swallowed hard. Then had to do it again. 'I'm glad.' One of them had finally got their life back on track. Was it possible to make that two out of two? Fear rose; sharp and solid. What if he had to choose between the woman he loved and someone else in another emergency? He couldn't do it. He couldn't. So he wouldn't put himself in that position. *Sorry, Kristina.*

There was a lot of throat clearing going on at the other end. 'I want you to be my best man at our marriage ceremony.'

Chase felt his legs soften. Dropping his butt onto the desk top, he took the weight off his boneless limbs. Best man? With their past? This spoke volumes about how far they'd come in a short time. It spoke of total forgiveness. He couldn't find it within him to be flippant, his usual way of dealing with difficult, emotional moments. This was do or deny. Working with Ethan, he'd learned he didn't want denial any more. Not with this man. They'd been through hell together, the outcome taken out of their hands by a larger force. Now they were taking tentative steps towards a real, honest friendship and he wouldn't be the one to screw that. 'I'd be honoured.'

He might now be able to work at dropping the denial on living a settled life in one place with one woman. Huh? Too soon. Way too soon. He still had to steady himself over his friendship with Reid.

'Cut the fancy words,' Ethan croaked. '"Yes" would've been fine.'

'Send me the details. When's this happening?' The last wedding he'd been to had been when Libby had married Jarrod, her childhood sweetheart, and they now had a posse of kids that would drive an army commander to drink. Army. Kristina. The two words clashed and melded in his head. Would he ever get her out of there again? Had he transferred his denial from Ethan to her? Now, *that* was getting complex. Forget it.

'A month after the *Poseidon* ties up at the end of summer. Hope that won't mess with your plans for heading out to Africa.'

The contract lay in his in-box. He hadn't been able to bring himself to sign it. Every time this past week when he'd thought he'd print it off to scrawl his signature across the bottom, Kristina's beautiful face had slipped into his mind, and he'd put it off. But the day was coming when he'd have no choice. Liam had already emailed to ask where the contract was. All that had done was remind Chase how unlike him it was to dither. He'd do it today. It wasn't as though he was changing his career path because of Kristina.

'You still there?' Ethan asked.

'I'll be available for the wedding. No matter what turns up.'

'Thanks, Chase. It's not a wedding. We're getting married in the Marseille Town Hall, just the four of us there.

Then we'll have big bash back at the family's village later on.'

'Four?' His stomach was tightening.

'Better warn you, Claire's asking Kristina to be her bridesmaid.' He laughed as though that was the biggest joke of the week.

'You're winding me up.'

'Not much.' Ethan was still laughing. 'Catch you.' He was gone.

Chase stared at the phone, ready to hurl it across the room. He and Kristina were going to be beside Ethan and Claire as they publicly declared their love for each other. They were being pushed together, want it or not. Considering how well the two women got on, he should've realised this would happen. Apparently Claire didn't have lots of friends, or at least none she wanted to stand beside her more than Kristina. And she was searching for permanency in her life, making him the wrong man for her. Unless he followed in Reid's footsteps.

Impossible or terrifying? Both.

'Chase, the next load of refugees is alongside.' Kristina stood in the doorway, hands on delectable hips, looking amused.

Had she heard his end of the conversation with Ethan? Or had she already been talking to Claire and knew they'd both be going to the wedding—as partners, no less? 'You heard from Claire today?'

Her brow creased. 'No. Should I have?'

He'd put his large foot in it again. 'Ethan mentioned she might be phoning you, that's all.' Standing up, he slipped the phone into his pocket, though there wasn't anyone else he wanted to hear from today. 'Let's go deal with our new patients.'

Then he'd be able to focus on what was necessary and ignore the rest.

* * *

Kristina wiped her face with tissues. They came away sodden. 'This heat is unbearable.'

'Be glad you're not on land.' Chase put his empty water bottle aside. 'There's a heatwave going on in Greece, Italy and southern France, with temperatures hitting the low forties in some areas.'

'How do people cope? I prefer the cold.'

Chase shivered. 'I don't.'

'Then again, when I've had to walk through snow and ice on my way to work I wished for the heat.' She grinned.

'No pleasing you, then.' His breathing was rapid, his smile forced.

'I used to enjoy snowboarding, whenever I had a chance to get up to the mountains, but it's been years since I gave it go. I'd probably make a right idiot of myself if I tried now.'

'Not my idea of fun.' There was something wrong about his tone, like she'd pushed the wrong buttons, upsetting him.

Yet she persisted. 'You've given it a go, then?'

'Not snowboarding.' He wasn't giving much away. All part of the 'don't talk a lot' in their quiet space on deck?

To her it was *their* place now. Over the past eight days she'd joined Chase every night for time out and not once had he told her to go away. It was special and she looked forward to being with him, to the lack of expectations put on her to fill in the minutes unless she wanted to. 'That's a yes to skiing?'

'It was a long time ago,' he muttered. The tension that had been tightening his arms and shoulders increased.

Desperate to undo the damage, she said the first thing that came into her mind. 'I don't like clothes that are remotely green or tan.'

His nod was short. 'I get that.'

'Heavy boots are no longer in my wardrobe either.'

One corner of his mouth lifted. 'Replaced with ten-inch high heels?'

'Ah, no. I fall off those too easily.'

'I'm disappointed.' He turned and leaned back against the rail, his gaze fixed on her now. 'I still can't get my head around you, so feminine and kind and fun, in the army. Why did you enlist?'

She should've stuck to the unspoken no-talking rule: instead, that sense of reaching for Chase, of feeling close to him, had got the better of her and now she was in the firing line. Looking out to sea, she wanted to tell him to leave her alone, wanted to put him back in the box where all people getting close went before they could hurt her by dumping her first. But something held her back. The need to find that future she wanted.

While Chase didn't stack up when it came to settling down, there was no denying he was helping her find her way. Telling him why she'd chosen the military couldn't hurt, might even help her get past the pain she carried into every relationship. 'I was looking for somewhere to belong.'

He studied her for a long time, before asking quietly, 'Did you find it?'

'Not really. This will sound weird to someone who comes from a loving family...' She paused, collecting the right words. 'Libby was always talking about her and Jarrod and the kids, and about your parents and you. She made it sound wonderful, having people behind you all the time no matter what you did.' Reminded her of her childhood.

'That's our Libby.' He sighed. 'She's not always right about everything.'

Kristina nodded. 'Who is?' Of course he didn't answer. There really wasn't one. Her gaze returned to the sea. There was anonymity in the heaving water and the hidden depths. 'I had this idea that being a part of the army would be on a par to belonging to a family.' She daren't look at Chase for fear there'd be mockery in his eyes. 'I wanted someone to have my back, to feel I belonged with them. I got all of that.' It still wasn't what she'd been hoping for.

'Where did it let you down?'

Chase got it. Again she watched him as she talked, basking in his ability to be non-judgemental, at least until he had all the facts.

'I *was* part of a dedicated group of people, working, training, playing together, and it appeared to be exactly what I'd been hoping for. Then I came to realise everything was on the army's terms, as it has to be. Going into battle as individuals would be disastrous. Every soldier has to be, and is, integral to each other.'

Then she had been discharged and the gate had closed firmly behind her. Bye-bye, Captain Morton. The two women she kept in touch with felt the same sense of being left out in the cold once they were no longer a part of the establishment, though they all agreed that could be their own fault because they'd expected too much.

'You obviously don't regret your decision despite not finding the right job yet.'

Again it sounded as though he understood where she was coming from. Just like that. With no follow-up questions about why, where and when. That earned him a lot of points. Other people like her father, who wasn't close by any stretch of the imagination, hadn't believed the truth, even knowing why she'd left the forces. Her mother had never understood her need to be loved for the person she was and not who her mum wanted her to be. Sitting on the Riviera or in the Bahamas, sipping cocktails, month after month with men who only wanted her beauty and body was not *her*. Yeah, her mum's American hadn't lasted more than a year.

Kristina could love Chase for his sensitivity alone. But

she wouldn't. Loving him for anything would only bring pain. At the end of the day he was still a man who didn't settle anywhere for long, didn't gather people around him, didn't want the same things she did. Though there was a real possibility he did want them, but wasn't prepared to risk finding them. He wasn't as straightforward as the man who presented himself as SARCO. That man was in charge, was friendly without getting involved. The man standing beside her hurt her deep inside where no one was allowed to go.

Again, she'd not be finding out why because to do so meant becoming involved, and as much as she'd like to be there for him, to make a difference, it would come with a price she couldn't afford. A broken heart was not on her horizon. Yes, getting close to Chase would mean love. Because she already felt twinges of emotion that only had one name whenever she was with him. Twinges only, not full-on, heart-totally-involved love. She remembered the lust that had dominated for weeks. 'I'm turning in. See you in the morning unless I'm required for an emergency.'

The haunting sound of a flute wafted over the air. She hesitated, listening as the sweet sound rose and fell. It was coming from the other end of the ship, striking her so that she didn't move in case it stopped.

'Kristina.' Chase's hand covered hers, his fingers slipping between hers. 'Stay with me for a moment.'

'It's beautiful,' she whispered, and slowly leaned back against him. Breathing deeply and slowly, she let the tension ease from her body while absorbing his warmth. A warmth unlike the heat from the sun that had finally dipped beyond the horizon. This was a warmth that filled her with longing and love and hope.

'It is.'

The notes rose and fell as though following the air. Who was playing the instrument? One of the medical people?

Or a refugee? They never brought much with them but a flute would take up no space in a small bag.

Chase wound his arms around her, tucked her closer to his body, his chest a wall for her back. His chin rested on the top of her head, his breaths lifting strands of her hair from behind her ear.

The music soared, and her heart rate followed the tempo.

Chase's hands spread over her waist, held her tightly yet gently.

She didn't want anything to move, could stay like this for hours.

Silence. Disappointment dripped off her. 'Oh,' she whispered. 'That was lovely.'

Then another note hung in the air, followed by more, a faster tempo, one that had her toes tapping.

Chase's hands were turning her, bringing her to face him. 'Let's dance.' He reached for her hands, drew her close as he stepped in time to the tune.

She went with him, unable to refuse, following his lead, hearing the music, hearing the beat in her veins, in her head.

When the music slowed, Chase slowed, held her close, and moved on the spot.

When the notes fell away, Kristina held her breath, waiting for the next tune.

Silence. This time it remained.

But Chase's hands were still holding her, his face coming closer to hers, and then his lips were touching her mouth, a light brush that woke her fully yet left her languid as his mouth covered hers and pressed harder, capturing her, teasing, sending waves of desire to her toes. To her fingers, her belly, her centre.

Winding her arms around his shoulders, she hung on and kissed him back with all the pent-up frustration of the last weeks. She kissed him deeply, hungrily. Kissed him as though to imprint herself on his mind for ever.

'Kristina,' he groaned against her mouth.

She didn't answer. Couldn't for the longing in her throat. Then she was being gently put aside. 'We have to stop.'

She didn't recognise his throaty voice filled with tension and need. Chase wanted her as badly as she wanted him. So why not do something about it? But as she opened her mouth to say so, she hesitated. He was right. They had to stop. Taking this any further would only exacerbate the differences between them. It would be a short-term thing, and knowing that would hover over her, make her feel uneasy instead of happy. She was too far gone over Chase to be able to have a fling and walk away in one piece. The pendulum was moving, from one side, lust, to the other, love, and she had to stop it going any further.

But couldn't she have one time with him?

He shook his head slowly, apparently good at mind-reading.

Stepping back, Kristina let her hands drop slowly to her sides. 'See you in the morning.'

His hand caught one of hers. 'Goodnight, Kristina.' His thumb caressed her skin, winding up the need tighter than ever. Then he let her go.

Loud banging on their cabin door had Kristina and Jane out of bed and pulling on clothes before hurrying on deck, where people from Libya were being brought on board after a small boat had capsized nearer the coast.

The scene was organised chaos. Small, bedraggled children sat crying and shaking in sodden clothes while distraught adults held them tight, their own tears tracking down ashen faces.

Across the deck Chase was doing CPR on a youngster,

the strain in his face saying there was no way he would fail to revive the lad.

She rushed to join him. 'Want a hand?'

'Get the defibrillator,' he demanded, sweat streaming down his cheeks and forehead.

Snatching the machine off the bulkhead, Kristina dropped down beside Chase, placing patches on the boy's chest to attach the wires. 'Stand back.'

The limp body jerked off the deck, slumped back down.

'Again,' demanded Chase. 'Again.'

When the flat line started to rise Kristina's hopes lifted. 'That's the boy. Where's the oxygen?' she asked.

'Coming,' Chase informed her through gritted teeth. 'Someone else needed it first.'

There was more than one tank and fittings, but when she looked around the deck she could see them all in use. 'What happened?'

'The boat was so overcrowded that when a wave from a passing ship hit, it rolled and sank. Luckily the other ship stopped and tried to save everyone, but it seems some haven't been found.' Chase's face was grim. 'But I've got this one.' He reached for the boy's wrist and felt for his pulse. 'Too weak.'

The boy's eyes flickered open. Water spewed from his lungs.

Chase quickly rolled him onto his side to prevent choking. 'I thought we'd got all that. Seems he's taken in more water than the Mediterranean holds. How did he survive that?'

'Here we go.' Kristina took the gear a nurse was handing her and placed a mask over the boy's face, turning on the valve.

'Hello. My name is Kristina. This is Dr Chase. You are safe now.' Hopefully her tone would do what her words couldn't and give the lad a sense of calm.

'Chase, over here,' called someone. 'We've got a major trauma.'

'You all right here?' he asked, but didn't wait for an answer, loping off across the deck like a wild dog was after him.

'I need a doctor when someone's free.'

Hearing Jane's voice, Kristina looked around. 'What's up?'

'Probably a fractured arm and torn ligaments.'

'Swap. This lad had heart failure, probable cause drowning. His lungs have been cleared, and he's breathing with aid from the tank. Can you watch him?'

'Be right there.'

Kristina counted the beats in her patient's wrist. Light, but regular. Was he really going to be that lucky? Her fingers crossed for him, she wiped his face and mouth.

Jane knelt down on the opposite side. 'Hi, there. I'm Jane. What have you been doing to yourself?'

Kristina headed for the girl with the fracture. 'Hello. I'm a doctor. Kristina is my name.' Her fingers felt the upper right arm that lay at an odd angle. 'I need to get you with one of the surgeons to put you back together.'

'I'll help you carry her down.' A nurse placed a stretcher on the deck beside them.

'Thank goodness for lifts.' Kristina nodded at him. Too much heavy lifting and carrying didn't do her back a lot of good.

'Kristina, over here,' Chase called. 'Now.'

'I'll get someone else to help me with this,' Bernie told her.

'What's up?' She squatted beside Chase, who looked fierce with determination.

'Blunt force trauma to the skull. He's not responding to stimulus, BP's way too low. I'm going into Theatre immediately and need you on hand while we take him down.

We can't wait for a chopper to airlift him to the mainland. He won't survive that long. Watch his vitals while I scrub up,' Chase added in no uncertain terms.

'Onto it.' This was like the day the bomb had blown up on the training exercise. With everyone in shock and frantic to do the right thing by the wounded, it had been chaotic. And she hadn't been able to move, to help. A chill settled over her. As long as the outcome was a hundred percent better. So far the chaos did appear to be under control, with everyone getting on with their jobs, all efficiency. She needed to relax. No one was dying from an uncontrollable bleed out. But she couldn't shake the sense of déjà vu, of not doing enough for the wounded. Which made no sense. Tonight she was not incapacitated with injuries and unable to help those who needed her.

As soon as Chase, his patient and a full tally of staff were at the operating table Kristina went looking for someone else to help.

'Over here.' Calvin waved at her.

'What's this one?'

'I suspect a miscarriage. There's heavy bleeding between her thighs and intermittent tightening of the gut at regular intervals. She's hypothermic, hence the survival blanket. We've stripped her of her wet clothes.' Calvin rubbed his chin with the back of a glove-covered hand. 'She's not responding to anything I say. Not a blink or a tightening of her hands. I wonder if it's because I'm a male.'

Kristina reached inside the blanket for a cold hand, and held it gently. 'Hello, can you hear me?' Where was Zala when she needed her? She'd disembarked along with everyone who'd come on board with her weeks ago, and Kristina still thought about her. If only they'd been able to keep her with them, but that was selfish as the girl was getting on with finding her new life. 'My name is Kristina and

I'm a doctor.' The words were starting to taste bland after so many times repeating them and not being understood.

The woman was shivering non-stop and her skin was frozen while there was a heatwave going on.

'Let's get her inside,' Calvin suggested. 'Away from the crowds she might be more receptive to help.'

'If that's possible. She's slipping in and out of consciousness.' Standing, she looked around for another stretcher.

In the full glare of the lights it was apparent Calvin's assessment was correct. The miscarriage was nearly complete, with the afterbirth coming away as Kristina began a thorough examination.

Calvin had put on a face mask. 'That way she might not see my masculine side and go all crazy. Though she's more settled since you joined us.'

'Seems pregnant women are my forté at the moment, despite having a midwife on board.'

'It's that soft, coaxing manner of speaking you have that gets them every time.' He grinned. 'I need to practise more.'

'I can see that working.' Kristina laughed. 'To be on the safe side, I'm doing a D and C.'

Calvin nodded. 'Onto it.'

'No problem.' They'd close the area off and scrub up after cleaning the woman down. 'You're helping me?'

'That's what I meant by *we*.' Again he grinned. 'Unless you want to do it alone.'

'Not at all.' They worked well together, and the woman was soon in a bed, tucked under a blanket with a nurse to watch over her until she woke.

'Back topside, I guess.' Kristina aimed for the stairs.

Chase was ahead, striding out hard and fast.

'Chase,' she called.

He didn't turn or slow.

'Chase, wait for me.'

His legs ate up the distance, his hands fisted at his sides. Why was he ignoring her? Or was he in a hurry to get to another urgent case? He should still be with the brain trauma patient. Uh-oh. She hesitated. Hadn't the patient made it? His injuries had been extreme, and they'd wondered if he'd been hit by the boat while in the water. Chase would be gutted if he hadn't saved the man. They all felt the loss of a patient but Chase seemed to feel it hardest. It was as though he was on a mission to save everyone who came under his care.

All doctors wanted that outcome, but with Chase she'd seen him go into despair when he'd lost a young girl even when the odds had not been on his side. Despair to the point of being over the top. Why? Was that just his nature? Or had he lost a patient he shouldn't have? Most doctors had failures on their conscience, but to the extent Chase seemed to go? No, there was more to this than he would ever let on.

Something terrible lay in both their pasts, something they'd both suffered, and still did, if Chase's reaction tonight was an indicator. He wouldn't tell her about it, she knew that. Didn't mean she couldn't offer her support. As soon as they were finished up he'd head for his—their—space, and she'd be right there for him.

Out on the deck there were few minor injuries left to deal with, and the nurses were handing out hot tea and bread with butter.

'We're done,' said Jane when Kristina came to a halt beside her. 'We're arranging bedding and dry clothes for those who need it and then we can stand down.'

'Sounds good to me. It's been quite a night.' From kissing Chase to fixing the wounded. Her gaze travelled the length of the deck and found Chase. He stood talking to one of the new nurses, his stance tight and unforgiving, his voice low and controlled, yet anger was coming off him in waves. Anger at the nurse? Or because of whatever had gone on during the operation?

Jane turned her head to stare in the same direction. 'The head injury guy died on the table.'

'I wondered.' Kristina's heart went out to the young man's family. And to Chase. He'd be chastising himself for days to come.

'Want a mug of tea?' Jane asked, now watching her.

'Best offer I've had all night.' What would Chase say if she took him one? Only one way to find out.

But it wasn't going to happen. He went past without acknowledging her, yet she'd swear he'd seen her as he'd stormed away to head down to the cabins, not up to his space. He'd have a lot to see to before knocking off for what remained of the night. Then he did an abrupt about-turn and charged up on deck.

She could give him some time to collect himself. Or she could join him. 'Make that a tea and a coffee,' she told Jane as she watched Chase charge over to the stairs heading to the deck.

Did she go to him or let him be alone and unhappy? That had been raw pain darkening those eyes to thunder clouds. She didn't let friends down when they needed someone to talk to. Not that she had friends who came calling in hours of need, neither was Chase likely to talk to her. But, 'One tea and one coffee,' she repeated.

'Sorry it's not laced with brandy.' Kristina handed Chase a mug when she finally made it to their space a few minutes later.

'Right.'

At least he accepted the proffered coffee. Settling against the railing, she sipped her tea and stared out into the darkness. 'Rough night.'

She was met with silence. Not that she'd been expecting Chase to burst into conversation. But nothing? Yes, that was the man she'd come here to lend a shoulder to. She sipped more tea. 'It never gets any easier, does it?'

Nothing.

'We can't save them all all of the time, Chase.'

Coffee splashed over the deck as the mug jerked in his fingers. 'Yes, I can,' he roared. 'I have to.'

Kristina held still, watched the play of emotions warring in his face and eyes—pain, anger, frustration, need—and knew she'd gone too far. But she wasn't about to back off. He needed help. Not that she was any expert about this kind of pain, only knew from her own experiences how it could destroy a person. 'You're wrong. I've been there. I know.'

'Go, Kristina. Just go.'

So much for that kiss.

CHAPTER FOUR

HE MIGHT'VE KNOWN.

Kristina didn't budge, looked as if she'd stay all night if he didn't respond, if he didn't beg her to leave him alone with his pain. Did she think that because he'd kissed her she had the right to encroach? Chase wanted to slam his fist into a bulkhead, throw a tantrum, yell at her for caring enough to be there. People weren't allowed to care about him—he'd made a career out of pushing away anyone who tried. Not that he'd succeeded with his family. They ignored his outbursts, his cold shoulder, the physical distances he'd put between them ever since that night. They loved him, no question.

Was Kristina made of the same stern stuff? Did he want her to be? It would only lead to heartache—for them both. He was beginning to feel involved with her. To feel the possibility of a future. That kiss had only increased his desire for her, complicating matters further. He had to be strong and push her away.

Chase remained upright with his back against the bulkhead, his hands jammed into the pockets of his shorts and his chin jutting out like an arrow aimed at the distant, unseen horizon. Trying to pretend Kristina wasn't within reach was a joke. Lift an arm and his hand would be touching that creamy skin that managed to survive the worst the sun sent her way without any blemishes. What he wouldn't do to touch, to taste, to kiss that sensational body. To take and to give, another kiss. To lose himself in her. Anything except surrender his heart.

'Chase? Talk to me.'

Why couldn't she leave him in peace? This was *his* place, not *theirs*. Though he had begun thinking of it as theirs. But right now he had to be alone to grapple with the bitterness of another failure. No one died on his watch. No one. Not any more.

But tonight a young man had. The odds of saving him had been long, too long as it turned out. But he should've succeeded. Even when he wasn't a neurosurgeon, and didn't have one on hand. Someone would be bereft, a mother, father, perhaps a wife. Because he'd failed. As he had with Nick.

'There's nothing to talk about,' he howled around the pain of his best friend lying trapped under an immovable beam, dying, pain that mixed with the loss of tonight's patient. 'Go away,' he shouted. Was it his memories he was hollering at? Or Kristina? Either, or: it didn't matter. It was imperative he turn her away before she saw through him to the guilt and fear that ruled him. It wasn't a lie to say there was nothing to talk about. It was called self-protection. Those wounds were not for opening.

They weren't open now?

'We work to save everyone, but it doesn't always pan out like that.' Kristina spoke softly, not daunted by his yelling.

'It has to,' he snapped. What didn't this woman understand? It was straightforward enough. Injured people came to doctors, to *him*, to be fixed, put back together, given another chance at living. 'It's what I trained for.'

'You're right, but sometimes it just isn't enough.' Did she take no umbrage with anything he said? 'Why can't you accept that?'

Get out. Stay. Suddenly he didn't want to push too far. Having Kristina on his side was like a balm he couldn't stop rubbing. Underneath that calm, friendly exterior was a will of steel. One he'd like to get to know. Damn it. Yes, he would. Around Kristina he didn't understand himself any more. It was as though by talking to Ethan so much lately he was allowing himself to dream. Hope rose when she came near. Was it possible to have a future with her? One where he planted his feet in the soil of his own property and felt like he belonged, like he had the right to stay and be happy with Kristina at his side? Deep breaths quietened his racing heart a little. Until he told her, 'Failure doesn't exist in my vocabulary.'

'Everyone knows that. It's the why I'm asking about.'

'Because the consequences are always unbearable for someone. A family, friends.' For me.

She waited. Not a movement, not a smile or a widening of those beautiful eyes. Nothing to get his back up. Nothing to make him believe she felt sorry for him. She was good.

Chase fell into the offer she was making.

'My best friend died. I couldn't save him. I blame myself regardless of the circumstances.'

Still Kristina remained quiet. No ranting about how that was silly, like so many had said to him in the past. Not Reid. He'd also lived with the consequences. Chase shuddered. Something he was accountable for.

'The national junior ski team was competing in the French Alps when an avalanche hit our chalet.'

Now Kristina did move, slipping beside him, her arm touching the length of his. Her warm hand wrapped around his cold one. Then she waited.

'I couldn't help him. Couldn't lift the beam that broke his chest and held him in snow and ice until he was frozen.' The memory of that ice and cold rippled through Chase, lifting his skin, turning his muscles taut.

Kristina's grip tightened. 'You were in the British national team? You must've been extremely skilful.'

'I was.' For all the good it did him or any of the team that night. 'But not the best. Nick Hariday held that ranking, and we were always after him to take over his position. Especially me and Ethan.'

'So that's where Ethan comes into it.' Kristina's nodded. 'Of course.'

'Of course what?' She intrigued him with her easy acceptance of his story. Had she read him correctly? He hoped so, or it was going to sting when he learned differently.

'The initial disquiet between the two of you during those first weeks he was on board. There was such tension between you. At first you both trod on eggshells whenever you were in the same room, but then something changed. You talked, didn't you? About what happened?' She shook her head.

Like he'd said, she was good. Where did that take him? Did he tie her to his side and never let her go so he'd always have someone who understood him to talk to? Or did he shove her away because he'd only drag her down as he hauled her all over the world, searching for more people to save? The one thing he was certain of about Kristina was that she wanted to settle, to stop wandering.

He answered her question in the vague hope it would turn her away. 'There were more beams on top of the one that pinned Nick down. He never stood a chance, but that didn't stop me trying, pleading with him to live. When the futility of my actions finally sank in I turned away to help Ethan. I had to save someone. But I resented him for that.' The words spewed out like poison and he let them come before the lump building in the back of his throat cut off all speech.

This was the second time in weeks that he'd talked

about that tragedy. Ethan had brought it up one night on shore during their first three-day break. They'd been downing bourbon, pecking around the past until Ethan had gone for the problem, boots and all, shocking Chase even though he'd known it had to happen. Ethan had put it out there about his guilt at being the one Chase had chosen to save thereby leaving Nick alone in those last precious moments.

For the first time ever Chase had admitted he'd been wrong to let him continue thinking that, how at the time he hadn't known how to cope with his loss and pain. Still didn't. After that they'd talked about the guys who hadn't made it, and the coach who hadn't had the courage to help anyone and who was now working for a charity gardening centre, possibly trying to assuage his conscience. It seemed every survivor from the tragedy had come away laden with guilt.

The resulting hangover had been a killer. Not something Chase was about to repeat, even if there was booze to be had on board, which as far as he knew there wasn't. It was MFA's policy, and anyone caught flouting it was politely asked to leave. Yet tonight, if there had been a bottle on hand, he might have been sorely tempted, needing the release that came with losing himself in the hit of alcohol. Not that he made a habit of doing that but occasionally it was okay.

Unable to resist her any longer, he drew Kristina close and wound his arms around that warm body, his chin resting on her head as he breathed in the salt air and her scent. As he waited for the lump to dissolve and his heart rate to return to normal, he absorbed her warmth, marvelled at the wonder of having a woman relax in his embrace, of not demanding anything for herself, letting him talk as he wanted to, or not if he preferred.

The lump of pain and despair slowly dissolved while

the throb of his heart began picking up its beat. His nerve endings came alive one at a time. His hands splayed on her waist. His mouth hungered for one more kiss. The rest of his body wanted everything, the whole naked, close, orgasmic thing. Tipping back in her arms, he gazed down into her eyes and asked, "Kristina?'

She must've felt the tightening in his body and known his need because she rose onto her toes and leaned forward. 'Yes.' Her husky voice brushed his skin, heightened his yearning. 'Yes.'

As her mouth opened under his he sank further into her embrace. She tasted sweet and strong and dangerous. He wanted to rob her of all awareness except for him. To take her where he was headed. To oblivion. Away from all that screwed him inside out.

There was no noise; no people talking or arguing, no birds squawking overhead, no boats heading towards the ship. Chase was deaf. And hot. And cold. And warm. He was lost in this woman who seemed to understand him when she shouldn't. She stole his ability to think, gave of herself and endorsed his feeling of being in the right place at the right time with the right woman.

His lips cruised over hers, devoured her mouth as he tasted. Her hands pushed under his shirt to caress and sensitise his skin, and he fell further into her. Rapid breathing made her breasts rise and fall against his chest, inflaming him more. He had to taste them. Her hips pressed against his rising, hardening need. Her scent swirled around them, enticing, erotic. His hands sought and found hot, bare skin, felt the frantic throb of a pulse, knew the warmth and care being given to him.

'Chase.' An urgent whisper against his mouth cut through the haze.

'What?' He wasn't stopping for anyone. He couldn't. Didn't have the brakes to haul on.

'Chase.' This time his name sounded urgent, and there was a cooling against his chest as the heat source pulled back. 'We've got company.'

His eyes ripped open. His hands dropped to his sides as he stepped back abruptly, the air suddenly chilly 'Who?' Damn it. Why couldn't he have one night to himself? With Kristina and no one to interrupt? *Because you're in charge of what happens on board this vessel where patients and medical staff are concerned.*

'Sorry, Chase, but we've got a problem below deck. One of the men is trying to steal food from the kitchen and the cook's going ballistic.' Calvin's words brought Chase back to reality faster than anything else could.

What had he been doing? About to do? Putting Kristina aside, he ran his hands over his face and straightened his back. 'On my way.'

'And that's that. He could've said something before rushing away. One word would've done.' Kristina stared after Chase as he bounded along the deck. 'Good to know where I stand.' Like a sticking plaster for his wounds that could be torn off at any moment.

Except the wound was a long way off healing. She wasn't so naïve as to believe she'd helped him on the first step towards forgiving himself. Only he could do that, and *if* there was anyone able to help him it was Ethan, not her.

Her fingers traced the outline of her swollen lips. Hell, could the man kiss. He'd exploded through her, taking away all sense of time, sound, location. All she'd known was Chase—and wanting more, wanting it all. His mouth, those large, strong hands doing a number on her skin, his erection hard against her soft stomach weren't enough. They'd been in a bubble. Until Calvin had turned up, spoiling the moment, bringing her back to reality in a flash. How she'd heard him calling Chase was beyond her.

If only he hadn't. Then who knew where she and Chase might've ended up? Or what they might've done? She should be thankful they'd been interrupted then, and not five minutes later. But she wasn't. She wanted him. Big time. Not sex. *Lovemaking.* She shivered. Yeah, she'd gone and lost sight of what she should be hanging onto and was starting to fall under his spell.

As for what Chase thought? Who knew? He'd rushed away without a backward glance, putting her in her place quick smart.

Chase had been through a lot. She understood his need to be in control, and wanting to save everyone who came his way. But he had to learn not to beat himself up when he lost a patient. As she'd begun accepting she couldn't have saved Corporal Higgs the day the owner of Merrywood's electrical business had been electrocuted while putting in wires at the garage she'd happened to be going past and she had made amends for failing Higgs by saving George.

Unfortunately, it wouldn't be her showing Chase how to move on. They might have shared kisses beyond her wildest imagination, their bodies might be hollering for each other, but they weren't *going* anywhere together. They had too many hang-ups to be able to have even a half-normal relationship. But she'd happily go for more here in their space. Though now she was coming down to earth she knew they wouldn't be making love here. Too risky that they'd be caught. Some people would say that was half the fun. Not her.

It was time to get some shut-eye. The horizon was lightening, and soon the ship would be alive with more people requiring attention. Another boat had been sighted and was due to be intercepted to remove the refugees later in the morning and she needed to be on her A game.

As if she'd get any sleep with those kisses so vivid in her mind. With how her body had reacted to Chase's touches.

She knuckled her back as she slouched along to her cabin. *Please let me sleep,* was her last thought for the night.

'Kristina, wake up. You're needed in the medical room.' Jane was shaking her arm.

Kristina rolled onto her back and stared at the apparition above her. 'What time is it?'

'You've missed breakfast.' Jane grinned. 'I'm not going to ask who kept you up so late.'

'Get a life,' she muttered. 'I was busy.'

'Sure you were. If it's any consolation, Chase looks terrible, too.'

'You're saying I look bad? How?' There was a low pounding going on in her skull, but how could she *look* a mess? They'd only kissed. *Only* kissed? Those kisses had been right up there with X-rated warnings. Her skin was probably scorched.

'Yuk, now you're looking dreamy. Definitely time you were downing strong coffee and dealing with malarial fevers.' Jane headed for the cabin door. 'If I don't see you in ten, I'll be back to prod you awake again.'

Kristina swung her legs out of the bunk and sat up to drop her head into her hands. Her eyes drooped shut. She forced them open. 'I'll be there. Give me five for a shower, and pour the strongest coffee that machine's capable of.'

'Will do.' Jane disappeared, closing the door behind her with a snap.

Hauling herself upright, Kristina's head floated and her body ached. If this was the result of Chase's kisses she was better off without them. Or had it been the reruns in her dreams that had wiped her out? Whichever, she didn't need any more.

Try telling that to someone who believes you. Imagine what making love with Chase would be like. Her imagination had already done that, now she was ready for the real thing.

The cold shower went some way to clearing the fog from her brain, and the coffee dispelled the rest, leaving her mind clear to focus on what was important around here—patients. 'That was perfect, Jane.'

'You're welcome.' Her cabin mate winked. 'Come and meet your next patient. He came on board yesterday, didn't complain of any ailments, yet during the night his temperature rose to thirty-eight point five and he developed sweats, chills and abdo pain. I'm thinking malaria so I've taken an EDTA blood and made a film. I'll stain it when it's dry.'

The thin, sweating man curled up on the mattress had a faint yellow tinge to his skin, suggesting his liver was reacting to whatever was causing the other symptoms. Kristina nodded. 'You're right. It looks like a case of malaria.' She'd seen a few since joining the ship. 'We need to determine which type but I'll give him a dose of chloroquine phosphate in the meantime.' It was the drug of choice for all but the rarest form of malaria and no harm would be done by administering it.

'I'll keep wiping him down and trying to get fluids into him. Shall we go for intravenous fluids as well?'

'Definitely. Dehydration needs to be kept at bay.' Kristina went to the drug cabinet and put in the code to activate the lock. Retrieving the chloroquine phosphate, she signalled Jane to check the vial and date, then returned to kneel beside the man. 'I'm giving you an injection,' she said, even though she wasn't sure he could hear her, and wouldn't understand her.

'Thank you.' His eyes flicked open, closed again.

He understood English. Yay. 'Have you had malaria before?'

'Yes.'

'Do you know what type?'

'Ovale?' Again he opened his eyes. 'Not sure.'

'Plasmodium ovale. I'll look at your blood film as soon as it's ready.' Sometimes a blood slide showed many parasites in the red cells, but more often they were difficult to find with less than one per field of a hundred or more red cells. This was work for a lab technician, and there wasn't one available. Chase had studied blood films and haematology so that he could diagnose some of the diseases their patients came with. She knew enough to recognise a parasite in the red cells when she saw one down the microscope and could run them by him for confirmation.

'I'm Kristina, a doctor. What's your name?' She pressed the plunger on the syringe she'd inserted into his arm.

'Abdal Matin.' A sheen of sweat covered his face. 'I worked in England five years ago as a reporter.'

How had he ended up here? It wasn't something she felt she could ask. 'Have you been taking prophylaxis?'

His mouth flattened and anger appeared in his unsteady gaze. 'I took chloroquine until it became impossible to get.'

Even when she had no idea where he'd come from or been, it was on record how difficult getting medical care had become in the places these people came from. 'Jane's going to set you up for intravenous fluids, and I want you to try and drink as much water as possible. You have a high temperature and those sweats aren't helping your fluid levels.'

'Thank you.'

Kristina got herself a top-up of coffee to take through to the tiny cabin where the microscope and glass containers of stain waited. A purple-coloured blood film lay on a blotter, ready to be looked at.

Perching on a stool, she applied a drop of oil to the slide and slid it in place on the microscope. Leaning forward, she focused the lens and began scanning the film, noting higher numbers of white cells than normal, mainly neutrophils and band forms, confirming the infection her patient had. The platelet numbers appeared normal. The red cells showed no obvious abnormalities but, then, she was no haematology expert. What was important was finding malarial parasites and they weren't exactly waving flags.

Thirty minutes later Kristina stood up to stretch her leg muscles and rub her lower back where the familiar throbbing had started up.

'Nothing?' Chase asked from the doorway.

She let her hand fall away. 'There's still a lot of film to go over.' Glancing over at him, her breath stuck in her throat. At the moment that mouth mightn't be soft but she had the memories, and they were turning her stomach into a swirling mess of need.

'You had breakfast?'

'I'm not hungry.'

His head tilted to one side. 'I could remind you what you said to me the other day on that subject.'

'I need to keep looking for malaria.' Her stomach would reject any food she fed it.

'You can eat and study the slide at the same time.' That wonderful mouth slipped into a smile, aimed directly at her.

And finished off any last hope of eating. 'I'll grab something when I've finished here. The man speaks English, by the way, so we currently have another interpreter, or will when the fever's abated.'

'What nationality is he?'

'I have no idea.'

'Let's hope it's the right one to be of use over the coming days.' The smile widened, lifting the corners of those delicious lips further.

What she wouldn't do for another kiss. 'At the moment he's too ill to be worrying about helping us out.'

Chase stepped into the small cabin, tall and lean and

sexy as hell, making her want to throw herself at him. 'Kristina.' He spoke softly. 'About last night...'

'Kristina, your malaria man is asking for you.' Jane stood where Chase had been moments before.

'Right, thanks.' Her eyes were still focused on Chase.

'We'll talk later.' His smile hadn't faded so he couldn't have been going to say something she didn't want to hear, like 'Sorry for kissing you' or 'That was wrong' or 'Forget the things I told you'. Could he?

That would hurt, she realised in a moment of clarity. The few men she'd dated she'd usually left without a backward glance on her part. This was a jaw-dropping shock. Not that there'd been many males in her life, as in affairs or the like, and none had got close enough to touch her in a way that raised hope and awareness for those wishes of a home and family. Was this what it was like to fall in love? It had better not be. Chase was all wrong for her. Given her history of mucking up her big goals, like joining the army to find a 'family', there was every possibility she'd get this thing with Chase wrong, too. Her parents had not shown her how to get it right.

'Sure.' Stepping around him, making sure not to brush against that delicious body in case he thought she was making a play for him, she headed for the door. 'I'll see Abdal Matin and then grab a sandwich.'

'I've got a few minutes going spare. I'll take a look at the slide.'

'Go for it.' If he found a parasite she'd try not to be disappointed she hadn't discovered it.

'Get out of here. You're needed in the medical area.' There might be a smile beaming out at her but she still felt let down.

She'd been hoping Chase wanted her—in a totally different way from how a patient might. At least he was still smiling. That was unusual in itself.

She'd take what she could get. *Pitiful, Kristina. Really, really pathetic. You're almost begging for his attention.*

'Plasmodium ovale,' Chase informed her when she returned to where he was.

'You found it? Damn, I wanted to do that.'

He shrugged a shoulder. 'That's the knocks you get in this work. Come and have a look.' He pushed the stool back enough for her stand in front of the microscope and study the cells at the other end of the lens. 'The ring form could be any type, but that parasite in the centre of the field? Definitely ovale.'

The purple, blue and red shades of the circle and dots were strong. 'It's incredible how something unable to be seen by the naked eye can cause so much harm to a human.' She glanced over her shoulder and stopped breathing.

Chase's gaze was fixed on her backside, nothing but longing gleaming out of his eyes.

'Chase?' she squeaked.

His head jerked up. 'Um, what were you saying?'

'Nothing.' Important, she added silently.

'I'll get back to the operating table.' The stool rocked as he leapt to his feet and stepped around her.

'Chase, stop it. You don't have to rush away.'

'Yes, Kristina, I do. For your sake, if not mine.'

Watching him stride out of the room as though he was being chased by a malaria-laden mosquito, she sank onto the stool he'd just vacated. Chase had just told her where they stood. Bluntly and purposefully. His beguiling smile didn't mean they had something going between them, had not meant what she'd begun dreaming about.

You didn't want anything happening with Chase. Other than more kisses. And making love.

All off the menu, by the look on his face as he'd fled the cabin.

Might pay to stay away from Chase's corner on deck

tonight. Every night? He could think she was staying away because he was a lost cause. That she couldn't cope with his past. Or he might be relieved because one of them had to see sense and call a halt to this attraction steaming between them.

Tossing her sandwich in the bin, she went to find a patient who needed her undivided attention. Chase could wait. She wasn't done with him, though. Not by a long shot.

CHAPTER FIVE

'I KNOW I should've phoned days ago, but it's bedlam here right now. Anyone would think our quiet little marriage ceremony was competing with the latest British royal wedding. Don't tell people you're getting married until the deed's done,' Claire said breathlessly. 'Honestly, you'd think the whole village had been waiting for ever for me to announce this marriage.'

Kristina laughed away the pain at the idea of her ever having to plan her own wedding. 'Says she who sounds very happy.'

'I am so happy it's scary. And we will have a party at home sometime later, but I won't be wearing a lace train that's twenty metres long or carrying a bouquet that would require a crane to lift. A glass of champagne will be enough, though with junior on board the bubbles will be water, not wine.' Claire paused, then went on in a quieter voice, 'I didn't know people could be so caring. Ethan's having fits about it.'

'I bet he is.' Kristina could imagine him glancing over his shoulder for an escape route. 'But he'll stay. He loves you.'

'I know. I truly believe that.'

Again Kristina had to swallow hard. She was happy for

this woman who'd befriended her on the ship. 'I'm glad for you both.'

'I rang to say you're going to be my bridesmaid. I won't take no for an answer.'

'But you haven't known me very long. You must have other friends for this.'

'No, it's you I want, and shall have. We clicked from the beginning, and that's what matters. Not even the fact that Chase is standing by Ethan on the day will let you out of this.'

He hadn't mentioned it. Was he unhappy about having to stand by her, all dressed up? Come on, they'd kissed and were still on speaking terms. There'd even been a second round of kisses. A frisson of excitement ran through her. Even small weddings had a photographer, didn't they? She'd keep one of those photos of her and Chase in her drawer to take out on the rainy days. 'Thank you. I can't wait.'

'Thanks, Kristina. It means a lot to me.'

'You asking means a lot.' Gulp. *Don't do the sentimental stuff. It gets messy.* 'What am I to do about a dress? Have you got ideas on style and colour?'

'Soft blue and off the shoulder. Anything else is your choice. Don't forget shoes with heels to die for. Make the men salivate.'

'I don't need men drooling over me.' Kristina laughed. Her feet were still more used to heavy-duty boots than killer heels. It really was time to get a girlie life. This could be fun.

'Might make Chase take notice in ways he mightn't have yet.' When Kristina gasped, Claire continued, 'Has he already? Come on. How *is* it going between the two of you?'

'You'd better have a stand-in ready in case I decide not to turn up for your wedding.'

Claire just laughed. 'Touched a nerve, did I?'

It was fun talking like this, even if her friend ignored the boundaries. It could be time to let go of more of her hang-ups. 'We're getting on better than expected.' *Oh, please.* 'We meet every night at Chase's no-go zone on deck.'

'Chase letting you be there says heaps.'

'There have been one or two interesting conversations.' Not to mention those kisses.

Claire went to the heart of the matter. 'What aren't you telling me?'

'That I like Chase a lot, really like him. But I doubt we'll take it very far as he's not into long-term relationships and, to be fair, he's made sure I understand that.'

'Ethan wasn't into them either until I came along and changed his mind.'

'I am not getting—' *Stop. Claire will be upset if you finish that sentence.* It wasn't as though she'd deliberately got pregnant, but she might misconstrue what Kristina had been about to say. 'Chase has told me a little of what happened when their ski team was hit by the avalanche. He has some huge issues to work through. The way I see it, he's not trying to move forward, instead seems focused on the past and how to rectify the impossible.'

Chase had told her that in confidence, but she needed to air her concerns, and to whom better than Claire, who already knew what drove their men? Their men? Chase wasn't hers. Yet there was something between them that went further than she'd ever experienced. Resisting him would be nigh on impossible—if they were ever to get hot and bothered together again.

'I shudder every time I think about that avalanche,' Claire agreed. 'I know the guys are still dealing with what happened and how they sort of hated each other, and are now becoming firm friends, but don't let Chase hold that up as a reason not to get involved if you're beginning to feel something for him.'

The many times Chase dominated her mind, not to mention her body, had not distracted her enough to put plans on hold for finding somewhere to settle and get a job. There was only one person looking out for her on that score, and that was her. 'You'd make a great agony aunt,' she joked, while the weight of what she might be losing out on dragged at her heart.

'Any time you have questions, you have my number. But, seriously, be open-minded about this. I'm speaking from experience here.'

'Thanks, Claire.' Swallow. Friendship. Wow. 'I've got to go. There's a boatload of refugees coming on board. We'll talk more about the wedding soon.' Without waiting for an answer, Kristina ended the call and slipped the phone into her pocket. Claire was too easy to talk to. Like Chase.

Looking around the deck, her gaze instantly found him. Standing with a nurse and a young man holding his meagre possessions in a ragged pack, Chase looked alone as he issued details of medical requirements. Tall, imposing and in control of all that was around him, there was no doubting his ability to oversee the comings and goings of the ship and its occupants. He was achieving what he desperately wanted, yet there was something sad about his stance. It spoke of disconnection, of deliberate composure to keep everyone at bay, of not letting anyone see the real Chase Barrington.

She was beginning to see behind that mask to the longing and fear, even the love he was capable of if only he'd risk himself. Strange how he allowed her into his corner. Only once had he told her to go away, and she'd chosen to ignore him, and look where that had led. Revelations followed by electric kisses, almost followed by making love.

Most times he seemed pleased when she turned up.

Sometimes she thought he was almost relieved, as if needing reassurance she wouldn't let him down. Since he wasn't into relationships it didn't add up. Could be she read too much into what for him was simply a friendship. A friendship with hot kisses and nearly sex? No, they'd moved beyond being pals. What came next was anyone's guess.

Chase turned, his eyes meeting hers. Then his mouth lifted into a soft smile that warmed her to her toes. That smile was genuine, and to be treasured. Bit by bit the man behind the caution was coming to light. Their kisses had softened her determination to remain strong against people who could hurt her, and had her wondering if Chase might be the one to eventually tear all her barricades down. Talk about a huge leap of trust that she wasn't ready to chance this side of the next ten Christmases. But she could give him a smile filled with happiness in return.

His eyes widened and his smile deepened. She'd get on with the day in a cheery frame of mind, and stop wondering if Chase was right for her. If he was, then things would unfold at the right time. If he wasn't, they'd move on from each other, maybe cross paths occasionally at events like the wedding. The naming ceremony for Claire and Ethan's baby perhaps. As if it would be that simple.

Claire had found her soul mate. What was that like? Finding a man who'd accept her for who she was and give her the love she craved? She'd have to love him back as strongly, or what would be the point? A rigid relationship like the one Kristina had with her parents wasn't happening. Chase might be aloof but he didn't do cold, much as he tried to pretend differently.

Did she truly believe that? The dreams that romped through her head at night where they were always together—working, playing, living—said so. In those he was always fun, kind and laughing. Which wasn't likely to become real. Dreams were nothing more than uncontrolled hope flitting through her mind when she wasn't in a position to stop them.

Moving away, she vowed to get on to looking into GP vacancies as soon as she had time to herself. It wasn't fair to expect Jarrod to come up with what she required.

'Why aren't there any jobs available where I'd like to live?' Kristina muttered as she shuffled her backside on the hard deck and leaned against the bulkhead, trying to stay out of the sun, still strong as it slid beyond the horizon.

'You being too picky?'

Chase. Where had he come from? How long had he been standing there? Why hadn't her radar warned her? 'Probably.'

'What are you looking for?' He sat down beside her, stretching those long legs for ever, and folding his arms across that expansive chest that stretched his T-shirt over interesting muscles that she itched to touch, to kiss, to lick.

In other words, diverting her attention to places it had no right to go. 'Something permanent.'

'So you've said. Are you sure you want to settle down? No more travelling the world, using your medical skills to help others?'

Did he have to make it sound so dull? So ordinary? It was what she longed for. 'Yes. My skills are just as useful at home, working in a medical centre, as here.'

'Home as in Manchester?'

'I have no wish to return to Manchester.' Now she looked up from the website listing medical positions all over Britain that she'd been scrolling through and focused entirely on her inquisitor. 'I prefer the south of England.'

'A small town like Merrywood.' When she gasped he added, 'It's written all over your face.'

She looked away. 'It can't be.' She'd become an expert at hiding her feelings.

'Was your boarding school in Manchester?'

'Yes, but Dad wasn't most of the time so no weekend catch-ups. Anyway, that's history, doesn't pertain to anything here. My problem is that I'll be unemployed in a little over four weeks, and that makes me nervous. I like to know where I'll be at any point in time. I plan my year to know what I'll be doing and where I'll be doing it, except I only got close to six months sorted this time.' She stared at him, hoping he'd understand her need to find her little spot in the world, a place that didn't require major worries about how to survive while making sure others could, too.

'You just argued with yourself. Your past is driving your future.' Breaking eye contact, his head tapped the bulkhead as he tipped it back and stared out in front of them.

The sea and sky had merged on the horizon so it was impossible to tell where one started and the other finished. 'Sometimes that's how I feel,' Kristina conceded. 'What you said is true for everybody.'

'Why this need to settle down?'

'It's what women in their thirties do.' She glanced at him. 'And, no, the biological clock's not ticking. I've been looking for somewhere to call my own since the day I overheard the girls at boarding school saying I didn't belong in their dorm, that I was dumb.' Following on from her mother not wanting her and her dad dumping her into someone else's care, the girls had only confirmed what she'd learned. She wasn't lovable, or likable.

Chase took her hand in his, clasped them together on his thigh. 'So why the army? Why *Medicine For All*? Why didn't you buy a house in any town and join the local medical practice when you qualified?'

'Shouldn't you be checking on patients? Or organising rosters?' She couldn't find the strength to withdraw her hand. It felt as though it was in the right place. Neither should she continue talking about her past. But there was nothing of interest to divert her attention on the medical jobsite. She closed that down with her free hand.

'The rosters are up to date, all vacancies filled again. The refugees are in capable hands or sleeping.'

Rare indeed for Chase to be letting go that easily. The blue in the sea was darkening to black, whereas in the sky it was as though the colour was slowly draining away to leave behind a star-studded canvas. Relaxing, she gave in to the need to talk.

'A recruitment officer for the armed forces was at a school where I was working on an immunisation programme and we had lunch together at the back of a classroom away from raging teenagers and bored teachers. He talked about the services and how he'd belonged to the army since he'd left school and it felt more like family than his parents and brothers ever had.' That had struck a chord with her. 'He mentioned how everyone in the unit always had his back in a way he'd never known before. I signed up within two months.'

'Was he right?'

'Yes.' She sighed. 'And no. I always knew the men and women around me had my back, wherever we were stationed. I belonged to them, to the greater picture. We ate, drank, worked together twenty-four seven, to the point it got claustrophobic and I'd wish I was out in the real world again. Until I was discharged. Obtusely then I wanted back in.' Much like the day her father had deposited her at that boarding school and told her she had to stand on her own feet and not be so needy. Apparently wanting to be loved by her parents was wrong.

'There were no jobs you could've done if you'd stayed in?'

'Nothing I wanted. The medical side was basic on home base. My back injuries stymied me from ever again being able to carry a twenty-five-kilo pack for hours on end. There were desk jobs, except pen-pushing didn't appeal.'

'It's always the paperwork that rubs me up the wrong way, but there's no avoiding it, I'm afraid. Not that I've found anyway.'

'When you do, copyright the idea. You'll make a fortune.'

'Now, there's a thought. But what would I do with said fortune? I'd want to be philanthropic but it takes time to look into charities and make decisions about who to donate money to. Time that would keep me away from surgeries and medical cases.'

'Which is what keeps you moving.'

Chase's hand jerked around her fingers. 'Yes.'

Kristina left it at that and studied the stars appearing in their thousands.

'There's a shooting star.' Chase pointed to the west.

The glittering light shot across the sky. 'I'm making a wish,' she chuckled. *To finally find what I've been searching for.* Her hand tightened around Chase's.

'Don't tell me what you wish for or it won't come true.'

Not a chance. Some things were best kept secret regardless of the consequences. Now she wanted another star on the move, because suddenly she really, really wanted to wish for Chase to kiss her. She could make the first move but what if he pushed her away? What if he told her the other night couldn't be repeated? Instigating a kiss then being rejected would humiliate and hurt. To hell with it. She'd take the risk.

But as she turned toward Chase he stood up and leaned down to tug her gently. 'Join me up here, will you?'

Then she was in his arms and his mouth was covering hers. No need for another shooting star. Certain dreams came true because they were meant to. Kristina gave up thinking and succumbed to Chase and his mouth, his chest pressing against her breasts and those hands splayed across her back. The hard rod pressing into her stomach. Heat spread slowly throughout her body, warming her in places that had been cold for far too long. This she could get to like permanently.

Her lungs squeezed tight. What?

Chase's mouth left hers. 'Kristina? You all right?'

Permanently? With Chase? It wasn't happening. *Am I all right?* 'Absolutely,' she whispered, before returning her mouth to his, afraid he'd walk away before she'd finished with him. More than all right. As long as she didn't think about that permanent word.

Chase deepened the kiss and she forgot everything except the man delivering this wonder. Forgot common sense, disregarded the warning bells clanging in the back of her head, and went with him to some place she'd never been before. And that was only with a kiss.

'Have you decided what you're doing for your days off?' Jane asked Kristina as the two of them worked on a young girl with a fever related to an infection in a wound in her thigh.

At the next bed Chase palpated a man's belly and held his breath as he listened for Kristina's answer. It was a question he'd been pondering, with an idea he wasn't certain was right brewing in the back of his mind.

Kristina drew up a dose of antibiotics. 'I'm thinking I'll do some sightseeing around Marseille, might even go to Nice for a day or into Italy. The trains run all the time. And I'll soak for hours in the spa at the hotel where MFA has booked our rooms.'

He had his answer. Two days before everyone headed off in different directions and he was already thinking how much he'd miss Kristina. Those times they had to themselves on the deck held him enthralled. 'The idea of the break is to get well away from the ship and the problems it's connected to.' The words spilled out of his mouth. True though they were, he suspected Kristina might be avoiding going back to England for her time off because there was no one she especially wanted to catch up with.

'I won't be on board, I'll be at the hotel. What's everyone else doing?' She was good at redirecting a conversation when it got too close for comfort.

Jane answered, 'I'm heading to Majorca, where my boyfriend's got an apartment. He's flying out from London to be with me. Three days of sun, swimming and lots of sangria. What more could a girl want?'

'It sounds sublime.' Kristina laughed, but there was a hint of sadness in the depths of her eyes.

Chase hated seeing that. He wanted to cheer her up, make her laugh. Stepping away from his patient, he told them, 'I'm going to my mother's sixtieth birthday shindig.'

After hearing about Kristina's sad family life, he'd rethought how lucky he was and had given in to the demands from Libby and his father to turn up for his mother's special occasion. Feeling like the heel he was for avoiding most family gatherings, he'd been mortified at his mother's joy. He really had become a terrible son, and while he believed he was protecting himself from further pain there no denying he'd hurt his family in the process. 'I'll be staying at my parents' farm.'

'Nice.' Kristina wiped the girl's arm and slid the needle in. The girl didn't wince.

'Want to join me?' he asked into a sudden silent moment. It was awkward because whatever her answer everyone would hear it, and know he'd got friendly with her when it was general knowledge he didn't do friendships. Except now he did. Reid had refused to be pushed away, had insisted they had a lot to work on and an underlying respect for each other despite Nick's death hanging between them. Despite, or because of?

During the weeks Ethan had been on board he'd begun to question everything he'd held onto since the tragedy and had realised how much he admired Ethan and always had, that what he'd believed to be strong dislike when they had been teens had actually been envy because the guy had been a better skier than him. None of that made him feel any better about himself.

Kristina's eyes widened and the empty syringe shook in her hand. 'What did you say?'

Here was the chance to backtrack, to reword the invitation. He didn't do inviting women to his parents' home on those rare occasions he visited. His mother and Libby would be asking questions there were no answers to. 'Want to go to Somerset for our down time? You already know half the clan.'

Get that, anyone listening in? Kristina's no stranger to my family. This is a friendly invitation, not what you might be thinking.

Kristina stared at him as though he'd lost his mind.

He had. He was going to regret it if she answered yes. Though right now disappointment was gathering like storm clouds the longer she remained quiet.

The silence around them grew, as if everyone was waiting for Kristina's answer. When Chase glanced around he saw one or two people watching them but most were engrossed in patients—or pretending to be. Returning his gaze to Kristina, he held his breath.

'Thank you for offering but I'll stay in France.'

His gut dropped. So did his heart. Why? 'Okay, if that's what you want, but in case you change your mind the offer remains until nine tomorrow morning when I leave for the airport.' Relief should be flooding in at her turning him down. Instead he felt piqued. Did he really want Kristina visiting his parents? Libby wasn't known for keeping her mouth shut when it came to her brother; all part of her agenda to make him get over the past and return home to settle. As for his mother, she'd see Kristina as a challenge, a woman to get onside. Still, the disappointment at his offer being declined was growing.

'Thank you.' The syringe rolled between her fingers.

'Careful. You could do yourself some damage with that.' Returning to his patient, he was soon left looking for something else to do. Seeing the doctor rostered to assist him with some minor surgical procedures shortly, he tracked through the waiting refugees. 'Calvin, see you in ten?'

There was a list as long as the table of these procedures to be done but since the cleaners had taken over scrubbing out the area after the last shift knocked off, they weren't able to start earlier.

'Not long now,' Chase told patients as he strode past, hands forced open, a tight smile stretching his face. What was wrong with joining him for a few days' R and R? 'Afterwards there'll be meals waiting for you,' he added when he noticed one of the men repeating everything to the others. Worried smiles broke out. They had yet to learn that when he gave his word it would be kept, and by the time they did they'd gone from the ship and on to whatever awaited them next.

A little after two, Chase and Calvin downed tools and went to grab a bite to eat. 'That was some line-up,' he muttered around his sandwich. He ached from head to toe from standing over the operating table for so long, but at least this intake would be ready to leave the ship when they docked at Marseille. 'You'd think I'd be used to it.'

'Throw in the late nights we work as well and the hours stack up really quickly.'

Kristina and Freja wandered into the room, picked up

plates of salad and bread rolls and came towards them. Both of the girls looked as exhausted as he felt. It was definitely time for that break.

'We had twin girls this morning,' Freja told them with a smile. 'So pretty.'

Kristina sat at the furthest end and tore into her roll hungrily.

'You helped with the birth?' Chase asked, because he wanted to hear her sweet voice.

Her ponytail swung as she shook her head. 'I've been assisting Jorge with vaccinations. Hope that's all right?'

'Of course it is.' He couldn't remember what she was rostered on, but he had no problems with what she'd done.

'I'll get to the children and their check-ups as soon as I've finished lunch.' Kristina lifted a water bottle to those wonderful lips and guzzled half the contents, her eyes closed.

Desire swiped him; hard and sharp. The air hummed. His lungs didn't know whether to breathe in or out. It would take one look from her and he'd be leaping up to sweep her into his arms and race along to his cabin where he'd make love to her, long and deliciously slow—if he had the stamina to hold on for long and slow.

Kristina yawned. 'Sorry.'

Chase collected his scattered brain cells and pulled himself together. This was absolutely silly. Losing control in front of staff in a place where he couldn't do a thing about what was ripping him apart, with a woman who kissed like a she-devil and had then said she wouldn't go home with him was doing his head in—not to mention other parts of his taut body.

Why wouldn't she go to Somerset? Though if this was how he reacted in a dining room where half a dozen medics were eating lunch then he should be grateful. He wouldn't be able to keep his hands to himself as they walked in the fields or sat at the local, having a beer.

Right now he needed to be busy. Very busy. Carefully adjusting his trousers before standing, he took his plate to the dishwasher, trying not to watch Kristina as she sat, chewing slowly, her eyes still half-shut, exhaustion leaking out of her like sauce on an upside-down pudding.

Grabbing a coffee, Chase headed for his office and the pile of paperwork that had come in on the helicopter that morning. Along with the papers there'd been a load of medical supplies they'd run out of due to the unprecedented number of minor surgeries performed over the last three days. At the time he'd have preferred that the satchel had been dropped on the other side of the railing so it could have sunk to the bottom of the sea, but now he was glad of something to occupy his restless mind.

Not that work calmed his rampant hormones. Hopefully getting deeply engrossed in refugee numbers and the amount of flour Pierre needed would eventually settle everything back into place. Until next time Kristina was in his breathing space.

'Chase, got a minute?' Kristina stood in the doorway.

No, his mind roared. 'What's up?' he said aloud. Now, there was a loaded question. He shifted from one foot to the other.

Her tongue wetted her bottom lip. 'Please, don't think I'm being ungrateful, turning down your offer.'

'I don't. But the dogs are going to be disappointed.'

'What?' Her head flicked back so she was staring at him, and then a soft smile lightened the moment, made him fight to stop himself wrapping his arms around her. 'You've got dogs?'

'Not me, my mother. She's bananas about her two German shepherds, and they go crazy around visitors, especially those who take them walking in the fields.'

'Low blow, mister. I love dogs. Once I settle I'm getting one, maybe two.' Her eyes were alight with excitement.

'So you might change your mind about going to the farm—because of dogs, and not me?' He grinned to show no hard feelings, and made a mental note to buy the biggest, juiciest bones in the village if she said yes to going with him.

'You push a hard bargain. But…' Her shoulders rose slowly. 'But I have a dress to buy, and I still need to look into finding a job.'

'You can do that in Somerset as easily as in Marseille.' At least his knees weren't on the floor as he all but begged. 'I know how much you want to resolve the employment problem, but there's nothing wrong with having some fun while you're doing it.'

'You're persistent, aren't you?'

'I've been known to be.' Usually when it was to get something for a patient, not when it came to a beautiful woman he couldn't get out of his head. But he'd never been faced with this dilemma before and was like a blind man trying to follow a track through the forest.

'Jarrod told me to drop by once I'd finished with MFA.'

'Kristina, can you take a look at Abdal Matin when you've got a moment?' A nurse appeared between them. 'His temperature's spiking again.'

'Coming right now.' She locked thoughtful eyes on him. 'Talk later.'

His heart sank. That meant she was still saying no to his invitation. He had to accept it, or risk looking like a prize prat.

So Jarrod kept in touch with her. He'd sung Kristina's praises when she'd worked for him. Who wouldn't? She'd do anything for her patients, and Chase believed she'd do the same for a partner and any children they might have. Lucky guy, whoever that man might be. Because she would meet someone to love and care about her. How could she not when she was so beautiful, inside and out?

You could be that man.

Using his heel to slam the door shut, he stomped across the narrow space to the desk. He did not want to be that man.

You're sure about that?

Very. His heart might get a few palpitations when they kissed, his body definitely lusted after hers, his dreams were filled of images of Kristina, his hands always wanting to reach for her—but he would not get emotionally involved. He wasn't ready to stop roaming the world, saving injured people. He never would be as long as the nightmares about that night on the mountainside persisted.

Nick had never got to win gold at the skiing championships, hadn't fallen in love, or studied to become the architect he'd wanted to be, or had had children—all because his best friend hadn't been able to save him, try as hard as he did.

Sorry, Nick. So damned sorry.

Time to sign the contract that'd take him to another continent at the end of summer.

Chase dug his phone out and punched a number. 'Ethan, got a minute?'

'Sure. What's up?'

Not answering that. He shifted in his chair. 'Nothing. Just thought I'd give you a call.' No excuses needed this time. 'I could do with some sensible talk.'

'So Kristina's giving you grief. I like it.'

He should've left the phone in his pocket and sat on it. 'I don't.'

'We going to talk about this?'

Deep breath. 'I invited her to the farm. She turned me down.'

'Don't give up at the first knock, man. Be as stubborn about this as you are about work.'

'Like you?' Finally Chase began to relax. This was why he'd phoned his friend. 'I recall you opting to be there but not as a couple when Claire announced she was pregnant and keeping the baby whether you wanted it or not.'

'Watch and learn. If you want Kristina, go after her, be persistent until you win or lose.'

There was the million-dollar question. Did he want her? 'Yes.' The word sighed out of his throat. Yes.

CHAPTER SIX

'I'M GOING SHOPPING in Marseille tomorrow for my brides-maid dress,' Kristina told Claire over the phone. 'I'll take photos if I find something special and email them to you for your approval.'

'Whatever you're happy with I'll like,' Claire replied. 'Have you docked already?'

'The city lights are getting closer by the minute.' She leaned on the rail in the space on deck and wished there was something more exciting to look forward to than buy-ing a dress. Which was grossly unfair to her new friend. She dug deep for enthusiasm. 'Is sky blue still your col-our of preference?'

'Unless you think you'll look hideous in it then yes. It's fashionable this season so it shouldn't be hard to find something.'

'If I don't have success here, I can try Nice or Genoa.'

'Remember to get something sexy, blow Chase's socks off. And his boxers.'

Kristina laughed hollowly. 'Yeah, right.' Her palm rubbed the scar line on her thigh.

'Kristina? Are you all right? Is something wrong?'

The concern in Claire's voice nearly undid her. 'I'm fine. Truly. With three days' leave about to start, why wouldn't I be?'

'Because you'll miss Chase.'

'Says who?'

'You weren't listening.' Claire paused. When Kristina neglected to fill in the silence, she continued, 'Still fancy him?'

'Yep.'

'The two of you need to get on with it, work whatever this is that you're denying out of your systems. Or make it something that's impossible to walk away from.'

This time Kristina was quick to speak, afraid of what else her friend might have an opinion on. 'Forget writing for an agony aunt column, you should try writing a romance. You've got the talent for making up stories.' Impossible to walk away from? She was already starting to think leaving Chase at the end of her twelve weeks was going to be hard.

This time Claire didn't laugh along with her. 'What's the problem? You're not sounding one hundred percent happy, so spill.'

Kristina glanced around, mindful Chase would come out here once he'd finished his paperwork. She was alone. But then her extra-sensory perception had already told her that. Chase only had to step onto the deck and her body would thrum with excitement. 'He invited me to go home with him. It's his mother's birthday and there's a party planned.'

'That's wonderful. You'll have a great time. Don't you already know his sister and her family?'

'You weren't listening,' she remonstrated. 'I'm staying at the hotel MFA has booked in Marseille to go sightseeing and shopping.'

'Come on, Kristina. Take this opportunity to have some fun. As in real, let-your-hair down fun.' Her laughter was naughty and left nothing to Kristina's imagination about what that fun should be.

She wanted to agree, to accept Chase's invitation and enjoy herself without worrying about getting a job or finding the right dress for the wedding or whether she'd ever find a town to call home. But the consequences? Suddenly she said, 'I was hasty in turning him down.' Then hadn't known how to retract without showing Chase how her increasingly mixed emotions were screwing with her head.

'You're afraid of where it might lead, of being hurt. But you'll get nowhere if you don't take a chance. Look at me. I was afraid Ethan would walk away and now I'm planning a wedding and dealing with morning sickness every afternoon.'

'Whoa, slow down, will you? It's only a weekend with people I mostly don't know, not a love fest with a man who has me in the palm of his hand.' Scratch that last bit. He only had to look at her and she'd melt into a pool at his feet, into his arms, against that lean, muscular body.

'Stop holding back. Get out there and live a little.'

Could she do that without coming a cropper? She'd give up parts of herself for him, but not her need to be in control of her life. Going to Somerset with Chase would be like putting a match to petrol, and she'd grab it with both hands. It was the afterwards that frightened her. There were no guarantees. They might fall head over heels in love with each other and ride off into the sunset, or they could say that was good, thanks very much, and get on with the last three weeks on *SOS Poseidon*, but most likely she'd settle further into the depths of love beginning to spread through her head and her heart, and then she'd be lost. Unable to get back on track and finally make her life happen. 'It's not that simple, Claire.'

'Yes, it is. What have you got to lose that you haven't already?'

My heart. 'My sanity.'

'Sure you haven't already?' Claire asked in all seriousness. 'A little nudge in a different direction doesn't necessarily mean getting hurt, and it might find you something fabulous you've never expected.'

Kristina cut in. 'Don't you dare say look what happened to you two again.'

'I don't need to. You're already thinking about it. Now, a certain someone is indicating it's time to go for a stroll around the village before hitting the sack. Text me when you make up your mind about what you're doing.'

'I already told you.' But Kristina was talking to herself. The distinct sound of a phone being cut off was the only reply she got. *Thanks, friend.*

She stretched her legs one at a time, the left one protesting at the effort, then she stood with feet wide and bent over into the V pose of Downward Facing Dog. With her hands flat on the deck and her butt sticking up, she tried to clear her mind of everything but banishing the aches in her leg and back. She needed quiet space in her head to get back on track.

'I brought you tea.'

She whipped upright, wobbling on her feet as her head caught up with the sudden change from hanging down to being upright. Chase stood a metre away, holding two mugs, looking like he was caught in headlights. How long had he been there? Her cheeks burned. He should be in his office, not gaping at her rear end. 'I hoped you were giving this a miss tonight.'

He shook his head abruptly, and tea spilled onto the deck. His eyes were still too wide, and there was a distinct look of want turning them to forest green. 'I've finished the paperwork.' His voice had darkened. Sexy.

'Oh.' She hadn't got that message.

'That stretch helping?'

It had until he'd turned up. Though now she could forget the aches in her back and thigh because the tension in her stomach was taking over, sending pulses of heat to her core. She nodded, speech beyond her.

'Here.' He pressed a mug into her hand and turned to lean on the rail, his mug clasped in both hands as he stared across the narrowing gap between them and Marseille.

It was a miracle she didn't tip the tea all over the place. Her knuckles whitened and the mug steadied. Now what? Keep quiet and see what he said. That wasn't hard considering the block on her brain and the pounding in her chest.

'That's a beautiful sight.'

He was talking about the panorama before them, wasn't he? 'Cities look so exciting from a distance. All those lights have me guessing at what's going on in the streets.'

'Want to go see when we dock? We could have a drink in a wine bar or go to a jazz club.'

Definitely talking about the city. Not her butt. 'You're into jazz?'

'What's not to like about it?' He continued watching the approaching shoreline, like he didn't know where else to look.

'I wouldn't know.' Music wasn't her thing.

'Then it's time to find out.' He glanced at his watch. 'Meet me at the gangway in thirty.'

She hadn't seen that coming. 'You're on.' Just like that she had a date—with Chase Barrington. The only man she wanted to go out with. What to wear? Her pack hadn't come filled with dresses and fancy shoes, just T-shirts, shorts and sneakers. 'See you soon.'

She tore down the stairs. 'Jane,' she yelled as she shoved their cabin door wide. 'I need clothes to wear to a night club.'

'I've got a skirt that might fit you—don't dance too vigorously unless you want to show what you've got. Who are you going with?'

Kristina caught her breath and eyeballed her cabin mate, trying for stern. 'Chase.'

'Brilliant.' Jane held her hand up, palm out.

Caught up in the moment, Kristina raised her own hand, slapped Jane's in return. 'Let me see this skirt. And thanks. I'll have it back before you leave for your flight in the morning.'

'Don't worry. I can replace it in Monaco. It's not the prettiest skirt you'll have ever worn but it beats those denim shorts you're so fond of. Now, a top. We'll go and see Freja. She's got enough clothes to go round all the females on board.'

'Really? Why?'

Jane's laugh would've been heard all over the ship. 'She likes to be prepared. Why not when the men are falling all over her?' She knocked on a cabin door. 'Freja, you in there? We need help.'

Chase watched the vision coming towards him and felt the tension holding him stiff let go and a low whistle rush across his lips. 'You look stunning.'

Kristina grinned. 'Not a bad effort considering what was in my half of the shoebox-sized wardrobe.'

He held out his hand. 'Let's have some fun. I can't believe you haven't listened to jazz.' He couldn't believe they were going on a date.

Her fingers tightened around his. 'I'm open to new experiences.'

There was a plus. Though how many new ones they'd face tonight was anyone's guess. One step at a time. Chase blinked. How many steps did he plan on taking? He wasn't thinking only about tonight. But she'd already turned down his invitation for the weekend.

He waved down a taxi and helped Kristina inside, trying not to stare at her delightful derrière. But how could he not when it was right there; rounded, filling out the red skirt perfectly?

The jazz club was heaving when they arrived, standing room only and a queue for the bar. 'Welcome to downtown Marseille,' he said against her ear so he was heard. That he got a whiff of pine and roses was a bonus. 'What would you like to drink?'

'A mojito would be great.'

'Wait here, and I'll try to be quick.'

'I'm coming with you or we might never see each other again.' Her hand slid effortlessly back into his and she stayed close as they pushed through to the bar.

'There's a bar upstairs and one through that door,' the barman told Chase as he mixed Kristina's drink. 'Different bands at each and you might find some seating upstairs.'

'*Merci,*' Chase said. 'We'll take a look.'

The only available chairs were at a table with three other couples, who happily let them join the group. Chase settled Kristina before sitting beside her and propping his elbows on his knees, his chin in his hand. 'This is a jazz club.'

'No complaints so far.' She tossed him a saucy smile.

Was she flirting with him? Two could play that game. 'I don't intend to give you anything to criticise,' he gave back, and felt strangely happy when she laughed.

'Sure of yourself, aren't you?'

'Oh, yeah.' What sort of man would admit to the butterflies that had come to life in the last minute? A woman didn't want an insecure guy trying to woo her. Wait, he was wooing her now? He sure was. Only for tonight. He'd see where they got to on mojitos and bourbon and loud music and hot moves on the dance floor. If they returned to the ship and separate cabins with the narrow uncomfortable bunks then that was how it would end. Standing, he held out a hand. 'Let's dance.'

'This could get tricky. These shoes aren't mine and

they're a little tight.' But she was already heading for the dance floor, her hand pulling at his.

Chase couldn't take his eyes off her as she raised her arms and rolled with the music. She mightn't be familiar with jazz but her body certainly knew how to move. He felt clumsy beside her, his own movements heavy and awkward, and he'd thought he knew what he was doing on a dance floor. But it didn't matter. No one would be watching him, all eyes would be on his partner. But, boy, did she know how to swing those hips and push out her breasts and move her hands in time to the music that seemed to get louder and louder. He was lost. In her. In the picture before him. In the music that she was responding to as though she'd been dancing to jazz all her life.

When Kristina whirled around and wrapped her arms around his neck his hands found her slender waist and he leaned in to kiss her. Who needed bourbon when he had this woman in his grasp? She was an aphrodisiac in a tight skirt and low-cut top, balancing effortlessly on ladder-high heels. Chase tipped his head back and laughed. He had not been this happy in a long, long time.

Kristina heard that laugh, felt it all the way to her toes, and smiled around the bubble of excitement bouncing up her throat. This was Chase as she'd never seen him, letting go and relaxing, having fun, truly enjoying himself. With her. Right now life couldn't get any better. Right now was what it was about. Not yesterday. Not tomorrow. Tonight. Her hands gripped together at the back of his neck and she stretched up to kiss that teasing mouth, to put a stop to the rampant sensations his smile caused in her belly. Much more and they'd have to find a bed, fast.

As her mouth caressed Chase's, those sensations went into overdrive, spinning through her body, touching everywhere, bringing her alive beyond what she'd ever imagined. Yet her limbs still moved in time to the jazz filling the air. Her feet hadn't stopped from the moment she'd walked onto the dance floor, while her eyes had been fixed on this sexy man holding her with those wicked hands, like he had no intention of letting her go. It felt like they were meant to be together, here, in this club, this city, on this night.

Then the lights flicked off then on again. A loud announcement broke through and brought her upright, still holding onto Chase, afraid to let him go in case that was the end of their time together.

'They're calling final drinks,' Chase interpreted. 'Let's get out of here and grab a taxi before the rush starts.'

She'd have hesitated, reluctant to go, but Chase took her hand in his and rubbed a thumb across the back, and her skin sat up to attention. 'All right.' Did he mean this wasn't the end of their night? 'We could walk. Our wharf's not too far away.'

'Are you sure your feet can stand it? Is your back playing up? You're walking a little lopsided.'

The concern in his voice touched her. She wasn't used to someone noticing and caring. Her back ached like mad and her thigh wasn't happy but she'd get over it. She was not spoiling a wonderful night by moaning about what couldn't be fixed. 'I don't want the night to end, that's all.'

'You're sure about that?' he asked.

'Absolutely.'

'I'm with you.' Chase pulled her up against him and kissed her forehead, then each cheek and finally, finally her mouth.

Oh, yes. She melted against him, kissed him back with all the passion pouring along her veins. So much for not getting involved. Right now there was nothing capable of stopping her. 'You're right. We need a taxi. Now,' she whispered from the side of her mouth, and went back to kissing him.

When she felt one arm lift from her shoulder she continued kissing him, pausing only to clamber into the cab and resume the instant Chase pulled her against him.

Then they were tipping out of the taxi at the security gate on the wharf. Kristina looked around. In the east the sky was beginning to lighten on the dark horizon. 'I can't remember the last time I was out all night.'

Chase placed an arm around her waist. 'I'd say you haven't been living, but it's the same for me. All work and no play makes for sad puppies.'

The guard waved them through. *'Bonsoir, Docteurs.'*
'Bonsoir, Louis.'

They reached the gangway. Chase murmured against her lips before his mouth covered hers, 'Come on. I can't wait any longer.'

'Chase, where the hell have you been?' a robust male voice interrupted them.

Chase ripped his mouth away from hers, though he kept his hands on her shoulders as she wobbled on those shoes, and asked the ship's captain, who was standing at the top of the gangway, 'What's the problem?'

'I've been phoning you for hours. Liam wants to talk to you urgently. He's in Manila and he isn't happy about something,' Josip told him.

The man was never happy about anything. Chase's hand automatically went to his pocket, pulled his phone free. 'Five missed calls.'

'You wouldn't hear it ringing inside the club. We couldn't hear ourselves think.' Not that she'd been doing much of that, unless it had involved the hot male body dancing before her. Hot and full of the promise of more heat. Kristina straightened, stepped back from those steadying hands, a sinking sensation going on in her stomach. Chase was back at work, whether he realised it or not, wanted to be or not. Being available twenty-four seven was what he did. Tonight had been uncharacteristic, not normal. She followed him up the gangway, trying not to drown in the disappointment flooding her.

He was telling Josip, 'I'm on leave. Have been since midnight.'

'Tell that to Liam. He's in a real mood, I'm warning you.'

Kristina reached the deck and stood watching Chase. The heat between them was gone, evaporated in a dose of reality. Though why should Chase let someone demand he phone them when he was on leave? But she already knew he would never walk away from his responsibilities. This was a timely reminder of how it would be if she took this any further. Her feet weren't yet back on the ground; she still wanted to follow through on their promises to go downstairs together. For her the night was not over. It might be out here where the sky was lightening to a grey shade of blue, but not within herself. No, her body was still afire with need. She laid a hand on his arm. 'Chase?'

Her heartbeat quickened as she watched the play of emotions on his face. Determination was winning. He was going to ignore Liam's calls and finish the night with her.

Then regret took over. 'Kristina, I'm sorry.'

'No, Chase. You don't have to be.' *You can come with me.* 'Phone Liam. I'll wait.'

He leaned in and kissed her. When he drew back his mouth lifted in a wry smile. 'I'll be as quick as I can. If I don't call back, Liam won't stop harassing Josip.'

Relief had her heartbeat slowly quietening. 'Remind Liam you have a life.'

'Unfortunately I don't really. Not outside MFA.' He leaned down to place the softest kiss ever on her lips. 'But for the first time I can remember, I want to. Thanks to you.'

'I'll be topside.' Could they make love in their space?

Most personnel were long gone. No, most likely they'd head to Chase's cabin.

'See you shortly.'

She watched him stalk across to the stairway leading to his office, her hope of finishing the evening in his arms making love still there but cautious, uncertain. So much for having a great night out and then getting over him. All she wanted was more. 'Chase?'

He paused, turned back. 'Kristina?'

'Is your invitation to join you in Somerset still open?' Her heart stopped, her lungs waited.

Caution crept into his eyes. 'Yes, of course.'

Thump, thump. Breathe. 'Then I'll be at the gate at nine. What airline do I book a seat on?'

'Leave that to me. I'll do it while I'm talking to Liam.' The next thing she was being lifted up and swung around in a circle before being placed back on her feet and receiving another kiss, this time on the tip of her nose. 'Somerset, here we come.'

'Multi-tasking? But you're a man.'

'Glad you noticed.'

How couldn't she? 'I'll fix you up for the flights.' They weren't in the sort of relationship where she'd accept him paying for her trip. Probably never would be. No reason not to have a load of fun over the weekend, though.

Up in 'their' space, Kristina toed off the shoes, which were killing her. It'd take more than one night to get used to glam footwear. Leaning on the railing, she soaked up the lights and tooting horns and shouts that was downtown Marseille at this hour, and let her excitement grow. How long would Chase be on the phone? Tempted to go down to his office and sit on his lap while he talked business, she wavered. That might be pushing the boundaries too far, too soon. One fantastic night would not change Chase into a relaxed, let's have fun with no consequences kind of guy.

She hadn't changed that much either, and being tense and nervous would spoil the moment. She'd wait here, let the anticipation in her veins grow and keep her warm.

'Liam, what's so important you have to phone in the middle of the damned night?' Chase growled. The phone was on speaker to allow him to pace around the poky office, trying to pacify the tension in his body that was all about Kristina and her seductive body, and nothing to do with work.

'Interrupt something, did I?'

Damned right you did. The best thing that's happened in a long while. Like for ever.

Chase held back on shouting. Liam would wind him up relentlessly. When he didn't feel like killing the Swiss national, they were friends. 'I'm on leave and was out having a drink with friends.'

Make that a friend who's within minutes of being my lover.

'My apologies. I didn't think beyond needing to talk to you before you left for England.' Liam paused.

Chase didn't rush in to forgive him, just waited and paced.

'We've got a lot to do in the Philippines. The people here are in need of urgent medical help.'

Chase clicked onto the internet and the airline taking him home in a few hours. Might as well get Kristina's ticket sorted while listening to Liam's rant. Once he started there'd be no stopping him. Except this morning his call wasn't going to be a long diatribe. *He* had somewhere to go, a woman to be with, and frustration was making him edgy. He could feel Kristina under his hands, taste that sensational mouth on his lips, wanted, needed her body joined to his. 'Liam,' he snapped.

'I need you in two places at once. We're short of doctors. These people, Chase, they'd break your heart. Today

I saw a three-year-old digging in the gutter for food. The boy needs urgent surgery for a displaced hip.'

The words came through the haze in Chase's head. There was a child who needed *him*. His skills. He pressed 'buy' on the flight details before him. 'You want me in Manila or Ghana next?' He'd be too late for the boy Liam was talking about. There were still weeks to go on the *Poseidon*, helping equally distressed people, but he'd go wherever he was most needed after that. It was why he was here, and would be there, or anywhere come tomorrow and all the days after.

Liam's sigh said it all. 'I guess Ghana. Who knows where you'll go after that? It's months away.'

'Whatever.' Chase saved Kristina's ticket, forwarded it to her phone. Kristina. She was waiting for him. Out in their space. 'I've got to go.' He wanted to make love with her. And then? Walk away? He stared at the screen where his copy of her ticket waited. There'd be no walking away for the next three days. And afterwards? After making love, and the party, and sharing his family, then what? Nothing would change. He still needed to save people.

Those demons still need to be placated, Nick. I can't stop moving from one crisis to the next. Can I?

Liam came through loud and clear. 'I don't like it when you go quiet. What's going on?'

'Sorry, doing two things at once.' It wasn't a lie, but it was the first time his mind was more focused on himself than on what Liam wanted. His gut churned with longing and the sense of missing out on something sensational. His trousers were uncomfortable, evidence of where his mind had been. Kristina.

'You need a break from all this? More than the three-day leave you've started?'

'Not at all.' But did he, though? The last nine weeks had knocked him around. First with Ethan landing in his life and insisting they sort out the past. That alone was enough to turn a man on his heel and have him running for the Sahara. Then along had come Kristina. Beautiful, mysterious, kind, fun and sexy. Don't forget the sexy. Like that was happening. She had his blood constantly running hot, and his ideas about his life sitting up and scratching at his head, as if to say, 'What am I doing? Do I want to spend the rest of my life going from one tragic place to another, to be always looking after those who can't look after themselves in faraway countries?'

Yeah, he did, because he had to.

'That's a relief.'

No pressure. He couldn't take any more. 'Talk to you later.' Stabbing the 'off' button brought that conversation to an end. But no relief.

Tonight had started out as an evening of drinks and dancing and music, and had ended with kisses, and sex about to happen. Except they'd been interrupted. He should've ignored Josip and Liam. Then he wouldn't have been responsible for the disappointment that had filled Kristina's eyes and face and tugged at her shoulders when she'd realised he would put work before her. He'd said he'd join her on deck, but he'd also let her down. Hell, he'd let them both down.

Chase took the stairs two at a time. Kristina was waiting for him.

But she wasn't. The space was empty, only a hint of her scent to confirm she'd been here.

His heart plummeted. Did she believe he hadn't intended to join her? Why had she left? Looking around, he could see the outlines of bollards and chains. The sun was coming up. His watch showed it'd been nearly an hour since they'd parted at the top of the gangway. Really? Liam had talked for that long?

Kristina must have thought he wasn't coming to her.

He wanted to rail against her for not trusting him, but couldn't. He should've cut the conversation short and joined her, but he hadn't.

He couldn't let the night finish like this. Couldn't. Sex was probably out, but an explanation—no, an apology was needed.

Kristina didn't answer his knock on her cabin door. The handle was locked.

Back in his office he texted her.

Liam took for ever.

No. He deleted the words, started again.

I am truly sorry. Can we try again? In Somerset? Airline tickets in your inbox.

Now he had a weekend to rectify things. If Kristina gave him a chance, which he so wanted. Of all the dumb things to have done, tonight's blunder had to be right up there. How close would he allow Kristina to get if she forgave him? Did they have a great time and walk away from each other come Sunday? Or did he give in to this crawling need coursing through his veins? For the first time in over a year he was going home, taking a woman with him who had his boxers in a twist and his heart holding its breath.

For the first time ever he was beginning to feel there was more to life than sick people in need of him. And it was scary.

CHAPTER SEVEN

'I'VE PREPARED YOU the bedroom next to Chase's,' Verity Barrington told Kristina much later. 'I wasn't sure if you two were friends or something more, so I've covered the bases.'

Kristina squirmed under the older woman's scrutiny. Was a man's mother supposed to say things like that?

There was a twinkle in Verity's eye that did nothing to quieten the hope knocking softly in Kristina's heart. It had started when Chase had apologised deeply as they'd waited for the taxi to take them to Marseille Province airport and it became real when his father, Alec, pulled up in front of the large double-storeyed farmhouse in Somerset and she'd climbed out of the four-wheel drive to stare around, with Chase standing beside her. The green fields where sheep grazed and the large implement sheds where tractors and machinery were stored made her feel she'd done the right thing in coming here. She was spending a weekend in Chase's territory.

'Watch out,' Chase had warned when German shepherds had charged out to greet first him and then her, making her welcome. His parents had accepted her without a barrage of questions, even hugged her on introduction. But that hope lurking in Verity's eyes when she'd mentioned the sleeping arrangements had Kristina questioning if she'd done the right thing in coming here.

'Thank you so much. I really appreciate you having me to stay.' She wasn't saying a word about bedrooms. For one, she didn't know the answer herself, and, secondly, Chase would put her on the next flight out if she talked about him to his mother.

'This couldn't get further from my cabin. It's enormous and I'm not sharing with Jane, who snores like a hungry pig. Nor are there people all over the place needing attention and fearful of asking for it.'

'It must get quite intense, dealing with those poor people.' Verity's eyes turned in the direction of her son, who was sitting in the conservatory with his father now that dinner was over. 'I know it takes a toll on Chase. Not that he's ever admitted it, but we see it in his demeanour. He's always tired, and doesn't laugh as much as he once did.'

'He takes his work very seriously.'

'Too seriously. While I'm not saying it's wrong, it breaks my heart that he doesn't lighten up a little. It's as though he doesn't want to enjoy life to its fullest.'

Kristina knew exactly where she was coming from. However, it wasn't her place to get involved in a deep and meaningful discussion about Chase. 'It's hard to put aside the things we see on a daily basis, which is why we have these breaks. They're essential to coping.'

'How long have you been on board the *Poseidon*?'

'I've done nine weeks, with three to go before I return to England and find a permanent job.'

'I wish Chase would do something similar.'

How long had it been since this woman had talked about her son to someone other than family? Why choose her? Hadn't she got the message that there wasn't a relationship going on, even if they were spending the weekend together? 'I'm sure he knows what he's doing,' she said softly, trying not to sound critical. The last thing she wanted was for Verity to turn her back on her. She liked the woman, and not just because she was Chase's mother. She was a charming, warm soul who adored her family and made strangers feel comfortable.

'I'll make a pot of tea. Would you like a cup?' Disappointment clouded the older woman's face.

Regret at having cut Verity off, but having had to before the conversation got out of hand, Kristina smiled. 'I'd love one. Shall I ask the men if they want one?'

'Alec will, but I don't know about Chase.' It was obvious she didn't know a lot of things about her son any more.

So he'd cut himself off from his family in order to stay true to his goal of saving people. Didn't he understand he could do that by living and working full time in Somerset? In the same country even? Saving people didn't mean only those who were in jeopardy of their lives because of politics. Helping a young girl overcome pain from a broken leg was as rewarding as removing a melanoma from a man's back before it metastasised.

'Where have you gone?' Chase stood in front of her.

She shook her head. 'I was coming to ask if you wanted a cup of tea.' Then, before he could ask more and she'd have to lie, she added, 'I'm looking forward to seeing more of the farm.'

'You ever been on one?'

'A couple of times when I was at boarding school I went home for long weekends with a girl who's a distant cousin. I didn't like the horses, too big and scary. But the cows and farm dogs were all right. More importantly, I loved the wide open spaces and how I could yell and laugh and no one heard me.'

'I'll take you to the farthest field tomorrow.'

'Or you could wait until the grandkids get here and

they can compete with Kristina.' Alec laughed. 'Those kids don't know the meaning of quiet.'

'I can't wait to see them again.' She meant it. It would be interesting to watch Chase interacting with them, too. Aloof, or down on his knees, hugging and playing, like he did on the ship? Could he remain uninvolved with them? Or would they knock his memories and fears aside for a short while? 'I met the boys at the medical centre. They certainly know how to create havoc.'

'Sounds like my nephews.' Chase grinned.

Suddenly Kristina's body slumped with exhaustion and it was hard to concentrate. A lack of sleep and being on edge about coming here was taking its toll. Now she'd relaxed everything was catching up. 'I know it's early but I think I'll go to bed, if no one minds.'

'Of course not. Take your tea with you,' Verity said. 'Make yourself at home and don't hesitate to use anything you want.' It was what any good hostess would say but it came with a huge dollop of kindness.

Kristina's eyes watered, and it took strength not to throw her arms around the woman. But she didn't. It might make her seem needy. Which she probably was. Why hadn't her mother been half as loving? Or her father? They did love her. They just had never shown it in the way she needed. It had been there in the trust funds and the expensive education her father had paid for, and the holidays to the luxury apartments her mother lived in with her latest billionaire. They didn't understand she'd have swapped it all for hugs and being cuddled when the cat died and having them watch when she acted in the school play. 'Goodnight, everyone.'

She scarpered to her room before emotion got the better of her, making her act like a blithering idiot. Coming here was beginning to look like a mistake.

'Kristina, wait,' Chase called as she began to close

the bedroom door. 'Are you all right?' He leaned an arm against the doorframe, studying her closely.

'Why wouldn't I be? Your parents are lovely.'

'So it's not their fault you're about to burst into tears?' His smile was gentle and undid the final cord holding in her emotion.

'No way,' she managed as those now familiar arms closed around her and drew her against the broad chest she'd touched last night. Why did she have to get so emotional? 'They're so open and friendly. It's not what I expected since they don't know me.'

'They're always like that, especially Mum. So, now what? Do I walk to my room and forget you're upset? Or shall I stay here and kiss you better?'

Kristina stepped backwards, her arms now firmly holding Chase, not wanting to let him go anywhere but up against her in her room. 'Option two.' She was only referring to a kiss, wasn't she? Yes, she had to be. For the sake of her head and heart. Not that she'd given those a thought last night when they'd been speeding back to the ship.

Bending towards her, Chase brushed his lips across hers and drew back a little. 'What made you sad?'

'Don't talk. Please,' she added, breathless around the electricity zipping throughout her body. Placing her mouth on his to shut him up and abate that current now debilitating her, she closed her eyes and went with the kiss. Went with being lost in Chase's arms, letting go of everything else, aware only of them.

A groan erupted between them, and opening her eyes she saw the happiness on Chase's face, in his eyes, and was happy to have given him that…and because his hands were circling her waist and his broad chest pressing against her breasts and awakening her further.

Kristina ripped her mouth away from his and stared at him. Making love was moments away—if she gave in to what she was feeling. It would be as easy as taking two steps and sinking onto the bed. She wanted it, needed Chase naked against her, pushing into her, taking her to great heights. And yet... 'Can we talk? I mean, I don't think I'm ready.'

His thumb rubbed across her lips. 'Damn.' He smiled. 'But it's okay. I think I understand.'

'I don't,' Kristina admitted, reluctant to remove her hands from him, wanting his strength and warmth. She backed away. 'I'm sorry.'

There was confusion and something she couldn't identify in his gaze. His voice was rough when he replied, 'Don't be. You're being honest, as you always are.'

If she was honest she'd admit to being afraid of where this could lead, scared of having her heart broken, of being left alone again. Better not to have loved than to love and lose him. Yet all she wanted was to fall onto the bed with Chase in her arms and forget the nagging memories from the past, to believe in a future filled with hope. She'd had time to think about this on the flight. She looked at him long and hard. If only she had the guts to follow through on the longing filling her from head to toe. If only. Early that morning nothing would've stopped her. What a difference a day could make. 'Goodnight, Chase,' she whispered.

'See you in the morning.' But he didn't move, remained standing there, watching her, a question in his eyes.

'What?' she asked finally.

He shook his head. 'It doesn't matter.'

The door clicked shut behind him and she was left feeling that she'd missed something big. 'I'm sorry,' she whispered.

She'd been looking out for herself. Sinking onto the bed, she hugged herself tight. And cursed silently. The more she came to know Chase the more she believed he was right for her—if he wasn't so determined to be alone.

Not that Verity had intended to but she'd reminded Kristina of the reasons she shouldn't fall in love with him. If it wasn't already too late. Double whammy, that. If this emotion that kept flooring her, stalling her was love, she'd found it with the wrong man. It had sneaked up and snared her when she wasn't looking.

Crawling into bed, she tugged the covers up to her chin and concentrated on forgetting Chase and his potent kisses, tried to think about the email she'd received from Jarrod that morning, asking if she'd drop into the medical centre tomorrow and catch up with everyone. There was something he wanted to discuss with her. Could there be a position going in Merrywood? A permanent one? If there was, how did she feel about it? Ha, that was one thing she did know the answer to.

It was exactly what she wanted, would be the perfect opportunity to get on with her life. She knew the staff, liked the locals, and could buy a cottage to suit her needs. She'd live alone. She'd meet people, and maybe a man would come along she would fall in love with.

Chase.

No, not Chase. She should never have come here. Now she had something else to put behind her.

Could be that she was getting ahead of herself. Jarrod might only want to catch up and offer her more locum work. And these feelings for Chase might be a figment of her overactive imagination.

Chase got up with the sun to take the dogs for a walk along the lane leading around the copse behind the house. So much for catching up on sleep. Impossible when Kristina reigned supreme in his head.

They'd come close to falling into bed together. So close he could still taste it on his tongue, feel it in his veins. But she'd backed off. That had nearly crushed him. He'd wanted her very badly, and he'd have sworn she felt the same. If not for Liam's phone calls the night before, they would've made love in his cabin. He'd have touched her everywhere, tasted her skin, felt her need, and held her to him as he pressed into her. He'd have known her intimately.

But he hadn't, though he wanted to more than ever. But he'd never force her to do something she wasn't one hundred certain about. Kristina had to come to him willingly. And had to want to make love as much as he wanted her. That was the scary thing. Because he did want Kristina, all of her, so damn much it hurt. He longed for the lovemaking, the laughter, the sadness, the history—and then a future.

'A future?' he roared at the blue sky looking down on him.

The dogs leapt, stared at him, their legs tense and shaking.

'Sorry, boys, but you don't know what it's like to be so damned afraid of grasping the chance at a future that might be on offer.' If only he could find the guts to front up to Kristina and lay these mixed-up feelings before her.

What do you reckon, Nick? Am I being stupid to think there might be a future with Kristina?

His head moved rapidly from side to side. It couldn't happen. That'd be a disaster. The desire crawling through his veins would become love, and he couldn't honour that in the way Kristina deserved. She needed a man at her side all the time, not when it pleased him to come home. She was not interested in travelling to different countries to put her medical skills to good use and he could not imagine himself staying in one place for ever. See? They were poles apart in their needs, and those poles could not be moved closer. He knew this in his bones. Nick was in the way.

The cool morning air made Chase shiver. Or could it be the sense of loss washing over him? Strange, when what he might be losing he hadn't actually gained in the first place. Deep conversations and off-the-scale kisses, a night on the town in a jazz club—that did not add up to a full-on relationship where both of them gave everything of themselves. Kristina had demons, too, but she was trying to work through them, unlike him.

Chase picked up his speed. He'd prepare breakfast, save his mum time when she already had plenty to do for the party.

'*Woof, woof.*' The dogs began trotting faster.

'Smell a rabbit, do you?' He turned and the air stuck in his throat.

Kristina stood in the ankle-high grass, hands clasped at breast height as she swung left and right from the waist, that stunning light hair, free for once and swishing back and forth across her back.

His mouth dried. 'OMG…' What little air was in his lungs hissed over his lips. Parts of his anatomy went rock hard. He couldn't move but he had to or she'd see him staring and think he was perving. He was. Couldn't help himself. 'Kristina,' he gasped. When she didn't acknowledge him he tried to swallow. It was impossible when his mouth was like a desert. Putting one leg in front of the other, he closed the gap, tried again. 'Morning, Kristina.'

Her eyes flew open and her arms fell to her sides. 'No wonder I couldn't rouse you. You were already out here.'

'You're up early.'

'Old habits. I never sleep late.'

Not lack of sleep because of thinking about how they could've spent the night together? Her eyes were puffy and dull. He sighed. They weren't doing each other any favours. 'Neither do I. I'm heading back to do something about breakfast.'

'Verity's got it in hand. She said it would be ready in

forty-five minutes and not to be late. I thought I'd limber up with a few yoga exercises before taking a short walk.'

'Want company?' He held his breath.

'I'd love it.'

Chase breathed again. 'We'll head to the top of the copse, then follow the track that comes out behind the farmhouse.'

'This place is wonderful. You were lucky to grow up here.'

'I know.' He tried not to stare at her butt filling those tight denim shorts as she strolled along, but his eyes had a mind of their own—until he tripped over a sod of grass-covered soil and nearly fell flat on his face. What had they been talking about? Oh, yeah. 'As kids Libby and I used to raise any calves rejected by their mothers for one reason or another. We had to do all the work and when they were sold at market we received half the money. The rest went to Dad to cover costs, though he was soft and didn't hit us with a large share of the expenses.'

'He was teaching you that nothing comes to you without working for it. I like that. My parents, especially Mum, thought the more they gave me the more I'd love them and not argue about who to stay with during the school holidays.' Kristina stopped to look around. 'Luxuriant green for miles and miles.'

Following the direction of Kristina's gaze, he admitted, 'I don't always see it like that. It's a big part of me, and still I don't get lost in being here.'

Drawing her eyes away from the view, she started walking again. 'You obviously weren't meant to be a farmer. Did that bother your father?'

'Dad's never been anything but encouraging in whatever I chose to do. This farm hasn't been in the family for generations like some around here. It was Dad's dream, and he went after it with everything he had. Then let his children follow their own dreams. I think he's hoping one of Libby's boys might be interested, but they're a few years off making those kinds of decisions.'

'The freedom of it all.' The wistful note in Kristina's voice caught at him.

'What did your parents want from you?' She can't have let them down by becoming a GP.

'Nothing I was prepared to give my soul for.' She strode out, leaving him behind.

Chase lengthened his steps and caught up. 'I hope you like a full English breakfast, because Mum's not going to let you away with anything less.' He wasn't going to follow up on that terse comment. There'd been pain in every word, pain she wasn't ready to share. Hopefully one day she'd find it in her to tell him. If he was still in the same country as her. Which wasn't going to happen so he wouldn't be hearing about her parents and how they'd raised her.

'My mother thinks marrying a millionaire is the only way to go.' Her laugh was tight. 'Lying by a pool for a couple of days a year is fine, doing it year round isn't my idea of fun.'

'I can't see you filling in time for the sake of it.' Surprised she'd given him a snippet, he waited to see if there was more.

'Dad wanted me to work with him, his company's specialty being hedge funds.'

Chase chuckled. 'Sitting in a high-rise, glass-encased office making millions online to please wealthy men who own fancy yachts isn't you either.'

'Dad isn't any good at knowing what makes me tick.' Again sadness tainted her voice.

And made him want to cheer her up. 'Do you want a lift into Merrywood this morning? I hear Jarrod wants to catch up with you. We could have lunch at the pub afterwards.' He was getting the hang of this dating caper.

Her mouth curved upward. 'Family, eh? Knows everything about everyone?' Then she blanched. 'I didn't mean I was part of your family.'

'Relax, Kristina,' he said, hating the worry clouding her eyes, wanting to see any other emotion there, even anger, toward him. 'No one's expecting more of you than to enjoy the time we're here and to join in all the fun.'

She suddenly grinned, a bright light in the cloud that had fallen over her. 'I'd like a ride into town, and especially lunch with you.'

With you. Two simple words and his chest was filling with pride and excitement. 'You'll be doing me a favour. Mum has a list a mile-long of groceries, meat, flowers and a million other things that need to be picked up.'

Her knuckles rapped his upper arm lightly. 'My shout at the pub.'

'It's a deal.' His blood warmed, his heart squeezed. Was this a second date with Kristina? So what if it was? He'd promised to have a good time, and not think about the future. 'We'll leave straight after breakfast.'

'I need to hit the shops. I haven't got anything to wear to the party.'

'Now she tells me,' he groaned. 'Is this going to take all day? Or are you a speed shopper?' Then it struck him as odd that she had no clothes for anything other than work. 'You must own more clothes than the shorts and shirts you carry in that backpack.'

'There's a wardrobeful at my father's Manchester apartment where I have a bedroom I use about once a year. Mostly it's for storing my gear. Another reason for finding a town to settle in, a home to live in. I'll be able to buy furniture I like, clothes I'll wear more than once before putting them in storage, collect recipe books and serving dishes.' She gathered a breath. 'Cooking isn't my strong point, mainly because I've never done any. Put that on my sheet of things to do—when I start one—take lessons on how to make duck *à l'orange* or tortellini in smoked mussel sauce.'

'You don't want to start with porridge or ginger-nut biscuits?' His mother had insisted he learn to make basic meals because cooking was her passion. Kristina obviously hadn't been given the chance. Because there'd been servants? Or no one could be bothered or patient enough to take the time to walk her through a recipe?

'Why start at the bottom?' She grinned in that way of hers that hit him in the gut and rattled his bones.

'Fair enough.' He opened the gate before them and breathed her in as she went through, her arm brushing his. 'Follow this path and we'll be through the trees and at the back door in minutes. Hopefully we haven't kept the bacon waiting.' What would that hair feel like on his skin?

Kristina felt a nudge in her belly as her arm brushed Chase's. Her feet tangled and she stumbled. Why hadn't she made love with him last night? She'd spent every hour until the sun rose regretting her decision.

'Careful.' Chase's hands caught and steadied her. His thumbs drew leisurely circles against her skin. His mouth was close, so close.

She had to kiss him, to feel his heat. 'Chase,' she whispered against his stubble-covered chin before her lips touched his. 'Chase.'

'Hell, Kristina, I've been wanting to do this since I saw you in the field.'

Her mouth peeled away far enough for her to reply, 'Good,' before she returned to kissing, this time trailing a line from the corner of his mouth to his chin and down his neck to the edge of his shirt. She yanked the shirt up and continued the kisses over his chest, down to his stomach where her tongue circled his belly button. They should've done this last night, she thought. Well, she wouldn't be stopping for anything this time.

'Those shorts should be banned. They cradle your butt like my hands need to. They outline your slim legs to the point that if I don't touch them, I'm going to die.'

'Help yourself,' she murmured against his stomach, while her hand sought the button holding his shorts closed and preventing access to the hard rod of need she had to touch, to wrap her hand around.

Chase groaned against her as she worked the button free.

Then his hands were on her pants, trying to push them down. 'Here.' She shoved his hand aside and tore the zip open, before returning to Chase's throbbing reaction to her. Reaching inside, her hands found him and slipped slowly down the satin skin stretched tight. She gasped at the wonder of his hardness, the heat, the throbbing need for her.

He dropped to his knees, his mouth finding her. Kristina gripped his shoulders, her head tipping back as Chase licked and nipped first one thigh and then the other. As his mouth reached the puddle of desire making her shake, her fingers grabbed his head, clung to him as he touched her, a lick, then another, and another, and she melted and tightened and let go all at once as hot, hungry need rocked her.

Chase rose before her, and gently laid her in the thick grass. His eyes were dark and intense, his erection throbbing when she enclosed it in her hands. She had to have him inside her. 'Now,' she cried.

Chase held himself above her. Winding her legs around him, she drew him down until his tip touched her. When she gasped he pushed, slowly, firmly, inside. Withdrew, pushed in. Her arms, wrapped around his shoulders, convulsed in time with her need exploding around him. Chase pushed hard, shuddering as he came.

Slowly her heartbeat returned to normal. Tipping her head back, she drew a long, unsteady breath. 'Wow.'

'Yeah, wow.' Chase rolled onto his back, sprawling her across him.

She clung to him, absorbing his heat. 'Guess we're officially late for breakfast now.'

'I don't think Mum will be too worried. She doesn't start cooking eggs until everyone's seated at the table. But we'd better get a wiggle on or there'll be a load of unwanted questions to deal with. If the dogs haven't already told them what's going on.'

Kristina laughed as she scrambled to her feet. 'What dogs?'

'Exactly.' Chase took her hands in his. 'What happened to "I don't think I'm ready"?'

'I spent the night regretting it.'

His smile devoured her. 'I nearly knocked on your door at three this morning.'

'It took till three?'

'Nah. I was playing hard to get, but it backfired.'

Winding her arm around his waist, she smiled for the short distance to the house, and then in her room where she quickly tidied up, and throughout breakfast, subtly ignoring Verity's amused glances coming their way. She was not sorry she'd made love with Chase. No, all she wanted was to do it again. Unfortunately the day ahead was about preparing for a party and catching up with everyone at the medical centre. Not that that was a bad way to spend a day, it was just that now she knew there was an even better one.

CHAPTER EIGHT

'KRISTINA, YOU'RE HERE.' The medical centre's reception-ist flew around the counter and engulfed her in an enor-mous hug.

Kristina's heart melted at the welcome. She felt like crying. 'Hey, Wendy, good to see you.'

'You're in time for morning tea. Libby sent blueberry muffins in with Jarrod.'

More tears threatened. Kristina straightened her back and dropped her hands to her sides. 'I am being spoilt.'

'Watch out, they want something from you,' Chase teased. 'Believe me, I know how this lot operate.'

'Dr Kristina, hello. Do you want to see my baby? She weighed in at four kilos and hasn't stopped gaining weight since.' A young woman held up a baby dressed in pink and held her out. 'We called her Lily.'

'Sherry, it's lovely to see you both.' Kristina took the soft bundle in her arms. 'Hello, little one. Aren't you the cutest thing? Look at all those blonde curls.' In the weeks Kristina had worked there she'd seen Sherry regularly.

'Lily came in a real hurry and I didn't make it to hospi-tal.' Sherry was smiling, her eyes full of love as she gazed at her daughter.

Kristina's stomach turned to goo. *I want that.* Handing Lily back, she managed, 'I'm so glad to see you both. I really am.' There was a sense of completing a circle, something that didn't usually happen for a locum.

'Me, too,' Sherry acknowledged. 'You were so kind to me when I panicked and cried for hours about my swollen ankles.'

'It was only minutes and every pregnant woman is allowed those moments.'

'Hello, Kristina. It's great to see you. Libby'll be along shortly. She's bursting to catch up on everything you've done since leaving here.'

Kristina turned to find herself slap bang in the middle of another hug, this time from Jarrod. When she was released she asked, 'Is she at the market?'

Jarrod nodded. 'Otherwise she'd be on to the list I presume is burning a hole in Chase's pocket. Come through to the tearoom where everyone's waiting.'

'But it's Saturday.' Merrywood Medical Centre had obviously been rostered to cover weekend emergencies for the area, but that didn't explain all the staff.

'They weren't letting you get away without seeing them.'

'Oh.'

Chase was biting on a smile. 'I prefer chocolate muffins so I'll leave you to it. Mum's list will take some effort to get through.'

'I said I'd help with it.' Kristina didn't want to let him down.

'I'm not tramping around behind you while you trawl the dress shops. Pick you up here at twelve-thirty, okay? We'll have lunch, then I'll put you to good use working on what's left of the list.'

'Sounds good.' Hopefully there'd be an outfit for the party in the first shop she went into. If there was sparc time, she'd look for a sky-blue, full-length dress as well.

'Thanks for coming in when I know it's bedlam at the

farm.' Jarrod led the way into the tearoom, where two nurses hugged her.

Were the hugs adding up this morning, or what? 'Verity's got everything under control, no sign of panic. How's everything here? I've missed this place.'

'Give this lot five minutes and then we'll go through to my office. Thankfully it's not too busy for a Saturday morning so we'll have some time to ourselves.'

Interesting. A fizz of excitement tickled her, and made the next five minutes the longest she could remember even when feeling so welcome.

'Bring your coffee.' Jarrod was on his feet and heading out the door.

As Kristina took a seat in his office the mug shook in her hand. Tension tightened her stomach. Was she about to get the offer of a lifetime or be sorely disappointed?

'Hey, there you are,' Libby bounded into the room and banged the door shut behind her before embracing Kristina. 'I'm glad you came with Chase for the weekend. It's great to see you again.'

This was getting out of hand. Kristina hugged her back fervently. 'Me, too. I thought you were selling cheese this morning.'

'I have been, but a friend's taken over. Jarrod wants me here while he talks to you. Probably thinks I can twist your arm for him.'

She straightened her back. This meeting was serious, then. *Please, be what I'm hoping for.* She waited, her breath stalled in her throat.

'I'll cut straight to the point. Campbell's leaving us, heading to New York where his wife's got a power job at some financial conglomerate.'

Kristina relaxed a notch. 'No surprise there. She's supposedly a whiz at that stuff. But can Campbell practise in the States?'

'He'll have to sit some papers, but he's decided to be a stay-at-home dad until the kids have settled into their new way of life, which will be very different from little old Merrywood.' Jarrod steepled his fingers. 'So, are you still looking for a permanent position as a GP? Because there's one going here and we'd like you to join us. Everyone would. You were so popular with the staff and patients during your two months, and I'm tired of patients asking when you're coming back.'

Lay on the feel-good stuff, why don't you? A smile split her face. 'I do want to work in a medical centre where I get to know patients for more than one visit.' Come on, say what you really think. 'Okay, truly? Merrywood feels right for me, and I would like to move here.'

Jarrod was watching her closely. 'Campbell intends to hold onto his partnership for now, in case things don't work out in New York. But even if he returns, this position is permanent. Our patient numbers are high, and could grow more if we opened the books again.'

'I don't need a partnership.' Maybe later on when she was settled in her own home with those dogs she'd begun thinking about. What about Chase? He was the snag in this otherwise perfect solution to her needs.

'Say yes, Kristina,' Libby said.

'So you're interested in working with us? Permanently?' Jarrod asked, before dangling a carrot in front of her. 'Campbell has suggested that whoever takes his place here might be interested in renting their home.'

That would take the pressure off finding her own place, give her time to look around and decide where best to put down roots. Kristina stared at her entwined fingers, looking for the answer to the main question, because now the offer had come, there were other things to consider.

These people were Chase's family. Libby and Jarrod lived nearby, his parents a few kilometres down the road.

He'd come home for visits, even if only occasionally, and she'd have to deal with seeing him, unless she took annual leave whenever he appeared. Despite the high she was on from that morning's lovemaking, come the end of her time with MFA their fling would finish. And it was definitely a fling. Chase was not ready for anything else.

Lifting her head, she looked at Libby, then Jarrod. 'Thank you so much for this opportunity. It's exactly what I want.' Deep breath. 'But there are things I need to consider. Can I have a few days before I give you my answer?'

Jarrod nodded. 'I didn't expect anything less. Just know that you're wanted around here by everyone, and that we'll all do whatever we can to help you settle in.'

'You're off to a head start, knowing my family,' Libby pointed out.

The snag in this whole deal. 'True, but I also have a need to see myself sorted, to find my feet. This would be a permanent move, and I want to get it right.'

'No problem.' Jarrod glanced at his computer and stood up. 'Sorry to rush you but I've a patient waiting.' He handed her an envelope. 'We haven't talked hours or salary, but it's all in there. Any questions or uncertainties, give me a call, or talk to me over the weekend.'

'I will.' She stood, surprised to find her legs a little shaky. Was this what finally finding what she wanted in life felt like? But it wasn't everything she hoped for. Until Chase, falling in love, possibly having a family, had been a distant dream to be followed when all else was in place and going well. Now she couldn't imagine life without Chase and yet that was exactly how it would be.

Libby slipped an arm through hers. 'Come and have another coffee, then we'll go to my favourite clothing shop because I hear you need an outfit.'

Two friends now? Special women she could talk to about anything. Except she couldn't with Libby because she had a brother who'd made love with her only hours ago, who no doubt would again before the weekend was up, and who, in the end, would walk away from her. No, she wouldn't be talking with Libby about what mattered. Unfortunately. But they could have fun shopping.

Sunday dawned wet and misty, and Kristina couldn't have cared less. Chase had taken her to his bed after the party had wound down and she was still there. He had one leg thrown over hers like he never wanted her to leave. That was an illusion, like the one that said summer was only about sun and warm temperatures.

'What are you looking so happy about?' Chase nuzzled against her neck.

'That was some party.' She grinned.

'The Barringtons are famous for putting on a good bash.' He was watching her now.

'I'll 'fess up. The after-party bash was even better.' Leaning over, she kissed his chin, felt the rough texture of beard growth.

'Glad you mentioned it. My ego was getting a little worried.'

'I'm glad I came. To the party,' she added as a grin began widening his beautiful mouth. 'It's been quite a weekend so far.'

'A great party, amazing sex, and then there's Jarrod's offer. What more could a woman want?'

'There is that.' The air dribbled out of her lungs, taking some of her happiness with it. To accept the job was the right thing to do. Yet she still hoped for something more with Chase. And if that wasn't possible then living in this district might encroach on his hopes for the future. Not that she could say why, but she did think that if she moved here he might stop visiting entirely and she wouldn't be responsible for that.

'Hey, if you don't want it, say so. You're not obligated to Jarrod.' Chase sat up and tucked an arm over her shoulders, drawing her close.

Why couldn't he see what they had? This easy rapport, a simple gesture of holding her, a kiss on his chin as they woke to a new day. 'We'd better get up. Your mother will need all hands on cleaning-up duties.' Kristina swung her legs out of the bed.

Chase took his time removing his arm from around her. 'You're avoiding my question. Haven't we moved past that?' He shook his head. 'Spill. What's bothering you?'

This so wasn't the time. But when would it be? Twisting to face him, she placed a hand on his arm, felt his strength and warmth. 'The job is perfect, the location is ideal, the future looks good.'

'But?'

No. She couldn't say she was falling for him. He'd shut down completely, and she wanted what was left of their time together. Today at least. Call her selfish, but this sense of belonging had never come along before. Why not make the most of what little time she had left? *Am I being greedy?* Yep.

'I get a little scared when I think about how lucky I am to have this opportunity. It's what I've been looking for and I'm scared it'll be snatched away. Part of me thinks if I don't say yes to Jarrod yet, the bubble won't burst too soon.' Now he'd think she was mad, but she always told him the truth—about most things. Those she didn't she avoided.

Chase's arms wrapped around her and drew her close. His lips caressed her brow, then trailed down to her mouth where he kissed her softly. 'Believe in yourself, Kristina. If this is what you want then grab it with both hands and never let go. You're strong because of what you've faced in the past. Draw on that strength. Keep on smiling and winning people over because that's also helped get you to where you can make a decision about your future.'

Tears streamed down her face. See? No wonder she loved him. Yes, full-blown love. That falling for him thing had arrived at its destination. She loved Chase Barrington. So tell him. Always truthful, remember? Avoidance, remember? She didn't need him saying, 'Thank you very much but nothing's going to change'. Her pride had taken enough knocks over the years to know when to look out for herself. Now was one of those times.

'Thank you.' She sniffed. 'I needed that.' If only she could give the same back. But they weren't talking about him and his plans after the *Poseidon*. Hopefully she'd get an opportunity over the next three weeks to do something about that. Who knew? She might even find the courage to tell him how she felt about him.

'Any time.' He grinned. 'Now, go shower. There's a party to clear up.'

Chase watched Kristina head out of his bedroom, his heart heavy despite that grin he'd given her. Go, Jarrod, for offering her the position at the medical centre. It was exactly what she wanted, and needed. She'd be mad not to accept. So why the hesitation? He didn't believe her explanation. Or rather he did, but it was only half the reason. What was the other half? He'd wanted to push for an answer but was wary of spoiling the wonderful time they were having together.

They'd be flying back to Marseille in the afternoon. No wonder he felt dispirited. He wasn't ready to go back to work, and that was such a rarity. He put his hand on his brow. Temperature normal. He and Kristina had hit it off so well the idea of giving it up so soon rankled. Hell, he'd come to enjoy her in his space, not only on the ship but also here amongst his family. She was special. Could they have a relationship after all? One that went beyond this weekend, further than the next three weeks on board the ship, out into the real future?

Chase leapt out of bed and snatched up his shirt. Pulling it over his head, he grabbed his shorts and jerked them up his legs. Time to give his mum a hand downstairs. He'd shower after all the hard work of packing up chairs and tables and taking down the marquee was done.

'Where do you want me to start, Mum?' Chase sauntered into the kitchen minutes later, a tight smile fixed in place.

'With eating breakfast,' he was told. 'Then you can do a rain dance in reverse, get the sun to beat away those pesky clouds and dry everything out.'

'Sure thing.' He hugged the woman who'd been there for him all his life, had never backed away when he'd lost his mind over Nick's death, who still believed in him no matter what he did and how often he hurt her. His throat started closing as he said, 'Happy birthday, Mum. You're the best mother a guy could have.'

She blinked, patted his face and said, 'I'm the only one you've got, that's why.' Then she smiled that special mum smile that always hit him hard, especially since the tragedy that had changed his life for ever. 'You're my best son, too.'

'I'm the only one,' he croaked the expected reply, and pulled her into another hug.

'Come on, you two. Haven't got all day to be mucking about, real birthday or not.' His dad strolled into the kitchen and dropped onto his usual chair, pulled the pan of bacon towards him and began dishing some onto a plate.

Chase sank onto a chair and tugged the dish out of his father's hand. 'You reckon?' Then the air crackled around his ears, the skin on his forearms tightened.

Kristina had arrived. 'That smells so good, Verity.'

'Help yourself, and don't be mean about it. You're going to be so busy you'll need all the energy you can muster.'

'Me, busy? I told the dogs I'd take them for a stroll down the lane, maybe sit in the field for an hour. Might even take them to the pub later.' She began buttering some toast, a soft smile lighting her beautiful face.

Damn, she fitted right in here. Almost as easily as he did, maybe more so considering those moments he got edgy about trying not to hurt his parents even knowing he would when he left to return to work. His mother always smiled and pretended she was all right with him heading off to places out of the norm to feed his need to fix people, while his dad would shake his hand, say 'Have a good trip' and go out to the shed.

Watching Kristina fork breakfast onto her plate as she chattered with them, Chase knew happiness. *She did fit in here.* And in doing so she was making him feel there was a chance he might, too. 'The dogs really enjoy a good burger and chips washed down with a beer.'

'I thought they might.' She fixed him with a dazzling smile, no trace of her worries of earlier darkening her gaze. 'Verity, what job have you got lined up for me? As long as it's got nothing to do with food, I can do pretty much anything.'

'I was hoping you'd bring the flowers in from the gazebo and arrange them in the lounge.'

She winced. 'I might be better employed dealing with the tables and chairs.'

Chase laughed. 'No flower arranging in the army, then?'

Kristina biffed him on the arm. 'I'll help your dad and you can take care of the flowers.'

His mother laughed, too. 'Whatever. As long as it's all done today. I see Jarrod's pulled up. They'll all want feeding.'

Chase leaned back in his chair and sipped his tea, soaking up the atmosphere. Even when the calm was shattered by three young boys racing into the kitchen shouting 'Happy birthday, Nana' so loudly his eardrums seemed about to burst, he felt the most relaxed he had in…well, in for ever. Funny how his eyes turned to Kristina. Come on. They were always looking her way, seeking her out, watching the play of emotions on her exquisite face, storing images for the months ahead when she was here and he was somewhere else.

Pushing up off his chair, he took his plate, cutlery and mug to the dishwasher. 'Right, let's get this show under way.' He had to get out of here, away from Kristina and her sweet voice as she chatted with *his* family. She was doing his head in, tinkering with his resolve to go solo for ever.

Placing fresh sandwiches and leftover bacon and egg pies on the table hours later, Chase pulled out a chair and sank onto it, trying to ignore the way his body ached in places it had no right to. It showed how out of practice he was when it came to making love. 'Anyone seen Kristina?'

'She took the dogs for a walk,' Libby answered. 'Said she'd be back shortly.'

'One of the dogs has probably taken off after a rabbit. She won't come home without them both in tow.' Tempted to forgo lunch and follow her, he remained seated. Like him, she sometimes needed time alone. He wondered if she was thinking about their lovemaking. It had been out of this world, and a running film kept going across the front of his mind. But with all that came decisions to make. He knew it, and so would Kristina. Nothing had changed in that they still weren't getting together permanently. He had obligations to fulfil—if he ever got around to signing that damned contract. Not once had he taken so long over something as simple as scrawling his name across a piece of paper. Hopefully Kristina wouldn't take so long with

Jarrod's offer. She wouldn't be doing herself any favours by procrastinating when it was exactly what she wanted.

His mother was pouring the coffee he'd forgotten. 'Jasper, naughty boy.'

Libby growled, 'No, Jasper, you cannot put all that in your mouth at once. Eat properly.'

Chase's nephew was working at shoving a whole bacon muffin in his mouth. 'Cute.' It was. All part of the family thing, everyone sitting around the table picking at food in a desultory fashion—except for Jasper—mulling over the party and generally relaxing together. He could get used to this all too easily. Where had that dumb idea come from? Usually he was bursting to get out of here before his family dragged him under with their love. But he'd never brought home a woman about whom he cared a lot, hadn't made love in his childhood bedroom since he'd been a horny teenager, and that had been more about sex than love. Face it, he hadn't felt so at ease with the whole scene in a long time.

'It's not cute at all,' Libby growled at him. 'Jasper, behave. You're disgusting.'

The kid couldn't reply with so much food in his mouth.

Chase wanted to laugh because he remembered doing something similar as a boy, but Libby would probably box his ears for encouraging him. Where was Kristina anyway? It was time she came back from her walk and joined in the fun. He'd seen in her demeanour how much she enjoyed interacting with this lot. 'Do you think Kristina will take the position you've offered her, Jarrod?'

'You'd know as much about that as I do,' his brother-in-law answered. 'I know she wants to, but something's holding her back.'

'That'd be Chase, I'm betting.' Libby added her two pence worth.

The hackles rose on the back of his neck. 'Anything

Kristina decides has nothing to do with me,' he said a little more forcefully than he'd intended. 'She's quite capable of making up her own mind.'

'Didn't say she wasn't.' Libby grinned. In other words, *Got you, big brother.*

'The job's everything she wants,' he said. 'She likes the town of Merrywood, too. She'll be wanting to buy a house as soon as possible.'

'We're all here for her,' Verity added. 'She can visit any time.'

His family liked getting involved with other people's business, whether asked to or not, but this went further. It was as though they'd accepted Kristina as one of them. He'd witnessed how comfortable she'd been at the medical centre yesterday. The staff had been fighting each other to talk to her. 'Kristina will make up her own mind without anyone putting pressure on her.' She didn't need this lot surrounding her with advice and—

Love?

Yes, from what he knew about them, they probably did love her in their all-embracing way. 'Her independence is important to her. You'd do well to remember that before you try to smother her.'

'Sure you're not talking about yourself, bro?' Libby really had sharpened her tongue overnight.

'That's ridiculous, and you know it,' he snapped. Sometimes Libby went too far. He didn't need to be reminded how he let his family down on a regular basis. 'I'm happy doing the work for *Medicine For All.*'

'Yeah, and when you're done with them you'll find another cause to hide behind. Don't you think it's time to come home and be a part of us again?' Libby gave back as good as she got, more so perhaps.

She had him between a rock and a hard place. Say no and he was telling his family he didn't care about them.

Say yes and they'd have interviews at the hospital lined up within days. He went for neutral. 'I'm not ready to stop what I'm doing yet. There are people who need me.' Then the hairs lifted on his skin. Twisting around, he swore under his breath.

Kristina stood in the doorway, sadness darkening her lovely face. Her gaze touched him briefly before she looked away, swallowing hard at the same time. As though she might've been thinking things between them had changed since they'd made love, and had now learned everything was exactly the same.

Guilt had him standing up and pulling out a chair for her. 'Come and have some lunch. Tea?' How much had she heard?

She stepped up beside him and smiled, a slow, soft movement that didn't reach her eyes. Then she turned to his family and said, 'What Chase does for *Medicine For All* is truly amazing and very important. They'd be lost without him.' She sat down and reached for a sandwich.

Libby stared at her, a slow smile finally breaking out and taking the sting out of her next words. 'So, big brother's got to you, too. Don't let that stop you coming to work for us. We need you.'

Kristina chewed and swallowed. 'There's only one person deciding on what I do next and that's me.'

Chase's hands were unsteady as he poured Kristina's tea. She'd had his back in front of his family. He should be squirming. He didn't need anyone taking his side, but while his head railed against that, his heart was lifting, softening. It felt good to have someone who wasn't family caring enough to support him. If he'd thought it was going to be harder than usual to leave the farm today, it was going to be a whole lot harder to say goodbye to Kristina in three weeks' time. Might be best if he backed off before then, stopped seeing her as anything other than a colleague, possibly a friend, but definitely not a woman to make love to in his cabin after he'd finished with the people needing his services.

But first they had the rest of the day to enjoy. Placing the cup in front of Kristina, he said to the room in general, 'How about we go to the pub for a beer before someone drops us at the airport? Let's have some more birthday celebrations. Family only. And Kristina.'

A wicked glint filled his sister's eyes and he wanted to growl at her but refrained. They'd always pressed each other's buttons, and this time he wasn't letting her win. Today was about him and Kristina, before he packed her away and got on with his real life. No, he wasn't exactly proud of himself, but there was no denying the need coursing through his veins.

CHAPTER NINE

'Big day.' The air was heavy as Kristina leaned on the railing in their corner of the deck. The horizon was lost in grey cloud. Her head was thick due to lack of sleep and a never-ending line of refugees requiring her attention since nine that morning. Many of today's boatload were suffering from fuel burns, and there'd been an outbreak of gastric flu on their cramped boat before they'd been picked up in the Gulf of Sirte.

The sleepless night had been exciting. For most of it. Chase had taken her to his cabin and made love to her with passion and hunger, and a need so great she'd wanted to hold him for ever, reassure him he was safe with her, but she'd held back, uncertain of his reaction. When he'd made love to her a second time he had been so excruciatingly gentle she'd cried. She'd been right to stay quiet. He was saying goodbye to their brief fling. Goodbye to the woman he'd taken to his bed, not to the doctor he'd still be working with.

Around four she'd kissed him softly on his cheeks and forehead, and lastly on his lips as he'd slept, then she'd crawled out of his bunk to head back to her cabin. He hadn't moved at all.

Now Chase was staring out to sea. 'They happen.' He hadn't budged an inch when she'd joined him. 'It's going to be as hectic throughout the night when the Sudanese refugees arrive.'

The message was so loud, so clear she wanted to shrink in on herself and pretend she was with a complete stranger passing the time of day before going below deck and catching up on much-needed sleep. Throughout the day they'd been so busy the only conversations had been about patients, and those had been abrupt. It was as though once she'd left his cabin that morning she'd left the man she loved, the man who'd let her in close.

Coming up here when it was obvious she wasn't wanted had been a mistake. Was she naïve, thinking he might miss her if she didn't? Damn, but she was pathetic. And hurting, and wishing she could change him, and knowing some things were plain impossible. She'd thought they'd have another three weeks together. Wrong. There weren't going to be any more stolen kisses up here. This area was reverting to *his* space. No making love in his cabin. Nothing.

Well, he wasn't getting away with not talking to her. Kristina watched Chase. 'I got my invitation to Jasper's birthday party today.' She'd checked her emails while downing a hurried meal between patients.

'Me, too.' Still no movement in that lean body she'd touched all over.

'I emailed straight back saying I'd be there.' She'd be living in Merrywood by then. 'His first day of school on the following Monday. How cool's that?'

'They grow up fast.' A sudden yearning flitted through his eyes, then was gone so fast she might've imagined it if she hadn't known what to look for.

Kristina swallowed the hurt she felt for him. She had her own to deal with. He loved his family, and if he thought they didn't know he was fooling himself. He needed shaking—hard. But was it her place to instigate it? No, but when had she ever let something like that stop her? Pressing on, she said, 'You'll be going to the party?'

'I'll be in Africa.' Again that yearning flared, died.

'So you've finally signed the contract?'

He winced and finally looked at her. 'No, but it's lying amongst the paperwork. I'll get to it later tonight.' The bleakness in those eyes was frightening. Did he not understand how much he was hurting himself, let alone everyone else, by being so stubborn about staying on his mission?

'Tell me again why you want to go so far away from those you love?'

'I've told you of my need to help people in difficult or dangerous situations. Nothing's changed, Kristina. There are people all over the world needing urgent medical help that's not easily available. Someone has to be there for them, to save them.' There was a warning in his voice. *Don't step any further over the mark.*

That wound her up fast. 'You think I won't save people in Merrywood? That being a GP in an English town won't rank up there with helping the sick and needy in your foreign locations? That diagnosing a heart condition before it becomes life-threatening isn't saving a life? You think you have to be at the coal face of danger all the time to be a great doctor?' Her disappointment in him, and knowing he wasn't about to change because of anything she said, further cranked up her temper, made it easy to say what she'd held in for days. 'Would you be more accommodating of a relationship between us if I followed you around, doing what you do?'

'No, Kristina, I don't think that. You're brilliant at what you do. I can't imagine you doing anything else. And before you even think it, I am not being condescending. The world needs more of you than of me.' His chest rose slowly. 'Further, I would never expect you to sign up for the work

I do—if I even wanted us to be together in a permanent relationship.'

'*Even* if you wanted us to be together?' she choked.

'I don't want to hurt you, but you've never hidden the fact you long to settle in your own home with a career you can become completely involved in. That's what you need, hanker for, have to have, and should make happen. What's more, if you take up Jarrod's offer you're halfway there. Those are the things I don't look for.'

'Avoid, more like.' He hadn't told her anything she didn't already know. But heck. 'Don't turn the conversation onto me,' she snapped around the ache building in her throat. 'You can't handle the heat whenever anyone starts talking about *your* future, can you? Fine, I'll shut up, but don't...' She poked her forefinger into his chest. 'Don't start on what I should be doing.' She'd find a way to accept that she was about to achieve half of what she wanted, which wasn't bad going. Not everyone was so lucky. Unfortunately she'd had a taste of what the other half could be like, and wouldn't be forgetting it in a hurry.

'Fair cop. Talking about my past is the hardest thing I ever have to do, so mostly I don't.' He was in his staring out to sea stance, arms folded across that chest she'd spent so much time kissing, his chin jutting forward with its tempting cover of light stubble, those long, sexy legs tense.

Even in the middle of this she was turned on. Damn him. 'You told me some of what happened in the French mountains.'

His nod was short and sharp. 'I don't regret it. Neither do I regret everything else we've shared,' he added almost as an afterthought, surprise shining out of his eyes for a moment.

Good to know. If it didn't hurt so much. But there was no point carrying on this awkward, snappy conversation. It only undermined the friendship and closeness they had, and if she could keep those alive she would. 'I also emailed Jarrod, accepting his offer.' Somewhere between leaving Chase's cabin and giving her last patient intravenous antibiotics she'd realised the decision was still hers alone to make, and if becoming more involved with Chase's family was the result then she'd grab the opportunity with both hands. He wouldn't stay away because she was there—he already did that.

'It's the right thing to do.' No heart-wrenching Chase smile for her this time. 'If I'm allowed to say so.'

Her heart rolled over. If only it could be different. They understood each other so well they really would work out as a couple—if they weren't looking for completely opposite lives. 'You take care of yourself. I'm sure Libby will keep me up to date with wherever you go and what you do.' To her own ears it sounded like she was saying goodbye. Which she was, despite the weeks ahead on the ship before she left for the final time.

There'd be no resolution for them, no seeing a path they could follow hand in hand. This was not a romance story with the predicable happy ending. Just her luck to fall in love with a man who could not meet her requirements. He was more intent on bashing his head against a brick wall, trying to save every endangered soul on the planet all by himself.

She took a step towards the stairs. It was time to accept what she'd known all along.

'Kristina,' Chase called, and when she turned he was watching her with an intensity that curled her toes and told her heart to move on. 'I am sorry.'

Did he love her at all? A tiny, weeny bit? They'd met equally on more levels than the physical. There'd been gentleness, kindness and, yes, something like love, if not total love, in everything they'd done together, including the times up here. This was the last time she'd come. Why prolong the agony? Stretching up on her toes, she leaned in and kissed him lightly on his mouth. 'I know.'

Then she was gone, out of there, away from the temptation to grovel. She'd only come off worse than she already felt. 'Goodbye, Chase,' she whispered.

Goodbye while they still had to work together. Should be a picnic.

Chase read all the documents that had come in with the medical supplies by boat that morning, signed the ones that were going back in the next outward mail bag, and dropped the rest into the cardboard box that served as his filing cabinet. The clock on the wall read seven-fifteen. Time for dinner, except he wasn't hungry. It had been a week since Kristina had slipped out of his cabin after a night of lovemaking. A week since he'd let her know that whatever they'd had was over. A week of wondering if he'd made the biggest mistake possible, of wishing she'd sneak back into his bed and ignore what he'd said about running alone. A week of growing tired and edgy, of avoiding her, and trying not to let Ethan's presence on board get in the way of his goals and his foul mood.

Pulling a large, over-full envelope towards him, he emptied the contents onto his desk. 'More damned forms to fill in. Why did I train as a surgeon?'

Yeah, why did he? Because of the driving ambition to save people's lives, to put them back together when life had made a mess of their bodies, to make their loved ones happy again. And had it made him happy?

Ramming his fingers through his hair, he dropped his head forward and stared at the tobacco-coloured carpet between his feet. He didn't have the right to be happy when Nick had lost out on so much.

The door opened and the sound of voices and laughter reached him before the door clicked shut again. 'Thought

I'd find you in here, sulking,' Ethan said conversationally, before banging a tray down on the desk.

Chase raised his head and stared at the man who'd finally become his friend, not his enemy. 'I'm not hungry.' The smell of sausages and chips made his nose screw up in distaste.

'Sure you're not, but you've got to eat.'

There were two laden plates, two glasses of iced water and cutlery for both of them. Ethan had returned for a final stint, as he'd said he would. He'd been working every hour he could, and still found time to harass Chase whenever he thought he needed reminding there was more to life than this.

'You been talking to Kristina? She told me the same a while ago.'

'Funny, that. I just gave her the same speech as I'm giving you. Eat.' Ethan sat down on the other side of the desk and used his fingers to pick up some chips. 'You two had a spat?'

'Not at all.' It was true. They hadn't.

'Then why are you burying yourself in work twenty-four seven? We're busy, sure, but there's more than enough staff to cover everything.'

'I need to catch up on all this.' He waved a hand at the files and documents Ethan had had no compunction about setting the tray on top of. 'I should've been an accountant or statistician, not a surgeon.'

'Getting withdrawal?'

From Kristina? Definitely. 'I sometimes wonder what it might be like working full time as a surgeon in one place, occasionally seeing repeat patients.' His head jerked back and a bleak smile lifted the corner of his mouth. 'Don't know why I'm telling you. You'll find a way to use it against me.' Something Ethan and Kristina had in common—taking what he told them and putting the onus back on him to do something about it.

'Because I know where you're at by rite of the same passage. I'm still getting used to the idea of putting my feet down in one place for as far ahead as I can see. I'll tell you this for nothing. I'm glad I'm doing it. More than glad. Happy beyond anything I could've imagined.'

'I'm happy for you.' Ethan deserved Claire and their unborn child, deserved that happiness.

'So am I.' Ethan chewed on a sausage and watched him. 'It's been quite a roller-coaster ride but I'm glad of every moment so far. I even look forward to the next phase: marriage and parenthood. Who'd have believed I'd be saying that?'

'Not you.'

'Isn't that the truth?' His eyes were still locked on him. Looking for what?

Chase began to feel uneasy, as though Ethan found him lacking. Picking up a handful of fries, he began to eat them one by one, swallowing with difficulty. He'd wait this one out.

Finally, 'You sent that contract back yet?'

It had been lying on the desk for five days, signed and ready to go to head office, gathering dust and more crinkles whenever he fossicked for particular documents to deal with. He shook his head. 'Not yet. But...' he shoved chips into his mouth and picked up the paperwork that would see him fixed up for work over the coming months '... I'll do it right now.'

Ethan's eyes were dark, unreadable as he watched him, more worrying than if he'd been angry.

Chase couldn't help himself. He had to ask. 'What?'

'Why did you ask me to do a spell with MFA?'

Kathump. The sound of his gut hitting the floor was deafening. 'There was that promise you'd come whenever

I needed your help. All I had to do was ask.' No cross-examination required. Or wanted.

'What took sixteen years for you to ask? And why ask me for help with something any doctor could do?'

His head joined his gut. 'Could be I wasn't ready to see your face or hear your cheek before.'

'Could be you're starting to think there might be more to life than how you're living? That in order to move on you had to deal with me, with your past—our past—first.'

'Never crossed my mind.' It hadn't. Not once. Never. Why would it?

'I'd been waiting for a damned long time to get that call. Thought it would never come.' A wealth of sadness dulled Ethan's words.

And sapped the resistance out of Chase. 'I wanted to call you, picked up the phone often enough, but then I'd think, Why spoil your day? Then one day I didn't put the phone down, just let the number ring. And here we are. No regrets. Don't ask why that day was any different from the others. It just was.'

'Sure.' Ethan stretched his legs out. 'Make sure you put in the dates you have to be in France for my wedding before you send in that contract.'

He was off the hook, yet relief wasn't rushing at him. 'Plus three days for my nephew's birthday and first day of school.' He owed Libby for upsetting her the morning after their mum's party. Nothing new in that, but he'd decided to go home for Jasper's birthday. If only he'd seen Libby's face when she'd read the email. Probably took an hour to close her mouth.

He had Kristina to thank for this. She'd managed to get him doing things with his family no one else had come close to. Could that be because she'd slotted in so effortlessly? Strange when she wasn't used to a close family who accepted a person for who they were. But if she hadn't had that, it made sense she might grab the opportunity when it came along.

'That's good news.' Ethan shrugged and put his empty plate back on the tray and stole some chips off Chase's. 'What are we expected to reach the next boat of refugees?'

Relief lightened Chase's mood and he stabbed a sausage with a fork. They'd moved past the sticky conversation. 'About six, just in time for breakfast.'

'Then I'll get things set up tonight.'

'You do that and I'll stocktake the pharmaceutical cabinet.' Something else to keep his mind occupied and off Kristina Morton. 'Then Josip wants to go over docking days and when the ship will be laid up for maintenance.'

'I'm sure you can come up with enough to keep you busy until six if you try hard enough.' Ethan sauntered out of the office like he hadn't a care in the world, so unlike the Ethan he'd thought he knew. This new Claire-enhanced version was slowly relaxing into the world around him. Did the man still think back to the avalanche? Of course he did, but he'd learned to go a little easier with what had happened and was beginning to live in the present without having to justify himself and his actions.

All assumption, really, based on how *he* reacted and lived, Chase admitted. He and Ethan had had too little to do with each other over the intervening years for him to be certain about the other man's thoughts and reactions.

Snatching up the drugs list and keys to the cupboard, he headed out of his office.

Less than twenty-four hours to go. Kristina sighed. The weeks since she'd left Chase's bunk had seemed endless and yet now, suddenly, it was all but over, and she'd leave for good in the morning.

The boat was quiet, and time lay heavily on her hands, with no patients needing attention. She'd done a round of those who were left, waiting for tomorrow and disembarkation. She'd accepted thanks and smiles in ever-increasing discomfort. These people deserved to be treated well. No one knew what lay in store for them next.

'Slow night.' Ethan looked up from a book he was reading. 'Claire's looking forward to you visiting for a couple of nights.'

This had felt like the longest period she'd done on the ship, all because Chase took up so much of her mind, and nothing else. The sooner she didn't have to see him countless times, work with him on patients, or hear his voice everywhere she went, the better. 'It'll be great spending time together. Talking baby things and dress shopping for my bridesmaid outfit.' Merrywood Fashion hadn't produced a sky-blue anything, let alone an off-the-shoulder dress fit for the occasion.

Ethan's eye-rolls were quite eloquent when he put in the effort. 'Think I'm washing my hair that day.'

'Thank goodness for small mercies,' she gave back. 'We really don't need your advice.'

'I *am* deciding what I'm wearing to my wedding. Though Claire has given me instructions.' He grinned.

It was amazing how much Ethan had relaxed since meeting Claire. He wouldn't have forgotten anything about the past he shared with Chase but he was so excited about the future it was lovely to see. If only Chase would take the risk, preferably with her. But it wasn't happening, and she had to remember that—all the time.

'Have you got Chase fixed for a suit?' Why ask? Because he was constantly in her mind. It wasn't because she needed to know the groom and his best man had their clothes sorted for the wedding. Claire was more than capable of doing that and, determined woman that she was, she had probably arranged weeks ago everything right down to the socks the men would be wearing.

Ethan's eyebrows rose and he tipped his head ceiling-wards. 'What do you think?'

'Yeah, I figured the moment I asked.' Wiping a tissue across her face, she laughed. 'This heat is diabolical. I still haven't got used to it.'

'I know what you mean, and yet we'll be complaining about the cold soon enough.'

'Probably.' That'd be when she was back in England, working as a GP and settling into a routine, maybe even moving into her own little house with lawns and gardens. Like she knew anything about plants and how to look after them. But wasn't that part of putting down roots? Not only her own but those of plants? Learning the day-to-day care and maintenance, pushing the barriers, extending her horizons. Exciting, if she didn't overthink it all. 'I'm heading up on deck for some air.'

Tomorrow she'd step off the ship for the last time. There'd be no coming back. Not that she hadn't enjoyed her time on board. It'd been a great experience, and she'd met lots of wonderful people, including Claire.

Chase. Yes, well. What could she say? She'd found the love of her life, and would be walking away from him. Not that they were together but, still, when the realisation of what little they'd shared was over and got too much to handle she could seek him out, breathe him in, file away more pictures of him working with patients or talking to crew, and pretend she was coping, pretend that her heart would recover, though bruised and wary for a long time to come.

'Your back playing up?' Chase asked from behind as she reached the railing.

Looking around, she gasped softly. She must've been in a different world to have walked into their space without realising he was here. It was the first time since the night she'd said goodbye to Chase and their relationship.

'You're doing the lopsided walk.'

Her hand automatically went to the spot where a steady throbbing had set up in the muscles an hour ago. 'I moved too quickly getting out of the way of some boys chasing a football. I'll have physio when I'm back on land.'

'Not a bad idea.' His smile was friendly, and warmed her down to her toes until he said, 'There was more to the story than being blown up, wasn't there?'

'Why ask now?' Was he tidying up loose ends?

His shoulder lifted. 'I feel I'm missing something.'

'It happened up north in Scotland. No enemy in sight. Something went horrendously wrong and a bomb exploded when there should've been no way it could. Corporal Higgs took a hit in his neck and I was impaled by a steel bar so I had no chance of helping him. I could only focus enough to tell others what to do.' She swallowed. 'Later, I learned nothing would've saved him, but I blamed myself for a long time, even though I understand how it was.'

The bright light from the sun reflecting back at them from the ground, the dust in the air, the silence moments after everything had literally blown up in their faces, the pain, the inability to move—it all raced back to her.

Chase remained where he was, but his arm was now somehow touching hers. 'Leave it if it's too hard.'

She shook her head. 'One day in Merrywood George Baines was electrocuted as I was walking past and I saved him. That made me realise I couldn't win them all and to be grateful for the ones I could. I started getting over the guilt that day.' Something Chase should try and understand.

'We have the guilt in common.'

But not how they dealt with it. 'We do. But neither of us deserves it.'

Chase went back to being silent. What was he thinking? That she'd done what she could and got on with her life in a way he hadn't? Or was he simply wondering why she hadn't settled down in a town as a GP from the moment she'd left the military? Or, even more simply, why was she standing here, talking to him?

'When do you head to Africa?' Might as well jump in and learn all she could to stop those pesky questions zipping around her brain.

'After I've seen Jasper go to school for his first day,' Chase said defensively.

Surprise made her gabble. 'You're going to be there? That's wonderful. Libby will be stoked. So will Verity.'

'Cool it, Kristina. It's no big deal.'

Okay, so he wasn't happy with her. Too late to retract a thing. 'It is to your family.'

'Once you get going, there's no stopping you, is there?' A hint of amusement took the sting out of his words. 'I should be used to it by now.'

'Chase…' How did she put this without sending him running for the stairs?

'Don't, Kristina.'

That automatically stirred her along. 'I was only going to say I'd like it if you'd call in to see me whenever you're visiting your parents. I don't think we need to break contact entirely.' Now she was being pitiful, clutching at any opportunity to see him and thrashing her heart all over again.

'You can count on it.' He gave her a small smile.

'Really?' Down, hope, down.

'Really.'

She'd have to be happy with that.

CHAPTER TEN

THE SHIP ROCKED, causing the gangway to roll as Chase made his way down it for the last time this year. Next stop Ghana.

He paused, waited for the rush of excitement. His heart rate remained the same, his stomach quietly went about its business. Sighing, he continued onto the wharf and stopped, placing his bag at his feet and his hands on his hips as he stared up at the *SOS Poseidon.*

'Will I see you here next summer?' Josip called from the bridge.

'Probably.' Again the exhilaration let him down, not a buzz in his veins at all. 'You take care.'

'I intend to. My wife says she's nailing me to the bed for at least a week.'

Chase laughed. 'Lucky man.' The laughter faded. It wasn't that he was jealous. But not having a woman waiting for him at home, to make love to and talk and laugh with—that made him feel even lonelier than he'd been every damned minute since Kristina had disembarked four weeks ago. No one could ever have made him believe how much he'd miss her. As though she'd taken his heart with her, leaving him struggling to breathe.

The days had crawled by, the nights hadn't moved at all. The hours spent in their space had been cold, despite the soaring temperatures blitzing the region as summer gave one last shove before handing over to autumn. He'd missed Kristina so damned much he ached in every part of his body.

'You going to stand there all day?' Ethan stood near the security gate, hands in his pockets, shaking his head. 'There's a cold one on tap waiting along the road.'

Hoisting his bag, Chase strode across to his friend. 'You're talking sense for once.'

'Who? Me?' Ethan laughed.

Suddenly a lightness settled over Chase. For the next twenty-four hours he could relax, enjoy being with his friend whose best man he'd be as he pledged his love to Claire in a week. 'My shout.'

'Already had that planned.'

They walked along the street until Ethan indicated an English bar. 'I'm missing beer from home.'

With frosty glasses in hand, they settled into a dark corner. 'Thanks for staying with us,' Ethan said. 'It means a lot.'

Chase took a deep mouthful of beer and swallowed slowly. It felt good, hearing that. 'We've come a long way in a short time.'

'No regrets?'

None whatsoever. 'We should've made the effort years ago.'

'Everything has its time and place.'

'Getting a bit sage, aren't you?' Chase wondered why they'd been at each other's throats so much as teenagers. The need to compete against each other had been huge, but at the expense of friendship? Who understood teenagers?

Ethan stared across the room, the fingers of one hand tapping on the table top, in the other his glass turned round and round. 'How're things with you and Kristina?'

What? 'I'll catch up with her in Merrywood.'

Slowly Ethan brought that inscrutable gaze round to fix on him. 'I don't think I'd have made it with Claire if you and I hadn't begun to repair the past, if we hadn't started to become friends. Without that happening I was too far off the rails, too afraid to trust my instincts when it came to love.'

Where was he going with this? Guys didn't talk amongst themselves about love. There was an awful feeling in the bottom of Chase's gut suggesting he wasn't going to like whatever came out of the man's mouth next, and he rushed in to halt him. 'You're moving on. That's enough.'

'You're in love with her.'

Chase sucked in stale air, stared at the apparition he'd thought he was getting to know. 'You think?'

'What are you going to do about it?'

'Nothing.' Was that admitting he did love Kristina? As in with all his heart loved her? 'I'm heading to Ghana straight after your marriage ceremony. Do you seriously think I should persuade Kristina to join me when she's finally found the life she wants?'

'What's wrong with you stopping in one place long term with her?'

'You know why I can't do that. More than anyone, you understand.'

'Before Claire I'd have agreed with you. Even after Claire I might've for a while. Not now.'

'Okay, you've found what you were looking for but—'

'I wasn't looking to settle down, certainly didn't intend to get married and become a dad for the same reasons you're denying yourself love. I was always looking for places to be, towns to slip through on the way to the next hellhole where people needed my undivided attention to make them better.' He banged his empty glass on the table. 'I was you. You are who I used to be.'

Chase sat back, gobsmacked. There was nothing to say.

He didn't understand, didn't *want* to understand the message Ethan was banging him over the head with. He could admit to himself he loved Kristina. To tell her would only hurt, because he'd have to follow up with the statement that he didn't intend to do anything about it. She already knew that. 'Want another?' He nodded at the empty glasses between them. If only that was all that lay between them, but it seemed Ethan was hell bent on prodding old wounds.

'Sure.'

Moving through the throng of men standing at high tables eating lunch with their beers, Chase fought the urge to run for the exit. What right did Ethan have to talk about his love for Kristina? He'd never admitted his feelings out loud, afraid that by voicing them he wouldn't be able to keep them under wraps. That was where they had to stay. For Kristina's sake. If that wasn't love, what was?

Back at the table they sat in silence as the beer slowly disappeared down their throats. Chase began to relax. That conversation was done. Now he could enjoy a night with his friend and Claire. It was such an alien idea that it excited him. 'How long does it take to drive to Claire's apartment?'

Ethan downed another mouthful of his beer, drew a breath, and locked his eyes on the table between them. 'Stop trying to save everyone, Chase. It's not possible. I know. We're sorry examples of men when it comes to what we want from life, but Claire has shown me otherwise. You…' his finger tapped the table top '…can have what you're hankering after—Kristina and love and a family, all in your own corner of the world. You want that as much as you want to save those people, so go about it differently. Get a job back home. I'm learning that saving a child by removing a ruptured appendix in a big hospital is as rewarding as debriding a refugee's burns. You can have it all. Go for it, man. You're entitled to happiness. We both are.'

There wasn't anything to say. It would take time to absorb the sincerity in Ethan's words, and even then Chase doubted if he could accept the possibility of following suit. 'You're staying on in France, not moving back to England?'

'Claire needs to be where she is, and that's enough for me. Have to admit I'm not keen on spending too much time with her family with the mountains that loom over their village, but as long as I don't go climbing or skiing I'll manage.' He drained his glass. 'And I need you here next week. I'm not waiting any longer to get married.'

There he went again. It all came back to the love of a good woman. Apparently Ethan would do anything to make his woman happy. Anything.

Wasn't that what he was doing by staying out of Kristina's way? Making her happy rather than dragging her around the world as he saw fit?

Ethan picked up their empty glasses. 'Let's hit the road. Gridlock starts when everyone heads out of the city at the end of work, and Marseille in gridlock is hell on wheels.'

Conversation was on hold until Ethan pinged the locks of his SUV. 'One last thing, then I'll shut up. We can't undo the past but we can change our futures. Start doing something about that now. Not tomorrow, not next month, now. Go home, stop wandering the globe.'

Chase's pack dropped into the back of the SUV with a loud thud. 'Never knew you could talk so damned much,' Chase snapped around the pain that was flaring in his belly and spreading throughout his body. Did Ethan believe he could change his life with the snap of his fingers? When he knew better than anyone what held him back?

But he does know. That's the whole point.

Was it possible to turn his life around?

Did he want to?

He was beginning to think he did.

And he knew where he had to start.

* * *

The hut sat on the brow of the hill behind the copse, the door closed but not bolted. The front was bathed in weak sunlight. The weatherboards had recently been painted. Dad doing his regular upkeep even when this particular tiny building had not been used since Nick had died.

Chase sat on the edge of the veranda and leaned back against the wall, deliberately letting the ache come and the memories start opening. Gazing out over the green pastures, he wished he'd brought a bottle of beer to raise to Nick. 'We were going to conquer the world, live in the fast lane, you as an architect and me a plastic surgeon. Women were going to fall at our feet, we were going to make millions, own our own houses and take holidays in exotic locations.'

Despite the tears tracking down his cheeks, he laughed. 'We were morons. Normal teenagers from secure backgrounds who knew the only way to get ahead was by working hard, and then harder still, and yet we dreamed.'

What a lot of fun they'd had up here, drinking illicit beers and talking nonsense. At least they hadn't been on the street, doing drugs or getting drunk, robbing the local grocer.

The biggest and likeliest dream had been that the team would win the European under-eighteens ski championships. 'You would've made it, mate. It was a given. You deserved to win.'

He sat looking down on the world that had been his childhood, his safe place, his home, and thought about Nick, then the night that everything had changed for ever, Ethan, and lastly Kristina. 'I love her, Nick. Everything about her. She's gutsy and strong and sweet and sexy, and why am I telling you this?'

Focusing on the farm, a sense of belonging stole through him. This *was* his place. He'd never live in the house again.

His children wouldn't grow up with these paddocks to run around in, and this hut would not be their hideaway, but his heart belonged here.

It also belonged to Kristina. If she'd accept him as he was—flawed, wounded, and willing to give life a go with no guarantees.

The sun was dropping beyond the distant hedges when Chase finally roused himself. Time to get started on the future. But first he had to close the past. He stood, hands in his pockets, feet splayed, and his eyes closed. 'Nick, I'm sorry, buddy, but the time has come for me to let you go. It's not fair you didn't get to do any of those things you wanted so much, and I've done everything I can to make up for that in other ways. Now I'm done.' He opened his eyes, looked around and felt okay about what he was doing. 'Goodbye, Nick.'

That night Chase slept the deepest sleep he could remember having. In the morning he joined his parents for breakfast then borrowed his father's four-wheel drive and headed into the city.

'Thank you so much, Dr Morton. Sorry to be a nuisance but I panicked when Lily went limp and quiet.' Sherry bounced a now happy baby in her arms.

'Stop apologising. I'd rather you came in and there was nothing wrong than you stay away because you're embarrassed and we find there's something to worry about. Most first-time mothers are the same.' Kristina tickled Lily on the chin. 'Your mother loves you, gorgeous.'

Sherry nodded. 'I still can't believe how that just happens, no warning, nothing. One day I was pregnant, and the next I was holding this precious little bundle I'd give my life for if I had to.'

Kristina's heart squeezed. Would she ever know the same love? 'Let's hope it never comes to that.' Placing

Lily's file on the receptionist's counter, she picked up her next patient's notes. 'I'll see you for Lily's six-month check-up. Unless you're worried about anything before then.'

Sherry nodded. 'I'm so glad you're back.'

Sherry's words registered in the back of her mind as she scanned the waiting room for Mrs Winter and instead found Chase sitting, watching her. Every thought went out of her mind as her blood heated and her body turned in his direction. He was sexier even than her memory of him, and that was off the scale. Those magical hands lying loosely on his thighs dried her mouth as more memories flooded her head. 'I've missed you so much.'

'I've missed you, too.' Chase crossed to her, those hands reaching for her, taking her close to that wicked chest.

She hadn't seen him move, didn't know she'd spoken aloud until his reply. He'd missed her? Really? In the way she hoped? 'I didn't know you were in town.' Libby hadn't mentioned it. Though Claire and Ethan were getting married shortly, so she should've figured he'd turn up.

'I got in yesterday.' His hands dropped away. His hug had been brief but warm. Friendly.

Ah, friendly. He hadn't come specifically to see her. But he'd said he'd missed her. What was going on? 'You're waiting to see Jarrod?' Not her. They weren't an item. She was getting on with her life, not stagnating while waiting for Chase to make random appearances.

'No.' His hand reached for hers again. His tongue licked his bottom lip. 'I—I'm hoping you'll spare me some time after you finish up. Go for a meal at the pub?'

'Oh.' She gulped. 'Oh.' Where was the strong, know-what-I-want Chase? This nervous version was new to her. 'I'd like that.'

There was relief going on in that gaze locked on her. 'I'm early, but I didn't want to risk you leaving before I saw you.'

'I've got two more patients.' Kristina dragged her eyes away to look around the room for her next patient, trying to get her brain functioning properly.

'I'll be here.'

She began to turn away.

'Kristina?' She turned back, still trying to fathom what was going on. "I'm glad you missed me,' he said quietly.

Thud. Was that her heart hitting the floor? 'Meaning?' She needed to find another doctor quickly because she was in no state to take care of patients. Not after that. Chase was either building her hopes up or about to kick her feet out from under her.

'Talk to you later.' His hand cupped her chin for a moment, dropped away. 'I'm not here to hurt you, okay?'

Okay? Her head dipped into a nod without thought. 'Fine.' Whatever that meant. First she had to get a grip. Just because Chase had strolled into her day didn't mean forgetting what, who her day was meant to be about. 'Mrs Winter?'

An elderly woman rose stiffly, and hobbled her way. 'Hello, dear. Are you Dr Morton, then?'

'I am. Pleased to meet you.' With all her willpower Kristina remained focused on the lovely lady before her and ignored the man who'd once again thrown her mind into a flap. 'Come through, and tell me what's bothering you today.'

Removing what appeared to be a basal cell carcinoma from Mrs Winter's lower arm took half an hour and made Kristina late for her last patient, who didn't seem fazed.

'I've been talking to Chase Barrington,' Tony Webster told her as he sat down by her desk. 'We went to school together. He always was a great guy. If only he'd come home.'

See what you're missing out on, Chase? People who know you and want to be a part of your life are as impor-

tant as the ones you see briefly before they disappear over the horizon on their own journeys.

'He's doing a wonderful job with *Medicine For All*.' Why had he asked her out for a meal? 'What can I do for you today, Tony?'

'It's my hip, Doc. It's getting more painful and I need to increase the diclofenac.'

The joint had been fractured a year ago when a cow had charged him, and he'd had problems ever since. 'It might be time for that hip replacement.' The wait-and-see approach hadn't worked and Tony needed to face facts. 'Up on the bed and I'll have a look.' After getting him to lift his leg, push sideways as she assessed his resistance level, Kristina returned to her desk and brought up the radiology request form. 'Get dressed. I'm sending you for an X-ray and referring you to the orthopaedic department.' She typed in details, printed off a radiology form and a repeat prescription for his anti-inflammatory drug.

'Only old people have hip replacements.'

Men. Stubborn creatures. Why *was* Chase waiting for her to finish work? 'Let's see what the X-ray shows, shall we?'

'I can't afford to take time off from the farm.'

'You'd rather lie awake in pain every night and hobble around the fields at half your speed. I get it. Make that appointment with Radiology today.' Then she glanced at her watch. 'Tomorrow. I'll be following up on you.' She smiled to soften the blow.

'I'm docking sheep tomorrow.' He limped out, a scowl on his face.

'Nice try,' Kristina called after him, before closing down the computer. Picking up her bag and keys, she slung her denim jacket over one shoulder and went to find Chase. And learn what this was about.

Pausing at the door, her gaze filled with the sight of

him leaning against the reception counter, talking with Jarrod. Even knowing Chase was here hadn't prepared her for the simple need to throw herself at him and wrap her arms around that tall, lean body, to feel his muscles under her palms and breathe in his man scent, just... Oh, just whatever. She'd missed him beyond reason. Missed the intimacy, his sexiness, their talks, everything about the guy. *Settle down, girl.* One evening sharing a meal wouldn't change a thing. He'd still head away on another adventure come tomorrow.

When he took her elbow, sparks flew up her arm. 'You all right to walk?' he asked calmly. No sparks for him?

'Definitely. I need to get the kinks out of my back. There's a lot of sitting with this job.' Which was never good.

'You been going to physio?'

'Twice a week. There's a physiotherapist connected to the medical centre, which is handy.' And the woman knew what she was doing. Always a bonus.

Chase placed two beers on the table and sat opposite Kristina so he could watch her face. He'd missed how her expression lightened when she laughed, how her eyes went deep blue in serious moments, how she scratched whatever surface was available with her forefinger when discussing those things that had shaped her life.

The moment he'd seen her in the waiting room he'd wanted to scoop her up and run to the nearest hotel room to make love, to show her how special she was. 'Jarrod tells me you've settled into the medical centre without any hitches.'

'It's early days yet.' She blushed.

He hadn't seen that before, and tenderness stirred throughout him. 'You've made the right move.'

The light blue shade of her eyes turned dark as she gave

a sharp nod. 'It's working out well. I'm going to look at two houses next week that have just come on the market. In for the job, in for everything.'

'You don't think you're rushing things?' She could come a cropper if she suddenly wanted to up stakes and head off somewhere else. Houses didn't always sell overnight.

'If I don't back myself, how can I expect anyone else to?'

She had an answer for everything. Way ahead of him. But he was racing to catch up. 'Point taken.'

'Hey, Kristina, see you at the make-up party on Saturday?' A woman in her thirties stood by their table.

'You sure will, Pam.'

See? She was fitting in in a way he struggled to envisage, yet was finally willing to give a shot. He'd listened to the young mother with her baby talking to the receptionist about how kind and caring Dr Morton had been, and how she was glad to have her as her doctor, and felt he was missing out on something big. When Tony came out of her room looking like he'd lost a battle, and grumping about Doc thinking she knew best, Chase had known exactly how he felt.

Weeks back when Kristina had had a crack at him about how he could do as much good for people here as anywhere he'd gone all defensive, believing she didn't understand what drove him. He wasn't going to be sucked into her way of thinking that home was best, didn't want to get involved with her or the town he'd run away from. Then Ethan had added his two euros' worth, saying the same thing even more directly. Who knew better than Ethan where he was coming from?

Throw in the four longest, dullest, most boring weeks of his life out at sea, and he knew he had to stop holding out for the lonely path he'd chosen when he'd been at his lowest. He had to do something different or end up a bitter, lonely old man with only himself to blame.

Kristina. He loved her. Without reservation.

Would the woman hurry up and leave? He had things bugging the hell out of him to share with Kristina. Now. Not later.

'Thanks for the invitation.' Kristina lifted her glass and took a sip.

The woman got the hint and said goodbye.

'You're popular already.' He needed to provoke that sweet blush, and was instantly rewarded.

'Join the medical centre, join the whole town.' Her smile was strained.

'That's how it is here, people watching out for each other.'

Her eyebrows rose, but she kept quiet.

'Everyone turned out to support me after the avalanche. I was overwhelmed by their compassion.' And his grief, but he'd put that to bed yesterday. 'I've spent the day visiting hospitals and surgical practices in Taunton and Frome. I'm looking for a job.'

Kristina leaned back in her chair, her eyes locked on him, disbelief warring with hope in her expression. 'Say that again.'

'I'm coming home, Kristina. It's time.'

'Why?'

'Because if I don't do it now, the chances are I never will, and I need to as much as I needed to stay away before.' Everything was so clear—how he'd wasted his life rushing after causes, how he'd let his family down when all they'd ever done was love and support him. But more than that, 'It's you. I love you. I want that future you're following. I want to…' He ran out of words as he watched Kristina's reaction.

Never a big talker, she was now silent. Shocked might

best describe her. Her eyes remained locked on him, her hands tight around her glass.

'Say something,' he croaked.

She picked up her drink in unsteady hands and gulped a mouthful, all the while watching him.

Raucous laughter broke out on the other side of the room.

Chase stood up and took the glass out of Kristina's hands, placed it on the table, then took her hand and tugged gently. 'Let's get out of here.' What had he been thinking to drop that on her when surrounded by people that had nothing to do with this conversation?

Outside he led her to the four-wheel drive he'd borrowed from his father that morning, and held the passenger door open as she climbed in. 'Where're you living?'

'Are you sure?'

'That I love you? Yes.'

'It's a bit sudden, isn't it?' Her tongue worried the corner of her mouth.

'I believe it started the day we worked together to save Antoine on the wharf. I didn't recognise love for what it was, or, if I did, I didn't want to.' She had to believe him. He wasn't making any of this up.

Kristina turned her startled gaze forward, so he couldn't read her any more. Not that he was having much luck interpreting what she was thinking anyway. 'Take me to the river. I need to walk.'

It would be dark soon, but the idea of being shut inside the house with Chase while she absorbed what he'd told her made Kristina feel hot and cold all at once. She needed space, not walls closing in on her.

Chase loves me. Who said dreams didn't come true? Her wildest dream had been that he'd fall for her and want to settle down here. So why wasn't she falling into his arms with excitement? Did she love Chase? Without a doubt.

Chase loves me.

So he'd been looking for work in the area. How long would he stay in one job before that crippling need to be actively helping those unfortunate people took over? Would he be able to stop in one town long term?

You have. It was early days, but she already knew she'd found her corner of the world. She was happy here—when she wasn't thinking about Chase. Sure, there'd be times when things went wrong, but this was home. But could Chase do the same?

He was pulling over. 'This do?'

'Yes.' The river walkway was devoid of locals, thank goodness. Now was not the time to be making idle chit-chat. She slid out of the vehicle and pulled on her jacket, zipped it up against the cool evening air. 'How did the job hunt go?' she asked as they began strolling along the river's edge.

'I have an interview tomorrow with the head of surgery at Collingwood Hospital. There are no positions right now, but there might be one coming up. In the meantime, I'll keep door knocking. Jarrod's contacting two surgeons in private practice he knows well.'

'You sound...excited.'

Chase looked down at her. 'You know what? I am. Now I've made up my mind I'm keen to get cracking on starting over.' Then his smile faded. 'You're not certain I'll stay around, are you? You're worried that I'll wake up one morning and wonder whatever possessed me to give up the life I've led for so long.'

'Yes, that's exactly what's going through my mind.' *I'm terrified my heart will be broken.* At the moment she could walk away and it would only be badly bruised, but to believe they had a future and then have it torn away—no, she couldn't survive that. 'I'm sorry.'

'It's right that you're looking out for yourself. I understand that.' Wrapping an arm over her shoulders, he pulled her out of the way of a cyclist. 'I'm going to Ghana the day after Ethan and Claire tie the knot.'

Her heart slowed. See? He hadn't made the change yet, was still hanging onto the old life. 'You finally signed the contract.'

His body touched the length of hers, strong and warm, making her want to believe in him. 'Yes, in a fit of uncertainty I did. I was grappling with missing you so damned much it hurt. Do I regret it? No, because I owe Liam time to find my replacement. Anyway, the contract is only for four weeks.'

Not long enough to know he'd made the right decision. Or was it? Was she being fair? Just because it had taken her a couple of years to realise the army couldn't give her what she'd been looking for, it didn't mean Chase needed as long. Kristina began walking again, pleased when Chase's arm remained around her shoulders. She'd missed him so much there'd been days when she'd wondered if she should walk away from what she'd found and re-join him on the ship. 'Four weeks and then you're moving to Somerset.'

'For good, Kristina. For good. This is where my heart is.'

She stopped in the fading light and turned into him, looking up at that face that was seared into her mind. 'I'm glad. You belong here. I've wanted to bang you over the head so you'd see what you've been missing out on.'

'Trust me, you did that more than once.' His smile was wry. 'Verbally, and in the way you fitted in with people I care about. That woke me up more than anything. If you could let your past go and be happy in a town that was new to you, slotting in as though you'd always lived here, why couldn't I return to where I'd grown up and have known people my whole life?'

'Because you're stubborn?' She raised an eyebrow and grinned, letting the wonder of his love take hold.

'There's that.' He grinned back. Then sobered. 'Kristina, I meant what I said. I love you with all my heart.'

She'd never told him how she felt. True, she had doubts about his ability to stay put, but while she'd only known his restless side she'd seen his strength in dealing with the day-to-day dramas and tragedies on the *Poseidon*. And he loved her.

'I want to marry you and settle into a home of our own and eventually fill the spare bedrooms with kids that have fair hair and summer-blue eyes,' he added.

Tears streaked down her face. 'Really?' she choked. Wasn't this what she'd been searching for?

'What do you think?' he asked as his arms wound around her.

Drawing herself up and taking a deep breath, she told him, 'You need to know I love you, too.' She'd always wanted the chance to love someone and to be loved back. And here it was. *Chase*. 'Yes, Chase, I love you,' she repeated.

'Oh, sweetheart.' His mouth touched hers, soft and warm and filled with love. The kiss when it came was long and slow and made her heart melt.

She didn't think it could get any better.

Chase lifted his mouth away from hers. 'Kristina, please say you'll marry me.'

Seemed she still got things wrong. This went beyond better. 'As soon as you return home for good.'

'Better start planning the wedding. From what Ethan tells me, it's quite a process.'

'Claire doesn't have Verity or Libby alongside her.'

'True.' Chase smiled. 'Family. They're going to be thrilled about this.'

'Want to go tell them now?'

He shook his head. 'No. We're going back to your place and I'm going to make love to you all night long.'

'Perfect answer, husband-to-be. Perfect answer.'

EPILOGUE

'I DECLARE YOU man and wife,' the marriage celebrant announced with a smile. 'You can now kiss your— Oh, right… Well, it seems I was a bit slow off the mark.'

Kristina would've laughed but she was too busy returning Chase's enthusiastic kiss. They'd done it. Gone and got themselves hitched, surrounded by family and friends.

'Okay, you two. There are children present.' Ethan clapped Chase on the back. 'Plenty of time for that later.'

Chase dragged his mouth away. 'Go and annoy *your* wife, will you?'

'Oh, no, you don't,' Claire shot back as Ethan reached for her.

Kristina grinned as she slipped her arm through Chase's. 'Get in line, you guys.'

'Did I tell you she's ex-military?' Chase turned back to Ethan.

'Didn't need to. I've known who's in charge in this relationship right from the start.'

'You haven't seen anything yet.' Taking her first step in her now complete life, Kristina tugged her husband and began the walk down between the chairs where everyone important to them stood and cheered.

Even her father, who reached out and placed a gentle dad kiss on her cheek. 'You're beautiful, my girl.'

On the other side of the aisle her mother dabbed at her eyes and nodded. For once her mum appeared to be in tune with her father.

Tears spilled down Kristina's carefully made-up face and she couldn't have cared less. The photos would show the real emotions of the day, smudged mascara and all. Her family mightn't know how to express aloud their love for her, but today they'd shown it by being here. It was all she asked.

Outside the tiny village church in the wintry sunshine they crossed the road to the wedding reception venue and were met by a waiter holding a tray of glasses filled with champagne and one with sparkling water for Claire. The four of them formed a tight circle and clinked the glasses. 'To the four of us,' Chase said.

'To us,' Ethan agreed.

After taking a sip, Chase dropped a kiss on Kristina's cheek then locked his gaze with Ethan's. 'We did it. Both of us.'

Ethan's hand splayed across against Chase's back. 'No regrets. This is real, and wonderful, and, yes, we made it.'

Chase looked at Ethan, then her. And raised his glass as he looked upward. 'To Nick.'

'To Nick.' Ethan nodded.

Kristina's tears grew heavier, but her heart was light. 'They're special, our men,' she whispered to Claire.

'I'm so glad they're happy, and have found a way forward.'

'I'll drink to that,' Kristina agreed.

'So will we,' Chase added as he smudged a streak of mascara off her cheek.

'Big ears.' His wife grinned. Tears maybe, but nothing today was going to wipe the smile off her face.

Then Libby was nudging into the group, breaking the moment, only to replace it with another. 'Welcome to the family, Kristina.' Then she broke down. 'And thank you for making Chase see sense at last.'

'Another glass required over here.' Chase beckoned a waiter.

Then they were surrounded by people congratulating them.

'It doesn't get any better than this, does it?' Chase whispered in Kristina's ear.

'Well…' She tapped her mouth thoughtfully.

'Don't.' He laughed. 'I love you. That's all you're getting.'

'That's all I need.'

* * * * *

OUT NOW!

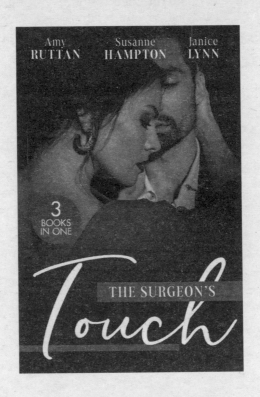

Available at
millsandboon.co.uk

MILLS & BOON

OUT NOW!

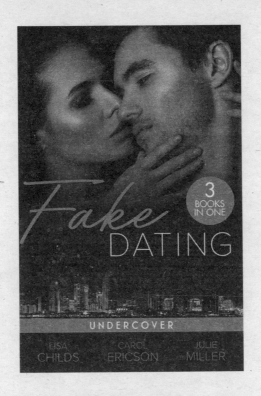

Available at
millsandboon.co.uk

MILLS & BOON